"If you think I'll stand idly by and allow you to get away with this deception, you're very wrong."

Anna yanked free of his grasp and warned, "You stay away from me, Brit Caruth!"

She rushed back inside and slammed the double doors behind her. She leaned back against them, trembling, afraid, upset.

This lusty man who lived under the same roof and was adored by LaDextra was intent, not only on exposing her, but on seducing her, as well. She wasn't quite sure of his motive for the latter. Perhaps it was simply strong physical attraction. Or maybe he wanted to show her that she was not only an impostor but a common tramp, as well.

Her anger flared anew. Her determination strengthened. She stalked to the bed, tore off the robe and vowed aloud, "You will never expose *or* seduce me, Britton Caruth!"

She had momentarily forgotten that Brit was still right outside on the balcony. Through the open windows he heard her impassioned oath.

Without making a sound, he mouthed a response. "You're wrong, Anna. I'm gonna do both."

Nan Ryan "writes beautifully. Her style, plotting and characterizations are skillfully developed."
—*Wichita Falls Times Record*

NAN RYAN

Wanting You

MIRA

ISBN 1-55166-521-2

WANTING YOU

Copyright © 1999 by Nan Ryan.

MIRA and the Star Colophon are trademarks used under license and registered
in Australia, New Zealand, Philippines, United States Patent and Trademark
Office and in other countries.

Visit us at www.mirabooks.com

Printed in U.S.A.

For
J. L. R.
who takes care of my cares

ACKNOWLEDGMENT

Special thanks to Dianne Moggy, editor and friend, with whom it is such a pleasure to work.

Thanks also to the wonderfully talented art department for giving this book such an outstanding cover.

And to all the gang at MIRA, thanks for making me feel so welcome and wanted.

One

The summer sun was at its zenith when Arizona Ranger Captain John W. Russell rode his winded roan gelding into the sleepy border town. The ranger's soiled white shirt was soaked with sweat and sticking to his broad back. His dark trousers were thorn-and-brush torn and so dirty they were stiff. His three day growth of black beard was matted with perspiration and alkali dust. His pale eyes were red rimmed and watering from the too-bright glare of the hot white sun. His thin lips were badly chapped and cracked.

Captain John W. Russell looked awful.

But as untidy as he was, the disheveled ranger looked all spit and polish compared with the screeching, struggling, clawing creature riding behind him on the lathered roan gelding. With her feet tied beneath the horse's belly and her wrists tied in front of the ranger's waist, the frightfully unkempt woman looked more animal than human.

Hair of an undeterminable hue hung in greasy

strings over her eyes and around her slender shoulders. A badly soiled garment of once-soft deerskin had one sleeve missing and the tattered skirt reached only to midthigh. Her slender legs were scratched and dirty and her bare feet were caked with dried mud.

It was impossible to tell what she really looked like. Her countenance was covered with dust and grime, and she constantly contorted her features, making mean faces as she hissed and snarled and swore.

Ignoring her antics, Captain Russell pulled his hat brim lower as he reined the tired gelding directly down Main Street. There was little diversion to be had in Nogales, so his unexpected appearance immediately caused a stir. Men loitering on the wooden sidewalks turned to stare, talking excitedly among themselves. Ladies, hearing the commotion, came to the door of Gamble Dry Goods Store to have a look. All eyes soon rested on the wild looking creature tied to the tall ranger.

"Say, Captain," shouted a toothless old-timer, "what you got there? Looks like a wild animal to me!" The aged man hooked his thumbs into his suspenders, gave them a brisk snap and spat out a string of tobacco juice.

"You're a long way from the reservation," shouted a tall, lanky cowboy leaning against the barber pole. "We don't much cotton to savages around here, so why don't you just ride right on out of town and take that there ugly squaw with you? We don't want her kind in Nogales, do we, boys?"

A resounding response went up from the crowd.

The taciturn ranger paid no attention to the shouts

and jeers. Looking neither to the left nor the right, he continued to guide the responsive gelding down the dusty street in a slow, comfortable walk. The hurled slurs and insults continued until the gelding reached the far end of town and turned the corner. Soon the buildings and the people were left behind and Captain Russell headed for the quiet, secluded Border Convent at St. Peter's Mission two miles east of Nogales.

When he brought the gelding to a halt before the tree-shaded adobe structure, he wrapped the reins around the saddle horn and, speaking softly, told the horse to stand still. He then untied the woman's hands from around his waist, but he clung to the rope encircling her wrists as he threw a long leg over the saddle and dropped to the ground.

Having no idea if she understood or not, he told her, "I am going to untie your feet now, but I don't want any more trouble out of you."

Her light eyes flashing fire, she glared at him and made unintelligible sounds as she thrashed wildly about. He gave the rope around her wrists a hard tug and said, "Be still or I'll leave your feet tied."

She spat at him and muttered under her breath.

The ranger managed to get her ankles untied. He hauled her down off the gelding, but the minute her bare feet hit the ground she shoved him and spun around. His long arm shot out and he caught her by the collar of her deerskin dress. He slammed her up against the gelding with such force it knocked the breath out of her.

The ranger was gently slapping her on the back

to help her regain her breath when two small, aging nuns, dressed identically in spotless, starched white habits, appeared on the convent's covered porch.

"Captain," said the taller of the two, as they hurried out to meet him, "is there something we can do? Can we be of help to you in some way?"

"No, but you can be of help to her," he said, indicating the angry, hard-to-handle woman at his side.

"Well, of course," said the other sister. "Anything we can do, we will."

"Thanks," said the ranger, relieved. "I really appreciate it."

"I am Sister Catherine Elizabeth," said one of the tiny women. "And you know our Mother Superior."

"Sister Norma Kate," said the other, offering her hand. "Shall we go inside?"

The dauntless nuns seemed totally unaffected by the shrill shrieks and stubborn struggling of the dirty young woman the ranger propelled toward the gleaming white convent. Just inside the convent's cool, quiet interior, Captain Russell explained his reason for seeking them out.

"I was down in Mexico when I stumbled onto a renegade Apache camp twenty miles south of the border. Some of Geronimo's bunch still have a mountain stronghold down there. I found this wretched girl there with them. She's white, although the only way you can tell is by her blue eyes."

Both sisters nodded in agreement.

Captain Russell continued, "The Apache said she

had been with them for a long time. They don't, or say they don't, recall where she came from or when. She doesn't know, either.''

He went on to tell the attentive sisters all that he knew about the girl, which wasn't really very much. To the best of his knowledge she no longer spoke or understood English, and he was certain she couldn't remember anything about her life before she was taken by the Apache. She had no idea who she was or where she came from.

Listening intently, the shorter of the two sisters soon clapped her hands, and a young, fresh-faced nun, who was exceedingly tall compared to the others, immediately appeared. In low, soft tones the Mother Superior repeated everything that Captain Russell had told them. That this poor young woman had been captured long ago by the Apache and held against her will. That she had no recollection of being taken by the hostiles. Nor did she have any memory of her white family.

"So, Sister Sarah Beth," said the Mother Superior, "if you will be so good as to take our guest upstairs now, I'm sure she would enjoy a hot bath."

The ranger quickly cautioned the young nun, "Better watch her closely, she's—"

"Don't worry, Captain," said the six-foot-tall Sister Sarah Beth, "I can handle her."

The ranger nodded, then stood twisting his sweat-stained hat in his hands as the no-nonsense nun firmly escorted the screaming, kicking girl up the stairs. Wailing and jerking and trying to pull free, the girl looked angrily back over her shoulder at him. A fierce hatred mixed with numbing fear glittered in her eyes.

Captain Russell felt his chest tighten.

Poor, pitiful child. In all likelihood, the safe haven of this secluded convent was just as frightening to her as the Apache camp must have been when she had first been captured. He hated to leave her, but he had no choice. He didn't know where she belonged.

If she belonged anywhere.

On the open landing above, Sister Sarah Beth forced the tearful, tussling girl through a door and out of sight. The ranger exhaled. And he wondered. Had he done the poor creature a favor or an injustice by bringing her back after all these years?

"Captain," one of the sisters said, breaking into his troubled reverie, "will you have a nice cup of tea or coffee with us? A meal, perhaps?"

Balancing a fragile china cup filled with steaming black coffee on his knee, Captain Russell sat on a stone bench on the convent's shaded back patio. The aged sisters sat facing him. He took a long draw of the strong coffee and, wishing he had a cigarette or a cigar, spoke again about the girl.

"I couldn't just leave her down there," he said, half-apologetically. "She doesn't look it, but she *is* white. There's no changing that."

"Are you certain," questioned Sister Catherine Elizabeth, "it was wise to take her from the savages if—"

"This girl is white!" Captain Russell interrupted

irritably. Immediately softening his tone, he said, "Can you imagine the life she's had with the Apache? Can't you tell by looking at her how she has been treated? Or rather, mistreated."

"Forgive me, Captain," said the contrite nun. "Of course you did the right thing by bringing her back."

Nodding, the Mother Superior said, "I wonder who she could possibly be?"

"And where she might have come from," added Sister Catherine Elizabeth.

"As I said," replied Captain Russell, "I don't know and neither does she."

The Mother Superior said, "Well, we will take good care of her, Captain."

The ranger smiled at last. "I knew I could count on you." He set his coffee cup aside. "I know as well that you will make every attempt to find her family." He looked from one to the other.

"Indeed we will," they promised, nodding their heads and smiling.

As the ranger rode away from the convent, the young woman he had brought to this peaceful place was upstairs being given—against her wishes—a none-too-gentle scrubbing. Sister Sarah Beth was determined to be neither bullied nor swayed by her charge.

The nun knew that her chore was to make the young woman as clean and pure as a newborn babe, and this she meant to do. So Sister Sarah Beth steeled herself to ignore the screams and growls and the splashing of the water all over her and the floor.

A good shampoo and a steaming hot bath revealed long, lustrous blond hair, a flawless complexion beneath a slight sunburn and, on her right temple, a fully healed scar indicating she had once received a severe blow to the head. It was perhaps the blow that had taken her memory. Below the scar, and mostly hidden by her hair, was an unsightly black tattoo, obviously put there by her cruel captors.

Sister Sarah Beth lifted the slippery, struggling woman from the tub and went about drying her slender body. Then managed, after several failed attempts, to get her dressed in fresh underwear and a plain, but spotlessly clean dress of gray cotton.

As she gathered up the wet, soiled towels, Sister Sarah Beth saw a small bundle on the floor and bent to pick it up. Before she could reach it, the freshly scrubbed woman screamed, fell to her knees, snatched up the bundle and pressed it to her chest, her eyes wild.

Frowning, Sister Sarah Beth forcefully took the bundle away from the girl, untied it and poured out the contents. The meager possessions included a short-bladed knife with a carved turquoise handle, some bits and pieces of faded fabric, a few baby teeth and a delicate gold locket with the letters *M.S.H.* inscribed on the face.

"M.S.H." Sister Sarah Beth said aloud, looking at the locket, then at the girl. "So your first name starts with an *M?*'' When there was no response, the nun continued, ''Then we will call you Mary. Now, come with me, Mary, I'm sure our Mother Superior will want to speak with you.''

Two

The Border Convent at St. Peter's Mission
March 1890

After nearly five years at the remote Nogales convent, Mary looked nothing like the wild, dirty savage who had been brought there by the Arizona Ranger captain. She had quickly blossomed into a beautiful young woman. Tall and slender, with long golden hair and enormous blue eyes, Mary was totally unaware of her striking good looks. Little attention was ever paid to her and she was almost as miserable at the convent as she had been with the Apache.

She was not a meek, quiet soul who fit in with convent life. A fiery, defiant woman, used to fending for herself—she'd have been dead otherwise—Mary often questioned authority and defied the nuns. Looked down on by the townsfolk, who considered her more savage Indian than civilized white, Mary had no friends.

A bright young woman who passed what little free time she had reading and daydreaming, Mary often wondered what awful deed she had done to deserve what the fates had handed her.

After several failed attempts to run away, she had given up and accepted her lonely lot in life. She would, she realized, spend the rest of her days at St. Peter's. Those days consisted of being tutored in English, mathematics and history, followed by endless hours of helping tend ailing sisters, ironing stiffly starched clothes, washing stacks of dirty dishes and scrubbing acres of dusty stone floors.

But Mary's fate and future were forever changed by a chance visit, early one spring afternoon, from an aged, ailing priest. Long retired, Father Fitzgerald had come to the convent to say goodbye to the sisters with whom he had once served. The frail priest saw Mary and was immediately struck by her strong resemblance to a woman who, years ago, had been one of his flock, in a little parish in the southwest Texas town of Regentville.

When Father Fitzgerald learned that Mary had been captured by the Apache as a child, he was certain he knew her true identity: Anna Regent Wright. The long-lost Regent heiress! The wealthy Regent family, owners of the state's largest working cattle ranch, had lost a little girl to the Apache in the summer of '73.

The child had been taken, along with the ranch foreman's two young daughters, as they played at a spring near ranch headquarters. The girl's frantic father and the foreman were killed in the ensuing melee.

The priest told the sisters what he suspected, and with their permission he spoke with Mary. Mary's blue eyes grew wide with interest as she listened to him tell about the rich, powerful Texas clan he believed to be her family.

He told Mary that a year after she was captured and her father killed, her mother had married again, choosing a widower with a young son. Sadly, the newlyweds were killed on a European honeymoon—swept away by an alpine avalanche.

"Who is left?" Mary asked. "Are there no Regents still alive?"

The old priest smiled. "There is still one Regent very much alive. The indestructible matriarch, LaDextra Regent, your maternal grandmother." He shook his graying head and added, "My, my, LaDextra's going to be overjoyed!"

Mary was not convinced that she was Anna Regent Wright. But she was more than willing to let Father Fitzgerald—and others—believe it. A woman whipped by many and unwanted by anyone, suckled by hate and reared by neglect, Mary had few qualms about pretending to be the missing Regent heiress.

Lying on her narrow cot that night in a little alcove off the convent pantry, Mary pondered the possibility of a better life. The prospect made her heart pound with hope. Never had she had a sense of belonging. Never had she had anything to call her own. No money. No name. No family. No home.

Knowing that his days were numbered, Father Fitzgerald told the Mother Superior and Sister Catherine Elizabeth that they must contact the Regent family's legal firm and express his strong belief that the missing Regent heiress was living at the convent in Nogales, Arizona.

The Mother Superior agreed to write the letter.

Father Fitzgerald then told the two nuns, "I am leaving what little money I have to Mary. She'll need it to get to Texas."

As the frail old priest's health rapidly declined, Mary spent every free minute with him, asking countless questions about the Regent ranch and its occupants.

Father Fitzgerald was completely convinced that this pretty young woman was Anna Regent Wright. Hoping to stimulate memories of her Texas home, he patiently drew detailed pictures of the huge, two-story ranch house. The sickly old priest fashioned from memory a carefully delineated map of the huge west Texas spread, complete with varying terrain, the location of springs and water holes, and criss-crossing roads.

Mary studied the map, memorizing every land-mark the priest had so carefully diagrammed. She envisioned the big cattle ranch with its imposing mansion in the foothills of the Guadalupe Mountains.

It was easy to picture herself inside that grand home.

The letter postmarked Nogales, Arizona, reached the William R. Davis Law Firm in Regentville, Texas, on the morning of April 18, 1890.

Will Davis was seated behind his mahogany desk in his Main Street office when his young law clerk popped in and handed him a stack of mail. On the very top of the stack was the letter from Nogales.

A puzzled expression crossed the face of the distinguished sixty-four-year-old, silver-haired attorney. He picked up an onyx-handled letter opener and swiftly slashed the envelope's top edge. He withdrew the letter, unfolded it and began to read. His heavy silver eyebrows knitted and his green eyes narrowed as he read, then reread, the letter.

Suddenly Will realized he was holding his breath. He released it in a loud exhalation, then dropped the letter on his polished desktop. A lifelong friend of the Regents, as well as their legal counsel, Will Davis was stunned. And skeptical.

It was, in his opinion, highly unlikely that Anna Regent Wright had, after all this time, turned up in an Arizona convent. He had long ago written Anna off as dead.

Will Davis was tempted to burn the letter and tell no one of its existence. If he did burn it, everyone involved would be better off. But he didn't dare. If he did and LaDextra ever found out... Will shuddered at the thought. He sighed heavily, ran a hand through his hair and rose from his chair.

He would do his duty.

Will wasted no time. He ordered his one-horse gig brought around, told his law clerk he might not be back all day, and left immediately on the six-mile journey to The Regent.

At the huge eight-columned mansion in the rocky foothills of the soaring Guadalupe Mountains,

LaDextra Regent was informed by a servant that a carriage was coming up the front drive. LaDextra immediately rose from her chair and began awkwardly smoothing her upswept white hair. Then she made her way to the front parlor and settled herself on a long velvet sofa.

Will Davis was shown into the parlor, and LaDextra smiled when she saw him. "Come, Will," she urged, patting the sofa cushion beside her, "sit here by me and let's gossip awhile before lunch. You are staying for lunch?" Her pale eyes twinkled with merriment. Will was her pipeline to the outside world. For the past few years now, LaDextra rarely left the ranch. But Will knew everything that went on in Regentville and kept her well informed.

"This isn't a social call, LaDextra," Will said as he plucked at the creases in his gray suit trousers and sat down beside her.

"Oh?" Her thin white eyebrows shot up. "Is there some kind of legal problem? Are we being sued for—"

"No. No, nothing like that," Will interrupted. He handed her the letter.

She looked at it; she looked at him. "What is this?"

"Read it."

LaDextra's eyeglasses, suspended on a heavy gold chain, rested on her billowy breasts. She lifted the glasses, settled them on her nose and began to read. By the time she had finished reading the letter, all the color had drained from her sun-wrinkled face.

Overcome with emotion, she couldn't speak for a moment.

Then she started to smile and said, "Dear Lord, can it be? Is my little Anna really alive? Is she coming home after all these years?"

"Now, LaDextra," cautioned a concerned Will, "please don't get your hopes up before we've even had a chance to meet this woman and check her out. Father Fitzgerald is old and dying. This may well be wishful thinking on his part. We have absolutely no reason to believe that the girl is actually Anna and I am not—"

"Get back to town, Will," LaDextra snapped, "and fire off a telegram to Nogales. Tell my granddaughter to come home to me!"

A week later, Mary stepped off the train on The Regent's private rail spur. Will Davis was there to meet her.

Mary wore a stylish traveling suit of crisp blue cotton and carried one small valise filled with new clothes she'd bought with the $278.27 that the late Father Fitzgerald had left her.

Tucked carefully among the folded dresses were the personal items from her captive days that she had not been allowed to see since they were taken from her that first day at the convent. When she was ready to leave, Sister Catherine Elizabeth had handed her the bundle containing her childhood treasures. The turquoise-handled knife. The faded bits of fabric. The baby teeth. The gold locket with the initials M.S.H. on its face.

Standing beside the parked carriage, Will Davis looked up, saw the young woman step out into the strong Texas sunshine, and felt his breath catch in his chest. She was stunningly beautiful, with pale blond hair. Fair porcelain skin. A tall, willowy body.

Will stepped forward, thrust out his right hand, smiled and said, "I'm Will Davis. LaDextra Regent sent me to meet you."

Mary flashed Will a blinding smile, shook his hand firmly and said, as if there were no doubt about it, "I'm Anna Regent Wright, Mr. Davis. Thank you so much for coming."

"You're very welcome," said Will as he put his hands to her small waist and lifted her off the wooden platform. He reached for her valise and guided her to the waiting carriage.

On the one-and-a-half-mile ride to the ranch, Will Davis learned that this charming young girl was more than just a pretty face. She was polite and friendly and intelligent and totally likable. Just as her mother had been. Enchanted, Will listened with interest to her earnest inquiries and forgot entirely that he was supposed to be the one asking the questions.

Mary looked around curiously as she talked. The long dirt road they traveled cut through fenced pastures where hundreds of cattle grazed.

"Do all these cattle belong to The Regent?"

"All these and more," Will replied with a smile. "Presently there are approximately fifty thousand head of cattle on the ranch. They only keep a few hundred head here in the *Tierra Verde* pasture."

Mary frowned. "*Tierra Verde?* Doesn't that mean green land? It doesn't look very green to me."

Will smiled. "No, it doesn't. We haven't had a lot of rain this spring, but hopefully we'll soon be getting some gully washers."

"So there are other pastures as large as this one?"

"Many more. This ranch is a million acres of land under two thousand miles of fence."

Mary started to comment, but the sprawling ranch house, now clearly in sight, arrested her full attention.

"Is that it?" Mary asked excitedly, pointing.

"Yes. That's it. The Regent."

Mary was overwhelmed. Since leaving the railroad spur they had been crossing the flat desert floor, moving steadily closer to a towering mountain range to the north. Now they were almost up into the Guadalupes, the road—graveled now—swiftly ascending into the rocky foothills.

A quarter of a mile ahead and a hundred feet above, a majestic white, two-story mansion with eight Doric columns rose to meet the blue Texas sky. Vast manicured grounds surrounded the huge house. Broad, hedge-trimmed terraces flanked the west side, and a completely level, velvety green lawn stretched out on the east, where a wishing well stood like a sentinel in the sun.

Mary stared at the enormous house, unable to believe that such an impressive dwelling actually belonged to one family. The house was so large and the grounds so immense, it brought to mind the pictures of European castles she had seen in books back at the convent. That's what this ranch house looked like—a magnificent castle in the clouds.

"Lawyer Davis," she said in awe, "the house...it's a palace. Royalty should live here."

Will Davis smiled and said, "Here in Texas, the Regents *are* royalty."

Three

At the imposing ranch house waited an alert, expectant LaDextra Regent. With the aid of her gold-handled, ebony cane, the eighty-one-year-old matriarch paced nervously back and forth on the mansion's sunny gallery. A statuesque woman with a halo of shining white hair and clear blue eyes, she was wearing her signature black, high-collared, long-sleeved dress.

LaDextra Regent looked formidable, indestructible, but her aging heart kept fluttering crazily as she anticipated the arrival of her granddaughter.

If it was her granddaughter.

How was she to know if the young woman was really Anna? Anna had been only eight years old when the Apache took her. Would she look anything like she had then? Would she, LaDextra, know at once, as soon as she saw her, that the girl was Anna? Or that she wasn't?

LaDextra suddenly frowned.

And if she was Anna, what about Brit? Would he feel threatened? Would he hate Anna? Would he hate *her* as well? The prospect of his hating her was too painful for LaDextra to consider. Britton Caruth was like her blood grandson, not just her stepgrandson. She loved him dearly. And Brit had been cheated enough in his life.

Orphaned at twelve, Brit had been an unruly, rebellious child who had caused her no small amount of grief. She had spent more than one sleepless night worrying about him. But from the start she had been fond of the troubled little boy. That fondness had grown as he grew, and as he began to feel that he was not in the way, that The Regent was his true home, his behavior had improved.

The devilishly handsome, twenty-eight-year-old Brit was, in LaDextra's opinion, the same cut of wild, rugged Texan as her dear departed husband had been in his vigorous youth. Like Robert Regent, Brit was a fun-loving, fearless fellow whom men admired and women desired.

A lusty hell-raiser, Brit was a natural charmer who enjoyed fine Kentucky bourbon, an occasional fistfight and the company of beautiful women. He was also intelligent, a hard worker and, for the past four years, the respected general manager of the vast Texas spread.

And presumptive heir to The Regent.

But if the girl was actually Anna...

If Anna was really alive...The Regent rightfully belonged to her.

LaDextra stopped pacing and frowned worriedly, her weak heart fluttering alarmingly.

LaDextra's worries of impending trouble were forgotten entirely when the young woman she hoped was Anna stepped onto the mansion's sunny gallery.

"Land sakes alive, let me look at you," said LaDextra, staring at the tall, slender girl before her. Her arthritic hands raised and clasping her own sun-wrinkled cheeks, her blue eyes misting with tears, LaDextra Regent felt as if time had turned backward and she was looking at her pretty daughter, Christina.

"Anna, my own Anna, welcome home!" said LaDextra. "May I hug you, child?" She didn't wait for an answer.

Mary found herself abruptly swept up and wrapped in the long, loving arms of LaDextra Regent. Mary was surprised to find that it was not unpleasant. The firm embrace gave her a feeling of being safe, a feeling she'd never had before. It came to her, as this woman rocked her back and forth affectionately, that she had *never* been hugged in her life. Her own slender arms lifted and went awkwardly around the statuesque LaDextra.

It was then, standing there in the sun on the wide gallery of the huge white mansion, that Mary decided she *was* Anna. From that minute forward, she would think of herself as Anna. She would *be* Anna and she would stay there forever. She would live in splendor and ease in the imposing mansion. She'd be accepted and loved and know that, finally, she belonged.

She belonged at The Regent!

This was her home and nobody could take it away from her. Nobody.

"Why don't we all go inside?" Will Davis suggested.

"Yes, yes of course," LaDextra agreed, reluctantly releasing Anna, but reaching for one of her hands.

The old woman led her inside, ushered her into the spacious drawing room, and once again Anna was astonished. Awed by the grandeur of the mansion and its impressive furnishings, she was tempted to slide her hand over the lid of a gleaming grand piano that sat in front of the large front window.

The room, square in shape and gigantic, held fine furniture of a kind Anna never knew existed. There were handsome velvet sofas, silk shantung chairs and marble-topped tables, frosted-globed lamps and fresh cut flowers in fragile porcelain vases.

Above a fireplace of shiny white marble hung a huge gold-framed mirror. Matching smaller mirrors graced the walls, along with paintings that Anna assumed were priceless original works of art.

LaDextra chuckled at the look on Anna's pretty face. She said, "I know what you're thinking. That this house looks out of place here in west Texas."

"No, I..." Anna began, shaking her head.

LaDextra's blue eyes twinkled. "It does look out of place. Sit down and I'll tell you why. I'm sure you've forgotten how I love to tell the tale."

Anna took a seat in a wing chair as LaDextra gingerly lowered herself onto a velvet sofa. The attorney, Will Davis, thoughtfully disappeared, slipping into the library to have a drink of bourbon.

Rubbing the soft arm of the sofa, LaDextra said, smiling, "Child, your granny wasn't always a wrinkled, sunburned old Texan. No sirree. I was a pampered Kentucky belle when your granddaddy met me. Robert Regent was a brash bachelor who had come to Louisville looking for blooded horses. My daddy brought him home to dinner one evening and it was love at first sight for us both. Robert said if I'd marry him and come to Texas and help him run the ranch, he would, within ten years, build me the mansion of my dreams."

Anna smiled, nodded.

"He kept his word," said LaDextra proudly. "I told him I wanted a fine antebellum-style Southern mansion with eight Doric columns and wide wrap-around galleries. Eager to please me, Robert imported the materials and craftsmen and had this home built for me." She laughed then, remembering, and said, "You won't see another house like this in west Texas."

"It's a beautiful home," said Anna.

"It's *your* beautiful home," said LaDextra.

At those words, Anna grew almost giddy with delight. It was all she could do to keep from laughing hysterically. She realized, with great relief, that this big, raw-boned, white-haired matriarch was more than eager to accept her as the long-lost Anna. The deception was going to be much easier than she could have dared hope.

Her future was secure.

Anna's newfound sense of security was shattered that very evening at dinner. She, LaDextra and Will Davis had gathered in the well-appointed drawing room as the April sun was setting.

LaDextra, glancing at a gold-and-crystal clock on the marble mantel, said, "We'll wait a few more minutes. Then we'll go on into the dining room."

Hungry, not used to eating at such a late hour, Anna wondered why they were to wait a few more minutes. Too soon she found out.

She blinked in confusion and apprehension when a tall, broad-shouldered, raven-haired man dressed in a spotless white linen shirt and a pair of dark, neatly pressed trousers abruptly entered the lamplit room. Flashing a dazzlingly disarming smile, he apologized for being tardy, walked straight to the sofa where LaDextra sat, leaned down and gave her forehead a quick kiss. Her face lit up like a Christmas tree.

The lean man then crossed to the attorney, shook his hand and said, "Good to see you, Will."

Then he turned directly to her, reached for her hand and took it firmly in his.

"Welcome home to The Regent, Anna," he said in a low, well-modulated voice, his dark eyes flashing in his tanned, handsome face.

Anna's heart sank.

She knew in that instant that this compelling stranger did not believe her claim. Would never believe it. She had no idea who he was or what he was doing here, but she knew, instinctively, that he was going to cause her trouble.

"I'm Brit Caruth," he said in a warm baritone, gently squeezing her hand in both of his own. "LaDextra's no doubt told you that my father married your mother."

"Now, Brit," scolded LaDextra, "I didn't want to bombard her with too much at once. She knows nothing about you. We haven't talked about you yet."

As if LaDextra hadn't spoken, Brit Caruth, his dark gaze holding Anna's, said, "So I suppose that makes me your big brother." He paused, grinned wickedly and added, "You need anything, little sister, you just let me know."

Caught off guard, Anna wished that Father Fitzgerald had warned her about this...this Brit Caruth. Or had he? She vaguely remembered the old priest mentioning that Anna's mother had married a widower with a young son. But she'd never considered the unlikely possibility that the man's son would still be at the ranch.

Anna sat stiffly throughout dinner. She had no appetite for the prime Regent beef that was cooked to tender perfection. The minute she learned that the dark man who managed the ranch for LaDextra also resided right here in the mansion, she was no longer hungry.

Dear Lord, she was to live under the same roof as Brit Caruth, whose lean, handsome face was cynically set and whose dark, flashing eyes silently told her he knew what she was up to.

Anna was horrified.

But she carefully concealed her feelings. Quickly she realized that LaDextra considered him to be a member of the family. So she sat across the table from him, pretending an ease and comfort she didn't feel. She listened politely to the pleasant dinner conversation, nodding at the appropriate moments.

She did her best to answer the casual questions posed to her by a beaming LaDextra, the amiable Will and the skeptical Brit Caruth. Anna had no trouble with LaDextra's and Will's harmless questions. But she faltered when Brit quizzed her. It was not just his probing questions that unsettled her, it was also the challenging gleam in his dark eyes when he addressed her. That, and the way the flickering candlelight cast menacing shadows on his dark face, accentuating the high cheekbones and firmly chiseled features.

Anna grew so nervous she felt beads of perspiration forming at her hairline as she noted how the fabric of the white linen shirt he wore stretched so tantalizingly across the flat, hard muscles of his chest, and that the shirt's collar was open, revealing his smooth, tanned throat. She stared, entranced, as the muscles there moved like well-oiled machinery when he drained the contents of his stemmed wineglass.

He set the empty glass down with both hands, the movement causing his shirtsleeves to pull taut over his muscular upper arms. Unable to take her eyes off those bulging biceps, Anna wondered involuntarily how it would feel to have those powerful arms around her.

Brit looked up, caught her staring at him and grinned accusingly at her. Anna shivered, quickly looked away and was greatly relieved when Brit dropped his dinner napkin on the table and pushed back his chair.

"Ladies, Will," he said, "if you'll excuse me, I think I'll run into town for a while."

LaDextra smiled fondly at him. "Who is it this evening? The brunette or the redhead?"

Brit just winked at her, said nothing. Rising to his feet, he said, "Good night now, Anna. Sleep well, you hear?"

"Oh, I will, thank you," she calmly assured him, knowing that she would not. Knowing that he knew she would not. Damn him.

Later that very evening, Anna was put to the first of many tests. She passed this initial one with flying colors, thanks to Father Fitzgerald.

Will Davis had, after a second cup of coffee served in the library, said his good-nights and gone home. Shortly after his departure, LaDextra had turned to Anna and said, "It's been an exciting day for us all, but you must be exhausted. I'm sure you need rest. I thought you could just take your old room."

"My old room will be fine," Anna replied with cool confidence.

As she patiently climbed the stairs beside the slow-moving LaDextra, the older woman said, "For years I kept your room just as it was the day you— you..." She shook her white head. "Finally Brit convinced me it was time to pack away everything that belonged to you. He was right, of course, so I did. But it was painful." She suddenly brightened and said, "The moment I heard you were coming home I had the room completely redone. I hope you'll like it. If you don't, we'll simply do the whole thing over again."

"I'm sure I will like it," said Anna.

The two women reached the top of the stairs. Anna decisively turned right at the landing and proceeded down the silent corridor to the correct room, thanks to the intense coaching from the old priest.

LaDextra was delighted.

"Oh, child," she said happily, "you remembered! You remembered! You *are* my darling Anna, I know you are. All the rest of it will come back to you in time."

"I hope so," said Anna.

"Now don't you worry about a thing," said LaDextra. "You just get yourself a good night's rest."

"Yes, ma'am, Mrs. Regent," said Anna.

LaDextra laughed. "Bless your heart, you don't know what to call me, do you, child?"

"No, ma'am."

"Well, it's a little too soon for you to feel comfortable calling me Grandmother, so just call me LaDextra. That's what everybody calls me."

"Thank you, LaDextra," said Anna.

"Now, good night, dear. My room is down on the first floor. For the past few years, I've had trouble with the stairs."

"Shall I help you down?" asked Anna.

"No, no, I can manage." LaDextra smiled then

and again put her arms around Anna and hugged her. "My sweet little Anna, you're home and safe and all's right with the world again."

"Yes," said Anna softly, "yes it is."

Four

His lean jaw set, his jet-black hair whipping about his face in the night wind, Brit Caruth rode hell-for-leather into town.

He was angry, although he had carefully concealed it from everyone. Everyone but *her*. He wanted her to know.

Brit was mad as hell that from out of the blue a slender, blond-haired pretender had turned up intending to calmly take advantage of the good-hearted LaDextra.

Damn her to hell, whoever she was. If it turned out that she wasn't Anna, and he was sure she wasn't, LaDextra would be deeply hurt. He hated the thought of that happening. LaDextra Regent was his only family and he loved her dearly, wanted to protect her from pain.

And if he didn't expose this woman claiming to be Anna for an avaricious imposter, he would lose everything he had worked so hard for all his life. Well, that was not going to happen. He wouldn't allow it. Tomorrow he'd get a wire off to the Pinkertons. Have them send one of their best agents down to Arizona and the Apache country to begin a thorough investigation of this woman claiming to be Anna Regent Wright.

When Brit reached the twinkling lights of Regentville, he began to relax. He was confident that the mystery woman would be exposed for the fraud she was and sent on her way.

And the sooner the better.

No getting around it, she was a pretty little thing, all right, with that long blond hair and porcelain skin and those luscious lips. And, Lord, that willowy body. A slender, beautiful body that looked as if it had been made to fit perfectly against his own. The very thought of holding her in his arms caused Brit's belly to tighten, his teeth to clamp down hard.

He impatiently shook his head to clear it.

To hell with her.

He had all the woman he could handle waiting for him a short half mile ahead.

Brit soon brought Captain, his iron-gray stallion, to a plunging halt before the pale yellow Victorian house at the end of Yucca Street. At his forceful knock, a voluptuous red-haired woman wearing nothing but a shimmering, black satin robe appeared in the lighted doorway.

"Evenin', Beverly," Brit drawled, smiling, and put his hands around her narrow waist. With total ease, he lifted her up before him and said, "Could a thirsty cowboy get a drink of whiskey around here?"

With laughter bubbling from her wide, red lips, the merry young widow Harris wrapped her long legs around Brit's hard waist and promised seductively, "Ah, my love, you can get a whole lot more than whiskey around here."

Smiling, Brit stepped inside the foyer and kicked the door shut behind him. He proceeded directly to the wide staircase, while the woman in his arms clung to his neck and scattered kisses over his tanned face.

Brit laughed and, holding her securely with one long arm, began dexterously relieving her of the black satin robe. Halfway up the stairs the robe fell to the carpeted steps and Beverly Harris was as naked as the day she was born. Her knees gripping his sides, ankles crossed behind his back, she impatiently slipped a hand down Brit's chest and began unbuttoning his white linen shirt.

By the time they reached the upstairs landing, Brit's shirt was open and pushed off one shoulder, and the wriggling woman in his arms was kissing and licking his bare chest. Brit lowered Beverly to her bare feet. Together they made short work of relieving him of his clothes. When he was as naked as she, Beverly purred like a kitten, wrapped her small white hands around his awesome erection and, backing away, led him by his pulsing member straight to her luxurious bedroom.

Once there, they moved decisively to the bed. Never releasing her hold on him, Beverly sank back onto the silk-sheeted mattress, drawing him down with her.

She licked her red lips, kept one soft hand wrapped around his erection and lowered the other to gently cup him. Letting her caressing fingers slide up and down his hot, heavy flesh, she murmured provocatively, "All day I could think of nothing but having your hard, beautiful flesh deep inside me." She looked up at him, smiled seductively. "Tell me that's where it belongs."

"Sure, honey," Brit said automatically, "it belongs in you and that's where I intend to put it very soon."

Beverly was not totally satisfied with his answer. She said coyly, "Brit, tell me it is mine. All mine. No one else's."

"Now, Bev, don't start with that foolishness," Brit gently scolded. Moving her hand away, he replaced it with his own and lowered himself against her. With his naked chest pressing her soft, warm breasts, his bare belly and throbbing erection resting against her stomach, he brushed a teasing kiss to her lips. Beverly flung her arms around his neck, eagerly lifted her parted lips to his and kissed him passionately.

She sighed into his mouth when his long, tapered fingers sought and found that soft wet heat between her thighs. His lips nibbling hers, Brit lay there partially atop her in the lamplight and teased and toyed with her until she was so aroused he knew she couldn't avoid a climax much longer.

So he stopped.

He took his hand from between her legs, his mouth from her lips. She moaned her protest, but was actually glad that he had stopped.

She knew exactly what he was doing and she fully approved.

He had left her right on the brink of ecstasy and would now wait until she calmed and cooled a bit before he started taking her there again. It was the way they liked to make love. Some nights they spent hours playing, pushing each other almost to sexual madness before finally allowing the much needed climax. And oh what a climax. Many a time she had screamed out as she thrashed about in the throes of fantastic sexual release.

Beverly sighed and lay back on the bed. Brit smiled and stretched on his back beside her. He folded his arms beneath his head and watched through heavy black lashes as the big-breasted, milky-skinned redhead ran her scarlet-nailed little finger up his rock-hard erection, from tight, drawn-up testicles to swollen, pulsing tip.

It was her turn to arouse him to the breaking point, and she was quite talented at the game.

Within a few short minutes she had stroked and caressed and licked and tongued his hard male flesh until he could stand it no longer.

Brit grabbed Beverly up, turned her onto her back and was poised to thrust eagerly into her when she stopped him.

"No, darling," she said, quickly putting a protective hand between her legs, blocking his access. "It's too early. You just got here." She agilely slipped out from under him and rose from the bed. She nodded to a tall silver stand near the bed where a corked magnum was chilling in ice. "Let's have a glass of champagne before we start again."

When the lusty pair finally made love fully, more

than an hour had passed. Both were pleasantly tipsy from the smooth wine and so hot they were on fire. Perspiring, slipping and sliding on each other, they were not on the bed, but on the floor beside it. There on the soft plush carpet, they finally let themselves go.

Afterward, Brit waited only a few minutes before saying, "It's getting late, I better go."

"No!" Beverly petulantly protested. "You never leave this soon. Why, we've just begun to have fun."

"Ah, Bev, you're too much woman for me," said Brit.

"I never have been before. What's wrong with you?"

"Nothing," he said, half-irritated that she'd suggest something was. "Not a thing," he assured her, easing her off of him and sitting up. Lifting his arms and running both hands through his thick hair, he said, "I'm just a little tired tonight. Had a long, hard day."

"Oh, very well," Bev replied, relenting. "You can go if you promise to come again tomorrow night."

"Can't," he said as he reached for his discarded trousers.

"Why? Have you something better to do?"

Brit flashed her a winning smile and said, "What could be better than you?"

At The Regent, Anna was still wide awake.

After LaDextra left her, she had gone inside the

room that had supposedly once been hers. Nothing about it was familiar. She had never been in it before. Nor in any room to compare. She had never seen anything so grand, so beautiful.

Anna had stared in amazement at walls covered in shimmering, pale beige watered silk. The high ceiling, the baseboard moldings and the oversize window casings were of gleaming ivory. Tall, ivory, many-paned French doors opened onto the wide balcony. The doors had been closed.

Now Anna opened one of them, stepped outside, moved to the balcony railing and gazed at the wide valley spread out below. A quarter moon sailed high in the cloudless night sky, and from somewhere nearby the subtle scent of honeysuckle sweetened the air.

Anna inhaled deeply, then turned and went back inside the exquisite room that was now hers. She left one of the French doors ajar to catch the cool April breeze.

A chaise longue covered in rich chocolate velvet sat before a tall front window near the French doors. A beige silk canopied bed had been turned down for the night. The sheets looked clean, cool and inviting, and there were a half-dozen pillows with lace-trimmed cases stacked up against the bed's tall headboard.

On the wall opposite the bed was an imposing ivory marble fireplace. A high-backed beige sofa sat near the fireplace, facing a pair of matching high-backed chairs across a low mahogany table. And wonder of wonders, there on a highly polished stand was a large, crank-up phonograph for playing music!

Anna kept turning round and round, staring at the large luxurious room. She clasped her hands together and pressed them to her heart. Tears of happiness filled her eyes. She gazed at the big soft bed and couldn't believe her good fortune.

Anxious to test the mattress's softness, Anna undressed, drew on a new batiste nightgown, blew out the lamp and climbed into the inviting canopied bed. How incredibly comfortable it was! In her wildest dreams, she had never imagined how absolutely wonderful it would be to lie in a big, soft bed with silky sheets and fluffy pillows. The hard ground and a narrow cot were all she had ever known.

Lying in that big bed, Anna sighed, stretched and smiled with pleasure.

But her elation was tempered with guilt.

I am a criminal, she silently accused herself, facing fully what she was for the first time. *A charlatan and a liar.* For an unpleasant moment, she struggled with her guilty conscience. Then she sighed and confessed, *But I've got what I wanted and it is worth it. Now, if only I can keep it.*

With that thought, the darkly handsome face of Brit Caruth flashed into Anna's mind. She frowned. She didn't want to think about him. She tried to dismiss him, but he wouldn't let her be. His image, the way he had looked at dinner with the candlelight casting shadows on his face, plagued her, frightened her. Anna tossed and turned fitfully.

She was worried.

Brit Caruth would surely do everything in his power to expose her as a fraud. He was not about to let her hurt LaDextra or get her hands on the Regent fortune. Anna knew instinctively that Brit Caruth was a dangerous man, at least dangerous to her. And in more ways than one.

Not only did she recognize him as being a powerful adversary, she was all too aware of his striking good looks and abundant animal magnetism. He was surely unsafe to any healthy, red-blooded female.

Including her.

Her hand still tingled from being enclosed in his lean fingers, and it was impossible not to speculate on how it would feel to have those beautiful brown hands touch her face, her throat, her lips.

Anna quickly turned onto her side and drew her knees up to her chin in a protective gesture. She would have to be always on her guard and, if possible, stay completely away from the incredibly masculine, menacing Brit Caruth.

Five

Anna awakened with the sun.

LaDextra had told her that she could sleep as late as she liked. But it was going take a while to break the habit of a lifetime. When she was with the Apache, they had prodded her awake each morning by five. When she was with the sisters, she'd risen regularly at five-thirty.

Anna turned her head, glanced at the delicate marble clock on the bedside table. Ten minutes of six. She yawned, got out of bed and dressed. At ten minutes past six, she ventured down the stairs and followed the pleasing aroma of coffee into the dining room.

The minute she stepped into the arched doorway, she wished she had stayed in bed.

His back to her, Brit Caruth sat alone at the head of the long dining table, hungrily devouring a huge plate of steak and eggs. Anna immediately turned away, hoping to make a quick exit before he saw her.

She never made it.

"Come on in, Anna," Brit said without turning his head. "Have breakfast with me."

Caught, she made a face and came forward, wondering how he had known she was there. And how he knew it was her.

"Where is LaDextra?" Anna asked, glancing at the seated man, who did not politely rise to acknowledge her presence.

"In bed, I would imagine," Brit replied. "She rarely rises before seven." He motioned with his raised fork. "Go ahead, help yourself."

Anna moved to the polished cherry-wood sideboard where silver domed covers and candle-heated platters held a dazzling array of breakfast edibles. Anna put a small piece of ham and a spoonful of scrambled eggs on her plate and went to the table.

Unsure where she was supposed to sit, she blinked, startled, when Brit kicked a chair out from the table. The chair was directly to his left.

"Sit right here by me, Anna," he said. "Let's get acquainted."

Anxious, sure he was going to bombard her with questions in an attempt to trip her up, Anna reluctantly sat down.

Brit picked up the gleaming silver coffee carafe and filled her cup.

"Thank you," she said.

"You're very welcome, *Anna*," he said, emphasizing the name as he poured another cup for himself.

His breakfast finished, he pushed the empty plate away and leaned back in his chair. His dark, hooded eyes resting on her, he said, "I would suppose one of the first places you'll want to visit is Manzanita Springs." The corner of his mouth lifted minutely in the hint of a sneer. He'd bet his best gray stallion that this woman claiming to be Anna had no idea what or where Manzanita Springs were. Or why she would want to go there.

"Yes," Anna said, looking him squarely in the eye. "Although I'm afraid it may be quite painful for me, I really feel I should have a look at the place from which the Apache took me."

Brit ground his teeth in frustration. His eyes darkened. He shook a cigarette from a slightly crushed package and stuck it between his lips. He said, "I thought you would. I'll take you there as soon as—"

"Hey, anybody home?" An intrusive masculine voice stopped Brit in midsentence.

Damn. He had completely forgotten that he'd told Buck to come up to the house for breakfast this morning, then ride into town with him.

"In here, Buck," Brit called out.

Anna smiled smugly at Brit, knowing that for now, at least, she was off the hook. Brit knew it, too, and it rankled him.

Big, blond, easygoing Buck Shanahan, grinning from ear to ear as usual, stepped into the dining room.

"Join us, Buck," said Brit, and the muscular cowboy strode directly toward the table, his smiling green eyes fixed solely on Anna.

"Anna, meet my friend Buck Shanahan," said Brit. "Buck, may I present Miss Anna Regent Wright."

Anna smiled, extended her hand. Buck nervously

wiped his own on his trouser leg before eagerly shaking hers.

"A pleasure to meet you, Mr. Shanahan," she said.

"Call me Buck, Miss Anna." Continuing to hold her hand, he grinned down at her and said, "Boy howdy, Brit told me you were awful pretty, but I had no idea you'd look like...like an angel."

Anna calmly withdrew her hand from his. "I'm no angel, Buck. Just a woman grateful to be back home after all these years—" she glanced at Brit, adding pointedly "—where I belong."

"Yes, ma'am, ah...I mean yes, Miss Anna," said Buck. "Miz LaDextra and all of us are mighty glad to have you home. Aren't we, Brit?"

"Ecstatic."

At midmorning LaDextra showed Anna throughout the sprawling mansion. They chattered companionably as they moved from room to room, LaDextra reminiscing, telling Anna that when they'd been young, she and her husband had wanted lots of children and were beginning to think that the good Lord was never going to bless them with a child.

"Why, honey, I was thirty-six years old when your mother, Christina, was born. Robert and I had just about given up. After she came, we kept trying for a boy, but..." She shrugged. "Christina was my only child and very precious because of it. Just as you are very precious because you're Christina's only child. My only grandchild."

Nodding, listening, Anna waited for an opportune moment, then said as casually as possible, "Tell me about Brit Caruth. Christina, my mother, was married to his father?"

"She was. Yes, she was. A year after you were captured and your daddy killed by the Apache, Christina met and married Douglas Caruth. He was a fine man, a widower, and he had a twelve-year-old boy, Brit. Brit stayed here with me while Douglas and Christina went on an extended honeymoon." LaDextra exhaled heavily. "Both were killed in an avalanche. Buried so deep in the snow their bodies were never recovered."

"I'm sorry, LaDextra," offered Anna.

"Well, it was a long time ago. I've done my share of grieving." She smiled wistfully and said, "Anyhow, poor little Brit was left an orphan. His father had been his only family. He had nowhere to go. So Brit had no choice but to stay on here at the ranch, and I had no choice but to keep him." Her blue eyes began to sparkle as she talked about the handsome young man she considered a grandson. "Those first few years were rocky, but I was crazy about the little scamp from the beginning, and I took good care of him." She laughed with pleasure and said, "Now Brit's grown and he takes good care of me. Runs the ranch better than your granddaddy—rest his soul—ever did. Brit's smart, industrious and as loyal as they come."

"He seems to be a nice man," said Anna, almost choking on the words.

"I'm betting that you and Brit are going to like

each other, that you become good friends," said LaDextra, hoping it was so. "I think the two of you will get along just fine, don't you?"

"I'm sure of it," said Anna with a sweet smile.

The two women swept on through the mansion, LaDextra introducing Anna to the house servants, hoping to spark a glimmer of recognition in the girl's eyes. Or in the eyes of the servants.

Directly after lunch, LaDextra summoned her personal maid, Connie. When the stocky, middle-aged servant appeared, LaDextra said, "Connie, I thought that while I have my nap you could assist Anna with her unpacking."

Connie nodded. "I'd be more than happy to help," she said. She glanced at Anna and smiled. "I'll get LaDextra settled in her bed, then be right up to your room."

"Thank you, Connie," said Anna, feeling suddenly uneasy. She suspected that the loyal servant would, once the two of them were alone, ask countless questions.

She was right.

As the two women worked together, shaking out the wrinkled dresses and hanging them up, Connie relentlessly quizzed Anna. Throughout, Anna managed to remain calm and collected. She had the answers to some of Connie's questions. To others, she freely admitted that she could not recall, did not remember.

As the seemingly casual, but intense interrogation continued, Anna knew she hadn't convinced Connie.

Still, she managed to keep a firm grip on herself, to smile and nod and act as if she were not the least bit flustered.

Coolly replying to yet another of Connie's questions, Anna turned and carried an armful of lingerie to the bureau. At the same time, Connie lifted a lilac summer dress from the open leather valise.

A small, curious-looking bundle tumbled out of the skirt's folds and fell to the carpeted floor. Puzzled, Connie laid the dress on the bed, stooped and picked up the bundle.

"What's this?"

Anna turned, saw what Connie was holding. Her composure shattering, she flew across the room in a panic.

"It's mine, give it to me!"

"Well, certainly," said Connie, eyeing her suspiciously as she handed it over. "I just wondered what—"

"It's nothing, nothing," said Anna, clutching the bundle, "just some silly sentimental keepsakes."

She could hardly breathe, she was so upset. If Connie had opened the bundle, had seen the locket with the inscription "M.S.H.," she would have immediately told LaDextra, "this girl is not Anna."

Connie never saw the damning necklace, but she didn't believe that this young woman was Anna.

On the other hand, Maggie Mae, the head cook at the ranch for the past three decades, was certain that the beautiful girl was Anna, now all grown-up. When Anna came into the kitchen later that afternoon, Maggie Mae said, "Honey, sit down there at the table and tell me what your favorite foods are."

Anna didn't hesitate. Smiling, she said, "Rare steak, of course."

"Of course," Maggie Mae repeated, nodding.

"And, um, let's see. Fried chicken. Baked ham. Potato salad." She tilted her blond head to the side and her blue eyes began to sparkle. "Oh, and blackberry cobbler with thick cream. And chocolate cake with rich fudge icing. Hot apple pie with melted cheese. Strawberry shortcake with ice cream and...and—"

"Honey, you haven't changed a bit," a laughing Maggie Mae interrupted. "Still have that sweet tooth!"

"I'm afraid I do," admitted Anna.

"Well, I'm going to bake you a big old chocolate cake for supper, that's what I'm going to do!"

"My mouth's already watering," said Anna with a smile.

When, shortly, LaDextra entered the kitchen and asked Anna if she'd like to join her for a cup of tea on the back patio, Anna left the cook beaming.

And certain that she was Anna.

Later that same afternoon, a visitor came to The Regent.

Unaware that LaDextra was entertaining an old friend, Anna came bounding into the drawing room and stopped short when she spotted a very frail, gray-haired woman seated on one of the velvet sofas.

As if she felt Anna's eyes on her, the aged woman slowly raised her head, turned it and looked directly at Anna. Anna stared, her lips open.

LaDextra looked from one to the other and said to Anna, "What is it, child?"

Anna didn't answer. Instead she walked into the room, smiled warmly at the old woman and said, *"Mein Liebling."*

Tears sprang to the eyes of the visitor and she struggled to rise. Anna was beside her in an instant, urging her to remain seated. Dropping to her knees beside the sofa, she firmly clasped the bony hand reaching for hers and laughed merrily when the woman repeated in her native tongue, *"Mein Liebling, Anna."*

"Yes, Helga, it's Anna. I've come home."

LaDextra, looking on in surprised delight, fondly recalled how Helga, Anna's German nanny, had always called the child *"Mein Liebling, Anna."* "My darling Anna."

And Anna had remembered! She had remembered after all these years. She was Anna, she was!

As Anna knelt and talked with the woman, neither LaDextra nor Helga could possibly have known how surprised she herself was that those words had come out of her mouth. Where had she learned any German? How did she know that this was what Helga had called Anna? How did she know the woman's name was Helga?

Was she, perhaps, really Anna Regent Wright?

In no time the household staff was firmly divided into two camps—those who believed and those who did not. Anna often confounded both sides. She couldn't remember things she should have easily recalled. Then she'd turn around and reveal something that only the Regent girl, or someone very close to her, could have known.

One member of the household was not so easily swayed by Anna's impressive flashes of recollection. There was no doubt in Brit's mind that she was an imposter. A pretender who had studied and learned all that she could about the Regent family. A dangerous dissembler spurred by greed.

Brit strongly suspected that she had a partner in crime. Perhaps someone who had worked at the ranch and knew the family. Probably a lazy lover who meant to cash in on the windfall. Only there wasn't going to be any windfall.

Not for her.

Not if he could help it.

Brit shoved the brief message addressed to the Pinkerton Detective Agency through the window of the wired cage at the telegraph office. "Dub, can you get this wire out in the next hour or so?"

"Is it important?" the balding operator asked.

"Only to me."

Six

Soon the strain of her ordeal began to wear on Anna. Ever fearful of giving herself away, feeling as if she was eternally on trial, she found her nerves beginning to fray. She had trouble sleeping.

After a full week at the ranch, during which she had been watched and questioned and checked on, she was so on edge she simply couldn't relax. Unable to face another night of restlessness, Anna finally slipped out of bed and drew on a silk robe, leaving it untied.

She crossed the darkened room, walked through the open French doors and stepped out onto the wide balcony.

And stopped abruptly.

Shirtless, shoeless, his black hair disheveled, his tanned shoulders and chest gleaming in the moonlight, Brit Caruth sat astride the balcony railing, smoking a cigar. He turned and looked at her, and Anna involuntarily shivered.

Brit took a long, slow drag from his cigar, then flicked it away. Anna tensed. Her pulse leaped. Her knees grew weak. Brit brought his long leg back inside the railing, pushed himself to his bare feet and came directly to her.

Anna couldn't breathe. She knew he was going to kiss her, but she didn't try to stop him. She was—and had been from the first moment she saw him—extremely curious. She wondered how it would feel to be kissed by this handsome, hard-faced man.

Brit stood directly before her, the width of his shoulders blocking out the moonlight. He smiled, and his teeth shone starkly white in his tanned face. Heat radiated from him, and Anna felt as if his tall lean body was one giant magnet. He was drawing her to him without even touching her. She felt herself helplessly swaying closer.

Brit's long, leanly muscled arms went around her and he drew her up on tiptoe. His dark eyes flashed in the shadowy light as he gazed pointedly at her parted, trembling lips. His eyes slowly lifted to meet hers, and for a long, tension-filled moment they stared at each other without blinking.

Then his long thick lashes began to leisurely lower as he bent his dark head to kiss her. All at once his mouth was on hers, warm and smooth and persuasive. Her response was automatic, as natural and as necessary as breathing.

With her arms hanging limp at her sides, her head thrown back, Anna stood there in the pale spring moonlight, pressed flush against this hard-muscled Texan, futilely demanding her wildly beating heart to slow its rapid cadence. Ordering herself to tear her seared lips from his scorching mouth. Commanding herself to pull away from the fierce heat of his lean, lanky body.

But she did nothing.

Brit's hands were inside her open robe. Gently he stroked her slender back through the thin fabric of her nightgown as his coaxing mouth molded her lips to fit perfectly against his. She offered no objections, so he deepened the kiss, his sleek tongue sliding inside her mouth. He allowed his warm, caressing hand to glide down over the swell of her hip and beyond.

Still she didn't stop him.

Couldn't stop him.

Didn't want to stop him.

And Brit knew it.

It was he who finally ended the heated embrace, abruptly releasing her. Anna immediately stepped back and struggled to gather her scattered wits. Trembling, longing for more of his devastating kisses, she futilely fought the frightening passion he had aroused in her.

Determined to conceal the weakness she felt, she said in a brittle tone, "Just what do you think you are doing?"

Brit smiled devilishly, laid a spread hand on his dark, hair-covered chest and let it slowly drift down his bare belly into the low-riding waistband of his faded Levi's.

"Why, welcoming the young mistress back to her ancestral home."

Instantly angry with him, and even angrier with herself for allowing him to hold her and kiss her, Anna said, "Don't ever do that—kiss me—again!"

His infuriating smile still firmly in place, he said,

"Now, now, little sister, is that any way to speak to your big brother?"

"You are *not* my big brother," she hotly declared.

Brit's smile vanished instantly.

"That's right, baby, I'm not," he said, his chiseled features set, his dark eyes gone cold. He reached out, took her arm, drew her close again and added, "Nor are you kin to that old woman asleep downstairs." Anna tried to pull away. He held her fast. "I don't know who you are, but I do know you are not LaDextra's granddaughter. And if you think I'll stand idly by and allow you to get away with this deception, you're very wrong."

Anna yanked free of his grasp and warned, "You stay away from me, Brit Caruth!"

She rushed back inside and slammed the double doors behind her. She leaned back against them, trembling, afraid, upset. Anna now knew for certain that what she had suspected from the start was true. He didn't believe her. She wasn't safe at The Regent.

This lusty man who lived under the same roof and was adored by LaDextra was intent not only in exposing Anna, but in seducing her. She wasn't quite sure of his motive for the latter. Perhaps it was simply strong physical attraction. Or maybe he wanted to show her that she was not only an imposter, but a common tramp as well.

Her anger flared anew. Her determination strengthened. She stalked to the bed, tore off the robe and vowed aloud, "You will never expose *or* seduce me, Britton Caruth!"

She had momentarily forgotten that Brit was still right outside on the balcony. Through the open windows he heard her impassioned oath.

Without sound, he mouthed a response. "You're wrong, baby. I'm gonna do both."

As vast as the Regent ranch was, it was too small for the both of them. Torn between not wanting to see Brit and wanting to see Brit, Anna was soon to learn that avoiding him entirely would be next to impossible.

Just two days after the unforgettable kiss, La-Dextra asked Anna if she would like to take a ride, see some of the ranch.

"Oh, yes." Anna jumped at the chance. "I would love that."

"Good. Brit will meet you here at—"

"Brit? I'm to ride with Brit? I thought..."

"What? That I'd let you ride out alone?" La-Dextra shook her white head. "I just got you back, Anna. I'm not going to lose you again."

Anna thought fast. "But surely Brit is far too busy to bother with me. I'll just wait until some other—"

"Nonsense," interrupted LaDextra. "You're forgetting that Brit's the boss. He can take off a couple of hours if he wants to."

"What if he doesn't want to take me riding?" Anna queried.

LaDextra smiled. "He does. I've already asked him. He said he'd be glad to show you around. Told me he'd come up to the house to get you at two o'clock sharp.''

Anna was trapped. "All right.''

At five minutes past two, Anna, dressed in a white silk, long-sleeved blouse, soft suede riding pants and shiny brown boots, stepped out onto the back gallery. Her long blond hair was twisted into a thick shiny rope and pinned atop her head, but a purposely loosened lock swirled down her right cheek, concealing the ugly black tattoo behind her ear. A rust-colored, flat-crowned hat swung from her hand by its braided drawstring.

Anna was not smiling.

The prospect of riding out to the far reaches of this huge rangeland with the tormenting Brit Caruth was not her idea of a pleasant way to spend an afternoon. If she could have thought of a reasonable excuse to get out of it, she would have used it.

"If you're not careful,'' drawled a flat masculine voice, "your face will freeze that way.''

Anna looked up.

Brit was standing just outside the manicured backyard. Arms crossed, he was leaning back against the hitch rail where his stallion and a white-faced sorrel mare with stocking feet were tied. He was rawly masculine and undeniably attractive in a sky-blue pullover yoked shirt, tight faded Levi's, tan shotgun chaps and black cowboy boots. He was smiling as if pleased with himself.

Anna wanted to slap his smug, handsome face.

She took a deep, spine-stiffening breath and went

to meet him. Brit continued to stand there unmoving, with his arms crossed over his chest, his slim hips resting against the hitch rail.

As she approached, he felt his heart skip a beat. She walked with a graceful, confident stride, and her suede trousers definitely enhanced her small waist, flat stomach, flaring hips and long shapely legs. Beneath the soft fabric of her blouse, her full, high breasts bounced provocatively.

Brit felt his mouth go dry.

Felt his groin involuntarily stir.

Anna reached him. She slammed her suede hat on her head, tightened the drawstring beneath her chin.

Her hands then went to her trousered hips and she said, "It really isn't necessary for you to ride with me. I am perfectly capable of—of..." Brit stepped forward, put his hands to her waist. She clawed at his fingers. "What in blazes are you doing?"

"Just offering my assistance in mounting Dancer, the mare you're to ride."

Anna stomped her heel down hard on the toe of his boot. "Let me go! I need no help getting into the saddle. I rode with the Apache, remember?"

"So you did." Brit dropped his hands away, stepped back. "What else did they teach you, Anna? Besides how to mount a horse, I mean."

She could tell what he was thinking by the expression in his eyes. He suspected that she had been some brave's squaw, had slept with an Apache. Or many Apache. Let him wonder!

"They taught me a great deal," she said mysteriously as she brushed past him, unwound the long leather reins from around the hitch rail, stepped over to the sorrel mare and swung agilely up into the saddle. "About everything." She wheeled the mare around and cantered away.

Brit felt his insides twist. Too clearly came the unwelcome vision of a grunting, sweating, red-skinned savage furiously pumping into her pale naked body. He gritted his teeth. He felt sick to his stomach.

Then he abruptly chided himself. What difference did it make? What the hell did he care if she had shared a blanket with half the tribe? It had nothing to do with him.

Brit climbed into the saddle, wheeled Captain around and galloped after Anna.

Despite the presence of her unwelcome companion, Anna enjoyed the ride. It was the first time she'd been on a horse in more than five years and it felt good. Right. Natural.

It was a perfect day—warm, but not hot. The sky overhead was a cloudless blue. And this part of the ranch, the high green meadows directly behind the mansion, was breathtakingly beautiful. Anna headed due north, straight toward the towering peak of *El Capitán*, its rugged spires shining in the bright Texas sun.

She knew—the priest had told her—that Manzanita Springs was in the shadow of the awesome monolith. Following the map in her head that she had so carefully memorized, she rode directly toward the springs. No more than a half mile from the house and perhaps two hundred feet above it, she could hear the splashing water.

Drawing rein on a rocky plateau, Anna dismounted. She carefully picked her way through the dense stand of shrubs and weeping willow trees enclosing the springs. She stepped out into a large clearing and, shading her eyes with her hand, gazed at the cool, clean water bubbling up out of solid rock. Her first thought was what a wonderful place it would be for a swim in the hot summertime. Totally concealed by the thick greenery, it offered a private, cozy place to swim and read and doze and daydream.

"Want to go for a swim?" Brit asked as he stepped up beside her.

"Don't be ridiculous," she said haughtily.

"Am I?" He shrugged wide shoulders. "Tell me that's not what you were thinking about just now."

"That's not what I was thinking about just now," she declared, annoyed with him for reading her thoughts.

"I stand corrected," he said. "I guess you were recalling the day the Apache took you from here."

"I don't remember that day," she said truthfully.

"I see. So how did you know where the springs were?"

"I remember some things, not others."

Brit nodded and let it drop. No use wasting his time asking questions. He would never get the truth out of her. His only hope was the Pinkertons. Surely he would be hearing from them soon.

"Come on," he said. "Let's ride on up to the

lower part of the mountain tract and head east toward Pine Spring Canyon. I need to check the water level of the tanks up there.'' He turned away, musing aloud, ''Damn, we need a good soaking rain.''

In silence they began to climb the face of *El Capitán* Peak, the last towering monolith at the southern end of the Guadalupes. In no time the scenery, and the flora, changed dramatically. The prickly pears, yucca and creosote bushes of the desert gave way to junipers and scrub oaks. As the two riders continued their ascent, the forest grew denser. Ponderosa pines, Douglas firs, evergreens and quaking aspen covered the peak's face, rising above them.

The temperature dropped at least ten degrees as they rode in and out of deep shade. Anna grew chilly.

''It must get really cold up here in the wintertime,'' she said.

Brit nodded. ''We try to get the cattle moved down to the lower pastures before the snow begins to fly.'' He smiled suddenly and said, ''Back when I was just starting to work on the ranch—I was fifteen or so, I guess—I spent many a cold winter night up here in a line shack.''

''Why did you stay up here?''

''Because I wasn't dry behind the ears and I drew the most hated job a cowboy can have—riding the fences.'' Brit drew rein, slowly turned his gray stallion in a tight semicircle. Anna pulled up on the sorrel mare.

She asked, ''Were you the only one who had to ride the fences?''

Brit chuckled. "No, it's the hated job of lots of our young cowpokes. That, and bogging—pulling cattle out of mud bogs. Talk about a tough day's work." Hands folded atop the saddle horn, Brit gazed down at the desert below. He said, "Lots of work to be done on a ranch and The Regent is no small operation."

"Are there really a million acres?" she asked.

"One million, one hundred thousand to be exact—all under fence."

"That's a lot of fence."

"More than two thousand miles of it," he replied, "and every mile of it has to be ridden every day."

"Every day?" She was incredulous.

"Yep."

"So some of the ranch hands actually live in line shacks scattered over the rangelands?"

"Yes. In line shacks and at the division headquarters. There are four divisions to The Regent, each with its own division boss. The main division, _El Capitán,_ is here where the mansion is." He turned in the saddle and pointed. "Out east is the Columbine. To the west is the Texas Star. And down south at the border is the _Agua Fria._"

Anna listened with interest as he told her about The Regent.

"We have thirty-seven separate pastures," Brit said. "You've seen only one, the _Tierra Verde,_ directly below the house."

"The name doesn't fit," she commented.

"I know. We need a rain," Brit said. "Anyway, thirty-seven pastures, fifty thousand head of cattle, a thousand saddle horses and a hundred cowboys and vaqueros.''

Anna noticed that Brit's chiseled features softened as he talked about the ranch. It was obvious that The Regent was a source of great pride to him, that he loved the land and his place on it.

''And you are responsible for running the entire operation?'' she said.

''Yes, I am,'' Brit stated, nodding. ''I'm the general manager.'' He paused. Then Brit's eyes narrowed slightly and his firm jaw hardened as he added, ''And one day I will be sole owner of The Regent.''

Anna didn't like the expression on his face or his tone of voice. A moment ago he had been so pleasant she'd almost forgotten that they were enemies. Now he looked cold and cruel.

''If I were you,'' she said icily, ''I wouldn't count on it.''

Seven

Sally Ann Horner was an outgoing young woman who loved life and adventure and excitement.

And gossip.

The short, pleasingly plump Sally had brassy brown hair that turned red in the sunlight and frizzed in the rain. Her slightly too wide mouth was usually turned up in a big smile, and her best feature—large green, almond-shaped eyes—often sparkled with merriment or mischief. The only daughter—she had four older brothers—of the wealthy town banker, Jameson Horner, and his gentle wife, Abigail, Sally Ann was a boisterous bundle of energy and curiosity.

Sally arrived at The Regent on a warm May morning in a cloud of dust. Driving the one-horse gig herself, she sped up the long pebbled drive and came to a gravel-flinging stop just outside the front gate. Tossing the reins to a stable boy, Sally leaped out of the carriage and went racing up the front walk. She lifted the door knocker and gave it a resounding whack.

"That'll be Sally," said LaDextra, smiling. "I'll leave you two to get acquainted."

Before LaDextra could rise from her chair, Sally

burst into the drawing room, all smiles and flushed face. "Morning, LaDextra," she said, nodding.

Anna, on her feet now, was both taken aback and genuinely delighted when the spirited young woman crossed the room, grabbed her in a firm bear hug and said, "Anna, I'm Sally Ann Horner. You may not remember me, but we were once the best of friends and we will be again."

"I'd like that," said Anna.

Sally released Anna, stepped back and announced, "We've a lot of catching up to do." She took Anna's hand, determinedly led her through the house, down the long corridor and out the back door, where she turned to the east. Sally eagerly ushered Anna across the lawn, past the wishing well and out to the old grape arbor at the far corner of the vast yard where they used to play.

"We shared many secrets here," said Sally, as they sat down together on a white settee beneath the shelter of dense, tangled grapevines. She looked at Anna and said, "Oh, Anna, Anna, I'm so glad you're home! I knew you'd come back one day. LaDextra never gave up hope and neither did I." She drew a quick breath, then said, "I'll fill you in on what's happened around here while you've been gone, shall I?"

"Yes, by all means," Anna said, smiling. Already she liked this lively young woman, felt as if she had known her forever.

"Well, actually, not all that much has happened, come to think of it. At least not to me. You may as well know, I'm an old maid." Sally made a face

and twisted a wayward lock of reddish-brown hair.
"I'll probably never marry, but so what! Marriage
isn't all there is to life. I almost got married a couple
of years ago." She frowned.

"Really?" Anna said. "What happened? Did you
change your mind?"

Sally snorted. "No, he did. He got cold feet at
the last minute. Jilted me at the eleventh hour, the
spineless cad." She shook her head and sighed
loudly. "Naturally I was humiliated and brokenhearted, so I took to my bed, decided I would never
leave my room again. I would become a pale, weak
recluse who never ventured outside the house, and
people would whisper and worry and wonder about
me."

"Oh, Sally," Anna said. "How sad."

Sally's frown vanished and she laughed loudly.
"Not really. After two or three days in bed I got so
darned bored I couldn't stand it. To heck with being
a mysterious recluse. That's not for me. I got out of
that bed, got dressed up in my finest and drove
straight into town. And you'll *never* guess who I ran
into on the plaza."

"Who?" Anna's eyes were wide with interest.

"J. Mitchell Pierce III, the weasel who jilted
me!"

"No!"

"Yes! And that's not all. He had the nerve to beg
for my forgiveness. Well, I told him straight out that
he'd be begging for his life if he didn't get out of
town and out of Texas and never come back." Sally
laughed again and told Anna, "I have four big

brothers, all of whom were just itching to get their hands on the scoundrel who wronged their sister!''

Anna smiled. ''So did he—did your fiancé—leave town?''

''With his tail between his legs and a promise that if he ever showed his cowardly face in Regentville again, it would be rearranged for him.''

Anna laughed.

The talkative Sally continued to regale Anna with amusing tales that usually involved her own escapades. The two laughed together, enjoying each other's company. After a pleasant hour during which Sally had talked nonstop, there was a lull in the conversation. The two young women sat for a time in companionable silence.

Then Sally placed her hand atop Anna's and said, ''You can tell me, Anna, if you like, about those terrible years you spent with the Apache. I'll understand, I promise.''

A tightness suddenly filled Anna's chest. She realized with surprise that she did want to talk about it. She had never told anyone about those horrible days and nights down in Mexico. Everyone, including the sisters at the convent, the old priest and even LaDextra, had always assumed that she wouldn't want to talk about her experience.

But she did!

She needed to tell someone about it so that she could put it behind her forever.

''Oh, Sally, it was a living nightmare,'' Anna began. ''The first thing I remember is waking up with a splitting headache and blood streaming down the side of my face from a wound on my head. A half-dozen fierce-looking Apache stood over me. I was bewildered and confused and terrified. I was alone and friendless in a wild mountain wilderness at the mercy of those brutal savages."

"Bless your heart," said Sally, squeezing Anna's hand.

Her narrowed blue eyes gazing into the past, Anna said, "I was made to walk for miles and miles with no shoes on my feet. The soles of my feet were lacerated and bleeding, but I was not allowed to stop, not even to slow down. The mounted braves were merciless. No matter how carefully I tried to pick my way, I stumbled on stones and sharp rocks, and when I fell, unable to put one bloody foot before the other, they beat me."

"Dear God," murmured Sally.

"In camp, I was awakened each morning at five and sent out to gather roots and berries for my captors to eat. Of course, I ate some of the roots myself—I would have died otherwise. There was never enough to eat. I was starving, weak and sick, but made to work all day, every day from dawn to dusk."

"I'm so terribly sorry."

"They made me take care of their children, and if I failed to heed every cry or whine of the babies, I was severely beaten." She inhaled, shook her head. "One day they lifted me up onto a pile of brush, then formed a circle around me—men, women and children, some naked, some dressed in blankets, some in skins. They started pounding on stones with heavy clubs, and one played a horn, another some crude kind of fiddle. They ran and jumped and danced and made bloodcurdling sounds. The women dashed up to me and pulled my hair and ripped my doeskin dress. I thought they meant to torture me to death, to light the brush and burn me alive.''

"Oh, dear God!''

"They only wanted to frighten me. After several dreadful hours they finally tired of the game and cut me down.'' Anna turned suddenly, swept back a portion of her heavy blond hair and showed Sally the ugly black tattoo beneath her right ear. "They did this.''

Eyes round with horror, Sally said, "How? It...it won't come off?

Anna shook her head. "They lacerated the skin with quills, and when the bleeding had just about stopped, they stuck a quill back into the wounds and used the juice of a berry to permanently stain the skin. It was painful and I was ordered to sit totally still throughout, but I didn't obey. I thrashed about and screamed when they told me they were going to tattoo my entire face. I fought and pleaded and howled until they gave up in disgust, saying I was not worth the trouble. My ear and jaw hurt afterward, and by night I was running a fever. The medicine man came and rubbed a foul-smelling salve over the wounds, and in a day or two I was back to hunting berries all day long.''

"Anna, dear Anna, why didn't you try to run away?''

"I did. I tried to escape many times, but they always caught me and took me back. And the last time I tried to get away, they taught me a lesson I would never forget." She shuddered, remembering. "They dragged me back to camp, shoved me down onto the ground, and two huge braves sat on either side of me, restraining me.

"An expectant crowd quickly gathered and I knew something horrible was about to happen. Then the music began, the throbbing of tom-toms, the chanting of the men. I looked up to see a poor captive Mexican girl being led to the center of the circle, and I stopped breathing. The wretched creature, who looked as if she hadn't been fed in days, was so sick and weak they had to drag her.

"They tied her to a pole not fifty feet away from me and began piling brush and sticks around her bare feet." Anna stopped speaking. She swallowed hard and goose bumps covered her bare arms. She gritted her teeth, took a deep breath and continued. "I can still hear the poor suffering woman's screams as the flames engulfed her. I begged them to shoot her, to put her out of her misery, but they refused. And they assured me that if I ever again tried to escape, I would suffer the same fate."

Anna trembled, hugged herself.

"So I stayed. And I was beaten and worked like a slave and treated like an outcast. The only form of mistreatment to which I was never subjected was sexual torture. I have nothing good to say of my captors, but I am eternally grateful that they never raped me, never touched me in that way at all. I don't know why. I saw other white women brutally raped, heard their screams, knew of their suffering. But I was spared.''

''Thank the Almighty,'' said Sally.

Anna continued telling of that terrible time, reliving those pain-filled days. She talked for a solid hour. She had needed, badly, to tell someone of the fear and horror of those lost years—and no one had ever let her. She poured out her heart, and when she was finished, the two young women were crying and clinging to each other.

By the time Sally Ann Horner went home that afternoon, Anna and she were the best of friends.

After that day, Sally was out at The Regent often, almost every day. She and Anna never again talked about Anna's wretched life among the Apache. The two young women gossiped and giggled and had a good time together. Sally helpfully supplied memories of the days when they were children.

And she talked dreamily about the sinfully handsome Brit Caruth, telling Anna that he was the catch of southwest Texas.

''All the pretty women are after him,'' she confided, ''and I don't blame them, do you?''

Anna shrugged noncommittally.

''Heck,'' Sally admitted with a laugh, ''I'd give myself to Brit in a minute if he wanted me!''

Anna did not comment.

And she was relieved when, finally, Sally changed the subject. When she wasn't swooning over Brit, Sally was great fun, and Anna enjoyed her company. She had never had a girlfriend, so her relationship with the effervescent Sally was precious to her. As was her relationship with the indomitable LaDextra, whose very presence made her feel safe and secure.

If not for Brit Caruth, everything would have been wonderful. For the first time in her life Anna was treated with respect and kindness. Already LaDextra doted on her, showed her the affection she had never known, had been starved for. Will Davis, the silver-haired attorney, had quickly become a kind, fatherly ally. She felt sure that Will believed she was Anna, and she suspected he hadn't expended a great deal of effort trying to prove otherwise.

Friends and acquaintances of the Regent family came to the ranch specifically to see Anna. Each had some small memory of her, and they had kept the memories alive because they cared about her, had grieved for her. Even people who were not close friends of the Regents were kind to Anna.

The first time she was to go into Regentville with LaDextra, Anna had been sick with apprehension. She remembered the reception she'd received on the streets of Nogales—the jeers and insults and threats. Would it be the same here? These people all knew she had spent years among the Apache. Would they look down on her, too?

To her relief, the townsfolk had come up to her, smiling, eager to welcome her home. They hadn't expected her to remember them, but they remembered her. All were kind and friendly and put her at her ease.

Anna had been deeply touched. She had never before felt loved or wanted. Now everyone seemed to love and care about her. It was heady stuff. She was happy. It all felt so right, so good. She wondered if it was because she really was Anna.

As the warm days glided pleasantly by, Anna became more and more at home on The Regent. She worried less and less about being found out. She realized that it would be next to impossible for anyone to prove that she was *not* Anna.

Or that she was.

Still, she did worry. She never completely relaxed.

Not with Brit Caruth on the premises.

Eight

"She is roughly the same age. Same slim carriage. Same big blue eyes. Same pale golden hair," said Will Davis thoughtfully.

"Sure, Will, but that description fits thousands of women," Brit replied. "It's hardly enough to convince me she's LaDextra's granddaughter. And it damned sure shouldn't be enough to convince LaDextra's trusted legal counsel."

"Now, Brit."

"Don't 'now, Brit' me. A stranger shows up after all these years claiming she's the missing Regent heiress and we're not to doubt it? To look into it? Jesus, Will, you're LaDextra's attorney. You're supposed to look after her interests, keep her from being taken in by a charming little swindler who just happens to resemble her long-lost granddaughter."

The two men were alone in Brit's office, sharing a drink at the close of the day. The last rays of a dying June sun slanted in through the half-open shades, bathing the dark, masculine room in a reddish-gold glow. Brit sat behind his mahogany desk, leaning back in his chair, his booted feet, crossed at the ankles, resting on the desktop.

The attorney, his linen suit jacket open, one hand

in his trousers pocket, paced nervously back and forth, feeling as if he were being interrogated. And loath to admit that he had done little or nothing to disprove Anna's claim.

"Look, Brit, I know how you feel, but—"

"Do you?" Brit cut him off. "I don't think so." He downed the last of his bourbon, swung his feet to the carpeted floor, set the heavy leaded glass on his desk and rose.

Torn between conflicting loyalties, Will said, "Son, LaDextra doesn't *want* me to do too much checking into Anna's past. She's the same as told me that. She's totally convinced that this girl *is* Anna, and she sees no need to investigate further."

"I can understand that," Brit said. "LaDextra's an old woman who has suffered more than her share of loss. But maybe you've forgotten that this is not the first time she's thought she had found her granddaughter."

Will looked sheepish. It was the truth. Over the years there had been at least three other young women who had shown up, claiming to be the missing heiress. None had favored anyone in the Regent family, and under intense questioning in Will's law offices, all had been easily exposed and sent on their way.

"That was different," Will said.

"The difference is that you were intent on denouncing them. But not this one. What's so special about her, Will? Why are you perfectly willing to believe her?"

Will's face flushed and he said nothing. Brit

shook his dark head in disgust. He came around the desk, headed for the door.

"Forget it. You won't hear another word out of me. You and LaDextra are convinced she's Anna. So be it."

"What would it take to convince you, Brit?"

Brit stopped in the doorway. "Ever hear of proof?"

"How can I prove that she is Anna?"

"You can't," said Brit. "But I *will* prove that she isn't."

It was mid-June, and still no rain had fallen in southwest Texas and the Guadalupe Mountains.

The once green pastures of the big Sunland spread were starting to turn brown, the grass was beginning to die from lack of water, the ground was becoming loose and dust-dry. The water tanks scattered out over the range were all getting low.

The lack of rain was accompanied by relentless century-mark heat. The long June days were scorching hot. The nights were not much cooler. Everyone was complaining of the heat, the incredible dryness.

Brit and some of the other cowboys and vaqueros rode the range bare-chested in an attempt to keep cool. LaDextra took to spending the hottest part of the afternoons in her darkened bedroom, wearing a dampened nightgown.

Anna, too, suffered from the sweltering temperatures. She became irritable, had little energy.

And as the Texas summer heat grew steadily fiercer, so did an unsettling heat of another kind.

Night after sleepless night, Anna lay awake in her stifling hot bedroom trying not to think about how Brit looked without his shirt. Or how a rebellious lock of his jet-black hair constantly fell over his high forehead. Or how his tapered brown fingers stroked his wineglass at dinner. Or how his tight Levi's appealingly outlined his slim hips and long legs.

Or how he looked at her with those smoldering dark eyes that held a promise of paradise.

She wondered, as she lay there tingling from head to toe from just thinking about him, if the fascination was mutual.

It was.

Brit couldn't help wanting Anna. He knew better. He knew that he should leave her alone. But he also knew that he couldn't. He wanted her. Wanted her badly. Wanted her more with the passing of each hot summer night. He had to have her at least once. Then he would let her be.

Brit knew women. Knew them well. Had plenty of experience at sensing exactly what a woman wanted, even before she knew it herself. He knew without a word passing between them what Anna was thinking, how she was feeling. He knew that she was lying in bed each night wide awake, unable to sleep.

Because of him.

He knew that she wanted him, just as he wanted her. He knew he was upsetting her, scaring her, tempting her. He knew that with the passing of each long, hot summer day she was growing a little more anxious, a little more attracted. Just as he was.

At first he had been only mildly interested. Curious, but not overly so. She was a beauty, and he had fleetingly wondered how it would feel to hold her in his arms, but he hadn't spent much time thinking about it.

Now he could think of little else.

Lying awake at night in the room right next to hers, Brit thought about the tempting swell of her pale bosom rising above the low-cut bodice of her frilly summer dresses. And the way her long golden hair ignited in the candlelight. And the sound of her rich, soft voice saying his name in a way that made his chest hurt. And how she prettily flushed and nervously licked her lips when he boldly gazed at her across the dining table.

Ah, yes, she wanted him.

Still, Brit wanted to make sure she was totally ready and willing before he went to her. So he intentionally let her twist in the wind. He bided his time, allowing the sexual tension to build, waiting for the opportune moment when he was certain she would sweetly surrender.

On a hot, hot late-June night, after a long, leisurely dinner during which the two of them had been unable to keep their eyes off each other, Brit felt sure the time had come. Unspoken messages had passed between them throughout the evening meal. Silent sexual communications going back and forth, unnoticed by the others. Invitations to intimacy extended through the flirtatious lowering of her thick lashes, the fierce beating of the pulse in his throat.

Now, finally, at well past midnight, the big house was silent and sleeping. Brit, lying naked on his bed, arms folded beneath his head, knew the moment for which he'd been waiting had finally arrived. He swung his long legs over the mattress's edge, sat up and got to his feet.

He stood in the darkness, anticipating what was about to happen. He padded into his bathroom, where the black marble tub, which had been filled earlier, was waiting for him. He stepped into the cooling water, sank down into its depths and lathered and bathed his lean body from the top of his head to the tips of his toes. He ran a hand over his jaw, wondered if he should shave again. He decided against it. He couldn't wait that long. He wanted her now.

After toweling his slippery brown body and thick raven hair dry, Brit slipped on a pair of freshly laundered Levi's, but didn't bother with shirt or shoes. He crossed the room, stepped out onto the moon-silvered balcony and drew a deep breath. He walked the short distance to Anna's room.

The French doors were open.

Inside the spacious room, Brit softly called her name and went directly to the bed. She didn't hear him. She was sound asleep. And, God, she was irresistible. His heart hammering in his naked chest, Brit stared at her, enchanted, fascinated.

She was wearing a lace-trimmed white nightgown, but the delicate fabric had become twisted and had risen up past her pale thighs, while the gown's bodice, partially open, revealed the soft curve of her breast.

Wanting her with a passion that quickly blazed out of control, Brit couldn't stop the immediate response of his body. With his swollen tumescence straining the denim fabric of his tight Levi's, he sat down on the bed facing her, bracing an arm across her slender body.

For a long moment he simply stared at her, trembling with need, excited beyond belief.

"Anna," he whispered, slowly lowering his mouth to hers. "Kiss me, Anna. Kiss me."

Before his yearning lips could cover hers, she was fully awake and fully furious. To Brit's stunned surprise, she pulled a sharp-bladed knife from under her pillow, stuck it against his naked ribs and snarled, "Don't you dare touch me, Britton Caruth."

Half frightened, half excited, Brit murmured huskily, "Ah, baby, don't be like that. Don't you want me? I want you. See?" he lowered his eyes, directing her attention to the awesome erection straining his Levi's. "See how much I want you."

Never taking the knife from his ribs, Anna purposely softened her expression and her voice. In a sultry whisper she said, "Oh, Brit, Brit, you do want me, don't you. Does it hurt? Shall I fix it for you?"

Sure she had capitulated, Brit urged huskily, "Oh, yes, yes." Then blinked in shock when she gave his hard, throbbing flesh a sound, swift thump with thumb and forefinger.

"There," she said sarcastically, smiling at the stunned man, "all better now?"

With fury flashing out of his dark eyes, Brit said, "Why, you cruel little bitch! I ought to—"

"Get up!" she ordered, cutting him off in mid-sentence, pressing the knife blade into his ribs. Brit hesitated "Now!" she warned.

Brit rose and Anna leaped to her feet before him. With the flat of the knife blade never leaving his flesh, she backed him across the room to the open French doors.

"Perhaps you've forgotten I was taught by the savages. I can take care of myself. If you ever again touch me," she threatened coldly, "I'll kill you."

Nine

Back in his own room, Brit poured a stiff drink of bourbon, downed it in one swallow, made a face and poured another. Angry and aroused, he paced restlessly in the darkness, more convinced than ever that this beautiful hellion who had pulled a knife on him couldn't possibly be Anna Regent Wright.

But, perversely, her unexpected rejection and reckless behavior had left him wanting her more than ever. Never in his twenty-eight years had a woman turned him down. This one had not only turned him down, she'd threatened to kill him if he ever tried to make love to her again.

He didn't doubt for a minute that she meant it. She had been, after all, raised by the Apache.

Brit involuntarily shivered.

The danger was intoxicating. It added a whole new dimension to his growing desire. Now he *had* to have her.

From that night, wanting her became an obsession that was equally as powerful as his need to expose her. Before the summer ended, he meant to settle both scores.

Then send the lying little wildcat on her way.

* * *

LaDextra noticed.

So did Will Davis.

Brit had stopped going into town in the evenings. He was present at dinner nearly every night.

Immaculate and handsome, he was charming and talkative, spinning humorous tales that made La-Dextra and Will laugh merrily. Anna didn't laugh, but she found it impossible to keep from smiling at his amusing, well-told stories. He was entertaining, no denying it.

He was also dangerously appealing. With his heavy-lidded, sensuous eyes and seductive noncha-lance, he was almost impossible to resist. But Anna had to resist him. She *would* resist him. And the only way to do it was to never, ever be alone with him.

She made it a point to check on Brit's where-abouts before she stepped foot outside the house, much less went for a walk or a ride. If he were anywhere on or near the premises, she didn't dare venture out.

But if she was absolutely certain he was gone for the day, was way out on one of the far ranges or visiting one of the division headquarters, she offered up silent thanks, feeling as if she'd been let out of jail.

On those welcome days, Anna waited until after lunch, when LaDextra was taking her afternoon nap. Then she flew out of the house and hurried up to-ward the mountain tract and her favorite spot.

Manzanita Springs.

Anna considered the gurgling, splashing springs

her own private paradise. She'd never seen any of the ranch hands or anyone else anywhere near the willow-enclosed waters. When she'd asked, La-Dextra had told her that no one went there anymore, hadn't ever since she, Anna, and the other two little girls had been taken from there by the Apache all those years ago.

The springs held no bad memories for Anna. And since no one else came here, she felt perfectly comfortable in stripping down to her skimpy white underwear.

She was at the cooling springs one scorching hot Wednesday afternoon in mid-June.

Brit posed no threat. Anna had learned from LaDextra that he and some of the cowhands would be up in the South McKittrick Canyon pasture all day, rounding up strays.

With him miles away, she could relax and enjoy herself. Eager to get into the cooling water, she was quick to slip out of her summer dress and petticoats. She kicked off her shoes, peeled down her stockings and stood there on the rocky banks for a long moment, anticipating the meeting of her hot body with the cold water.

Squealing with childish delight, she jumped in and swam across the crystalline stream with long, graceful strokes. Loving the feel of the water lapping around her and over her, Anna swam back and forth several times before getting out.

Her delicate underwear now sopping wet and clinging to her chilled skin, she shook herself like a great dog, laughed and sat down on a smooth,

slightly tilted flat rock. She sighed with satisfaction
and stretched out on her back, folding a bare arm
beneath her head. Squinting against the hot glare of
the summer sun, she considered reading, but quickly
decided against it. She felt drowsy, wonderfully relaxed. She didn't want to do anything.

Nothing at all.

Lying there in the warm June sun, Anna was
struck anew with how good, how easy her life was
here on The Regent. She was never allowed to do
any work. When she offered, the servants just smiled
and shook their heads. It had taken a while to get
used to a life of leisure. At first it had seemed
strange not to be constantly scrubbing floors and
washing dishes and ironing clothes.

Anna sighed with sweet contentment.

Soon enough she had grown accustomed to the
amazing freedom enjoyed only by the wealthy. She
was emancipated, did as she pleased when she
pleased. And oh how wonderful it was to go to bed
each night not suffering from an aching back or
chapped, red hands.

And acute loneliness.

Smiling dreamily, lazily counting her many bless-
ings, Anna soon fell asleep.

"Damnation!" Brit swore, as the sharp thorns of
barbed wire punctured his fingers through his protective chamois gloves.

Groaning, Brit shoved on the huge Hereford bull
he was attempting to free from the tangle of wire.

"Hang on," shouted Buck, dismounting, hurrying

to Brit's aid. The big blond cowhand easily pushed the angry, snorting bull away from Brit, then freed Brit's hand from the wire. Bright red blood immediately appeared in the pierced fingers of Brit's work gloves.

"Son of a bitch!" Brit muttered. Peeling off his ruined glove, he took the bandanna Buck offered and wound it around his bleeding fingers.

"We're about finished here," said Buck. "Why don't you go on down and have that hand tended?"

Brit nodded. "I will. See if you can get this big brute out of the wire, but be careful."

"I can handle him," Buck said with confidence. "When you get that hand bandaged, what say we go into town tonight, see if we can't find us some wild women?" He grinned broadly.

"Another time," Brit said noncommittally.

He mounted his iron gray, turned him in a semicircle and rode away with his best buddy frowning after him. Buck was puzzled by Brit's strange behavior. Lately, Brit never wanted to go into town, and that wasn't like him. Buck wondered what was bothering him.

Brit knew a shortcut down to the mansion. It was rarely used because it was extremely treacherous, but he trusted his sure-footed stallion. He'd take the route and be at the house in less than an hour. Man and stallion soon left the broad, high-country pasture behind and started the rocky descent out of the canyon and off the mountain.

Upon reaching the most dangerous section of the trail down, Brit spoke softly to his stallion and guided the big beast out onto a narrow jutting shelf of rock spanning the south face of the mountain. The ledge, steadily descending, was barely three feet wide. One misstep, one loose pebble causing a misplaced hoof, and man and horse would fall to their deaths far below.

Brit was not worried. Trusting his dependable stallion completely, he sat relaxed in the saddle, hand loose on the reins. The treacherous trail finally reached a much wider shelf of rock at a spot known as Wilderness Ridge.

At the ridge, Brit abruptly pulled up on Captain. Squinting, his heart beginning to pound alarmingly, he kneed the iron gray farther out onto a rocky overhang, which afforded an unobstructed view of Manzanita Springs not fifty feet below. The water shimmered in the sun like a million tiny mirrors. But it was not the water that arrested Brit's attention.

It was the beautiful girl sleeping on the rocks in the sun. She looked almost naked in a flimsy white camisole and skimpy underpants, both of which were wet and sticking to her flesh.

Brit swallowed hard as he stared at her, entranced. The thin batiste fabric clung wetly to the creamy curves of her rounded breasts, the twin points of her rosy nipples clearly outlined.

Her delicate ribs and flat belly were well defined, as was the shadowed triangle of thick gold curls between her pale thighs. Her long hair was fanned out around her head, gleaming golden in the sunlight. Her eyes were closed, her lips parted.

She was the most beautiful creature Brit had ever seen.

His initial impulse was to ride straight down to her, grab her up and kiss her senseless. He shuddered and swiftly dismissed the insane idea. She might have that mean-looking, turquoise-handled knife with her.

Such a shame. Here she was, all gleaming wet, nearly naked and stretched out below him like an exotic offering from the gods of love. And he couldn't touch her. Couldn't even go down to where she was.

Frowning, Brit sat there atop his stallion, gazing down on the beautiful woman to whom he longed to make love, wondering if it was ever going to happen. He was beginning to doubt it. He was at a loss. She didn't behave as other women did, didn't respond to him like she should have. Yet he knew she was attracted to him. As much as she tried to hide it, he was not deceived. She was as sexually aware of him as he was of her.

But obviously she was bound and determined not to let anything happen between them.

Brit ground his teeth in frustration. Perspiration dotted his hairline and a vein throbbed on his forehead.

If she even knew that he was up here right now, spying on her, she'd have a fit. Never speak to him again. Call him a dirty, disgusting voyeur who—who…

Abruptly Brit began to smile wickedly as a devilish idea suddenly came to him, a plan that was foolproof. His dark eyes began to twinkle with mischief and his smile broadened.

Brit took one last long, lecherous look at the near-naked woman below, then quietly backed the iron gray off the rocky ledge and carefully skirted the springs on his way down to the ranch house.

At the mansion, LaDextra fussed over him and told him she'd send a vaquero to get young Dr. McCelland to come take a look at his injured hand.

Brit wouldn't hear of it. "I don't need a doctor," he assured her, heading for the kitchen. "A little iodine will fix me right up."

Nodding, LaDextra said, "I'll get Connie."

LaDextra stood over them as Connie carefully cleaned the puncture wounds on Brit's fingers, generously painted them with iodine, then wrapped his hand in a clean white bandage.

Eyeing the bandage at dinner that evening, Anna wondered, miserably, if this meant he would be lurking around the house for the next few days. The prospect automatically brought a frown to her face.

"Something bothering you, Anna?" Brit's smooth baritone voice broke into her troubled thoughts.

"No," she replied too hastily. "Certainly not."

Smiling then, knowing exactly what she was thinking, Brit mentioned casually, "This hand's a little sore, but it won't slow me down. I'll ride on down to Fort Davis tomorrow as planned to see about that new army beef contract."

"Now, Brit," LaDextra mildly scolded, "there's no need for that. Why don't you wait a few days, let those fingers heal?'' She turned and looked at the attorney. ''You tell him, Will.''

''Maybe you should listen to LaDextra, Brit,'' Will said evenly. ''That beef contract can wait. Or you could send one of the division bosses down to the fort.''

Brit looked thoughtful, as if he were mulling it over in his mind. Then he looked directly at Anna and asked, ''What do you think, Anna? Should I go or stay?''

You can go to blazes for all I care. Sweetly she said, ''I'm sure you know better than any of us how badly your hand is hurt.''

''Is that a yes or a no?'' he needled.

''Make up your own mind!'' she snapped.

While Will and LaDextra exchanged puzzled looks at her harsh tone of voice, Brit merely grinned, amused.

He drawled, ''Yep, I'll just ride on down to the fort tomorrow.'' He looked pointedly at Anna when he added, ''Probably won't be back for a couple of days.''

Anna returned to the springs the very next afternoon.

Smiling as she approached the stands of thick green willows enclosing the cool, sparkling waters, she felt deliciously wicked. She had decided that since no one else ever came to the springs, she would, this very day, take everything off.

She never had before. She had always left on her underwear. Not today. Today she meant to experience the provocative pleasure of swimming totally nude!

The only person who posed any kind of threat was miles away from the ranch. Brit would be gone—thank God—for at least today and tonight, leaving her free to relax and enjoy herself.

Anna picked her way through the tall willows. Soon she stepped out into the large clearing, dropped her leather-bound book and blanket to the sun-heated rocks and kicked off her shoes. She was starting to unbutton her dress when she turned her head and saw him.

She almost had a heart attack.

Sound asleep, Brit Caruth lay stretched out on a huge flat rock, sunning himself like a big, sleek jungle cat.

Naked save for a battered Stetson hat placed strategically over his groin, he was unquestionably the embodiment of stark masculine beauty.

Anna couldn't take her eyes off him.

He looked like a perfectly carved Greek statue, all bare and bronzed and lean and muscular. Her throat gone dry, her heartbeat erratic, she warily studied his dark, chiseled face. Long sooty lashes were closed over those beautiful dark eyes. High, prominent cheekbones cast shadows on his smooth tanned cheeks. His perfectly shaped mouth, in repose, was soft, sensual, tempting.

Anna's wide-eyed gaze moved cautiously down from his handsome face to his tanned throat and bare, sculpted shoulders. She noted the bulge of his hard biceps, the bands of muscle that shaped the wide, symmetrical chest that tapered to a trim, hard waist.

Her fascinated gaze slowly slid lower.

Only his groin was covered. Everything else was bare. That splendid masculine body was fully exposed to her eager eyes. Anna stared at the well-molded juncture where his hard muscled thigh joined his slim hip. She studied the prominent hipbones. The flat, drum-tight brown belly. The thick line of raven hair leading down from his navel. The dark, shadowy hint of inky curls peeking out from beneath the well-placed Stetson.

Swallowing hard, Anna stared at the hat and found her herself guiltily wishing that it was not there. She had an overwhelming desire to go to him, fall to her knees and lift the Stetson so that she could see everything.

She didn't dare.

Her breath short, she allowed her gaze to travel on down his long, muscled legs to his bare brown feet.

Then she started back up.

And all the while she stared at him, she was telling herself that she had better turn away right now and leave. Go before he woke and caught her looking at him.

But he was so brown and so beautiful, and, sleeping as he was, harmless.

Anna edged closer, admiring him, desiring him. How, she wondered, would it feel to take off her clothes and stretch out beside him? To lie there naked in the warm caressing sun with him? To feel his heated bronzed body touching her own?

Her nervous gaze climbed slowly back up his long, lean frame, returning finally to his face.

And she froze, horrified.

Brit's dark, hooded eyes were open and looking straight at her. For a long tense moment, they stared at each other in silence.

It was Brit who finally broke the spell.

He drawled lazily, "Usually I stand to acknowledge the presence of a lady, but..."

"Don't you dare get up!" she warned. Then added accusingly, "What are you doing here? You said you were going to Fort Davis today!"

Brit shrugged his bare, tanned shoulders. "Changed my mind. Decided I'd better take care of these injured fingers." He lifted his bandaged right hand.

Anna's own hands went to her hips and her eyes flashed with anger when she said, "You did this on purpose!"

"Did what?" He was all little-boy innocence.

"Led me to believe you would be away from the ranch today," she said heatedly. "You never meant to go to the fort. You intended all along to come here and...and ogle me. Catch me without my clothes!"

Brit laughed. "You've got it backward, haven't you, sweetheart? You're the one who intruded on my privacy, caught me naked and leered at me."

"I did not! I would never leer at—"

"I don't mind," he told her, smiling wickedly. "Look to your heart's content."

"I do *not* want to look at your...at your..."

"Well, I sure want to look at yours," he coolly interjected. "Why don't you just shed all those hot sticky clothes and lie down here beside me?"

Her face now a bright, flaming scarlet, Anna, backing away, shouted angrily, "Are you out of your mind?"

"Just about," Brit said truthfully. "You're driving me crazy, Anna."

Ten

Furious and upset, Anna hurriedly spun away. She slammed headlong through the thick willows, clawing at the branches slapping her arms and legs, desperate to get away, to reach safety.

Dislodging pebbles and stirring up dust, she scrambled swiftly down the mountainside, feeling as if Satan himself were after her.

And, in a way, he was.

Brit Caruth was surely the devil incarnate. A handsome, seductive, dangerous demon who took evil delight in tempting and tormenting her. The sexy, sinister son of a bitch meant to seduce her, corrupt her, rob her of her virtue and her will, and strip her of her inheritance.

This latest incident at the springs would not be the last of his diabolic schemes to slowly, surely chip away at her defenses. The base, brazen bastard wouldn't rest until she surrendered.

"That's not going to happen!" she told him under her breath. "Never, never, never!"

Fighting back threatening tears of frustration, Anna reached the border of the mansion's manicured back terrace. She stopped to catch her breath and compose herself. She straightened her dress, smoothed her hair and remembered, suddenly, that she had left her book at the springs. Cold fear clutched her chest. Would Brit bring it back? And if he did, would he quietly give it to her or would he shame her by letting LaDextra and the entire Regent household know that the two of them had been at the springs together?

Anna took a deep breath, crossed the vast terraced lawn and slipped in the back door. She immediately heard voices. She looked down the long, wide corridor and saw young Dr. McCelland handing his suit coat to a servant.

Forcing herself to smile, Anna went to greet him.

"Hello, Dr. McCelland," she said, offering her hand.

"Miss Wright," said the doctor, his eyes immediately lighting up and a shy, boyish smile touching his lips. He shook her hand gently, as if it might break.

Dr. J. Bryan McCelland Jr., only son of the recently retired Dr. J. Bryan McCelland Sr., looked much younger than his thirty-two years. A very shy, very nice man, he was barely taller than she. The slimly built physician had sandy hair, a fair complexion and green eyes that lit up noticeably each time he looked at Anna.

"What brings you to the ranch today, Doctor?" Anna inquired politely, smiling at him.

"Just a routine visit to LaDextra," he said, his shy smile still very much in evidence. "I spent the morning down at the bunkhouse and at the married ranch hands' quarters—checking on the men, their wives and children, tending a few sick people. Thought I might as well stop by at the house since I was out this way."

"Yes, of course," Anna said, then extended her hand toward LaDextra's room. Accompanying him down the corridor, she said, "You see to the health of the hired hands as well as...?"

"Yes, yes I do. I come out here every couple of weeks and I also travel to each of the division headquarters at least once or twice a month."

"I see," Anna replied with interest. "So the cowboys and vaqueros show up at division headquarters if they need medical attention?"

Dr. McCelland nodded. "Their wives and children as well."

Anna again smiled. "You must be a very busy physician."

The bashful young doctor smiled back at her. "Not so busy that I'd miss the big Fourth of July celebration." He turned a pale shade of pink when he said, "You will be there, won't you?"

"Yes. Yes, of course."

"The biggest blowout in all Texas!"

That's how Sally Horner described The Regent's annual Fourth of July celebration as she and Anna lay across Anna's bed the next afternoon.

"*Everybody* comes," she told Anna, throwing out her arms in a wide encompassing gesture. "The Regent cowboys and vaqueros and their families will all be there. Plus the entire population of Regentville turns out for the festivities. And there are old friends of LaDextra's who come from as far away as the Panhandle, El Paso, Pecos and San Antonio." She laughed and warned, "Be prepared to have a houseful of overnight guests."

"LaDextra mentioned the celebration at dinner last night. She said that I would go into town with her some afternoon next week to make the arrangements and to get a new dress for the occasion."

Sally nodded. "I've already picked out a lovely yellow piqué dress that definitely makes me look slimmer and quite sophisticated as well." Twisting a reddish-brown curl, she mused, "We'll want to look our very best, since every eligible bachelor in southwest Texas will be there." She glanced at Anna, then suddenly frowned. "Heck, you needn't worry. You'd look good in anything." Sally sighed enviously.

Ignoring the statement and the sigh, Anna said, "So this Fourth of July festival is a Regent tradition?"

"Yes, indeed," Sally replied. "For as long as I can remember I've been coming out to the ranch for the Fourth. It's such fun, Anna, you'll absolutely love it. Games and gossiping and food and flirting and champagne and fireworks and dancing and—"

"Dancing?" Anna interrupted.

"Yes, of course. Everyone dances the night away." Sally's eyebrows lifted. "What? What is it? Why are you making a face?"

"I don't know how to dance," stated Anna dejectedly. "The sisters educated me, but dancing was not part of the curriculum."

"Is that all?" Sally said. "Don't worry. We've got two full weeks before the Fourth. I'll teach you to dance. There's nothing to it." She jumped up and raced across the room to the phonograph player. She cranked it up and said, "Heck, let's get started."

The dance lessons began that very afternoon in Anna's spacious bedroom. The somewhat scratchy sound of the music, as well as their clear girlish laughter, floated down the stairs to LaDextra's ground floor sitting room. The old woman smiled with genuine pleasure at hearing her beautiful young granddaughter laughing, happy.

Her eyes were closed, but LaDextra was still smiling when, half an hour later, the two young women came racing down the stairs, giggling and whispering. Sweet, sweet music to LaDextra's ears.

The young women burst out the door and onto the front gallery. They were rushing down the sidewalk when Sally suddenly stopped and grabbed Anna's arm.

"Look who's coming!" she said excitedly.

"Who?" Anna asked. She lifted a hand to shade her eyes, looked down the long pebbled drive, but saw no one.

"Over there!" Sally pointed to a couple of mounted horsemen a hundred yards away, cantering across the broad pasture directly toward the house. "It's Brit and Buck Shanahan. Do you suppose I'd ever have a chance with Buck? He's not as good-looking as Brit, but—"

"I have to go inside," Anna interrupted, anxiously pulling free of Sally's grip.

"Go inside?" Sally was nonplussed. "And miss a chance to flirt with these two handsome cowhands? You could at least wait until—Anna...!"

But Anna was already to the gallery and she didn't look back. She disappeared inside. Shrugging, Sally sighed, headed for her one-horse gig, waving madly at the approaching horsemen.

The two men waved back at Sally.

Anna's speedy retreat had been missed by neither. Buck commented, "Guess Miss Anna is too busy to come out and visit with us."

"I guess."

"I'll bet she's never too busy to visit with Doc McCelland though."

There was no reply from Brit.

"Yes sir, looks like Doc McCelland is pretty much smitten with Miss Anna," Buck said as the two rode knee-to-knee, heading home after a hard day down at the *Sierra Blanca* pasture.

Brit's dark head finally swung around. "What the hell are you talking about?"

Buck shrugged. "Well, all I know is the good doctor has been out to the house several times recently, and I figure it's to see Miss Anna."

Brit was involuntarily irritated. "Jesus, you're as bad as an old woman," he scoffed. "Doc McCelland isn't interested in the girl. He routinely visits the ranch to check on LaDextra. Make sure she's in good health."

"Maybe," said Buck, "but one of the house servants said just yesterday she heard the doctor ask

Anna if he could sit at her table for the evening meal at the Fourth of July celebration.''

"So?''

"So, sounds to me like he's sweet on LaDextra's granddaughter.''

"Damn it to hell, Buck, I've told you a thousand times, this woman is *not* LaDextra's granddaughter!''

One evening a few days later, LaDextra and Will Davis lingered at the dining table long after Brit and Anna had both hastily excused themselves. The two old friends drank their after-dinner coffee and discussed plans for the upcoming Fourth of July celebration.

"Brit's driving me into town tomorrow so I can make the final arrangements,'' said LaDextra.

Will took a pull from his cigar and nodded. "Engage the musicians, order the food and liquor?''

"Yes, and I plan to hire a couple of carpenters to build a temporary dance floor out on the west lawn.''

Again Will nodded. "The Hall brothers would probably be your best bet there. Shall I have them come to my office tomorrow to meet with you?''

"Why don't you? Make it afternoon, though. I have to get the food and liquor ordered. Then I'll need to check with Hap Kinney, see if he'll come out twenty-four hours early again this year and start the barbecue.''

"He's the best,'' commented Will.

"I know, and I really want this year's celebration

to be the best one ever." Will was puzzled by the wistful look that came into LaDextra's expressive blue eyes as she spoke.

"I'm sure it will be a huge success, just as always," he offered. "What about the fireworks?"

LaDextra nodded. "I contracted an El Paso outfit some time back. They've promised to put on quite a pyrotechnic spectacle at straight-up midnight."

The two continued to discuss the upcoming Fourth of July festival, recalling amusing incidences that had happened at past celebrations. Fondly remembering old friends who came every year, some of whom were no longer alive. Laughing about the liquor-induced arguments and fistfights that occasionally broke out.

"We've had some mighty good times out here on the Fourth, haven't we, Will?" LaDextra mused, tears of laughter shining in her pale eyes.

"We sure have, my dear," said Will with a smile. "And we'll have many, many more."

Eleven

Brit's trousered knee slowly slid across the smooth leather and lightly brushed Anna's thigh. She quickly scooted nearer to the far edge of the carriage seat. She cast a covert glance at him and caught him grinning.

Anna clamped her jaw angrily. She couldn't say anything to him and he knew it. She could do nothing but quietly simmer.

Anna folded her arms over her chest and gazed unseeingly out at the stark, flat countryside.

If she had known that Brit was the one who'd be driving LaDextra and her into town today, she would have begged off and stayed home. Since the unnerving meeting at the springs, she had managed to successfully avoid him. Except at dinner when both Will and LaDextra were present, she hadn't so much as caught sight of him.

And that's just the way she wanted it.

Now here she was, seated beside him, his strong masculine presence making her both angry and anxious. She would have gladly done without a new frock for the Fourth of July shindig if she'd known that it meant spending a day in his presence. She was more than a little annoyed with LaDextra for not telling her Brit would be driving them into town. It was almost as if LaDextra had kept it quiet on purpose. Although why, Anna could not imagine.

She made a face and softly sighed.

For days she had been eagerly looking forward to this all-day outing. She'd been as excited as a child when she'd come out of the house that morning. She had skipped down the steps, rushed down the sidewalk, then looked up and seen Brit lounging negligently against the big double-seated carriage.

Her face had immediately turned red with irritation and embarrassment. After what had happened at the springs, it was impossible for her to look at him and not recall him naked.

"I'm fully dressed today," he said when she reached the carriage, as if he'd read her guilty thoughts. "Which way do you like me best, Anna?"

"Will you lower your voice!" she had scolded hotly under her breath, looking nervously over her shoulder at the slowly approaching LaDextra.

Unfazed, Brit leaned close, whispered, "Tell the truth, don't you like me best bare assed?"

"I don't like you at all, Caruth!" she muttered. "With or without clothes, I do *not* like you!"

"I don't believe you," he said with calm assurance. "You don't want to like me, but you like me. Too much."

"Shh!" Anna warned as LaDextra neared them.

She would just die should LaDextra ever find out about their meeting at the springs. But she suspected that the devilish Brit wouldn't much care if La-

Dextra did find out. He would probably think it was amusing.

Grinning sunnily, Brit reached for Anna. But she was having none of it. She swiftly slapped his hands away. "See to LaDextra," she snapped. "I can get into the carriage with no help from you." She turned away and started to climb up into the rear seat.

"No, no, dear," LaDextra called out, stopping her. "You ride up front with Brit, please. I'd like the entire back seat to myself so I can stretch my stiff old legs. If you don't mind."

Anna forced a smile. "Of course I don't mind."

While Brit very gingerly helped LaDextra into the rear seat of the carriage, Anna irritably swung up onto the leather front seat, smoothed her skirts and folded her arms across her chest. She would, she decided, silently stare straight ahead for the entire six-mile journey.

But she didn't do it.

Brit wouldn't let her.

Much as she wanted to totally ignore him—pretend he didn't exist—it was impossible. By the time they reached the outskirts of Regentville, Anna was grudgingly laughing at Brit's humorous stories, just as LaDextra was. He was funny. And he was fun. Lively and entertaining, with a self-deprecating wit that made him likable. Lovable. It wasn't fair. It just was not fair for one man to possess so much natural charm.

Anna was loath to admit it, but she was helplessly, hopelessly fascinated with this tall, dark Texan. He was, it seemed to her, everything that a man should be and more. Innately intelligent. Strikingly handsome. Incredibly captivating. Seductively virile.

But, she reminded herself, he was, above all, extremely dangerous.

Regentville, Texas, was a small community set on the high flat southwestern desert in the middle of nowhere. Built around a central plaza, it was named for the Regent family. The town had sprung up to serve the many people who worked at the big cattle ranch, but it had grown over the years as more and more settlers migrated to far west Texas.

Elm trees had been planted on the plaza, their spreading limbs casting welcome shade on a scattering of stone benches. The benches were always filled, with friends and neighbors visiting, talking, eating, enjoying a day in town.

Built around the plaza were the usual businesses. A blacksmith shop, a feed store, a saddle maker and a funeral parlor lined the square's east side. On the south was a bakery, a butcher shop, a general store, the telegraph office, the William R. Davis Law Firm and Dr. McCelland's clinic.

The west side was home to all of the town's rowdy saloons, lined up in a row. The Red Rose. The Last Chance. The Bloody Bucket. The Plainsman. The Corral.

Dominating the north side of the plaza was the brick, three-story Regentville Hotel. Next to the hotel, its only entrance located inside the hotel's grand lobby, was Lily's Ladies' Wear Salon. Lily offered the finest in ladies' ready-to-wear garments. Well-made, stylish clothes that couldn't be found at the general store. Or anywhere nearer than San Antonio.

Brit pulled up on the reins directly in front of the Regentville Hotel. A smiling young boy rushed out to assist the ladies and tend the carriage.

"Will you be staying in town long, Mr. Caruth?" asked the boy.

"All day," Brit told him. "Make sure LaDextra's room is ready in case she wishes to rest."

"Yes, sir." Brit handed him a silver dollar. The young man smiled broadly. "Thank you, sir."

Expecting—and secretly hoping—that Brit would part company then and there and go directly to one of the saloons, Anna was surprised, and grudgingly impressed, by his insistence that he help LaDextra with the many celebration arrangements. Anna could see that LaDextra depended on Brit, took his counsel, deferred to him.

He completely took charge. Slowing his steps to match hers, he patiently escorted LaDextra around the square, stopping at those establishments where provisions for food, drink, flowers and the engagement of musical groups were to be made. If LaDextra was indecisive, couldn't make up her mind how many cases of champagne or how many gallons of ice cream would be needed, Brit did some fast figuring in his head and promptly supplied the numbers.

By one o'clock, when the three of them returned to the hotel for a late lunch, they had taken care of everything, save hiring Hap Kinney to cook the barbecue and meeting with the Hall brothers to discuss the cost of building a temporary dance floor.

For Anna, there still remained the pleasant chore of choosing a pretty new dress for the festivities.

Brit noticed, as they were having a leisurely lunch, that LaDextra was looking extraordinarily tired and pale. It had been a busy morning for her. She needed to rest.

"I've a suggestion," he said, as they finished the rich custard dessert.

"Which is?" said LaDextra.

"You go upstairs and have a nice long nap. I'll run down Hap Kinney and then meet with the Hall brothers at Will's office."

"I would agree to that," said LaDextra, "but I promised Anna I'd help her shop for a new dress to wear on the Fourth."

Brit looked at Anna, but addressed LaDextra. "Anna's a grown woman. Surely she can select a dress by herself."

Feeling somehow as if this were a trap into which she was falling, Anna said, "I can choose a dress, LaDextra. You do look tired. You really should rest."

LaDextra sighed. "Well, children, I believe I'll take you up on that suggestion. A little nap sounds mighty tempting." She smiled at Anna and said, "Get any dress you want, dear. Two or three if you like. Just tell Lily to put them on my bill."

"One will be plenty. Thank you so much," said Anna.

"You're very welcome, child," said LaDextra,

then turned to Brit. "Will you get the room key and help me up the stairs?"

Together, Brit and Anna got LaDextra settled into the luxurious second-floor suite that the Regent family had retained since the hotel's opening. The suite was reserved solely for the family. Brit stayed there overnight occasionally. LaDextra used it for long day trips into town.

Closing the door on the weary woman, Brit and Anna silently descended the hotel's broad center staircase. At the base of the stairs, Brit paused, laid a hand on Anna's forearm and said, "Come with me to Will's office, then I'll help you choose a dress."

"No, thank you," she said, brushing his hand away, genuinely nervous at the prospect of being left alone with him. "As you pointed out, surely I can select a dress all by myself."

She turned and flounced away, hurriedly crossing the marble-floored lobby and rushing out the open front doors, her full skirts swaying with her quick, determined steps.

Unhurriedly, Brit exited the hotel after her. He stood on the wooden sidewalk under the portico and watched Anna. She was several yards down the sidewalk now, having reached the glass-fronted ladies' wear shop. She hesitated, stopped, looked around, puzzled. Then it hit her. The only entrance into Lily's was through the hotel lobby.

Brit knew the exact instant she realized it. She made a sour face and slapped her hands against her full skirts. Brit grinned and leaned a muscular shoulder against the hotel's heavy door frame. He crossed his arms over his chest and waited.

Anna had no choice but to return to the hotel. Whirling around, she started back.

But when she saw Brit standing there, radiating amused arrogance, she did a quick about-face. She would do without a new dress forever rather than be subjected to his infuriating insolence.

Brit's cocky smile remained in place. He knew why she had turned away. With his heavily lashed lids lowered, he watched her stroll aimlessly around the plaza, stopping to look in store windows, killing time, waiting for him to leave. Bent on avoiding him. What, he wondered, would she do if he stayed here all afternoon?

Brit fished his gold watch out of his vest pocket. Time to meet with the Hall brothers. Afterward, maybe he'd have a couple of drinks or a card game at the Plainsman.

Twelve

Anna waited until she knew it was completely safe.

If the tormenting Brit watched her, she watched him as well. She kept a close eye on him until, finally, she saw him disappear into Will Davis's law office. She then heaved a great sigh of relief and hurried back toward the Regentville Hotel.

A bell above the door tinkled softly as she entered the plushly carpeted Lily's Ladies' Wear Salon. At the back of the elegant shop, rose velvet curtains parted and a tiny, handsome middle-aged woman with upswept dark hair appeared.

Smiling warmly, she came directly toward Anna. "I am Lily," she said, extending her bejeweled hand. "And you are Anna Regent Wright."

"Yes, I am," said Anna. "But how did you know?"

"Two ways, really," said Lily, with a musical laugh. "LaDextra sent word that the two of you would be coming in today. And you're so extraordinarily pretty. Blood does tell. You would have to be Christina Regent's only daughter." Anna nodded, smiled, said nothing. Perfectly arched eyebrows lifting, Lily asked, "And where is LaDextra? Not ailing, I hope."

"Oh, no. She's fine, just a little tired," Anna assured the woman. "She's upstairs in the hotel resting. I told her I could choose a dress myself."

"But, of course, you can," said the diminutive Lily, clasping her hands together. She looked Anna up and down, determining her size. "Shall we gather several for you to choose from?"

"Yes," said Anna, eager to get started. "Please do."

The tightly corseted, stylishly bustled Lily swept around the large salon, selecting those dresses she thought most suited the tall, slender beauty. Leading the way to the dressing room, Lily carried a half-dozen frocks over her arm. She hung them around the large room, turned, smiled and asked, "Shall I help you dress and undress?"

"No, thanks," said Anna. "I can manage."

"Very well. You change your mind, just call me."

When a half hour had passed and Anna had not emerged from the dressing room, a concerned Lily called out, "You are having trouble deciding, no? Come and let me have a look."

Anna came out into the main salon wearing an emerald-green organdy. The dress had small puff sleeves, a high round collar and at least thirty tiny, covered buttons going from throat to waist.

"Ah, yes, how lovely you look!" exclaimed Lily. "I knew this dress would suit you."

"You think?" asked Anna doubtfully, not at all certain that this was the dress for her.

She stood in the middle of the large, plushly carpeted shop before a freestanding, full-length mirror, critically studying herself. When she turned slowly about to look over her shoulder at the back of the dress, she promptly frowned.

Brit Caruth was standing on the sidewalk just outside Lily's, looking directly at her through the clear plate glass window. Leisurely he inspected her, his unhurried gaze sliding over her slender frame before he finally lifted his eyes to meet hers.

Looking straight at her, Brit shook his head. His dark expressive eyes clearly said, ''That's not the dress for you. Don't get it.''

Flustered, Anna turned away and rushed back into the dressing room, determined she wouldn't come out again. She hurriedly shed the green organdy, dismissing it as a possible choice. She didn't like it. It didn't suit her. Not at all. Her decision had nothing to do with Brit's disapproval. She couldn't have cared less what he thought.

Anna slipped on a pale blue silk with a square neckline, tight bodice and elbow-length sleeves. It suited her better than the green organdy. Still she wasn't sure. It was of the latest style and the color was flattering, but...

As she stood there scrutinizing herself, Anna couldn't help but wonder what Brit would think of the gown. Chiding herself for being so vain and so foolish, she nonetheless ventured back out into the salon, wondering if he would even still be there.

Probably not.

He was.

Brit was standing just as she had left him, booted

feet slightly apart, arms crossed over his chest, looking through the plate glass at her.

Anna shyly glanced at him, blushed, then stepped up before the full-length mirror and turned this way, then that. Knowing he was watching her every move, she drew in her breath so that her breasts would swell against the tight, blue silk bodice.

She slowly turned to face him.

Brit stared at her for a long contemplative moment, then raised a hand and rubbed his chin thoughtfully, as if trying to decide. After what seemed an eternity to Anna, he held his hand out before him, palm down, and tilted it slightly from side to side several times as if to say, "So-so."

She knew just what he meant. She felt the same way about the blue silk. It was expensive and attractive, but it wasn't *the* dress.

Back into the dressing room she went.

Her pulse now pounding with growing excitement, she slipped into a matching skirt and blouse of crisp white cotton eyelet. The peasant-style blouse had a low, wide, off-the-shoulder ruffle encircling the gathered bodice and delicate short sleeves. The full, full skirt, draped over rustling white underskirts, was three tiered. A wide sash of flaming scarlet broadcloth encircled her small waist and fell almost to her feet.

Anna gazed at herself and shivered. This was the one. This was her. She could hardly wait to show Brit.

Anna made no pretense of stopping at the mirror. Nervously clutching the full white eyelet skirts, she walked directly up to the window and turned slowly about so that Brit could carefully examine her.

It wasn't necessary for him to gesture, shake his head or mouth any words. His midnight-black eyes, shamelessly riveted on her, said it all.

"I'll take this one," Anna announced decisively, backing away from the window, purposely lifting her right shoulder so that the wide eyelet ruffle would slip a little farther down her bare arm.

By four that afternoon, the three of them, Anna, Brit and LaDextra, were ready to start home. Anna, still flushed from the thrill of her impromptu fashion show, was looking forward to wearing the beautiful white eyelet dress on the Fourth.

Brit, aware that he'd made inroads with Anna this afternoon, was looking forward to her wearing the beautiful white eyelet dress on the Fourth.

So he could remove it.

LaDextra, refreshed from a nice long nap, waved away Brit's offer of assistance and crossed the hotel lobby with only the aid of her gold-headed cane. Anna followed, with Brit right behind them.

The carriage had been brought around and Brit was helping LaDextra into the rear seat when a woman's slightly shrill voice called out, "Mrs. Regent! Brit!"

Brit, Anna and LaDextra all turned at once to see the well-dressed, red-haired woman eagerly approaching.

"Oh, Jesus," Brit swore softly under his breath.

The widow Harris reached them, gave Brit an accusing look, then smiled warmly at LaDextra. "So very nice to see you, Mrs. Regent."

"My pleasure, Beverly." LaDextra was cordial. "I don't believe you've met my granddaughter."

"No, no I haven't," said Beverly, her eyes shifting to Anna.

"Anna, this is Mrs. Beverly Harris," LaDextra announced. "Beverly, my dear granddaughter, Anna."

Anna smiled and extended her hand. Beverly reluctantly shook it, nodded, acknowledged, "Anna." She immediately dropped Anna's hand, glanced at Brit, then back at Anna and said, "We must scold Brit, Anna. He never mentioned that you were so pretty."

"Thank you, Mrs. Harris," said Anna.

But Beverly had already turned her attention back to LaDextra. "Tell me, Mrs. Regent, will you be having the Fourth of July celebration this year, despite this terrible drought? Brit says the continuing lack of rain is becoming a very serious problem for the cattlemen."

"Nothing could stop the Regent Fourth of July festivities, Beverly. You know that," LaDextra assured her. "Rain or no rain, we'll have the big party, just as always." She shook her white head for emphasis, then asked, "You're coming, I hope?"

Those were the words Beverly Harris wanted to hear. Smiling prettily, she said, "I wouldn't miss it for the world." She slid a hand possessively around Brit's biceps, said to LaDextra and Anna, "Would you two excuse us for a moment?"

Before either could reply, Beverly was urging Brit away from the parked carriage. Never releasing her tight grip on his upper arm, she maneuvered him down the sidewalk a few steps until Brit balked and stopped walking.

Annoyed, he said, "What's on your mind, Bev?"

"You, darling," she cooed. "I haven't seen you in ages and I've missed you terribly."

"Been pretty busy," he said.

"Oh, I'm sure you have," she replied, unable to conceal her jealousy. She glanced pointedly at the golden-haired girl now climbing into the parked carriage, and added accusingly, "And I can just imagine what—and with whom—you've been so very busy."

"Christ, Bev, don't be absurd."

"Don't *you* be absurd, Brit Caruth. You think I can't see that there is something between you two?" Beverly's green eyes turned glacial. "For heaven sake, she's a member of the family. Surely LaDextra wouldn't approve of you sleeping with her granddaughter. There's a word for this."

"That's it!" said Brit, turning away in disgust.

Immediately contrite, Beverly hurried after him. "Wait, darling, wait, I'm sorry I said that. I didn't mean it. I know you'd never really be interested in a child, even a pretty one."

His firm jaw clamped tight, Brit kept walking. Beverly caught up with him. "Don't be angry, Brit," she said anxiously. "Please forgive me. Take the ladies home, then come back and have dinner with me." She laughed nervously, adding naughtily,

"Or have me for dinner if you like." Unsmiling, Brit shook his dark head. Beverly grabbed his arm, pressed her voluptuous body close, rose up on tiptoe and whispered, "I have a new black lace nightie I bought just for you."

"Some other time," said Brit, his disinterest evident.

Truly worried now, Beverly hid her disappointment and said, "Come when you can, darling. I'll save the black lace nightgown for you. And, please, Brit, save yourself for me." Brit gave no reply. Desperate now, Beverly said, "Well, then I...I will see you on the Fourth of July? Brit? Brit?"

Thirteen

The final days of a dust-dry June slowly waned, with southwest Texas suffering the worst drought it had seen in more than three decades. Not a drop of rain had fallen since early spring. All the many Regent pastures, save the high, lush mountain tract, were turning brown, the grass dead or dying. The precious water holes were drying up. Fire was a real and constant threat. Day after day of heat was taking its toll on The Regent cattle empire. But the parched, thirsty land was not the only thing suffering.

Brit was miserable.

Anna was, too.

Achingly aware of each other, sharing identical feelings of growing desire and painful longing, the two of them felt the raw sexual tension between them escalate daily until it was almost palpable. The anxiety Brit had aroused in Anna was now completely overshadowed by the building passion he had so effortlessly incited.

It was the same for Brit. His deep distrust and resentment of Anna's impersonation had been eclipsed by a basic, burning hunger to possess her physically. The attraction that had smoldered from the very beginning was now threatening to blaze out of control. Unspoken between them was the awareness that they could not stay out of each other's arms forever. Brit was impatient. Anna was apprehensive. Both were obsessed.

The blinding white-hot days were interminable. The dark sweltering nights endless. Night after sultry night, an edgy, restless Brit lay in his room unable to sleep, hot and miserable, his naked body gleaming with perspiration. He could find no relief from the awesome summer heat. Or from the raging desire that had him so hot for Anna he could hardly stand it.

It was sheer agony knowing that she was asleep and vulnerable in the room right next to his own. His body automatically responded as he pictured her there in bed wearing only her thin white batiste nightgown, her long unbound hair spilling across the pillow like a gold, silken fan.

Brit cursed himself for the unwanted erection now pulsing on his bare brown belly. He had never been this way about a woman before and it both frightened and annoyed him. There were far too many times of late when no more than a glance at Anna made his knees buckle, his heart pound. It was as if she were now the one in control, not he.

And he sure didn't like that.

Brit balled his hands into fists and ground his teeth. He reminded himself—one more time—that this golden goddess who robbed him of his rest was a greedy lying thief who meant to hurt LaDextra and steal The Regent from him.

It did no good.

He still wanted her. God, how he wanted her. He wanted her so badly he felt as if he couldn't stand it one more agonizing minute. Yet he couldn't risk being rebuffed again. He would have to wait. Like it or not, she was, temporarily, the one who wielded all the power.

But she was, he knew, steadily weakening. He was going to have her and soon. And he was confident that all it would take to put this debilitating madness behind him for good would be to make love to her.

Once. Just once.

No more.

Just one long, dark, hot, passionate night in her slender arms and he would be cured of this insanity.

He exhaled heavily, turned over onto his belly, allowing his heavy erection to press into the mattress, hugged his pillow and silently cursed the beautiful woman who was sleeping soundly while he suffered.

Brit would have been surprised—and pleased—had he known that Anna was not sleeping as soundly as he imagined. While he lay in the dark, naked and hurting from wanting her, she, too, was wide awake and suffering.

Night after steamy night, Anna lay awake in the hot darkness, her gown damp with perspiration and sticking to her skin, her slender body painfully tense with a kind of powerful longing she didn't fully understand.

It was not the summer heat that kept her awake

each night. It was the awesomely masculine man in the room next to her own.

Anna pictured Brit sound asleep in his bed. She didn't envision him in pajamas. She saw him gloriously naked, like he'd been at the springs. Only without the Stetson covering that most virile part of him. She visualized the smooth darkness of his lean, hard body against the snowy whiteness of the sheets, imagined his jet-black hair appealingly ruffled on the pillow.

The vivid vision brought on a new surge of heat, and Anna was plagued by the rising fever in her blood. Her slender body on fire, she felt as if she couldn't draw a breath, was smothering. She rose from the bed, impatiently lifted the damp nightgown up over her head and dropped it to the plush beige carpet. She exhaled shallowly. Naked, she got back into bed, stretched out and closed her eyes, certain that blessed sleep would finally come.

It did not.

Now the wicked thought kept running through her mind that Brit was in bed and she was in bed and he was naked and she was naked and he was uncomfortably warm and she was uncomfortably warm and he wanted her and she wanted him.

Anna was hot and cold at once. She trembled even as she perspired. Her teeth chattered, while her body felt feverish. Her stomach fluttered as if butterflies had taken wing inside. Her bare breasts swelled and her nipples tightened and ached. A gentle throbbing began in her lower belly.

Anna gritted her teeth and curled her hands into

tight fists. She reminded herself—again—that this dark Adonis who stole her sleep was a hard-hearted adversary who meant to deny her her heritage and have her tossed right off The Regent.

It did no good.

She still wanted him. Wanted him so badly she would have welcomed him warmly had he crept into her room the way he'd done that night she'd pulled the knife on him. Right or wrong, foolish or wise, she wanted Brit Caruth. She wanted him to take her in his arms and make love to her. He wanted her, too; she knew he did. They wanted each other, so it was, she realized, inevitable that one night soon it would happen. They would come together in their shared passion, unable to fight the deep yearning for one more minute. She hoped it would be soon. She didn't think she could stand it if it took much longer.

Tingling with the anticipation of being enclosed in Brit's strong arms, Anna told herself resolutely that if he made love to her once and never wanted her again, she wouldn't be hurt or disappointed. If once was enough for him, it was enough for her, too. Hopefully that's all it would take. Surely the fierce fever in her blood would cool once he had given her that sweet, mysterious release.

July 4, 1890, dawned clear and hot in the parched deserts of far southwest Texas and in the rocky foothills of the towering Guadalupe Mountains.

Anna awakened with the sun.

As soon as she opened her eyes, she smiled. Delicious aromas wafted up from the kitchen below.

Maggie Mae and her helpers were already hard at work preparing tempting foods for the daylong celebration.

Anna bounced out of bed, despite the fact that she'd slept little. She was excited. The Fourth had finally arrived and she had the delicious feeling that this was going to be one of the most exciting days—and nights—of her life.

Just as Sally had predicted, the mansion was now full of out-of-town guests, old and dear friends of LaDextra's. Petra, Anna's young maid, had told Anna that every single guest room was filled.

Anna had met most of the visitors at dinner last evening. And, as far as she could tell, she had passed muster with all of them. She was hugged and patted and told repeatedly, "You look just like you did when you were a little girl."

Anna heard voices coming from outdoors. Curious, she drew on a robe and rushed out onto the balcony. Praying that Brit was either still sound asleep or already up and gone, she anxiously tiptoed past his room, then hurried on down to the east end of the mansion. She followed the wide balcony around the corner and looked down on the terraced lawn, where the festivities were soon to begin.

Directly below, on the terrace nearest the house, and at the very back edge of the yard, a skinny man wearing a tall chef's hat and a white apron stood beside a huge pit and its roaring fire. A long-handled brush in his hand, he was basting the slow-cooking beef with some secret, spicy barbecue sauce. A platoon of white-garbed assistants were engaged in

similar tasks. Anna watched as the great sides of
beef were slowly turned on the spits. LaDextra
swore that Hap Kinney's barbecue was the best to
be had in all Texas because of his secret sauce and
the slow, patient cooking of the beef.

Near the smoking pits were several long utility
tables. Soon servants would be carrying huge platters of food from the house and placing them on the
service tables.

On the middle terrace, workers were busy setting
up dozens of tables that would later be covered with
white cloths and place settings. A couple of Regent
gardeners were filling dozens of white porcelain
vases with red roses to serve as centerpieces. Stacks
of folding chairs had come out of a storeroom and
were ready to be set up and placed at the tables.

Anna gazed down and wondered at which table
she would be seated that evening. And she wondered
where Brit would be sitting. Would they be at the
same table?

On the third and lowest terrace of the vast east
yard, the sound of hammering echoed in the early
morning quiet. A team of carpenters was construct-
ing a large wooden dance floor. As soon as the platform was completed, dozens of colorful Japanese
lanterns would be strung overhead to cast their mellow light on the dancers. At the north end of the
new dance floor was a raised dais for the orchestra.
Anna pictured herself turning round and round on
the dance floor in Brit's arms.

Soon her attention was drawn to the south side of
the lower terrace. Workers were very carefully

stacking fireworks for the midnight display. Anna smiled. Exactly where, she wondered, would she be at straight-up midnight? What would she be doing? And with whom?

A thrill shot through her at the thought and she turned and dashed back to her room.

By midafternoon everyone had arrived. Hundreds of guests were milling around the manicured grounds, sipping iced lemonade, greeting friends, laughing and talking, totally oblivious to the searing July heat.

On the flat west lawn a huge striped tent offered welcome shade to those seeking it. For the younger and heartier in the crowd who needed no protection from the broiling Texas sun, games were underway. A crawling-baby race—complete with wagering— had just ended. A gurgling, chubby nine-month-old girl had beat out some strong competition, much to the delight of her proud parents and the gamblers who had put their money on her.

Contestants were now being sought for the men's three-legged race. Brit and Buck Shanahan immediately volunteered. Anna, standing on the sidelines with Sally, clapped excitedly as the gun was fired and two dozen laughing, scrambling men awkwardly took off. The spectators yelled and whistled and took bets on which team would finish first.

Her sparkling eyes fixed on the laughing, hobbling Brit, Anna was startled when a woman's low, sultry voice said into her ear, "In case you've been getting any ideas, he belongs to me."

Anna quickly turned, to see the beautiful, red-haired Widow Harris standing close beside her. Speaking on impulse, Anna replied, "I wouldn't be so sure, Mrs. Harris."

Beverly's eyes narrowed minutely, but she smiled and said, "Ah, but I am. You can't compete with me, my dear. You're a sweet, pretty young girl, but Brit doesn't like sweet, pretty young girls. He prefers women."

"Oh, really?"

"Yes, really. And *I* am the woman he prefers," Beverly boasted. "Brit wants no one but me." Again she smiled and warned, "Stay away from him."

Quickly rising to the challenge, Anna smiled back at her and said, "You're warning the wrong one, Mrs. Harris. It's Brit who can't stay away from me." And she turned back to watch the races just as Brit and Buck tripped and went down.

The girls' egg races came next, and Anna and Sally were among the first to line up. Fourteen girls and women participated. With their hands behind their backs and a silver spoon holding a boiled egg clamped between their teeth, the contestants waited nervously for the starting gun.

At the sound of the shot, off they went, moving as quickly as possible while attempting to keep the egg from falling off the spoon. Again the crowd cheered and whistled, and Anna heard people calling her name, rooting for her.

It was exhilarating.

From the corner of her eye she saw Sally drop

her egg. Anna kept going. Others were dropping out now. The finish line was only twenty short yards away. Anna wanted to win. She was out in front of the others. Victory was within her grasp. Her heart was pounding with elation. Everyone was cheering her on. Brit's deep baritone voice rose above all the others. She was giddy with delight.

And then a moment's distraction spelled defeat.

Beverly Harris, standing at the finish line, her red hair aflame in the sun, purposely moved across Anna's line of vision and slipped her arms around Brit's hard waist from behind.

Anna made a misstep.

The egg teetered and fell to the grass. The Methodist preacher's wife raced across the finish line, the winner.

Beverly Harris laughed.

Seething, Anna silently vowed to have the last laugh.

Fourteen

Exhausted, but content, the imposing, black-garbed LaDextra, mistress of all she surveyed, sat at a white-clothed table on the east lawn's middle terrace as the searing summer sun finally slid below the string of distant western mountains. As the fiery red gloaming preceding full twilight bathed the guests in its warm pastel glow, LaDextra sighed with satisfaction.

It had been a wonderful day and she had enjoyed it to the fullest. She had spent most of her time seated comfortably beneath the shade-giving striped tent on the broad west lawn, surrounded by a circle of her closest, dearest friends, visiting, gossiping, watching the young folks act as friendly rivals in various competitive events.

She had laughed and applauded as she'd watched her golden-haired granddaughter compete in the ladies' egg-in-the-spoon competition. But her wrinkled face had fallen and she'd loudly exclaimed, "Dangnation!" when, almost to the finish line, Anna had lost the race. For no apparent reason Anna had made a misstep and the egg had toppled from the spoon.

But much to LaDextra's delight, Anna had proved

to be an extremely good sport. She had laughed at herself, kicked the dropped egg with the toe of her slipper and hurried forward to congratulate the winner. *Such a sweet, thoughtful child,* LaDextra mused complacently. *Such a priceless joy in this tired old woman's life.*

Now LaDextra looked down the table at Anna, who was presently lifting a spoonful of rich peach ice cream to her lips. LaDextra watched, amused, as Anna tasted that first bite, pursing her lips and rolling her big blue eyes with ecstasy. Looking even lovelier than usual this evening, she was nothing short of a vision in the new white eyelet dress.

The wide ruffle encircling the blouse's low neckline had slipped off Anna's right shoulder, but she was so caught up in relishing her ice cream, she hadn't even noticed. She looked incredibly young and innocent, more like a fifteen-year-old than the twenty-five-year-old she was. The dying sun touched her golden hair, setting it aflame and tinting her pale pearly skin a warm winsome pink. She was by far the prettiest girl at the party. And LaDextra would bet anything that the young man seated beside Anna would heartily agree.

Dr. McCelland was on Anna's right. He, too, was enjoying the frozen dessert, but he was, it was apparent, enjoying Anna's company even more.

Friendly by nature and always kind to everyone, Anna chattered companionably with the bashful physician, who said little, content just to listen. Anna easily made him laugh and blush and have a good time. Anna, too, seemed to be having a good time. Which made LaDextra especially happy, since the girl was as dear to her as life itself.

Satisfied that Anna was enjoying herself, La-Dextra temporarily shifted her attention elsewhere. Squinting in the fading orange light, she glanced around at the many tables crowded with laughing, talking diners, many of whom were still on their second or third helpings of Hap Kinney's delicious barbecued beef. She searched doggedly for the dark, handsome face of the only other living human being who was as dear to her as life.

LaDextra's wrinkled face broke into a wide grin when she spotted the smiling Brit holding forth at a table of vaqueros and their wives and children. He might have been one of them, so olive was his skin, so black his hair. And when he abruptly stood up to gesture for Buck Shanahan to come join them, she saw that he was dressed this evening in the vaquero's native garb.

He had at some point in the day gone to the house and changed out of the soiled blue cotton shirt and faded Levi's he'd worn for the three-legged race, the softball game and finally the impromptu bucking-bronco rodeo down at the stables.

Now he was immaculate in a snowy white shirt open at the throat and a pair of snug-fitting black *charro* trousers with silver conchos going down the outside of each long leg. The circular silver disks winked in the fading light before he sat back down. He, too, LaDextra could see, was enjoying himself. The beautiful, red-haired Beverly Harris was seated beside him, and Beverly, like the others, was laughing at something he had said.

Brit was a charmer, no doubt about it. Lately, LaDextra had noticed that he had even managed to halfway captivate the reticent Anna. Where once Anna had remained distant and stone-faced no matter how amusing a story he told, she had now begun to loosen up and laugh like everyone else.

Thank goodness.

There was nothing LaDextra wanted more than for the two people dearest to her to get along, to like each other. Each night she prayed that Brit and Anna would become good friends, would, as the years rolled by, grow genuinely fond of each other, become close, like brother and sister.

Her dream was that the two of them would be content to share The Regent. She could not bear the thought of either one of them taking everything and leaving the other with nothing. She worried constantly about being fair to them both. She worried about breaking Brit's heart if she left The Regent to her true heir, Anna. And she worried about breaking Anna's heart if she left it to Brit, who had worked so hard and so tirelessly to make it the profitable, renowned empire it was.

And to divide the ranch would be to kill The Regent and everything it stood for. Unthinkable!

Will Davis abruptly drew LaDextra out of her reveries when he leaned over and said, "You look quite tired, my dear. Shall I escort you into the house for a half hour rest?"

LaDextra shook her white head and said to her

old friend, "Not on your life, Will. I don't intend to miss a single minute of the fun." She reached out, patted his hand where it lay atop the table. "You having a good time?"

The distinguished-looking attorney smiled and said, "Yes, I am, and everyone else is as well. I've heard more than one guest say that this is your best Fourth of July celebration ever."

"It has to be," said a suddenly pensive LaDextra. Then she quickly waved away the questioning look her offhand remark had brought to Will's eyes.

Full darkness had fallen.

Colorful paper lanterns cast their mellow light over the diners at the tables and over the polished dance pavilion on the terrace below. An orchestra was taking its place on the raised dais, and soon lively music filled the still night air.

Before the first tune was finished, couples were eagerly making their way down to the floor. Old and young alike danced to the upbeat music. Those who didn't immediately join in turned their chairs toward the dance floor and clapped their hands in time with the music.

Anna, clapping enthusiastically, urged Dr. Mc-Celland to do the same. Sally Horner, seated on Anna's left, didn't need any prodding. The boisterous, fun-loving Sally not only clapped, she stood and tapped her foot, setting her yellow skirts astir.

The first several tunes the orchestra played were all upbeat. The dancers whirled rapidly about, their feet moving fast, their hearts beating faster. Their faces soon flushed, and they laughed, fought for breath and anxiously clung to each other, spinning wildly about on the polished floor while the onlookers cheered and whistled, enjoying the spectacle.

Anna, intensely aware, as she had been all evening, that Brit was with Beverly Harris at a table nearby, forced herself to keep her eyes off him, to watch only the dancers whirling below.

While Anna determinedly watched the dancers, Brit covertly watched her. He, too, clapped and laughed and carried on with his table companions, but he was distracted. He kept glancing at Anna and Dr. McCelland. Brit was looking directly at her when the young physician leaned close, whispered something in Anna's ear. She laughed with obvious delight and laid a hand on McCelland's forearm.

Brit felt his heart squeeze in his chest. He was jealous, but it was an emotion so foreign to him, he didn't recognize it for what it was.

"Well, will you?" Beverly's voice, close to his ear, broke into his troubled thoughts.

"Will I what?" Brit asked.

"Dance with me, of course," she said, reaching for his hand.

"Later," he said, begging off. "I'm too full to dance right now."

"Oh, very well," she said petulantly.

Brit pushed back his chair and took a long, thin cigar from his shirt pocket. As he struck a match and cupped his hands around the tiny flame, he again glanced at Anna. And he kept glancing at her often, could hardly take his eyes off her.

He stood it for as long as he could. When finally the orchestra changed its rhythm dramatically, concluded the up-tempo tunes and went into a slow romantic song, Brit crushed his cigar out in a crystal ashtray and, ignoring Beverly's shrill protestations, excused himself.

"I'm sorry I don't dance," said Dr. McCelland. "I know you'd enjoy dancing and I wish—"

"No, it doesn't matter," Anna sweetly assured him. "It's fun just to watch."

Dr. McCelland nodded and turned his attention back to the dance floor. Anna quickly seized the opportunity to glance at Brit's table. He was gone! With her brows knitted, her bottom lip caught between her teeth, she looked anxiously around.

And she jumped, startled, when she felt a warm hand on her bare shoulder and heard a deep masculine voice ask Dr. McCelland for permission to dance with her.

"Certainly. By all means," the doctor said, graciously rising to his feet.

Brit thanked the physician, took Anna's arm and guided her down to the dance floor. Once there, they clasped hands, stared at each other with deep meaning and began to dance.

Neither said a word.

Anna was breathless to find herself in Brit's arms, which was where she had wanted to be all evening.

Holding her close against his tall, hard body, Brit

silently glided Anna around the crowded dance floor. Her heart beating with his, her temple resting against his firm chin, Anna made no attempt to fight what was happening to her, to them.

Neither did Brit.

While they swayed seductively together, he gently took both her arms and raised them up around his neck. She locked her wrists behind his head. He laced his fingers behind her narrow waist. She sighed and leaned back in the circle of his arms.

They looked into each other's eyes, their expressions identical—wistful, yearning. Their bodies moved perfectly together as if they were one being. Brit's muscular thighs brushed against Anna's through the folds of her white eyelet skirts, and his flat, rock-hard belly was pressed flush against her slender frame. Mesmerized by the growing fire in his midnight eyes, she softly gasped when he drew her even nearer. Unobtrusively inserting a black, trouser-clad knee between hers, he drew her so close that her breasts flattened against his solid chest and she felt his hot breath fan against her cheek.

Feeling weak and shaky, Anna laid her forehead on his shoulder for a moment. Slowly she turned her head until her face was very close to his tanned throat. She saw the strong pulse pounding there and had an overwhelming desire to press her mouth to it. She could almost feel that throbbing power beating against her open lips, making her dizzy, thrilling her.

Vowing that one day she *would* kiss that pulse

point, Anna raised her head, tipped it back and again looked straight into Brit's dark, smoldering eyes.

Gazing down at her, Brit read the clear message in her beautiful blue eyes. He shuddered against her because he felt exactly the same way.

The music ended.

They stopped dancing, exchanged quick looks of regret that this sweet closeness was over. Without a word, Brit escorted Anna back to her table and reluctantly released her into the company and care of the good doctor.

But before he returned to his own table, Brit gave Anna one last fleeting glance.

That look spoke volumes.

Fifteen

And the merriment continued to escalate.

The dancing became more spirited as a grandly uniformed mariachi band took the dais shortly after eleven. The laughter and talk grew louder as freely flowing champagne was consumed by young and old alike.

Anna, sipping the bubbly wine from a stemmed glass, moved her shoulders in rhythm with the music while she watched smiling vaqueros spin their wives and sweethearts around the dance floor.

Whistles and shouts rose from the crowd when the band, led by a burly, mustachioed cornet player, broke into a rousing rendition of the a Mexican dance. Sally, draining her second glass of champagne, slammed the glass down on the table, licked her lips and reached for Anna's hand.

"Come on, Anna! Let's go down and join them."

Feeling warm and giddy and totally confident from the effects of the champagne, Anna thought it sounded like a fine idea. She laughed, nodded, reached out and plucked a red rose from the table's centerpiece. She snapped the stem, stuck the scarlet rose in her hair above her left ear and said to Dr.

McCelland, "You will excuse us, won't you, Doctor?" And didn't wait for a reply.

Eager to get down to the floor, Sally, clinging to Anna's hand, pulled her firmly along. As they maneuvered through the mob, Anna cast a quick glance at Brit's table. Her heartbeat instantly quickened. He was looking directly at her. Their eyes held for one fleeting second, sending shivers of excitement through Anna.

At last Sally and Anna reached the crowded dance floor.

Their hands clasped behind their backs, bright smiles on their olive faces, vaqueros lifted their knees high and struck the heels of their boots against the wooden floor as they turned and spun and danced around their female partners.

Anna studied the movements of the pretty señoritas and imitated them. She was a quick study. In less than a minute she had the steps down and was whirling around, stamping her heels and swirling her skirts with the best of them.

With the white ruffled bodice slipping low down one arm, Anna flirtatiously flashed her skirts, moved her bare shoulders provocatively and swished her long hair about as she turned her head one way, then the other.

She quickly drew an appreciative audience. Soon other dancers stopped to watch and applaud. Laughing, feeling flushed and wonderful, Anna danced ardently, bringing her own special brand of playfulness and passion to the lively tune. Lost in a world of her own, she was oblivious to those around her.

She was unaware of all the attention she attracted by dancing with happy abandon.

But if she was unaware, Brit was all too cognizant. His dark face set in hard lines, his firm jaw ridged, he watched unblinking as the whirling, laughing Anna easily beguiled dozens of other men, just as she beguiled him. He saw the way they looked her, knew what they were thinking, what they were feeling.

His chest uncomfortably tight, his teeth clamped so hard his jaws hurt, Brit manfully fought the fierce temptation to go down and yank her right off the floor. To scold her hotly for behaving so seductively and making a spectacle of herself. To let her know in no uncertain terms that she was *never* to dance and flirt and flash her skirts for anyone but him.

Brit exhaled heavily when the rollicking dance finally ended and a breathless Anna left the floor and headed back to her table, amidst much appreciative applause and shouts for more.

Pushing her heavy hair behind her ear, Anna again glanced at Brit. And a jolt of unease shot through her. He was looking at her, but his eyes were icy cold. Anna was baffled.

Back at the table, she gratefully accepted another glass of chilled champagne and drank thirstily. And she laughed, delighted, at the shocked expression that came to Sally's flushed face when big Buck Shanahan walked up, nodded to everyone, paid his polite respects to LaDextra, then looked at Sally and asked, "Miss Sally, would you care to dance?"

Her eyes wide, her mouth rounded into an O,

Sally couldn't speak. Could only nod. But she shot to her feet so fast her chair overturned. Grinning, Buck righted the chair, took Sally's arm and led her down to the dance floor.

"You're looking mighty pretty tonight in that bright yellow dress," Buck said as he took Sally in his arms.

Sally replied brashly, "You're looking mighty pretty tonight in that starched white shirt."

Buck threw back his blond head and laughed. His arm tightened around her waist and he said, "Say, you've lost some weight."

"A pound or two perhaps," said Sally, cleverly concealing the fact that she'd been starving herself for the past two weeks so she could fit into the new yellow dress.

"Well, I hope you don't lose any more," said Buck.

Sally stopped dancing. "You mean you don't think I'm fat?"

"Fat? You?" Buck snorted. "No sirree, Miss Sally. Anything I hate it's a scrawny woman." His arm again tightened around her. "You feel just about right to me."

Overjoyed, Sally tightened her hand possessively on Buck's strong neck and said coquettishly, "And you feel absolutely perfect to me."

Buck's face reddened. But he squeezed her other hand and said, "There's something I've been meaning to ask you, Sally."

"Ask me now."

"How come you and me never got together?"

"I've been wondering the same thing."

"Well, you reckon I could come call on you one of these evenings?"

"Is tomorrow night too soon?" was her quick reply.

Anna smiled with amused pleasure as she watched Sally and Buck spin around the dance floor. Sally was obviously thrilled that Buck had noticed her. And from the wide grin on Buck's face, the feeling must have been mutual. When the song ended and another began, the couple stayed on the floor.

Anna continued to sip the smooth champagne and converse with the attentive Dr. McCelland. The two of them were discussing how much they were looking forward to the midnight fireworks display when they were abruptly interrupted. A young Regent vaquero came rushing up to the table, out of breath, excited.

"I am sorry, Dr. McCelland. *Por favor*, forgive me, señorita," the man said apologetically. "Doctor, it is time. My Maria, she has gone into labor. She needs you!"

Dr. McCelland was on his feet immediately. Calmly patting the shoulder of the nervous, expectant father, he said, "I'll get my bag out of the carriage, Rio. You hurry on back to Maria and I'll meet you at your adobe in ten minutes."

"*Sí. Gracias, gracias!*" The young man turned and rushed away.

To Anna, Dr. McCelland said, "It's Maria Alverez's first child, so I probably won't be back for the fireworks."

"I'm sorry you have to miss them," said Anna.

The doctor smiled. "Next year perhaps."

"Yes, next year," Anna replied. "Now go. Maria needs you."

"Good night, Anna," he said, and left hurriedly.

"You haven't danced with me all evening," Beverly complained for the dozenth time. "Please, Brit. Let's dance."

Tired of hearing her whine, Brit said, "All right. One dance, but then that's it."

Certain she could make him change his mind, Beverly gave him a full-lipped smile and said, "Whatever you say, darling."

They rose and headed down toward the dance floor. As they wove their way through the crowd, Brit took the opportunity to glance at Anna's table. He saw Dr. McCelland rise, bid Anna good-night and leave. Brit's heart kicked against his ribs.

He and Beverly reached the dance floor just as the orchestra changed tempos, began a romantic Latin ballad.

Anna took a drink of champagne. The band suddenly changed tempos. A slow Spanish love song floated on the still night air. Anna sighed, closed her eyes dreamily and imagined herself floating about the floor locked in Brit's long arms.

She could almost feel his lean legs brushing against her own, could nearly catch his clean, masculine scent. Inwardly shivering, Anna opened her eyes, took another drink of champagne and turned in her chair to look down on the dance floor.

In the sea of couples swaying to the music, her attention was drawn to something winking and gleaming in the lights from the Japanese lanterns. She carefully focused. Several small silver disks were sparkling, reflecting the light.

Anna's face immediately fell.

Those shiny silver disks winked and glittered from the long, black-trousered leg of Brit Caruth. He was turning slowly about on the floor, and in his arms was a radiant Beverly Harris. Anna swallowed hard as the strikingly handsome pair swayed and spun and moved gracefully to the slow romantic ballad.

Sick with jealousy, Anna bit her lip and fought the overwhelming desire to rush down to the floor and snatch Brit from the tenacious grasp of the sophisticated, red-haired temptress. To rebuke him scathingly for dancing with Beverly. To make it crystal clear that he was *never* to hold any other woman but Anna herself in such a sensuous, intimate way.

"Anna, where did Dr. McCelland go?" La-Dextra's firm voice shook her from her troubled reveries.

Anna forced a smile to her face and, speaking loudly to be heard, explained the doctor's abrupt departure. "Maria Alverez is having her baby."

"Ah, good," LaDextra said, nodding. Then, motioning, she added, "Move on down here by Will and me."

Anna complied. She pulled up a chair beside LaDextra.

"You having a good time, child?"

"The best time of my life," Anna assured her, knowing that's what LaDextra wanted to hear and feeling, somehow, that before the night ended it *would* be the best time of her life.

LaDextra beamed.

Anna spent a few pleasant minutes visiting with LaDextra and Will. At the same time she managed to steal covert glimpses at Brit as the love song ended and he and Beverly headed back to their table. She saw Beverly say something to Brit, then leave him to weave her way alone through the crowd and up toward the house.

Anna tried, but could not hide her restlessness. Astute, LaDextra sensed it.

"You've spent enough time with us old folks, Anna," said the older woman. "And you've spent the entire evening at this table. Why don't you walk around a little? Mix and mingle. Circulate. Meet some new young folks. See what mischief you can get into." Her light eyes twinkled.

Anna smiled, kissed LaDextra's wrinkled cheek and whispered, "You're a wise woman, LaDextra Regent."

LaDextra chuckled merrily. "I don't know about that, but I was once a young woman, and after all these years I can still remember what it was like." She inclined her white head toward the dance floor.

"I see lots of good-looking young men who'd be thrilled if you said hello."

Anna took one last drink from her champagne glass, set it aside and rose. "Good night, LaDextra. Good night, Will."

"You be careful, you hear?" said the fatherly Will.

"You enjoy yourself," said the understanding LaDextra.

Anna wandered away.

Brit noticed the moment she left the table. Grateful that Beverly had decided to go to the house and freshen up, he hurriedly rose to his feet.

Anna did as LaDextra had suggested. She mixed and mingled, moving unhurriedly through the crowd, introducing herself, shaking hands with men and women alike. But she managed to always keep Brit within sight, watched him as he, too, maneuvered leisurely through the gathering, greeting people, sharing a word here and a laugh there.

For the next half hour the two of them distractedly circled each other. Both migrated steadily toward the far north end of the packed dance floor. As if they had verbally communicated, had told each other exactly where and when they would finally meet, each gravitated toward the same spot.

Without a word being spoken, the two of them shared an exciting secret. They were, both knew, now on a steady course toward that long-awaited clandestine meeting. Players in an exciting drama, they were the principals, obeying a strange, bewitching mating call. They were partners in a seductive, well-orchestrated, perfectly choreographed dance of desire.

It was a marvelous, magical game that only they knew they were playing. Each was adept at his and her part. When Anna stopped to talk with guests, she never failed to look at Brit and let him know she was aware he was following her and that she wanted him to continue to follow her.

If Brit, moving through the multitude, was temporarily lost from Anna's view, he made it a point to step out into the open and nod to her. The game proved to be great fun. So much fun they were reluctant to end it. They purposely made the thrilling exercise last, stretched it out, played hide-and-seek with each other. And with every moment that ticked away, their shared excitement grew, their mutual anticipation heightened.

Finally they could stand the sweet agony no longer.

At last they met.

Face-to-face, they stood in the shadows just beyond the lighted dance floor. As naturally as if it had all been preordained, Brit gently took Anna's hand in his, clasped it close to his chest and commandingly led her a few yards farther into the starlight.

He stopped beneath an old elm tree, turned to her and, gazing into her sparkling eyes, anxiously took her in his arms and kissed her.

It was a long, intrusive kiss of such fiery passion that Anna shuddered against him, melting completely. As if he were afraid to release her lips lest she run away, Brit continued to kiss her hotly, masterfully, molding her mouth to his, teaching her how to kiss, taking her breath away. Her wits scattered, her heart pounding, Anna clung to him and gloried in the prolonged, devastating kisses. Deeply penetrating kisses that thrilled her, overwhelmed her, conquered her.

Brit's hot lips and probing tongue drew all the strength from Anna until she was weak and totally limp in his arms.

Finally he tore his burning lips from hers, again took her hand and eagerly drew her along with him, moving steadily away from the lights and the music and the crowd.

Hurrying to keep up with his long, determined strides, Anna could only nod when he said, "The house is full of guests, we don't dare go there." Again he stopped, bent his head, kissed her, then said, "There's only one place where we can be alone."

He held his breath and waited for her answer.

"Take me there," she said, putting her hand to his tanned cheek and drawing his face back down to hers so that she could kiss him.

And in her kiss was all the need, all the passion, all the love she had saved for a lifetime. Brit's knees buckled and his heart thundered in his chest. He quickly moved his booted feet apart to brace himself, wrapped his arms around her, tore his lips from hers and pressed hot, desperate kisses to the warm curve of her neck and shoulder, waiting for his strength and his equilibrium to return.

When finally they did, he scooped Anna up off the ground and sprinted down a narrow, winding path toward the only place where they could be alone without danger of being caught. Brit was so eager to get her there, he ran every step of the way, while Anna, her arms looped around his neck, clung trustingly to him.

In minutes they reached a sturdy stone structure totally isolated from all the other ranch outbuildings. With Anna held high against his chest, Brit ducked inside the stable where he housed his prized stallion, Captain.

The stallion whinnied happily at the sight of his master, anticipating a soothing rubdown or a few cubes of sugar. Ignoring the big gray, Brit shoved Anna none too gently up against the wall and hungrily kissed her. His tongue aggressively delved deep, touching and stroking all the sensitive places inside her mouth.

And as he kissed her his hands captured and flattened hers against the wall, and he firmly thrust his trousered knee between her legs, boldly pressing his hard muscled thigh flush against her groin through the skirts of her white eyelet dress.

He sighed into her open mouth when she eagerly began to rub herself against his bent knee. On fire, completely carried away, Anna slipped her hands free of Brit's and lowered them to his slim hips. Her eyes closed, her tongue stroking and mating with his, she moved rhythmically against him, seeking the partial balm to this burning passion that his hard, muscular thigh afforded.

For a time they stood there like that, mimicking the erotic movements of full-fledged lovemaking. Her hands on Brit's hips as they moved together, Anna grew so excited she twisted one of the silver conchos on his trouser leg until it came off in her hand.

She was clutching the silver disk tightly when Brit's hot lips finally lifted from hers. Her eyes came open as he raised his head and said in a husky baritone, "You're not going to kill me if I make love to you, are you?"

Breathless, yearning so much she actually hurt, Anna whispered, "I will kill you if you don't."

Sixteen

"Ah, sweetheart, you'll let me hold you and love you all night?" Brit murmured, scattering kisses over her face, her throat, her bare shoulders.

Tingling from head to toe, Anna, sagging weakly back against the wall, whispered, "For as long as you want to love me, Brit."

Pressing a kiss to the sensitive spot just below her left ear, Brit inhaled deeply of the fragrant red rose tucked into her golden hair and said, "God, baby, I've been going crazy watching you tonight, wanting you, waiting for this moment."

"Me, too," she said with appealing honesty.

Knowing he had her now, that she wouldn't bolt and run away, Brit warned himself to slow down, to take it easy, to love her the way a woman liked being loved. To make this encounter as pleasurable for her as he knew it would be for him.

He raised his head, smiled down at her and said, "Will you do something for me, sweetheart?"

"Yes. Anything," she quickly replied.

"Unbutton my shirt, please," he urged. "Take it off."

Anna didn't hesitate. Her nimble fingers went to the buttons of his snowy white shirt and in seconds it was open down his dark chest. She pushed the shirt apart, looked up at him and said, "May I... I want to kiss your chest."

Brit shuddered. "Sure, honey," he answered, then cupped the back of her head as she bent to him and brushed her soft lips to his hot flesh.

It was then, while she was sweetly sprinkling kisses over the broad expanse of his naked chest, that the midnight fireworks display began. A boom reverberated, then a great profusion of light illuminated the inside of the stable. And the couple embracing there.

Her golden hair shimmering in the rocket's fleeting light, Anna did what she'd wanted to do since she had danced with Brit earlier in the evening. Slowly she slid her lips up his chest, across his collarbone to his throat. Her hands gripping his ribs, she raised herself on tiptoe and, whispering, "I've wanted to do this all evening," opened her lips against the firmly beating pulse at the base of his throat.

She pressed the tip of her tongue to the powerful throbbing there and shivered with pleasure at the strange sensation. His heartbeat was pounding into her open mouth. Toying with him, she stroked that throbbing pulse with her tongue and playfully plucked at it with her lips. At last she sighed, released him, raised her head and said, "Is there anything you'd like to do to me?"

"So many things," he said huskily, and whipped off his shirt in one fluid, masculine movement.

Shirt in hand, he turned and walked away from

her. From a shelf he took down one of Captain's newest, softest horse blankets, one that had never been used. Anna watched as he spread the blanket atop a bed of hay against the far wall. He dropped his shirt, turned about and sat down on the blanket with his bent knees spread. He leaned back against the wall, looked at her meaningfully and extended his hand.

His voice low, caressing, he said, "Come. Sit here beside me, sweetheart."

Before she could take a step, a great shower of fireworks lit the night sky and sent a burst of light through the darkened stable. For a few seconds it was as bright as day, and the thought struck Anna that if the fireworks display continued, it would be intermittently bright as day when they made love. She shivered at the thrilling prospect.

As Anna crossed to Brit, the gray stallion loudly snorted and blew, clearly demonstrating his disapproval. His big eyes wild, he reared his forelegs high in the air and brought them down with a loud thud.

Sinking to her knees before Brit, Anna said, "I don't think Captain wants me here."

Brit smiled, reached out, encircled her narrow waist with his hands and slowly drew her forward to kneel between his raised knees.

"Doesn't matter. I want you here," he said. "Don't worry about Captain. He's showing off. Ignore him and he'll settle down."

She nodded, placed her hands on his steely biceps. "I hope so."

"Don't worry about anything, baby. Just relax here in my arms and allow me to love you."

Brit leaned closer, kissed the warm, shadowy valley between her breasts, where the ruffled white blouse dipped low. Anna exhaled anxiously and threw back her head, arching her throat, giving him better access. Brit's burning lips slid slowly upward and he kissed the delicate hollow of her throat, painting it with his tongue. Anna's eyes closed and she gripped his upper arms so tightly her nails cut into his flesh.

When his mouth began its downward slide, Anna held her breath, wondering where he would stop.

If he would stop.

Brit's hot face reached the top edge of the wide white ruffle going around her bare shoulders. Anna gasped when he snagged the ruffle's edge with his teeth and steadily eased it down until finally a pale pink nipple was exposed.

"Brit, Brit," she said breathlessly as his handsome face hovered a scant two inches from her bared breast.

He said, "You asked if there was anything I wanted to do to you." He lowered his lips to her breast. "This is what I want to do, sweetheart."

And before she could respond, his warm, wet mouth closed gently over the nipple. Anna involuntarily gasped with pleasure. She arched her back, breathed through her mouth and watched, transfixed, as Brit's full, sensual lips plucked and sucked at her breast until she felt a strong infusion of heat radiate outward from where his mouth was. She winced and wiggled when she felt his sleek tongue tease and toy with the now diamond-hard nipple, and secretly she hoped that he wouldn't take his marvelous mouth from her aching breast.

Brit was an experienced, perceptive lover. He could tell that Anna was, like most women, thoroughly enjoying this particular part of lovemaking. He had learned long ago that a woman's breasts were incredibly sensitive, that females wanted, needed, had to experience this ingredient of lovemaking to be absolutely satisfied.

So, with his lips never leaving her flesh, Brit gently drew her down, carefully turned her about and laid her across his lap, cushioning her head against his supporting arm. She sighed softly, snuggled close, closed her eyes and lay there in his arms while he continued to suckle, lick and playfully bite her stiffened, stinging nipple.

Anna was so completely carried away with this new kind of pleasure she was hardly aware that as he kissed and caressed her swelling breasts, he was skillfully sliding the full skirts of her dress up until finally they were gathered and bunched around her thighs.

Anna whimpered in protest when Brit's magical mouth left her breasts. Her eyes opened and she looked up at him questioningly.

And experienced an immediate ripple of added excitement when, gazing directly into her eyes, he announced in a low, husky baritone, "I'm going to take off your underwear, sweetheart." His supporting arm tightened around her shoulders and he lifted her up so that she was in a sitting position. "Watch me, baby. Watch with me."

Shocked to the roots of her hair, but so thrilled and aroused she could hardly breathe, Anna could only nod. She did as he asked. Her feverish cheek pressed to his, she watched, entranced, as he effortlessly found the tape of her full petticoats, unhooked it and pushed them down. In seconds the white petticoats lay in a heap at her feet.

Her breath caught when he laid his hand on her stomach atop her thin batiste underpants. Anna was now tingling and nervous and unsure if she wanted him to go further. Brit read her thoughts, knew her doubts. As his lean dark fingers began to ease the lacy underwear down, he murmured, "It's all right, baby. You're here in my arms and we're all alone. There's no one in the world but us. Just you and me."

A little gurgle of tumult laced with rising desire escaped Anna's lips as indecision plagued her. The party's music and laughter carried on the still night air and, just as her lace-trimmed underwear slid down her belly to her thighs, a booming skyrocket filled the stable with a blinding white light.

During those seconds of bright illumination, Brit whisked her underpants completely off. He got only a fleeting look at her bare loveliness before the darkness enveloped them. But it was enough to make his already heated blood surge through his veins, scorching them.

Her stomach was so flat as to be almost concave. Her prominent hipbones rose appealingly beneath the pale, luminous flesh. Her navel was tiny and turned inward, and a wispy line of golden hair trailed downward from that cute belly button to the shimmering triangle of dense golden curls between her thighs. Sheer silky stockings, supported by flirty, blue satin garters, encased her long, shapely legs. He decided to leave the stockings on. He liked the look of her in the stockings, found it incredibly sexy.

A muscle twitched in his jaw.

The sight of her lying trustingly in his arms, naked from the waist down, made his heart hammer in his bare chest.

He cautioned himself not to give in to the fierce animal lust threatening to overcome him. Already he was tired of waiting, tired of wooing. He wanted to sweep the rest of her clothes away, free his aching tumescence from his tight trousers, push her stockinged legs apart and implant himself deeply within her. Then thrust forcefully into her until he shot off inside that slick wet warmth and shuddered in his release.

Brit was sorely tempted to do just that. And more than likely it wouldn't have mattered if he had. She was, after all, hardly an innocent. It surely wouldn't be the first time an overly aroused male had pounded ruthlessly into her. A woman as fair, blond and beautiful as she couldn't possibly have spent all those years among the Apache without...

He didn't want to think about that. Not now. He wanted to pretend that he was her one and only lover. To keep up that pretense, he would treat her as if it were true.

Brit spread his hand on Anna's bare, flat belly and felt the muscles quiver at his touch.

"You are," he said honestly, "the most beautiful woman I have ever seen."

"As beautiful as Beverly Harris?" Anna's reply was totally feminine.

"Much more beautiful," Brit assured her. Pressing her head back against his supporting arm, he kissed her.

His hot, insistent mouth holding hers prisoner and his warm hand on her trembling belly filled Anna with an all-encompassing heat. She sucked at his thrusting tongue and squirmed against his spread hand, unable to be still. When finally Brit ended the long, penetrating kiss, he left his lips on hers and said into her mouth, "I'm going to touch you now, baby. You want me to, don't you? Make you feel good? Love you with my hand?"

He kissed her again as his spread hand slowly slipped down between her parted legs and gently cupped her. For a long, lovely time he did nothing more. Just kissed her and kissed her while he possessively covered her soft groin with his hand. It felt very good to Anna and she sighed into his mouth, relaxing, enjoying the closeness.

Finally Brit took his mouth from hers, raised his head and looked directly into her shining eyes as he parted the dense golden coils with his middle finger and gently touched that tiny button of slippery flesh he had exposed. Anna winced and immediately began to struggle.

"No," she whispered, "no, Brit. Stop, you must stop."

"Shh," he soothed, and hugged her more closely to him. "Just let me touch you for a minute, baby. If you don't like it, I'll stop."

And his long, lean finger began to slowly, skillfully circle that sensitive little bud of pure sensation. In seconds a silky wetness was flowing from her, and Brit dipped his fingers into that fiery liquid and spread the natural lubrication from the very top of her swollen cleft to that small, tempting opening that his hard male flesh would soon fill.

"Stop, oh, stop," Anna weakly whispered.

But Brit knew she didn't mean it. She was becoming so excited she was actually frightened by the depth of her desire. The longer his masterful fingers stroked and circled and caressed, the hotter she became, until she was near to hysteria.

Brit stilled his fingers, gave her a chance to calm a little, to catch her breath. Then he started again. His middle finger, wet from her arousal, slid and stroked and teased until Anna was arching her hips and pressing herself against that teasing, torturing hand.

Panting, jerking involuntarily, Anna felt as if the entire universe was located there between her legs where he was caressing her. As the incredible pleasure rapidly escalated, the terrible thought flashed through her mind that any minute he might take his hand away. Oh, God, she couldn't stand it if he did. She'd die of agony if he left her like this before...

"Don't," she murmured anxiously. "Don't...stop. Oh, please, don't ever stop."

"I won't," he assured her. "We've all night, sweetheart," Brit added soothingly. "And there's nothing I love more than touching you like this."

"Oh, Brit, Brit!" she sighed, and closed her eyes.

He smiled as he watched the changing degrees of joy spread across her lovely face as he continued to patiently please and pleasure her. After only a few short moments, her ecstasy was quickly rising toward that badly needed climax.

Brit knew just what to do to take her the rest of the way. He slipped his middle finger down and put the tip inside her for a moment. Then withdrew it and returned it to that pulsing nubbin of flesh. He repeated the exercise until she was left gasping and trembling. In seconds she was anxiously saying his name, her eyes gone wide with fear and delight.

Then it happened.

While the music played and the fireworks lit the stable and Brit's nervous stallion snorted and whinnied in excitement, Anna's release began. Brit stayed with her, holding her, stroking her, as her ecstasy built and grew so intense she could stand the burning bliss no longer. She screamed when the rising heat exploded deep inside her, even as a great barrage of fireworks exploded outside.

Her awesome release came as the powerful fireworks again illuminated the lovers. Watching her, Brit got almost as much pleasure from Anna's orgasm as she did. She was wild in her ecstasy, pitching and bucking and screaming his name.

He held her and soothed her, kissing her temples and calming her until she sighed, collapsed and went totally limp in his arms. He allowed her to rest for a while. Then he sat her up on his lap and began tugging her white eyelet blouse out of her skirt's waistband.

"Now," he said, slipping the blouse up over her head and tossing it aside, "I'm going to make love to you." He unhooked her lace-trimmed camisole, swept it apart, cupped a warm bare breast.

"I thought you already had," she replied dreamily.

"That was just the preliminaries," he told her. "I haven't begun to really make love to you."

Anna sighed, put her arms around his neck, brushed a kiss to his lips and said, "Well, before you do, may I do to you what you just did to me?"

Seventeen

"You can do anything you want to me, sweetheart," Brit calmly assured her, wondering worriedly how long he could continue to control his raging passion if she put her soft warm hands on him. "Anything at all."

He continued to dexterously undress Anna. Amazed by how adept he was at the task, she couldn't help but wonder how many times he had done this. With how many women. Then his lips, warm and persuasive, brushed the side of her throat and she wondered no more.

His hands gently caressing each portion of pale flesh he bared, then his lips paying homage, Brit adroitly swept the remainder of Anna's clothes away, right down to the silk stockings, which he peeled swiftly off her long, slender legs. The entire task was completed with her sitting on his lap.

Anna was now as naked as the day she was born, but she felt no embarrassment or shame. It seemed to her that it was the most natural thing in the world to be naked in Brit Caruth's arms. She sighed and smiled and squirmed as he kissed her and whispered to her all the things he wanted to do with her, told her of the many ways he wanted to love her.

The blood raced through her veins and she thrilled to the sound of that deep, masculine voice speaking of all the shocking, forbidden things that they would do together. She tingled from head to toe when Brit promised that before the night ended, he would possess her totally, would love her as she'd never been loved before.

Excited by his amorous vows, Anna finally interrupted. Hugging his dark head to her bare breasts, she murmured against his midnight hair, "Brit, you promised you'd let me..." She inhaled deeply, whispered barely loud enough to be heard, "I can't do what I want unless...you...you'll have to take your clothes off."

She cupped his cheeks in her hands, lifted his face and looked at him. She said, "I want to touch you and please you the way you pleased me. You said you'd let me."

"How could I possibly refuse?" Brit replied. He kissed her quickly, then lifted her off his lap and sat her down gently beside him on the spread blanket. He removed his freshly polished black boots and socks, set them aside. He smiled at Anna and asked, "Want to turn your head now, while I undress?"

"No," she said truthfully. "I don't. I want to watch you."

Brit swallowed hard. "As you wish."

He was on his feet in a flash, his hands at the buttons of his tight black pants. Silver conchos running down the outside of each trouser leg flashed in the darkness as he undressed. Her eyes riveted to him, Anna hastily lay down and stretched out on her back. From below she watched every move Brit made. In seconds he was discarding his trousers. Just as he tossed them aside, a bright explosion of fireworks bathed him in its radiant, revealing light.

Staring, Anna found her breath caught in her throat.

He stood there in all his wild naked beauty, his bronzed skin aglow in the brilliant light. He was godlike, splendid, a Greek statue come to life. A perfect male specimen so divine, so arresting, she felt as if she would be content to just lie and look at him forever. Before her curious gaze could focus on that powerful phallus thrusting horizontally from the dense growth of blue-black hair covering his groin, the light was gone.

Darkness returned.

Brit sank to his knees, stretched out on his back beside Anna. He sighed, took one of her small hands in his, raised it to his lips and kissed it. Then he carried her hand down to his belly, gently spread her fragile fingers and placed them squarely atop his heavy erection. He took his hand away.

He folded his arms beneath his head and said, "Sweetheart, it's all yours. *I'm* all yours."

Awed by the heat and hardness of him, Anna, never taking her hand from his flesh, eased up into a sitting position. Curious, enthralled, she carefully examined him, wanting to learn all there was to know about this beautiful bronzed body that was so different from her own.

Innocently unaware that her stroking, seeking fingers had Brit in a state of unbearable arousal, Anna lovingly explored and inspected, thrilled by the way his responsive flesh seemed to have a mind of its own. The lightest brush of her fingertips caused the smooth, mushroom-shaped tip to rise and seek her touch.

Guided by instinct, Anna, cupping him gently, possessively, suddenly popped a forefinger into her mouth. Then she painted the stirring tip of his throbbing erection with her wet fingertip and heard him groan deep in his throat.

She looked at his face, saw that it was contorted. "Does that hurt?" she asked.

"No," he managed to reply. "No. Feels good." He ground out the words.

"Good," she said, and returned to her delightful diversion.

Brit allowed her to play, but it was pure agony for him, all he could do to keep from climaxing. Biting the inside of his bottom lip until he drew blood, he watched her through heavy-lidded eyes. The sight of her small, white hands enclosing him was so powerfully erotic he had to look away.

His heart almost exploded when, gently gripping him with both hands, Anna impulsively bent her head and brushed a soft kiss on the jerking tip.

Brit instantly rolled up into a sitting position, tore her hands from his flesh, drew her to him and kissed her passionately. While he kissed her, he eased her down onto her back.

When their lips finally separated, he said hoarsely, "I can't wait much longer, sweetheart. This body of mine wants to be on yours. In yours. Buried deep inside you.''

"I'm yours for the taking," she told him, and meant it.

"Do you want me, baby?"

"Yes."

"Then say it. Say 'I want you, Brit. I want you inside me.'''

Anna didn't falter. Gazing lovingly up at his dark, handsome face, she said softly, adoringly, "I do want you, Brit. I want you inside me. I want you to stay inside me all through the night.''

"Jesus," Brit groaned, and anxiously swept a warm hand down her slender body. Anna involuntarily arched up to meet it. Looking into her eyes, he slipped his fingers between her legs and tenderly touched her. She was, he learned, not quite ready for him. Brit withdrew his hand, licked his fingers until they were gleaming wet, then returned them to her. As he caressed her, he leaned over and kissed her. Settling his lips warmly on hers, he kissed her again and again while his gentle fingers prepared her for total lovemaking.

In a few short minutes she was hot and wet and ready. Brit's lips left hers, slipped down over her chin. He nibbled and nuzzled his way downward, kissing her breasts, her stomach, her prominent hipbones.

Then, urging her legs wider apart, he quickly moved between and lay lightly atop her. Bracing his weight on an elbow, Brit carefully inserted the stirring tip of his pulsating erection just inside her. He felt her body respond to his heat and hardness. But he didn't immediately plunge into her.

For several heartbeats he lay there unmoving between her spread thighs, letting the anticipation build, the passion burn higher. While he lay totally still with his hot rigid flesh cushioned by her soft, swollen sweetness, he lowered his face and pressed kisses to her feverish cheeks, her small ears, her open lips, her pale shoulders, her surging breasts.

Raking his teeth over a distended nipple, he told her, "From the first minute I saw you, I dreamed of you being just as you are now. Naked and beautiful and hot and wet. And just for me. For nobody else but me."

"For you, Brit. Just for you, only for you."

"Baby," he murmured as he changed positions slightly, put his hand between them, guided his throbbing flesh more securely inside her. He took his hand away, saw that her eyes had slid closed. "Open your eyes, sweetheart. Look at me. I want you to look at me while I love you."

Anna complied. She looked straight into his dark, sultry eyes as a new flash of fireworks washed over them, lighting their faces and bodies as if it were midday. It was then that Brit thrust deeply into her. Their gazes remained locked throughout that swift, deep insertion of his rock-hard flesh in her yielding softness. With that first driving invasion, Anna experienced a shockingly intense pain. A burning, white-hot pain so acute, she wanted to scream at him to take it out, to stop, to let her go, she couldn't stand it.

But she didn't.

Anna was used to bearing pain without showing how much it hurt. Her years with the Apache had conditioned her to endure varying degrees of torture without so much as a whimper or change of expression. So she suffered this excruciatingly painful invasion of her body without resistance or altered countenance.

Looking into her eyes as he thrust into her, Brit saw nothing on her face that gave away her distress. But her hot, sweet body was so incredibly small, so unbelievably tight, he momentarily wondered at her past sexual experience. He had such a difficult time forcing himself into her, it was almost as if she was a virgin. Untouched. Unused. Unprepared for what he had done to her.

But that couldn't be.

The nagging possibility of her innocence quickly fled as her yielding flesh gripped and squeezed him, driving logical thought out of his head. He began to move within her and heard no pleas for him to stop. Soon she was moving with him, catching his rhythm, following his lead. And as they moved together, her sweet, hot body was relaxing and expanding to better accept him.

The terrible discomfort Anna experienced with that first forceful thrust was now totally gone. Being stretched and filled with him no longer hurt. It felt good, right, wonderful. Pain had been replaced with pleasure. That growing pleasure was enhanced by the sight of Brit's darkly handsome face above her own. It was incredibly thrilling to feel him moving inside her while she looked into his dark, beautiful eyes.

It was glorious.

For him.

For her.

While the rip-roaring party continued, with the music playing and the fireworks cannonading, and the gray stallion whinnied and kicked at the stall not ten feet from them, Anna and Brit lay on their bed of hay and made hot, passionate love as if there were no one else in the world but the two of them.

Thinking how perfectly their bodies fit together, Brit playfully teased and tormented Anna. He would slide almost all the way into her, then slowly pull almost all the way out. After only a couple of times she was frantically tilting her pelvis up to his and gripping his ribs with her hands, anxious to have him back in her. Pleased with her reaction, Brit made her wait for only a few tense seconds, then he drove deeply into her, giving her all he had, making her take every hot, hard inch of him.

Anna clung to the bulging biceps of her experienced lover and gave herself wholly to him, loving the feel and sight and scent of him. The electrifying sensations touched off in her by his artful lovemaking were both fantastic and frightening in their intensity. She'd had no idea such ecstasy was possible.

His weight supported on his flattened palms, Brit watched the changing expressions march across her beautiful face and promised himself that he would hold back, would keep the pace of his lovemaking slow and easy, for her sake. He wanted, he realized, to bring this beautiful woman to climax again and again before he sought his own.

He shuddered involuntarily at the stark realization that her pleasure meant more to him than his own. Or anyone else's. He'd made love many times in his life, but he had *never* cared as much about making a woman so completely happy as he did now.

Perversely, the fact that it meant so much to him kept him from performing as planned.

It was too good.

She was too sweet.

The hot softness so snugly gripping him was already threatening his tenuous control. He couldn't believe it. He was in danger of losing it, of going over the edge.

Brit quickly closed his eyes so he couldn't see her beautiful face, couldn't be pulled into the depths of those fathomless eyes. He tried to distract himself. He guessed the number of cattle in each Regent pasture. He named each division boss who'd ever worked at The Regent. Finally he reminded himself that this silky-skinned beauty stirring beneath him was his adversary, a lying, cheating vixen bent on stealing his inheritance.

It didn't work.

His climax was coming and there was nothing he could do to stop it. Instinctively, Anna knew what was happening to him and took pride in the fact that she was responsible. She felt a delicious surge of female power and she eagerly accommodated his swift, powerful thrusts, speeding her movements to match his.

His eyes were closed, but hers remained wide-open. She watched in wonder as his release came and his handsome face, already hardened with passion, grimaced as if in great pain. A vein stood out on his forehead; he gritted his teeth and groaned low in his throat.

And as he shuddered in satisfaction, she could feel the hot, thick liquid of love fill her to overflowing.

Spent, Brit collapsed atop her.

Anna sighed with contentment and cradled his dark head on her breasts. He panted heavily, loudly, and his heartbeat was rapid and forceful, pounding against her, through her.

When his breathing began to slow and his pulse decelerated, Brit apologized. "Forgive me, sweetheart."

"For what?" she asked as he moved off her, stretched out on his back beside her.

He said, "Give me a couple of minutes to rest and I'll make it up to you."

Eighteen

It was past two o'clock in the morning.

Only the diehards remained.

Most of the tired, sleepy guests had gone home. But not all. A number of people milled around, visiting the recently refilled buffet tables, eating, laughing, enjoying themselves. Others were scattered about the white-clothed tables beneath the lanterns, drinking, spinning yarns. An orchestra was still on the dais, playing slow, mellow ballads. Several couples leisurely spun about the dance floor.

One of those couples was Sally Horner and Buck Shanahan. Since their first one, they had danced every dance together, and they meant to stay on the floor to the very end.

Shortly after midnight, Sally's father, the distinguished Jameson Horner, had interrupted the dancing couple to tell Sally to say good-night to Buck and come along, it was time to go home. Sally had strongly protested, not wanting to go, exclaiming that it was much too early to leave.

Buck hadn't wanted her to leave, either, so he had nervously asked Jameson Horner if Sally could please stay an hour longer. Buck quickly assured the frowning father that he would be more than happy to see Sally home. He could borrow one of The Regent's buckboards and drive her straight to her house.

Jameson Horner had started to object, but Sally had made a mean face at him, and his wife, Abigail, standing close beside him, had squeezed his arm meaningfully, so he had relented.

Now Sally and Buck swayed languidly on the floor, flirting and laughing, caught up in the first thrilling stages of a budding romance. Both agreed that although they had known each other all their lives, it was as if they were seeing one another for the first time.

"Excuse me again, Buck, Sally." The red-haired widow, Beverly Harris, stepped up and tugged on Buck's shirtsleeve.

Sally and Buck both blinked, abruptly brought back to reality. One glance at Beverly Harris and they knew she was furious. The pair stopped dancing, but Buck kept his arm around Sally's waist.

"Mrs. Harris," Buck acknowledged. "What can we do for you?"

"You know very well what you can do for me! You can tell me where Brit is. Where is he? I know you know."

It was not the first time she had asked. Growing increasingly short-tempered, Beverly Harris had spent the last hour anxiously searching for the mysteriously missing Brit.

Buck shrugged broad shoulders, looked over Beverly's head at the sparse crowd. There was no sign of Brit. "Ma'am, as I told you before, I really don't know where Brit is, but—"

"He's been missing for two solid hours!" Beverly declared impatiently.

"Two hours? That's a long time," Buck said thoughtfully.

"I went to the house to freshen up. I told Brit it would take only a few minutes and I'd be right back. But when I returned to our table, he was gone," Beverly complained. "Can you imagine that? Just left me high and dry and never came back! I've looked everywhere for him, asked everyone if they've seen him." Her face flushed scarlet and her eyes snapped with anger.

"Well, now, I'm sure he's around here somewhere," Buck said, trying to placate her. "He surely wouldn't have gone off to bed—"

"Bed is exactly where the son of a bitch has gone!" Beverly declared. "The question is, with whom?"

"Now, now, Mrs. Harris, calm down," Buck cautioned. "Brit wouldn't do a thing like that."

"No? How can you be so sure? When did you last see him?"

"Lordy, I don't remember," said Buck truthfully. "Sally and I have been dancing for the past couple of hours..." he looked at Sally, grinned, squeezed her waist "...and we kinda forgot about—"

Interrupting, Beverly shifted her narrow-eyed gaze to Sally. "I notice your little friend Anna has been missing since midnight."

"Has she? I wouldn't know," said Sally. "Last I

saw of Anna she was at the table with LaDextra, Will Davis and Dr. McCelland."

"Dr. McCelland left hours ago. LaDextra retired shortly after midnight and Will Davis left a half hour later."

In a gay mood, Sally smiled at the irate widow and said, "That's amazing. You know where everybody went and when."

"Don't get smart with me, Sally Horner," Beverly warned. "Where is she? I want to know. Is Anna with Brit? Are they together? You tell me right now!"

Until Beverly had raised the possibility, it had never occurred to Sally that Anna might be with Brit. Come to think of it, she hadn't seen either of them in hours. Could it be that they were together? Had they discovered one another the way she and Buck had discovered each other? Had they slipped away to kiss in the moonlight? She hoped so. She disliked this bossy red-haired widow and thought Brit could do much better.

"Oh, very well. We just can't hide anything from you, can we, Beverly?" Sally said, enjoying the stricken look that came to the redhead's pretty face. "I promised Anna and Brit I'd keep quiet, but what's the use. You've already guessed, so..."

"Then they are together?" Beverly's voice lifted an octave and her eyes burned with outrage.

Sally didn't have to verbally confirm. All she had to do was smile as if she knew a delicious secret, and lift her shoulders in a shrug.

"That two-timing bastard!" Beverly hissed, red-faced and shaking with anger. "And that simpering blond bitch! Damn them both to eternal hell!" Muttering under her breath, cursing them both, she stormed away, imagining the worst.

Wondering miserably what the two of them were doing at that very minute.

At that very minute Anna, serenely nude and glowing with happiness, lay on her stomach atop the blanket covering the soft bed of hay. In her right hand was the shiny silver concho she had twisted loose from Brit's black trousers.

Purring and stretching like a lazy cat, Anna smiled dreamily as Brit tickled and teased her with the fragrant scarlet rose he'd taken from her hair. As he brushed the petals of the rose over her pale, luminous skin, he kissed her bare shoulders and back. His lips spreading wonderful warmth, Brit lay partially atop Anna. One hand was underneath her, cupping her breast, toying with her tingling nipple.

Wiggling and stirring from his fiery kisses, Anna couldn't believe that she was becoming aroused again. It had been only a few short minutes since Brit had brought her to an incredible orgasm.

And that had been the third time she had climaxed tonight.

The first time it happened had been when Brit had stroked and pleasured her with just his hand.

The second time he'd made love to her fully and she had been greedy in her carnal pleasure, bucking and pitching against him, wanting it, begging for it. And then it had begun, a release so intense she was shattered by the fierce explosion of her body. Waves of incredible fulfillment shuddered through her until she had screamed his name and clawed his smooth brown back with her sharp nails.

When finally she had stopped quivering and went limp in his arms, she had realized that he was still hot and hard. He had not yet climaxed.

Then she'd heard him say in a low, caressing voice, "I'm going to lie here close beside you and kiss you and touch you until you want me again."

Anna had softly sighed and answered, "I'm sorry, Brit, I don't think that will happen. You loved me too well. I'm too satisfied, too spent."

He had simply smiled down at her, brushed a kiss to her temple and said, "We'll see."

For a time they had lain there like that, she on her back, limp and blissful, he close beside her, fully aroused and burning. Certain that she was incapable of becoming excited again, Anna was passive and pliant as Brit worked subtly at arousing her.

Totally tranquil, an indolent Anna had allowed him to kiss and nuzzle her, not actually participating herself. She couldn't. She was simply too tired, too content. He didn't seem to notice or mind. Kissing her parted lips, murmuring words of passion in the darkness, he soon moved between her legs and slowly, gently penetrated.

After a long moment to allow her to adjust and relax, Brit wrapped a hand around the back of her right leg and urged the leg up until her knee was pressed against her chest. Then he pushed her left leg outward at a cocked angle.

Anna was shocked at how this new position made her more acutely aware of his hard flesh throbbing inside her. Her sweet lethargy swiftly subsided and she exhaled heavily. She bit her lip when he drove forcefully into her, and she felt her entire body rapidly starting to heat.

"Brit, Brit," she breathed, as he adroitly slid her bent knee up over his shoulder.

It was the strangest of sensations, having one leg raised and draped over his shoulder, the other stretched out and cocked to one side. And then he began the slow, rhythmic movements of lovemaking and Anna knew why he had positioned her like this. She felt as if she were open wide to him and therefore able to take more of him in.

She relished it.

And she relished it even more when he primitively pounded into her, conquering her with deep, commanding strokes. The powerful throbbing of his rhythmic thrusts matched the savage beating of her heart. The hot, still air was filled with the perfume of love as they ascended toward that waiting sexual nirvana.

Her body now blazing hot, Anna gripped and squeezed her lover, determined that this time she would take him with her to paradise. But before she realized what was happening, *it* was happening. She was spiraling up toward total ecstasy again and there was nothing she could do to stop it or even slow it down.

"Oh, Brit, I—I..."

"I know," Brit murmured, pumping fervently

into her. "Let it happen, baby. God, you're so sweet, so beautiful when you come."

His words triggered her already threatening release. She felt great explosions of white-hot heat, and the rising ecstasy was so unbelievably potent, she was frightened by its intensity. Tears sprang to her eyes and she screamed as the final burst of pleasure detonated deep in her belly and spiraled outward.

It was several long minutes before she realized that, once again, Brit had not attained fulfillment. She had supposed that he had because he'd slipped off her and stretched out on his back beside her. So she had been astounded when, her breathing finally returning to normal, she had sighed, turned, looked at him and seen that his erection was still fully formed and resting on his belly.

Frowning, she lifted her eyes to his face. "You didn't...?"

His answer was a smile, a quick kiss and a request for her to turn over and stretch out on her stomach.

So now she lay here on her stomach, squirming and sighing, clutching the silver concho, as the fiery lick of Brit's tongue brashly dipped into the beginning crevice of her bare buttocks. While he kissed her there, he laid aside the red rose and slid his hand down her stomach to explore and excite her.

She gritted her teeth when his lean fingers went between her legs to touch and tease. Breathlessly Anna surged against that insistent hand, and she emitted a strangled little cry of shocked delight when he playfully bit the pale rounded cheek of her bottom.

Anna came up on her elbows when he slipped his other hand between her legs from behind. She exhaled shallowly when his hands met and his skilled fingers did marvelous, forbidden things to her that quickly set her afire.

"Wh-what are you doing to me?"

"Loving you," he said, as his fingers gently caressed that concealed, feminine flesh in an intimate exploration that aroused Anna beyond belief. Her eyes slipped closed and she panted with building excitement.

His fingers caressing, toying, his lips sprinkling kisses over her bare squirming bottom, Brit said huskily, "I want you on top this time, baby."

"On top?" she repeated dreamily, having no idea what he meant.

"Yes," he said, "you on top of me."

Abruptly releasing her, Brit moved off her and lay down on his back beside her. Anna levered herself up onto her knees and sat back on her heels, unsure what he wanted, still ignorant to the many ways of making love.

"Come here to me," he said, and put out his hand.

Reaching for her, Brit effortlessly lifted her astride his hips. He sat her down atop his supine body, then he raised his arms and folded them behind his head. "Mount me, sweetheart," he said. "Easy. Slowly."

Anna gave him a puzzled look. "We can make love in this position?" she asked innocently.

"With great pleasure," he assured her. "Rise up onto your knees." Anna went up on her knees and looked to him for further instruction. "Now take me, baby. You do it so we can go at a pace that's acceptable to you."

Anna nodded.

Finally she put aside the silver concho she'd been gripping tightly in her palm. She laid the shiny disk on the hay beside them, then wrapped a soft, warm hand around his immense erection. Bottom lip caught between her teeth, she gingerly guided him up inside her.

Both sighed simultaneously as she slowly lowered herself down on him. She gasped and he groaned as he penetrated deep inside her. For a long moment, neither moved. Brit waited, not wanting to hurt her, allowing her the opportunity to settle herself comfortably on him before he began the actual movements of loving. As she enveloped him in her warmth and sweetness, Brit gazed at her through lowered lids and felt his heart hammer in his chest.

The sight of her, naked and fragile, seated astride him, was an image he would never forget. She was perfect in every way. Her skin was like alabaster. Her hair like gold silk. Her breasts were soft and round and topped with satiny pink nipples. Her waist was small, her hips gently flared.

And between her thighs, where her body joined his, a down-soft cushion of golden curls was now intimately meshed with the blue-black hair of his groin.

Brit's arms came from beneath his head. He laid his hands lightly on her thighs and sighed with exquisite pleasure when she began to slowly gyrate her hips. Anna licked her lips, arched her back and flung a hand up to her forehead. Her thighs tightened on his waist and she moaned, wanting him to do more, wanting him to move inside her.

Brit read the message and began to unhurriedly thrust into her, giving them both a quick rush of sweet ecstasy. Soon they were moving together rapidly, their rhythm almost frantic. Anna rolled her hips and rode her lover with wild abandon. Brit thrust his pelvis upward, impaling her deeply, and watched the delightful dance of her breasts, the swish of her unbound hair, as she bucked and bounced on him.

God, she was a wonder.

A beautiful, wild, wanton creature with no inhibitions, and he wished he could keep her like this forever. Naked and passionate and impaled upon him. He wanted time to stand still. Wanted the two of them to be caught forever in this magical state of building bliss. Yet he knew that nothing this perfect could last.

Within minutes both had lost all control. They were two pagan lovers, drenched in perspiration, sliding and slipping on each other. They mated like a couple of animals, gasping and clawing and moaning, each intent on taking everything the other had to give. Avaricious in their quest for the ultimate, they were rash and reckless, caught up in the blazing need for total, blinding release.

Anxious, panting, Brit rolled up into a sitting position, cupped Anna's bouncing bottom in his hands and drew her closer, tighter against him. At the same time he flexed the muscles of his buttocks and surged into her.

Soon it started for them both—a deep, all-consuming orgasm that left them weak and powerless in its throes. Both Brit and Anna could feel his full-to-bursting erection exploding inside her, and they cried out in their shared ecstasy. Frantically they clung to each other, trembling and gasping for breath as burst after burst of intense physical pleasure rocked them.

When, finally, all the tiny aftershocks had passed, their breathing had slowed and their heartbeats had returned to normal, the pair continued to stay as they were. Holding each other. Sighing contentedly. Savoring the perfect peace that follows such splendid lovemaking.

Nineteen

Anna awakened when strong morning sunshine, streaming in through her tall bedroom windows, touched her face. Lying on her stomach, clutching her pillow, she drowsily opened her eyes.

The first thing she saw was the hammered-silver concho.

The small circular disk lay on the bedside table, glittering brightly in the summer sunlight. Beginning to smile, Anna levered herself up on her elbows, reached out and scooped up the shiny ornament. A shiver of delight surging through her, she raised the shimmering disk to her lips and kissed it reverently.

Then she flopped over onto her back, pressed the concho to her breasts and squeezed her eyes shut, sighing dreamily. A rush of recollection washed over her and she blushed as she recalled with vivid clarity the wonderfully forbidden things that she and Brit had done during their long, unforgettable night of lovemaking.

The flood of fresh memories made her squirm and tingle. Anna could almost feel Brit's long tapered fingers on her face, his amazingly soft, sculptured lips tasting hers, his lean, hard body pressed against her own.

"Oh, Brit, my love," she whispered in the silence. "Do you love me half as much as I love you?"

Sure she knew the answer to her question, Anna tossed back the silky sheets and got out of bed. Like a child she laughed and spun wildly around in a circle, so happy she wanted to shout it to the rooftops. To tell every single soul on earth that Brit Caruth was in love with her and she was in love with him.

Careening to an abrupt stop, the slightly dizzy Anna was struck with the thought that Brit might very well be downstairs in the dining room right this minute. LaDextra had said that today's breakfast would be served from shortly after dawn right on through midmorning, so that the departing house guests could enjoy the morning meal at an hour best suited to their travel plans.

Kissing the silver concho one last time, Anna carefully laid it back on the night table. Then she yanked her nightgown up over her head and tossed it aside. Naked, she dashed into the bathroom where, thankfully, a tub had been run for her. Sinking down into the sudsy depths, Anna hurriedly bathed, blushing again when she saw that her breasts were still pink from Brit's fiery kisses.

Even more telling was the novel soreness between her legs, a mild discomfort that gave her more pleasure than pain. A secret, silent reminder of her passionate lover's intimate invasion.

Bathed and toweled dry, Anna sped into her dressing room, yanking down the first dress she saw.

It was a girlish-looking, pink cotton shirtwaist with short puff sleeves, tiny covered buttons from throat to waist, and full, billowing skirts.

Eager to get downstairs to hopefully see Brit, she dressed quickly, brushed her long hair a few strokes, pulled the left side back behind her ear and secured it with a gold clasp. Twenty minutes after awakening, Anna was out the bedroom door and descending the center staircase.

Midway down, she paused on a carpeted step and listened. Voices and laughter carried from the dining room. Anna recognized the various voices of the visiting San Antonio contingent. Everyone else was to have gone home earlier in the morning. These half-dozen party-loving San Antonians would be the last to leave the ranch.

Justin Box, a favorite cousin of LaDextra's, was speaking, telling an amusing story. When he concluded, laughter followed. Anna felt her pulse leap when she heard Brit's low distinctive baritone. So excited she felt like she might burst out giggling, she skipped down the remainder of the stairs.

Just outside the high-ceilinged dining room, Anna paused, drew a deep, slow breath, then walked through the wide, arched doorway.

"Ah, here she is now," LaDextra announced, and everyone turned to greet Anna.

Almost everyone.

Having eyes only for the dark, handsome man seated on the opposite side of the table, Anna felt her world come crashing down abruptly when Brit finally looked up.

Not the slightest flicker of fire lit his eyes. Instead he touched her with a brief, chilly glance, then dismissed her, returning his attention to the plate of food before him.

There was no warmly drawled "good morning." No meaningful exchange of sweet secrets shared. No silent, private messages.

Nothing.

Stunned, shaken, Anna had to put her hand on the back of LaDextra's chair to steady herself.

"Well, lazy bones, we thought you were going to sleep all day," LaDextra accused affectionately. The others merrily chimed in, teasing her.

I wish I had. I wish I had never awakened. I wish I could go back to sleep and never wake up!

As calmly as possible, Anna said, "I'm not fooled. You're all still at the breakfast table, so how long could you have been up?"

LaDextra laughed, nodded. "Get yourself something to eat, honey, and sit down there between cousins Justin and Olivia."

Anna gave no reply, but turned and went to the heavily laden sideboard, grateful for the opportunity to temporarily have her back to Brit and the others. Fighting the tears that were threatening, Anna was so upset her hands shook as she spooned scrambled eggs from the silver warming platter. Wishing she could turn and run out of the room, she continued, with difficulty, to fill her plate.

Inhaling shallowly, Anna firmly gripped the plate with cold, stiff hands, turned and went to the table. Justin Box, the gangly, bearded, sixty-five-year-old

San Antonio cousin, quickly rose to his feet and pulled out a chair for her.

"Thank you, Cousin Justin," she said, and sat down.

"You're mighty welcome, Anna," said the cheerful Justin Box. "Olivia and I were just saying to LaDextra that we sure want you to come to San Antone one of these days soon and spend a couple of weeks. We'd love to have your company, and there's lots to do and see there."

"Justin's right." His soft-spoken wife, Olivia, seconded the notion. "Come for a nice long visit and we'll go shopping and to the theater and to all the fine restaurants. And we know several handsome young bachelors who would be thrilled to meet you."

"Sounds lovely," said Anna, forcing a smile. "I might just take you up on your kind invitation."

So saying, she hazarded a quick, nervous glance at Brit, hoping against hope that she had jumped to conclusions earlier, that he would, if he had the chance, make eye contact, signal her, silently reassure her.

It never happened.

He didn't give her a look.

Or a thought.

Throughout the endless meal, Anna sat directly across the table from the stunningly attractive man who had been so burning hot last night. And who was now so icy cold. She was devastated. Brokenhearted. And totally baffled. What had she done wrong? How had she displeased him? Had last night meant nothing to him, when it had meant everything to her?

In agony Anna pushed her food around her plate, made obligatory small talk and carefully hid her disillusionment and pain. She was, after all, a master at concealing her innermost feelings, at facing terrible dilemmas alone, at keeping her own counsel. To those around her, she appeared to be at ease and perfectly placid. No one in the dining room suspected that she was so hurt and miserable she could hardly retain her composure.

Relief flooded Anna when finally the long meal ended. It was time for the last of the visitors to leave The Regent. Amid much talk and laughter, they all began to drift out of the house and toward the waiting carriages that would take them to The Regent's private train spur. In the confusion, Anna managed to slip unnoticed up the stairs and to the welcome privacy of her room.

Once inside, with the door closed behind her, she began to tremble and jerk uncontrollably. Tears stung her eyes and she felt cold to the bone, as if she were getting a bad case of chills. On weak, rubbery legs she crossed to the bed, stood there for a long moment staring down at the gleaming silver concho lying on the table, recalling how she had twisted it from Brit's trousers in a fit of passion.

She could no longer hold back. The tears began to spill down her cheeks. Weeping, her shoulders shaking, Anna sagged to her knees beside the bed, pressed her face into the mattress to muffle her sobs, and cried her heart out.

She wept and wept until her eyes were red and swollen and her head ached with a relentless, pounding pain. She sobbed and shook and choked. She coughed and gasped and could not stop weeping. She cried for a solid hour, until she had no strength or tears left.

Red-faced, exhausted, Anna raised her aching head from the mattress. It was the first time she had cried in fifteen years. She vowed that it would be another fifteen years before she cried again.

The sparkle gone from her eyes, the joy gone from her heart, Anna rose weakly to her feet, a wiser woman. She had, she realized, been a fool to believe that Brit Caruth could love her.

She sat wearily down on the edge of the bed and shook her aching head. How foolish and gullible she had been. How unforgivably stupid to have willingly gone with him to the secluded stables. How naive of her to believe that if a man made love to a woman the way Brit had made love to her, he surely loved her. At least a little.

Brit didn't love her, had never loved her, would never love her. And now, after having had her, he no longer even wanted her.

Her hurt and humiliation slowly giving way to anger and resentment, Anna silently promised the hard-hearted Brit Caruth that he would be sorry for his callous use of her.

He would pay.

He would pay with the only thing that meant something to him.

The Regent.

She would, she pledged, wage an immediate campaign to convince LaDextra to leave the ranch to her, the true and rightful heir. She could do it. She *would* do it.

Then the vast Sunland spread would one day belong solely to her, and when it did, she would promptly banish Britton Caruth from the premises.

At twilight that evening a tired LaDextra and Will Davis sat alone on the front veranda after dinner. The two old friends had also dined alone. Anna, they were told by her personal maid, was nursing a bad headache and had requested a tray sent up to her room. As for Brit, he had left the house around noon and hadn't been seen since. Rocking slowly back and forth, her arthritic hands clutching the chair's wooden arms, LaDextra mused, "Mighty quiet with everyone gone."

"Mmm. Peaceful," said Will. "Nice and peaceful."

"Yes. Yes it is," LaDextra agreed. "I'm kind of glad it's all over."

"Amen."

"It was one heck of a blowout though, wasn't it?"

"Indeed it was."

Smiling, recalling the merriment, LaDextra said, "I suspect Anna's headache is from drinking too much champagne last night."

Will nodded, smiled. "I wouldn't doubt it."

"Bless her heart, she'd never tasted champagne before and I think she had two or three glasses."

"I know," Will said. "She got a little tipsy, but no harm done, as far as I can see."

"No, not really. She's a responsible young woman, wouldn't do anything foolish."

"Never."

They fell silent for a while, enjoying the gathering summer dusk, watching the fireflies dart about on the front lawn, hearing the crickets start their rhythmic croaking chorus.

"I swear that Brit," LaDextra was the one who broke the silence. "I guess he never runs down."

"Doesn't seem to."

"I'd wager that right this minute that restless scamp is either at Beverly Harris's house or in town playing poker at one of the saloons." LaDextra laughed, adding, "Everybody else might be tired from the celebration, but not Brit. He'll likely stay out tonight until the wee hours. No telling when he got in last night. Or more likely, this morning."

Will Davis nodded, then yawned. "Then he's a better man than I. I'm exhausted. How about you?"

The smile left LaDextra's wrinkled face. "Tired, Will. Dead tired."

"I thought as much. It's getting dark. Let's get on inside and call it an evening."

"A capital idea."

LaDextra, starting to rise from her rocking chair, faltered badly, almost fell. She sat heavily back down in the chair and all the blood drained from her wrinkled face. A worried Will, who knew her better than anyone, realized that something was very wrong. This was more than just exhaustion or weakness. It suddenly dawned on him that LaDextra Regent was ill. Seriously ill. That's why Dr. McCelland had been at The Regent so often of late.

Hovering worriedly over her, Will said, "My God, LaDextra, what it is? Are you...?"

LaDextra shook her head and admitted to her old friend, "I haven't long, Will, but you must not tell anyone. I don't want the children to know just yet."

His face a study in distress, Will helped the feeble woman up and into the house. "I'll get Dr. McCelland out here right away and—"

"No use, there's nothing he can do," said LaDextra. "It's my heart."

"But surely—"

"No, Will. It's too late. My days are numbered."

Will exhaled heavily and asked, "How long, my dear?"

The ailing Regent matriarch smiled wistfully and said, "When the summer dies, so will I."

Twenty

His hat brim pulled low over his dark, squinted eyes, a troubled Brit Caruth crouched on his heels in a distant lowland pasture of The Regent. He was alone on this blistering July morning.

Brit reached down and scooped up a handful of dry, crumbling soil, then let it slowly sift through his gloved fingers. He shook his head, exhaled heavily and rose slowly to his feet.

Hands resting lightly on his hips, he stood in the desert wasteland with the west Texas wind and dust blowing into his face and pressing his shirt against his chest. The useless sea of sand had, until this summer, been a verdant valley pasture carpeted with gamma grass and stocked with pure-blooded Polangus and Hereford stock.

Now the huge pasture was silent, empty.

The cattle that had once grazed contentedly here had been shipped to market at a loss or moved to higher pastures where patches of scrub grass still grew and shallow water holes still offered some degree of relief from constant thirst. Some of the cattle had perished. Hundreds, maybe thousands more would die if it didn't rain soon.

Water was a bigger problem than grass.

The ground water here was too deep for windmills, and the closest unoccupied water hole was the Hueco Tanks, midway between the Guadalupes and the Rio Grande. The ranch was solely dependent on adequate rainfall. Without it the land, the cattle, the people could not survive.

This drought had been a long one.

It was now late July and no rain had fallen in months. Not a drop since early spring. Brit couldn't recall so much as a sprinkle since just before the April roundup. God, if he'd known then what he knew now, he would have sent fifteen or twenty thousand more head to market.

This was not the first time the area had suffered from a lack of rain. Brit could remember a particularly long drought that had stretched all across southwest Texas, but that was before The Regent was stocked with blooded cattle. Back then, when he was young and just learning to be a cowboy, scrubby longhorns had dominated the Texas cattle country. They had filled the many pastures of The Regent, the clacking of their horns a constant sound on the open range.

They were a breed apart, those ugly, gangly creatures. Tough, strong-legged, the longhorns could survive almost anything. They could be driven ten to twelve miles a day for a hundred unremitting days or more through heat and cold, drought or deluge, across mountains or plains, or rivers that weren't bridged.

Too bad these pampered Angus and Herefords

weren't a little more like those rugged Texas long-horns.

Brit tipped his head back and looked up.

Not a cloud in the sky.

No hope of rain.

He sighed, reached into his shirt pocket and took out a long, thin cigar. He stuck the cheroot between his lips and lit it, cupping his hands around the tiny match flame. He shook out the match, inhaled deeply of the cigar smoke and gazed wistfully across the endless barren acres of the land he loved, to *El Capitán's* towering peak standing sentinel in brilliant morning sunshine.

From where Brit stood he could pick out the cow trails up Guadalupe Peak and Pine Canyon that were cut—he had helped cut them—into the mountains to allow the cowmen on horseback to reach the stock in the high country.

If he had ridden up those mountain trails once, he had done it a thousand times.

He had, he reminisced, done it all on this immense Texas spread. He had spent his entire adult life riding line, bogging, haying, rounding up cattle, plowing fireguards, feeding cattle, freighting supplies. You name it, he'd done it. And, hopefully, he would continue to do all those things until he was too old and too tired to mount a horse.

Brit blew out a plume of cigar smoke, then, thinning his lips over his teeth, whistled for Captain. The gray's ears pricked up and he immediately came to his master. He nuzzled Brit's shoulder, and Brit smiled and affectionately patted his jaw.

Brit dropped his cigar, crushed it out beneath his boot heel and swung up into the saddle for the long ride south to the *Agua Fria* division headquarters of The Regent. He planned to spend at least three or four days at *Agua Fria,* the area hardest hit by the drought because of its location down near the border.

An extended visit to *Agua Fria* would serve two purposes.

First, he could work alongside and reassure the anxious vaqueros that no one would be losing his job on The Regent.

Second, and more importantly, it gave Brit an excuse to stay away from the mansion.

On that same sweltering July morning, Anna smilingly greeted Dr. McCelland and ushered him directly back to LaDextra's ground floor sitting room. She then left the two of them alone, closing the door behind her, but she paced just outside.

Anna was worried about LaDextra.

Since the Fourth of July party more than three weeks ago, LaDextra had seemed uncommonly tired, had spent a great deal of time resting in her room. Which wasn't like her. Yet every time Anna asked if anything was wrong, if she was feeling weak or ill, LaDextra assured her that she was fine, just fine.

Anna stopped pacing when the door opened and Dr. McCelland said, "You can come in now, Anna. We're finished here."

Anna anxiously hurried inside and straight to

LaDextra's chair. Dropping to her knees beside the chair and taking the older woman's hand in both of her own, Anna said, "Tell me the truth, are you okay? Are you really feeling well?"

LaDextra squeezed her hand. "Fit as a fiddle."

Skeptical, Anna, glancing at the doctor, asked, "Then what is Dr. McCelland doing here again so soon after his last visit?"

"You tell her, Doctor," said LaDextra.

The doctor smiled, took a chair and, leaning forward, explained, "As I may have mentioned to you before, Anna, I make regular calls on all the division headquarters of The Regent. Today I'm due at the Columbine. So I just stopped by here on the way."

"Satisfied?" LaDextra asked, smiling down at Anna.

Nodding, Anna released LaDextra's hand and rose to her feet. "I suppose." Then she asked, "How far is it from here to the Columbine?"

"Five, six miles," said the doctor.

"Take me with you!" Anna said impulsively.

The doctor blinked. LaDextra, starting to frown, asked, "Whatever for, child? Dr. McCelland will likely stay at the Columbine all day. You'd get very bored sitting around waiting for him."

Anna said, "But I wouldn't just sit around and wait. I would help out. Don't you see, LaDextra, The Regent is my home and I love it as you do." LaDextra smiled, pleased with the statement. Anna continued, "I love this ranch and the people on it, and I'd like to be more useful, to help out in some small way."

"Why, honey, you're a great help and comfort to me," said LaDextra.

As if she hadn't spoken, Anna said, "When I was at the convent, the sisters taught me to tend the sick, and I became quite good at it." She looked anxiously from one to the other. "Don't you see, I could assist Dr. McCelland. I'm not the least bit squeamish. I've dressed wounds and bathed frail bodies and held the hands of the dying and—and surely an extra pair of hands would come in handy."

"Oh, Anna, I don't know," LaDextra said thoughtfully, "it's hot as Hades out there and—"

"I don't mind a little heat," Anna quickly assured her. "Oh, please say yes. Please. I want to go."

LaDextra sighed heavily. "You'll wear a hat and take a canteen of cold water?"

"Absolutely," Anna promised. "Then I may go? You don't mind?"

LaDextra looked from Anna to the doctor. "What about it, Doctor? Would she be in your way?"

The doctor needlessly cleared his throat. He said, "On the contrary, I am sure Anna would be a great asset, very helpful."

"Then it's settled!" Anna declared excitedly, leaping to her feet. "I'll go change right now."

A half hour later Anna and Dr. McCelland were riding through the bushy slag below the Pine Spring Canyon trailhead, heading due east. Her hat brim pulled low over her eyes, heavy hair tucked up under the hat, Anna felt the hot winds stinging her face, the perspiration pooling between her breasts.

She didn't mind.

The heat, the wind, the ride made her feel alive again. It was the first time she'd felt anything since she had come down the stairs the morning after the Fourth of July celebration and seen the unmistakable indifference in Brit's dark eyes. Since that horrible moment she had been imprisoned inside the house, hardly leaving her room, afraid that she might bump into Brit. Thankfully, she hadn't. She supposed it was because he was rarely home of late.

LaDextra bemoaned the fact that Brit was never home for dinner anymore, that she never got to see him. She blamed his absence on the worsening drought, saying that Brit, as the general manager of the entire operation, was working even harder than usual this summer. He was, she explained—although Anna hadn't asked—dividing his time among the four division headquarters. It fell to him to keep the worried cowboys' spirits up, to reassure them that they would all get through this terrible drought together, that The Regent would survive and prosper.

Anna always politely listened as LaDextra extolled Brit's unflagging dedication to the ranch's operations. But she doubted he was all that dedicated. She suspected his nights were not spent in a narrow cot in some distant bunkhouse, but in the comfortable bed—and possessive arms—of the red-haired Beverly Harris.

"Anna?"

Brought back to the present, Anna, realizing her sorrel mare, Dancer, had slowed to a walk, blinked at Dr. McCelland and said, "I'm sorry, I—"

"I said we're here." Pointing, he directed her attention to a long, low adobe building a hundred yards ahead, baking in the hot Texas sunshine. Baking along with the sand-colored building were the ailing people gathered there, anxiously awaiting the doctor's visit.

Their eyes lit up when they saw the kind physician, whom they trusted to make them feel better. A mannerly bunch, they lined up to patiently wait their turn as Anna followed Dr. McCelland inside the adobe to the large, sterile room where he treated his patients.

Minutes after their arrival, Anna found herself elbow deep in coughing, feverish children, worried young mothers, bruised and battered vaqueros and cowboys.

Her hat tossed aside, sleeves rolled up, Anna worked tirelessly alongside the gentle doctor, cleansing dirt-and-gravel-encrusted abrasions, assisting as he set broken arms and legs, holding crying babies as he gave them medication.

The work was so demanding, so steady, there was not a single minute when the examining room was empty. The hours rushed by in a blur. In fact, the summer sun was slipping toward the horizon when the very last patient, a leathery old cowhand with a badly swollen thumb infected from an imbedded prickly pear sticker, was finally tended and sent on his way.

Anna had been so busy she hadn't had time to think about anything other than helping Dr. McCelland. It was a welcome respite from her own personal pain. For the past several grueling hours her heart had not hurt, because she had been too busy to think about Brit.

Nor had she realized that she was tired. Now her back was aching badly between her shoulder blades and her legs felt as if she couldn't possibly stand for another minute.

She must have looked as exhausted as she felt, because the concerned doctor, urging her down onto a straight-backed chair, said, "I shouldn't have brought you here, Anna. It was too hard on you. I should have known better."

"No, no it wasn't," she argued. "Please, Dr. McCelland, don't tell LaDextra you think I'm not up to it, because I am, really I am. This day has meant so much to me. I feel so peaceful and happy and, yes, tired, but a good kind of tired. Can you understand that?"

Standing above her, his arms crossed over his white-jacketed chest, he smiled and said, "Yes, I can. Caring for the sick is a rewarding occupation. But I'm afraid that you are too fragile to—"

"I am not." She jumped to her feet to face him. "I'm a strong, healthy woman and I want to do this. It means so much to me. Please, say you'll allow me to accompany you to the other division headquarters."

"But, Anna," he explained, "that's out of the question. Why, *Agua Fría,* the southern division headquarters, is a good twenty miles from the ranch house. It can't be done in a day. You can't ride all that way, tend the patients and come back the same night.''

"Oh," she said, her brows knitting. "No, of course you can't.... So, when you visit the *Agua Fría,* do you spend the night?"

"Yes, I usually ride out late the afternoon before, spend the night, then get up early and treat my patients."

"Then I will spend the night, too. Surely they have facilities to put up guests."

"Hardly the kind of quarters you are used to, Anna."

"You're forgetting, Dr. McCelland, until a few months ago the quarters I was used to were nothing but a cot on the floor behind the convent kitchen. Before that, when I lived with the Apache, my accommodations were the hard, cold ground, without benefit of blanket or pillow. I am no hothouse orchid, Doctor."

"No," he said, gazing at her with frank admiration, "I guess you're not." For a long moment he said nothing more, just looked at her. Then, his voice soft, he said, "Anna, I—I..." Impulsively, he raised a hand to touch her face, leaned close and started to kiss her.

"No," Anna said gently, turning her head slightly. "Don't, please...."

"I'm sorry." He immediately dropped his hand and stepped back.

She turned back to face him, and looking directly into his eyes, she told him, "I think the world of you, Doctor, you know I do, but I..."

He nodded, said, "It's Brit, isn't it?"

"Brit? Brit Caruth? Certainly not! Never in a million years. Whatever gave you such a ludicrous idea? Good Lord, if he were the last man on earth, I wouldn't—"

Interrupting, Dr. McCelland said softly, "I saw the way he looked at you at the Fourth of July celebration."

Anna shrugged slender shoulders. "Well, I can't help it if he—"

"And I saw the way you looked at him." Anna gave no reply. She lowered her head. The doctor again apologized. "I shouldn't have said that. Forgive me. What's between you and Brit is none of my concern and I swear to you that I'll never mention it again." He paused, then quickly changed the subject. "If LaDextra will allow it, I look forward to having you work with me in the days and weeks to come."

Anna slowly raised her eyes to meet his. She caught the wistful expression in his light eyes. Then it was gone and he smiled at her. He looked amazingly fresh and boyish despite the long, hard day, and Anna wondered sadly why things couldn't be different. Why couldn't she feel about this kind, caring physician the way she felt about Brit Caruth?

She sighed wearily and said, "Be my friend, Dr. McCelland."

"I am your friend, Anna," he replied. "I will always be. Now I'd better get you home before LaDextra sends the ranch guards out looking for us."

Twenty-One

" ... And then he said, 'You look even prettier than you did last night,' and I said, 'Oh, go on, you're just buttering me up,' and he said, 'No, I'm not, I think you're just about the most beautiful girl in all Texas,' and I said...''

A starry-eyed Sally Horner was regaling Anna, happily repeating every word she could remember of last night's conversation with her attentive new beau, Buck Shanahan.

The two good friends, wearing only their lacy underwear in a futile attempt to stay cool in the broiling summer heat, were lying across Anna's soft wide bed.

It was midafternoon, the hottest part of the blistering late-July day. The big house was quiet. LaDextra was napping in her room. The servants were in their quarters. Siesta time at The Regent.

Anna yawned.

She was tired, sleepy. Had she been alone she would have taken a much needed nap. Yesterday's long, hard hours spent helping Dr. McCelland at the Columbine division headquarters had left her exhausted, and yet, when bedtime came last night, she hadn't been able to fall asleep. Had stayed awake into the wee small hours of the morning.

It was the same every night.

No matter how tired she was or how late she went to bed, sleep would not come. Only painful memories followed by wrenching regret. She suffered, but she was determined to suffer in silence and in secret. She had told no one what had happened at the Fourth of July celebration, would never tell anyone.

Not even Sally.

"...And then, after a late dinner with my family, Buck and I took a carriage ride in the moonlight. And you'll never guess who we ran into. Brit." At the mention of Brit's name, Anna involuntarily tensed. "He was leaving town at about the same time we were leaving the house. He stopped and talked with us for a few minutes." Sally, lying on her stomach, bare feet in the air, ankles crossed, frowned suddenly, twisted a rebellious, reddish-brown curl around her finger and added, "I think he'd been drinking heavily, he was slurring his words."

Anna made no comment, instead yawned dramatically to indicate she wasn't the least bit interested in Brit Caruth's whereabouts or his level of sobriety.

Sally continued, "Something's bothering Brit. Buck said so himself."

Anna felt her heartbeat quicken, but she said levelly, "Of course, something's bothering him, Sally. This terrible drought. He's worried about what's going to happen to The Regent."

"Well, sure, that too, but... Mmm, I don't know,

it's something more. Buck thinks so, too. He says Brit is just not himself lately. He's distant and irritable and..." Sally suddenly turned questioning eyes directly on Anna and said, "When are you going to tell me what really happened the night of the Fourth? I have waited patiently for three long weeks, supposing that since I am your closest, dearest friend, you would, when you were ready, tell me the truth about that night."

Anna, lying on her back, knees bent, bare feet flat on the mattress, stretched lazily and said as casually as possible, "Nothing out of the ordinary. I had a lovely time at the party, just like everyone else." She forced herself to smile, adding, "Well, perhaps I didn't have as good a time as you."

"Or," Sally said thoughtfully, "perhaps you had an even better time."

"What a ridiculous thing to say," Anna replied, hoping her hot face had not turned beet-red. "You're the one who collected a new beau."

Sally put her hands on the mattress, levered herself up to her knees and sat back on her bare heels. Narrowing her eyes, she stared down at Anna and asked bluntly, "Just where were you from midnight till 2:00 a.m. on the Fourth? Tell me the truth."

"At the party, of course—where else would I have been?"

"I don't know," Sally admitted, "but I do know that Brit was missing for those same couple of hours."

"Really?" Anna tried to sound nonchalant. "Well, you might want to check with the red-haired widow, Beverly Harris. She could probably provide the answer.''

Sally shook her head. "I've told you repeatedly that Beverly Harris was beside herself searching for Brit. If she asked Buck once, she asked a half-dozen times if he'd seen Brit. She was frantic." Sally paused, waited for Anna to respond. Anna said nothing. Sally accused, "You know more than you're saying. I know you do. You were with Brit that night, weren't you?''

Her heart now drumming inside her chest, Anna was determined she would not give herself away. Ashamed of her wanton behavior and crushed by Brit's cold rejection, she could never let even Sally know what had happened. She worried constantly that Brit would tell—or had told—Buck all about it. That he had bragged that he'd had her in the stables like a mare mounted by a stud, and then the two men had laughed about it. The only thing she was sure of was that, even if Buck knew, he hadn't discussed it with Sally.

If he had, Sally would have told her.

Determined to distract her friend, to get her off the subject, Anna said, "Are you seeing Buck again tonight?''

The frown of puzzlement on Sally's face turned quickly to a smile of pleasure. "Yes! Can you believe it, Anna? We've been together every night since the Fourth and he says he just can't get enough of me. Isn't that romantic? Am I the luckiest woman in Texas?''

"You are," said Anna, "and I'm happy for you."

"I know you are," Sally said. "Oh, by the way, I want you to do me a big favor."

"Sure, if I can. What is it?"

"Well, since I've been with Buck so often, I'm running out of different things to wear. I certainly don't want him seeing me in the same dress twice, so I must do some serious shopping."

"Yes. So?"

"So you must go shopping with me, help me choose some pretty new clothes. I thought, if you agree, you could come into town this Saturday and help me pick out some things at Lily's Ladies' Wear Salon. You have such good taste and, Lord knows, I don't. I'd love to find something half as attractive as that white eyelet dress you wore the night of the Fourth."

Anna inwardly cringed. The beautiful white eyelet dress, with bits of hay still sticking to it, was wrinkled and soiled and hidden from the laundress, tucked up on a high shelf in the back of her closet. She now hated the dress she had loved so much. She never intended to wear it again.

"You'll help me choose some dresses," Sally was saying. "Afterward, we will have a late lunch at the Regentville Hotel. Buck is meeting me there at—"

"You're having lunch with Buck?"

"No, *we're* having lunch with Buck," Sally said, smiling.

"I don't know, Sally. Buck might not appreciate me intruding."

"Don't be silly! He'll be tickled to have your company. Say you'll come, please."

Anna smiled at last. "All right, I'll come. Sounds like a pleasant way to spend Saturday afternoon."

On that same hot July afternoon, two good friends worked side by side under the blistering Texas sun.

Wearing big straw, shade-giving sombreros, Brit and Buck, along with several dozen vaqueros, were laboring to dig deep, furrowed fireguards in the *Sierra Blanca* pasture along the northern edge of the *Agua Fría* division. Bare chested and sweating profusely, the men shoveled tirelessly despite the sweltering heat, their constant thirst and aching muscles.

Every man on the job knew how dangerous the bone-dry conditions were. One carelessly tossed match, one flash of heat lighting, and an inferno would rage out of control, racing across the barren, brushy acres. Unstoppable. Destroying everything in its path. The prospect of fire was so frightening, the vaqueros were as eager as their boss to take every possible precaution to protect their land and livelihood.

Brit was fully aware that his mere presence both calmed and spurred them on. Made them feel a little more secure. Made them work harder. They were, he knew, nervous, worried, just as he was.

But he carefully concealed any anxiety from them.

He laughed and teased and joked with the men as if he didn't have a care in the world. When he spent the night at one of the division headquarters, he drank whiskey and played cards with the cowboys and vaqueros. And when, in the quiet of the evening, someone pulled out a guitar and started strumming, he sang along with the others in their native tongue, his Spanish flawless, his inflection decidedly romantic.

Now, at the hottest part of the day, Brit pushed the wide brim of his sombrero up, tipped his head back and squinted at the white-hot sun. He quit shoveling, lodged his shovel in the dirt, put two fingers to his lips and give a loud, piercing whistle.

Everyone stopped what they were doing, turned to look at Brit.

Brit smiled sunnily, said, "*Mis amigos,* it is siesta time!"

Loud cheers went up from the hot, tired men. Shovels were immediately laid aside and everyone hurried to the tall water can on a wooden table beneath a huge black tarp stretched between four tall poles. Chattering and wiping sweat from their faces and chests, the thirsty workers lined up for a nice cooling drink, then sought out a spot where they could lie down.

Ten minutes after Brit had whistled, all was quiet. Sombreros pulled over their faces, the men lay slumbering in the century-mark-plus heat.

Brit and Buck didn't sleep, but they rested.

Buck lay on his back with an arm folded beneath his head. Brit sat leaning against the sturdy table where the water can was, his long legs stretched out before him, crossed at the ankles. A cup of water in his hand, he drank slowly, sparingly, saving a little of his precious ration. His dark torso and leanly muscled arms were glistening with sweat, so he turned the cup up and let the water spill down over his chest.

He set the cup aside, raised his hands and spread the water over his chest, belly and arms, sighing with the simple pleasure of it. He reached for a cigarette, lit it and slowly blew out the smoke.

"You sleepy?" Buck asked softly, so as not to disturb the others.

"Nope," said Brit, drawing on his cigarette.

"Me, neither." Agilely, Buck rolled into a sitting position, locked his arms around his knees and exhaled heavily. He studied Brit for a long moment, then asked, "Are you okay?"

Brit shot him a narrow-eyed glance. "Why the hell wouldn't I be okay?"

Buck shrugged massive shoulders. "No reason, I just..."

"You just what? Spit it out, for Christ sake."

"Now that's exactly what I mean, Brit. You're so damned testy. Something's eating you."

Brit took a long drag from his cigarette, blew out the smoke. "In case you're the only human being in Texas who hasn't noticed, we haven't had any rain since early April. You think that might have something to do with my mood?"

"Well, sure, I know you're worried about the drought, but..."

"But what?"

"It's something more."

"Buck, you've gone loco."

"No, I haven't. I'm not crazy. I've known you for years and I..." Buck paused, debating whether or not he should continue. His curiosity winning out, he said bluntly, "When are you going to tell me what happened on the Fourth?"

"Jesus, how many times do I have to say it? Nothing happened. *Nada.*"

"You say nothing happened, but Beverly Harris was frantically hunting for you and—"

"So you told me."

"Anna was missing all that time, too."

"Was she?"

"Yes, she was. Where were you from midnight to 2:00 a.m.? Were the two of you together?"

His dark eyes starting to snap with anger, Brit said through thinning lips, "You're not my keeper, Buck, so drop it. I don't know what you're driving at, but I'm sick and tired of your questions. Not a damned thing happened the Fourth other than I got separated from Beverly. Typically, she got angry and went home. That's it. There's no more to it and I don't want to hear any more about it. *Comprende?*"

"*Comprendo,*" said Buck, knowing Brit was on the verge of really losing his temper.

Brit crushed out his cigarette, leaned his head back and closed his eyes.

"Brit?"

Brit cocked one eye open. "Can't you be quiet for five minutes?"

"I can and I will, but first, I wanted to tell you I'm planning to take off Saturday afternoon. I promised I'd meet Sally in town for a late lunch. That okay with you?''

''Sure. I'm taking the afternoon off myself. Got some business to handle in town.''

''You're going to be in town Saturday, too? Why don't you join Sally and me for lunch at the hotel?''

Brit tilted his head to one side. ''Sally might not appreciate me horning in on—''

''Why, she'd be thrilled to death,'' Buck interrupted. ''Honest, she would. How about it? Say, two o'clock? We'll meet you in the Regentville Hotel dining room. Say you'll come.''

''Sure. Why not?''

Twenty-Two

In need of a shave, his faded Levi's dusty, his gray chambray shirt wrinkled and sweat stained, Brit Caruth took off his Stetson and walked into the Western Union office at noon on Saturday, the second of August.

Dub Harrison, the balding telegrapher, was seated on a stool inside the barred cage. He looked up from behind his wire-rimmed glasses when Brit came in.

"Britton Caruth? That you?"

"In the flesh," said Brit, and stepped up to the window.

Dub climbed down off the stool, shaking his bald head. "Why, I like not to recognized you, Son." He chuckled then and added, "Thought for a minute you was one of them bad outlaws come to hold me up."

Brit grinned good-naturedly, his teeth showing starkly white in his dark, whiskered face. Scratching an itchy jaw, he said, "Guess I do look a little rough."

"A visit to the barbershop wouldn't be a bad idea."

Brit nodded, then pointed to a yellow pad at

Dub's elbow. "Hand me one of those blank message forms. I need to send a wire."

"That's what I'm here for," said Dub, shoving the entire pad through the window.

Brit tore off one page, turned and walked away. At the front window, he placed the blank paper on a high writing table, took a pen from its well and wrote out a lengthy, urgent message to the Pinkerton Detective Agency in Denver, Colorado.

He repeated the request he had made several weeks ago, and asked that they put a high degree of urgency into their ongoing investigation of the woman calling herself Anna Regent Wright.

Concluding, he penned, "Time is running out."

Brit replaced the pen in its inkwell, blew on the message paper to dry it, turned and crossed to the caged window. He passed the message through and said, "Dub, see to it this telegram reaches the Pinkerton office within the hour."

"It's as good as there," said Dub, already reading the missive with undisguised interest.

"One last thing, Dub."

Dub peered at Brit over his glasses. "Yes?"

"Be sure you exercise that strict Western Union policy of total secrecy you swore to when you took this job."

"Why, I wouldn't think of revealing——"

"Good day, Dub."

"What about this gunmetal-gray organza?" The petite Lily held up the dress for their inspection.

"It's the latest style and quite exquisite, don't you agree?"

"Mmm, I don't know," said Sally, rising from the velvet sofa where she and Anna were seated. "I do like the tiered skirt, but..." She looked back at Anna. Anna quietly shook her head. "No," Sally told Lily decisively. "It doesn't suit me. I won't be trying it on."

"Very well," said the sedate Lily, smiling. "Not to worry, Sally. I've dozens of lovely dresses to show you." With the gray organza gown tossed over her arm, she hurried away. Moments later she returned with a couple of fashionable choices—a frothy, rose-colored chiffon and a shimmering lavender silk. She held both up.

"The lavender silk!" Anna and Sally said in unison, then laughed and hugged each other.

Anna stayed in the main salon while Lily ushered Sally to the dressing room to try on the silk dress. No one else was in the shop. Anna was alone. She glanced at the gold-trimmed, freestanding mirror at the center of the big salon.

A wistful smile tugged at her lips as she recalled standing before that mirror in the lovely white eyelet dress. She remembered how she had saucily turned from the mirror and moved purposely up to the salon's front window, where Brit had stood looking in.

If she lived to be ninety, she would never forget the expression on his handsome face as he'd gazed at her. Without a word he had told her that the white eyelet was *the* dress and that she looked incredibly beautiful in it.

Anna sighed sadly, recalling the fun and flirtation of that day.

She shook her head to clear it, rose from the velvet sofa, and moved restlessly around the spacious salon, idly looking at dresses with no real interest. Soon she returned to the bench, but before she sat down, she glanced out the plate glass storefront. Her lips fell open and she hurriedly moved closer to the window, squinting to see across the plaza.

She couldn't be sure, but she thought that she had caught a glimpse of Brit's iron-gray stallion being led inside the livery stable by a young groom.

Dear Lord, was Brit in town this very minute? Was the stallion she saw Captain, or just a look-alike?

Anna sat down heavily on the velvet bench, put her hands to her hot cheeks and told herself she was being foolish. It wasn't Captain she'd seen. Brit wouldn't be in town at noon on a Saturday. She was imagining things. She took several long, deep breaths to calm herself, turned and again glanced through the clear plate glass.

She saw no one on the street resembling Brit. He wasn't in Regentville. He was miles away, working on the ranch. After all, Captain wasn't the only iron-gray stallion in southwest Texas.

"How do I look, Anna?" Sally asked, rushing toward her wearing the lavender silk.

"Absolutely elegant," Anna replied.

* * *

"The key to The Regent's suite, please," Brit said to the desk clerk.

"Right away, Mr. Caruth." The hotel employee was pleasant. He fetched the key, handed it across the polished counter and said, "I believe you will find everything exactly as you requested. Your bath has just been drawn, should be the right temperature by the time you get upstairs. And you'll find a fresh supply of your favorite cigars and a bottle of fine Kentucky bourbon on the drink trolley in the suite's sitting room." He smiled, added, "If there's anything else you need or want, please let us know."

"Will do," said Brit, before he turned and walked across the spacious, marble-floored lobby, his big roweled spurs jangling with each step he took.

Upstairs, Brit let himself into the quiet, spacious suite, crossed to the tall front windows and yanked the heavy drapes open, flooding the room with hot August sunshine. He turned, went directly to the drink trolley and poured himself two fingers of bourbon. He drank it down in one long swallow, wiped his mouth and exhaled.

He poured a second, but did not down it as he had the first. He leisurely sipped the whiskey while he lit a cigar, then stood there in the sunny sitting room, undressing, not stopping until he had disrobed right down to his bronzed skin.

His soiled clothes left in a heap on the sitting room's plush carpet, Brit stood blinking in the wide shaft of sunshine slicing through the room. Finally he frowned, stuck the cigar in his teeth and crossed to the open drapes. Quickly he closed them and then nodded in approval. It was cooler with the curtains closed and the room dim.

Brit returned to the drink trolley, snagged the bourbon bottle in two fingers, plucked a shot glass from a neat stack and headed for the master suite with its adjoining bath. Just as ordered, a full tub awaited him, along with a fresh bar of soap, a long-handled brush and a half-dozen white towels.

Brit placed the bourbon bottle and shot glass on a low tubside table, stepped into the steamy water and sighed as he sank down in its depths.

His intent was to lie luxuriating in the tub for at least an hour. Sipping his bourbon. Smoking his cigar. Relaxing. It was not quite one o'clock. He was to meet Buck and Sally downstairs at two. There was plenty of time to rest and unwind.

Brit stretched his long legs out full length, laid his dark head back against the tub's rim, placed his arms along the sides, closed his eyes and sighed, preparing to take a little catnap.

But his dark eyes opened almost immediately. A muscle flexed in his jaw. He ground his teeth in frustration. Damn it to hell. He found no peace here. Not here, not anywhere. Would there ever be any again?

His darkly whiskered face set in rigid lines, Brit bolted up into a sitting position, reached for a washcloth and the soap. He vigorously scrubbed his body, as if in so doing he could wash away more than just sweat and dirt. He wanted to cleanse away the nagging, persistent memories that so tortured him.

After his bath, Brit carefully shaved away the three-day growth of beard. He studied himself in the mirror, turning his head one way, then the other. He needed a haircut, but there wasn't enough time. Maybe he'd get one after lunch.

Naked, Brit opened the door of a large closet, which was filled with his clothes. Garments kept here for just such occasions as this one. Uncaring what he wore, he took down the first suit he saw, grabbed a shirt, a pair of shoes and got dressed.

When he was ready to leave the suite, he paused for a moment before the gold-trimmed mirror mounted above the mantel. He hardly recognized himself with a fresh shave and a clean suit of clothes. It was then, while he was inspecting his image in the mirror, that he realized this was the first time he had bothered to be well groomed and nicely dressed since...since...

Brit turned and stalked out of the suite.

"There he is!" said Sally, waving madly as she and Anna entered the wide arched doorway of the hotel's partially deserted dining room. "And look, Brit's with him."

At the mention of his name, Anna's heart stopped beating. Then almost pounded its way out of her chest when she glanced across the room and actually saw him. Horrified and instantly furious with Sally, Anna felt like a trapped, frightened animal. She couldn't turn and run, although that's exactly what she wanted to do. She was held powerless by some indefinable force that emanated from him.

Surprised that her feet and legs still worked, Anna found herself crossing the capacious dining room, moving steadily closer to the two tall men, who had risen to acknowledge the presence of ladies.

His dark head cocked a little to one side, Brit stood there looking handsome as the devil in a suit of crisp beige linen and a shirt of powder blue, open at the throat. His tanned face was smoothly shaven, his midnight hair brushed and shiny and a trifle too long, curling appealingly over his shirt collar.

Though she was horribly uncomfortable, it was apparent that he was not. That habitual air of egotism clung to him like his finely tailored suit, and it was insulting to her. Was he eagerly anticipating her crushing embarrassment and chagrin at his unexpected presence? Had he come here purposely to upset and shame her for his own selfish amusement? Was he hoping she'd be so flustered she'd make a spectacle of herself?

Her throat was so tight it hurt, and her pulse was pounding with apprehension, but Anna's innate pride quickly rose to the surface and she told herself she would survive this ordeal with her dignity intact.

If the cocksure, coldhearted bastard was waiting for her to make a fool of herself, he would have a long wait. She *was* a fool; she had proved that the night of the Fourth. But she wasn't about to let Sally and Buck and half the population of Regentville know what a pitiful fool she was.

After the first moment of surprised astonishment, Anna quickly regained her self-control. She had to get through this ordeal somehow, so she pretended that she was a great stage actress and this was the most important role of her entire career. Her performance had to be flawless.

Anna crossed the dining room looking cool, unruffled, even pleased, as if she were delighted that Brit had decided to join them. When she and Sally reached the two men, Sally and Buck embraced and whispered to each other like the lovesick pair they were.

Anna tilted her face up to Brit's and favored him with a dazzling smile.

"What a nice surprise," she said in a soft, level voice. "I do hope you're staying for lunch." She held her breath, praying he would make some excuse and leave.

"I wouldn't miss it for the world," he replied calmly.

Brit held out a chair for her and Anna slid into it. Then instinctively drew in her breath when he sat down directly beside her.

"How are you today, Miss Anna?" Buck had finally released Sally and was grinning broadly as he held out her chair.

"I'm fine, thank you, Buck," Anna said, and picked up a white linen napkin.

Buck dropped down into the chair beside Sally, saying, "Sally didn't tell me you were coming today, but we're sure glad you did. Aren't we, Brit?"

Brit smiled easily. "Delighted."

Anna was in agony throughout the meal, but she was keenly aware that Sally and Buck were watching, so she smiled serenely, made pleasant table conversation and did her best to ignore the close, troubling presence of the heartless, handsome man seated beside her.

She longed to move her chair away from his, but didn't dare. She tensed each time his shoulder brushed hers. She inwardly bristled when he laid an arm along the back of her chair. And when, beneath the cloth-draped table, she felt his knee brush hers, she drew a quick breath, but did not immediately recoil and therefore allow him to know he was upsetting her. She purposely waited a couple of heartbeats before moving her knee away from his.

Anna was careful not to look at Brit, but just as careful not to let Sally and Buck know that she was ignoring him. Since Brit was seated beside her, it was quite normal for her to look across the table at Buck and Sally. Neither noticed that she avoided looking at Brit. She was sure Brit noticed, and she wanted him to. She wanted him to know that she never wanted to look at him again for as long as she lived.

At least she wanted to never *want* to look at him again.

Midway through lunch, Anna couldn't help herself. She hazarded a quick sidelong glance at Brit. He was smiling sunnily as he told some amusing tale, effortlessly charming both Sally and Buck. Anna gritted her teeth. He had them fooled. He had everyone fooled—LaDextra and Will Davis and the cowhands on The Regent and the townspeople of Regentville. Everyone liked and admired Brit Caruth.

She didn't.

She didn't like him. She didn't admire him. She hated him and she would hate him to the grave. He was, whether anyone else knew it or not, cold, callous and unbelievably selfish. He had teased and flirted and wooed her until she had surrendered to his abundant masculine charm. Once he'd conquered her, he had held her and kissed her and loved her until she was his completely and forever.

And when he was sure she belonged to him, body and soul, he had tossed her aside like a soiled garment.

Despite her inner turmoil, Anna continued to carefully conceal her feelings as lunch progressed. She laughed with the others when Brit's entertaining story was completed. As the leisurely meal continued, Anna wore a mask of repose and agreeableness that appeared as genuine as Brit's easy air of affability.

Twenty-Three

Anna thought the meal would never end.

It was nearing three-thirty when finally Buck Shanahan swallowed the last bite of his second piece of apple pie and drank the last drop of his coffee.

He sighed loudly, shoved back from the table, patted his full stomach and said, "Well, I guess that'll hold me 'til suppertime." He winked at Sally, who giggled.

"An excellent meal," commented Brit, pushing back his chair. "It's getting late and I—"

"Naw, now, don't be running away," Buck objected. "You said yourself you were taking the afternoon off. I thought we might all go over to Sally's house and—"

"No, I can't," Anna and Brit protested in unison.

"I really must get home," Anna said. "I'm sure Roberto, my driver, is waiting for me out front."

"I have some things to take care of," said Brit.

"Well, if you both have to go..." Sally's face brightened. "But today's been such fun, I've a great idea! A traveling opera troop out of Fort Worth is going to be in Regentville next week. Why don't the four of us get together and go see—"

"I won't be here," Anna said, thinking quickly.

"You won't?" Sally was puzzled.

"No, I—I'm going to San Antonio for a visit with cousins—Justin and Olivia Box. They've been after me to come and—" she smiled coquettishly, adding solely for Brit's benefit "—they're most anxious to introduce me to some of the city's eligible bachelors."

"You didn't tell me you were going to San Antonio," Sally said, frowning.

"Didn't I? Well, I am." Anna laid her napkin on the table. "I really enjoyed lunch. Thank you for inviting me." She smiled at Buck and Sally, then nodded when Brit rose to pull out her chair.

Holding hands and whispering, Buck and Sally led the way out of the empty dining room. Walking side by side, not looking at each other, not talking, Brit and Anna followed. The foursome exited the dining hall, crossed the marble-floored lobby and stepped out into the blistering August sunshine.

A Regent carriage and driver waited at the curb.

Shading her eyes from the sun's glare, Anna said a hasty goodbye to everyone. Buck and Sally turned and walked away, strolling down the sidewalk hand in hand. Left alone with Brit, Anna anxiously brushed past him to get into the carriage.

Before she could climb up onto the leather seat, his strong fingers encircled her waist. He effortlessly lifted her up into the carriage, and his hands remained on her for a heartbeat too long as his dark, fathomless eyes snared hers.

Aware that passersby were watching, Anna knew she had to be civil. Under her breath, she hissed,

"Get your hands off me." Then she smiled at him, placed her hands atop his and gently removed them from her, saying sweetly, "Thank you so much, Brit. I'll see you back at home. Bye, now."

Brit gave no reply. He closed the carriage door and stepped back. He was still there where she'd left him when the gleaming black brougham turned the corner of the plaza and Anna glanced back.

He stood unmoving in the sunlight, his raven hair glistening, his distinctive profile etched against the cloudless Texas sky. A sudden, hot breeze blew up and pressed his blue shirt against his chest, his beige trousers against his long, lean legs.

Anna didn't realize she was holding her breath until Brit abruptly turned and walked away. She released her held breath, relieved that she was leaving him behind, that this trying afternoon was finally over.

She leaned back against the plush, tufted leather and closed her eyes. Her head was throbbing. Her stomach was on fire. She was miserable and she was angry, as well. Angry with Brit. While she had suffered through the endless, strained meal, struggling to maintain her self-control and hide her discomfort, he had been totally unruffled and at ease. It maddened her to know that his mere presence could so upset her, while her presence bothered him not at all.

As the carriage rolled down the dusty street leading out of Regentville, Anna sighed, opened her eyes and crossed her arms over her chest. She set her jaw and silently told the insensitive man responsible for her despair that he wouldn't be so infuriatingly calm when she was finished with him.

He had better enjoy his days on The Regent, because they were numbered.

Brit went straight to the Red Rose Saloon.

Unsmiling, he pushed through the slatted, batwing doors and made his way to the long wooden bar at the back of the saloon.

"Bourbon, Sam," he said, when the beefy bartender appeared.

"Coming right up," Sam replied, nodding.

The barkeep set a shot glass before Brit and filled it to the brim from a full bottle of Kentucky bourbon. When he started to move away, Brit reached out, clasped his forearm and said, "Leave the bottle."

"Whatever you say."

Brit stood at the polished bar in the hot, airless Red Rose Saloon for the rest of the afternoon, drinking whiskey straight and frowning darkly at anybody who jostled him or got too close.

The regulars murmured among themselves, wondering what was bothering Brit Caruth. He wasn't himself today. He was mean-looking and short-tempered and in no mood for fun and high jinks.

"If you ask me," said one old-timer under his breath, "Brit's itchin' for a fight."

"Well, I wish to hell he'd find one," said a poker player at a table nearby. "I'm tired of looking at that ugly scowl on his face."

The old-timer chuckled and challenged, "Then why don't you fight him?"

"Not me," said the man, picking up the cards just dealt him. "I've seen him fight. He'd make mince-meat out of me."

Brit continued to sullenly drink his bourbon, mindless of the talk going on around him. He stood at the bar looking neither left nor right, having nothing to do with anyone, determined to drink himself senseless.

At shortly after seven on that hot Saturday evening, the saloon's doors swung open and Jackson "Tiny" Crandall, a troublemaker from Carlsbad, New Mexico, strode inside, puffing a fat cigar and sporting a brace of pistols.

A hush fell over the crowd.

Most all of the Red Rose patrons were admittedly afraid of the muscular, six-foot-four ruffian, who enjoyed browbeating and harassing people.

The crowd held its collective breath when Tiny, thumbs stuck into his low-riding gun belt, teeth chomping on his fat cigar, sauntered toward the bar, his beady eyes fixed on Brit's back.

The insults started immediately.

"Well, lookie here, what have we got? I do believe it's Pretty Boy Caruth," said the ugly, grinning Tiny. "Is that you, pretty boy? Old Lady Regent let you come to town all by yourself?"

There was no response from Brit. He didn't turn around, didn't say a word, just continued to drink his whiskey and stare into space.

"Hey, I'm talking to you, Caruth." Tiny's voice

grew louder. "You hear me? You afraid to turn around and face me?" He laughed and looked about the crowded saloon, clearly enjoying his attempts to humiliate Brit. "You know, I keep hearing how fast you are with your fists, but I ain't never seen any sign of it."

Stony silence filled the room.

Tiny pressed on. "Know what I think, Caruth? I think you're a yellow-bellied coward. I think you're afraid to fight a real man, that's what I think." Tiny crushed his cigar out on the bar at Brit's elbow and said, loudly enough for everyone in the saloon to hear, "Maybe you ought to shimmy down them fancy pants you're wearing and let us all have a look. I got a feeling there's lace sewed on your underdrawers."

There were loud guffaws from Tiny.

Gasps from the crowd of men.

No response from Brit.

Big Tiny Crandall continued to needle Brit for the next half hour, doing his best to get a rise out of him. It didn't work. Brit didn't take the bait. He didn't give a tinker's damn what Tiny Crandall said about him.

At last Tiny gave up on antagonizing Brit.

Only then did he finally get Brit's attention. Tiny made the mistake of turning his goading and tormenting on a slightly built young cowboy who had lived and worked on The Regent all his life. The youth had been left mute after a fall from a mustang when he was just five years old. His name was Gilberto Baca and he was a hard worker, intelligent, likable and dependable.

"Hey, Barkeep," Tiny bellowed, lowering his face to within inches of Gilberto's, "I see you're still letting this dummy drink in here like he was as good as anybody." Tiny spat on the floor and said to Gilberto, "Get out of here, dummy. I don't like lookin' at your stupid brown face when I—"

"Excuse me, Tiny." The deep, resonant voice was accompanied by a firm tap on Tiny's beefy shoulder.

"What the...?" Tiny turned around, and his broad face immediately met with a hard driving blow from Brit's right fist.

The surprise punch staggered Tiny, but he didn't go down. Brit didn't wait for him to recover, but shot a fast left hook up under Tiny's whiskered chin. The big man flew backward and landed on his rear.

Shedding his beige linen suit jacket, Brit advanced on the downed man. "Get up," he said through thinned lips, his fists raised.

"I'll get up, all right. I'll get up and kill you, Caruth," threatened Tiny as he struggled to his feet and came at Brit.

The fight was on.

Card games stopped in midhand. The piano player quit playing. Everyone loved a good fistfight, and within seconds bets were being taken on who would be the victor.

Big Tiny Crandall was the taller of the two and his arms were longer, so he had the reach on Brit. But Brit had the edge, nonetheless. Each swing he took at Tiny's ugly face released some of the pent-up tension that had been building inside him for weeks. For too long he had been like a tightly coiled spring, wound up, ready to break. The feel of his fist slamming into flesh was just what he'd been needing to relieve the pressure.

Brit fought like a madman, swinging, jabbing, landing punch after punch, grinning when he heard Tiny grunt and groan.

"Look at Brit," shouted one of the raucous spectators. "He's smilin'. He's havin' a good time!"

And he was.

Brit couldn't avoid all of Tiny's punches. He took some glancing blows to the jaw and a couple of haymakers to the belly. But he hardly felt the pain. Nor did he tire. He followed the retreating Tiny around the floor, knocking over chairs and tables, relentless in his pursuit. He connected with so many punishing blows that the bigger, taller man was soon swaying on his feet, his face battered and bloody.

Brit didn't let up.

He continued to weave and dart and strike with well-aimed fists until his opponent was clearly beaten. One eye swollen shut, blood dripping from his nose and various cuts, Tiny tottered and tried futilely to finish Brit off.

Tiny was the one who got finished off.

Brit, suffering no more than a bruised cheek, a split lip and torn clothes, knew it was all over and was almost sorry that it was. He hadn't felt so good in weeks. Advancing on his beaten opponent, Brit said, "You had enough, Tiny?"

Tiny, struggling to stand on rubbery legs, spit a glob of blood on the floor, raised his battered fists and said, "Go to hell, Caruth."

Brit stepped in and easily landed a forceful blow that ended the fight. Tiny Crandall went down and lay unconscious on the floor. Patrons whistled and applauded. Men crowded around Brit, anxious to shake his hand and pat him on the back. Young Gilberto Baca couldn't vocalize his gratitude, but his dark, flashing eyes thanked Brit, and Brit smiled and ruffled the boy's hair. The beefy bartender shouted above the din that drinks were on the house.

Brit celebrated his lauded victory for the next half hour, then quietly slipped away.

Out on the wooden sidewalk, he inhaled deeply of the still night air. He felt good. Relaxed. In charge. Better than he'd felt in weeks. Like his old self.

Brit whistled a lively tune as he walked to the livery stable for his stallion. He rode out of the stable, but didn't head home to the ranch. He was, he realized, finally thinking straight again instead of like some lovesick schoolboy.

All he needed was a woman. A beautiful, warm, willing woman, and one woman was just like the next. Always had been. Always would be.

In minutes Brit dismounted before a well-lit, pale yellow Victorian mansion on the outskirts of town, and knocked loudly. The red-haired widow, Beverly Harris, answered the door herself.

Her face reflecting her surprise, delight and concern, the negligee-clad Beverly threw her arms around Brit's neck and exclaimed worriedly, "Brit, you're hurt!"

Brit rubbed his bruised jaw. "Not really. I'm okay. I do need to wash up, though."

"Oh, my love, come inside and I'll give you a nice hot bath."

Twenty-Four

Anna hurried to LaDextra's room the minute she got back from Regentville that Saturday afternoon.

She knocked gently on the door and heard La-Dextra say, "If it's Anna or Brit, come on in. If it isn't, leave me alone."

Anna smiled and went inside. Crossing to the easy chair where LaDextra sat by a tall window, she leaned down, gave the woman's wrinkled cheek a quick kiss, then sank to her knees beside the chair.

"You look tired," LaDextra said. "Are you feeling all right?"

"You've stolen my lines," Anna replied. "I'm supposed to be asking you that question. So I will. Are you feeling all right?"

"Yes, yes." LaDextra waved a dismissive hand. "But you..." She shook her white head worriedly. "What is it, child? Are you running a fever?" She cupped Anna's cheek. "Are you ill? Has something happened? What's wrong?"

Not daring to tell LaDextra what was bothering her, Anna shrugged and said, "It's the heat. It was so hot in town and I stayed too long. I'm a little tired, that's all."

Convinced, LaDextra nodded. "Tell me about it.

Did Sally and you have a successful shopping day? Did you enjoy lunch with Sally and Buck?''

Anna said, ''Yes. With my guidance, Sally picked a half-dozen pretty new dresses at Lily's.''

''And the lunch?''

''Very nice.'' Anna looked down, picked some imaginary lint from her full skirts and said, in a voice that she hoped held no emotion, ''Brit joined us.''

''Brit was there for lunch? What was he doing in town?''

''Said he had some business to take care of,'' said Anna.

''I can't imagine what kind of...'' LaDextra's words trailed away, and she looked momentarily puzzled. Then she brightened and said, ''Well, I'm glad to hear he took the time to have lunch with you. He's been working so hard lately, I swear, I've hardly seen the rascal since the Fourth of July. How was he?''

Anna lifted her head. ''Brit was Brit. Cocky and handsome as ever.''

LaDextra chuckled, pleased.

Anna rushed on, ''LaDextra, tell me the honest truth. Are you really feeling well? Because if you are, I thought maybe I—I'd...''

''You'd what, child?''

''You remember cousins Justin and Olivia inviting me to come to San Antonio for a visit?''

''Sure, I do. And they meant it, too. They'd love to have you.''

''I want to go.''

"All right. Fine. I think that's a real good idea. A visit to a big city would be good for you," said LaDextra. "Let's see, early fall would be a perfect time to—"

"No. Now. I want to go now."

"Now? This month?"

"This week. Monday if possible."

"Well, honey, what's your hurry?" LaDextra's brows knitted as she studied Anna's upturned face. "Something *is* wrong. You're hiding something from me."

"No. No, I'm not." Anna couldn't tell LaDextra the truth, that she had to get away from The Regent—from Brit—if only for a week or so. "It's just…" Anna smiled reassuringly and said, "I'm like you, LaDextra—impulsive." She lifted her slender shoulders, adding, "I've decided I'd like to go to San Antonio. So why wait?"

LaDextra nodded, charmed. "Why, indeed? I'll have Will wire Justin and Olivia to let them know you're coming. There's a morning train out of Regentville. You can leave Monday if you like."

"Oh, thank you," Anna said, rising up on her knees and giving the elderly woman an affectionate hug.

Brit didn't object.

He stood in the middle of Beverly's big bath and allowed her to help him get undressed. He had kicked off his shoes and removed his socks, and now, while he unbuttoned his blue shirt, Beverly unbuckled his belt and undid the fly of his beige linen trousers.

When the pants were open, she put her hands to the waistband and pulled both the trousers and white linen underwear down over his hips. She followed the trouser's descent, sinking to her knees on the plush carpet as she peeled the pants down his long legs until they pooled at his feet.

Brit watched as she carefully lifted one foot, then the other, freeing him of the trousers. She then tilted her head back and looked up at him. He was Adam naked now, and Brit could tell by that familiar hungry look in Beverly's eyes that she could hardly wait to get him bathed so that she could get her hands—and her mouth—on his flaccid flesh, which was now at her eye level.

If he read her thoughts, she read his as well. She boldly cupped him, gazed adoringly at the soft male flesh, raised her eyes to his, and announced brazenly, "I will show it—and you—that no sweet-faced, slender blonde can make this magnificent male member stand at attention as quickly as I can!"

Brit hoped she was right.

He stepped into the hot, sudsy tub and relaxed while Beverly lovingly bathed him. Kneeling beside the tub, she dabbed gently at his discolored jaw with a soapy washcloth, then cleansed away a streak of matted blood in his right eyebrow.

When she moved the washcloth to his chest, Brit noticed she was pulling one of her favorite tricks. She purposely leaned over the tub so that the sudsy water would saturate the nearly transparent fabric of her white negligee. Instantly the gossamer gown clung wetly to her full breasts, delineating her large nipples.

To Brit's astonishment, the sight of her pebble-hard nipples peeking through the wet gauze did little to his libido.

Beverly scrubbed Brit's back, washed his long arms and legs and then, smiling seductively at him, lowered the washcloth slowly down his belly to his groin. He caught her mild surprise when she found that he was still as soft and harmless as a baby even after his extended bath with her talented hands.

Still, he wasn't worried. Yet. She could arouse him; he was sure of it. She would get him out of the tub, dry him off and do what she did best. No need to be nagged by doubt. She could get it up if anybody could.

Her wet negligee outlining her hardening nipples, Beverly dropped the washcloth in the water and said, "Now, get out, darling, and I'll help you dry off."

While Brit vigorously rubbed his wet hair with a large white towel, Beverly dried his tall, lean body. His hair still damp, Brit tossed the towel aside.

"That's it, Bev," he said, "I'm dry."

She smiled up at him, tossed her towel away, removed her dampened negligee and said huskily, "Well, I'm wet."

"Good, let's go to bed." He started to turn away.

She stopped him. "Not just yet. Let's start in here." She nodded to a mirrored wall of the luxurious bath and said, "Let's watch ourselves get hot and hotter and hottest."

With that, she leaned toward him, kissed his broad chest, nuzzling her nose in the crisp black hair that grew like a large fan across the wide, flat muscles. Her hands resting lightly on his trim waist, she put out her tongue and made wet, teasing circles around a flat, brown nipple.

Brit was stunned at how little it affected him.

Her lips never leaving his flesh, Beverly slowly sank to her knees before him. Kneeling now, she was clearly shocked to see that he still had no erection.

"It's the water, Bev," Brit said sheepishly.

She whispered, "Doesn't matter, darling. I'm glad, really. It will be thrilling to feel your flesh grow and stiffen in my mouth."

Her hands brushed tenderly through the thick, crisp hair of his groin and again she cupped him. Then she tilted her head back, looked up at him, licked her lips wetly and said, "Watch in the mirror while I arouse you to a fever pitch, darling. When you're fully erect and ready to pleasure me, we'll watch together."

With that she took him gently in her hand, opened her mouth wide and slipped it over his soft, limber flesh.

Brit stood in the mirrored bath and watched as the naked, red-haired woman knelt between his legs and gamely attempted to awaken his sleeping flesh. He gritted his teeth and silently cursed himself for his body's mysterious lack of response. What in hell was wrong with him? Jesus, if this didn't make him hot and hard, he was hopeless.

For several minutes Beverly Harris stayed on her knees with her mouth on Brit's flesh, in a futile attempt to make him spring to pulsing life.

It didn't work.

"I'm sorry, Bev," Brit murmured, his hands in her hair, urging her head up. He gently drew her to her feet and said, "I'm very tired and half-drunk and—"

"You've been tired and drunk before and we made love all night," she said irritably. "That's not it. You don't want me."

Her accusation hit home.

He had thought that he wanted her. Or that she could make him want her. He wanted to want her the way he used to want her. But he didn't.

There was only one woman he wanted and it wasn't Beverly Harris.

"Of course, I do."

"Liar!" she accused, growing angry now. "Liar, liar, liar. I know exactly what's wrong with you!" She reached for her discarded negligee, raised it up before her. "It's Anna. Anna owns your body now, doesn't she? Has she stolen your heart, as well? You bastard, you've been thinking of her the whole time you've been here with me."

"Ah, Bev, that's nonsense."

"You want her? Well, get out of here and go home to her!" Beverly was shouting now, her eyes tear-filled and flashing with anger. "See if *she'll* get down on her knees for you, because I never will again!''

It was nearing midnight when Anna undressed. She slipped a cool white cotton nightgown over her head and smoothed it down over her hips. She wasn't sleepy, but she got into bed and picked up a book from the night table.

She didn't read.

She couldn't see the words because Brit's handsome face kept intruding. The image of him as he had looked at lunch today plagued her, wouldn't let her alone. Never had he been more strikingly handsome, more potently masculine. Throughout the meal it had been almost impossible to keep her eyes off of him, when all she'd really wanted to do was gaze at him forever.

Each time he had lifted his wineglass to his lips, she had felt her stomach flutter and turn somersaults. His beautiful tanned hands cupping the fragile glass made her recall all too clearly how it felt to have those lean, dark hands gently caressing her sensitized flesh.

And when he drank the wine, oh God, that mouth, that marvelous, magical mouth. She had watched that sensual, full-lipped mouth open to take a drink of the wine, and couldn't keep from remembering the feel, the heat of those sculptured lips opening on her own.

Anna sighed and laid the book aside.

She had to stop thinking about Brit. She *would* stop thinking about him. She reminded herself—one more time—that while Brit Caruth might be masculinely beautiful and almost impossible to resist, he was a ruthless, self-indulgent scoundrel who cared nothing for her. She was in his way, just as he was in her way. He was, she knew, as intent on evicting her from The Regent as she was on seeing to it that he was permanently exiled.

She could hardly wait for that day to come.

Determined to put him from her thoughts and think about something pleasant, Anna told herself she was eagerly looking forward to her upcoming trip to San Antonio.

Justin Box was a gregarious man who liked everyone, and Olivia was a wise, genteel lady who had a knack for making people feel comfortable. Anna would, she knew, feel right at home with the likable couple, and she was sure they would be happy to have her come for a visit.

Besides, never in her life had she been to a big city, and she was quite curious. She couldn't imagine what it might be like, but from all she'd heard and read, San Antonio was a bustling, exciting place where there was so much to do and see she wouldn't have time to think about Brit Caruth.

Anna yawned, blew out the bedside lamp and closed her eyes. Minutes later, they opened at the sound of drumming hoofbeats. Curious as to who might be riding toward the mansion at this late hour, she got out of bed and went out onto the wide front balcony.

There was no mistaking the lone horse and rider. Captain's gray coat shone silver in the moonlight as the mighty stallion galloped up the pebbled drive, his dark master astride. Brit's linen suit coat was missing, and his shirt was open down his dark chest and billowing behind him in the wind.

Anna's pulse quickened at the sight of him. She whimsically imagined that he was a big, brave knight from days of old, that she was his ladylove, whom he had come to whisk away from the castle.

She wished that it were so.

She wished she could slip down the stairs, rush out to meet Brit and feel those strong arms lift her up into the saddle before him. Then the two of them would ride away in the summer moonlight and make love in some secluded spot until sunrise.

Scolding herself for her foolishness, Anna turned and hurried back inside before he could spot her. She got back in bed, turned onto her side and was immediately distracted by something glittering brightly on the bedside table.

Her eyes narrowing, Anna reached out and picked up the shiny silver concho she had twisted from Brit's trousers that fateful night in the stables. She forcefully threw the offending silver disk across the room.

It hit the wall and fell to the plush carpet below.

Twenty-Five

Brit brought the lathered, snorting Captain to an abrupt halt directly in front of the mansion. He dismounted and turned the big stallion loose. He knew that Captain would dutifully circle the immense manicured lawns, pick his way down the path to the outbuildings far behind the house and go directly to his private stable, where a sleepy groom would unsaddle him and give him a rubdown.

"Well, what are you waiting for? Go on," Brit said to the big iron gray, which had not yet moved. He pointed a finger in Captain's face and warned, "And don't go tromping through LaDextra's flower beds or we'll both be in big trouble."

The stallion whinnied, nudged Brit's shoulder, turned and pranced away.

Brit inhaled slowly and automatically looked up at Anna's room. It was dark. She was asleep.

Quixotically, he wished that she was awake and standing on the balcony in the moonlight, eagerly awaiting his arrival. He envisioned her there. And he envisioned himself anxiously scaling a vine trellis to her, taking her in his arms and whisking her off to his room, where he could make love to her through the long, hot night.

Brit exhaled heavily and scolded himself for being a fool.

His hands thrust deep in his trouser pockets, he went up the front walk, circled the huge mansion and quietly let himself in the back door. In the shadows cast by the dim wall sconces, he climbed the back stairs to his room.

Inside, a lone lamp burned low on the bedside table. The rest of the room was in shadow.

Brit sat wearily down on the bed, but was up immediately. He crossed to the drink trolley, poured himself a bourbon. He took one small swallow and set the glass aside. From a silver box on a marble-topped drum table, he snagged a cigar. He lit it, took a couple of drags, then impatiently snuffed it out in a crystal ashtray.

He started to undress. He took off his open blue shirt, tossed it aside. His hands went to the waistband of his soiled and torn beige trousers, but fell away before he unbuttoned them. He wasn't sleepy. He was edgy, restless, haunted by the bedeviling vision of an angelic face with enormous blue eyes framed by spun-gold hair.

And a tall, willowy body that had fit so perfectly against his own.

Brooding, Brit shook his head as once again he relived that terrible moment on the morning after he had made love to Anna in the stable. There had been at least a dozen people in the dining room enjoying a late breakfast when she had stepped inside, silently commanding everyone's attention.

Including his.

Especially his.

She had been so appealingly fresh faced and glowing. Her long hair had been pulled back on one side, and she'd worn a girlish pink dress with puffed sleeves and full skirts. She might have been sixteen years old, so pure and guileless she'd appeared. The sight of her looking so young and innocent, coupled with the fresh memory of all the intimate things they had done just hours before, had taken his breath away.

Her cheeks flushed, her beautiful eyes sparkling, she had looked at him shyly, expectantly. And he had pointedly glanced at her, then quickly dismissed her.

Brit swallowed hard now, remembering.

He knew what his indifference had done to her. She had been crushed by his coldness. Bewildered and badly hurt. She had immediately assumed exactly what he had wanted her to assume—that he was already bored with her. That their night together had been a mindless diversion, nothing more. That he'd had all he wanted of her, was no longer interested in her.

Oh, God, was she wrong.

He hoped she'd never learn that the reason he had been so pointedly cold to her that morning, and ever since, was because the lovemaking *had* meant something to him. It had meant too much to him. It had meant as much to him as it had to her, and that had angered and frightened him.

Scared him half to death.

The last thing he wanted was to fall in love with

a beautiful imposter who intended to steal his inheritance. He couldn't let that happen. He wouldn't let it happen. So he had purposely let her believe that he was a callous cad who had taken what he wanted from her and then promptly lost interest.

Nothing could have been further from the truth.

She was on his mind constantly, and it was driving him crazy. He could think of little else. Since that sweltering Fourth of July night when exploding fireworks intermittently illuminated her beautiful face as he made love to her, she'd been on his mind and in his blood and under his skin. Jesus, he couldn't even get it up with Beverly because he wanted Anna.

Only Anna.

No one but Anna.

Brit shook his head, disgusted with himself. There was little he could do about the fever in his blood. This beautiful blond thief had a definite hold on his body. But he'd be damned if he'd let her get her hands on his heart.

Or on his inheritance.

He had to remember at all times that no matter how sweet her kisses or how pliant her body, she was a cunning imposter with but one goal in mind. To swindle LaDextra out of The Regent and leave him holding the bag. He knew it as well as he knew his own name.

But he had to have proof. God, why were the Pinkertons dragging their heels? Why was it taking so much time to learn the woman's true identity? When was he going to hear something?

Brit shook his dark head, determined to dismiss her from his troubled thoughts. He was tired and he was finally getting sleepy. He finished undressing, turned off the bedside lamp and crawled between the silky white sheets.

He lay perfectly still in the darkness for several long minutes, then turned his head on the pillow. And saw, lying on the bedside table, the leather-bound book of poetry that Anna had left at the springs that day she'd come upon him naked. Brit raised up onto an elbow, reached for the book. He laid the book on the mattress and opened it to where a brittle flower lay pressed between the pages.

The rose.

The bloodred rose that Anna had worn in her hair the night they'd made love. Brit's hooded eyes darkened and a muscle danced in his lean jaw as he carefully lifted the fragile flower and touched it to his lips. He shuddered, recalling how he had plucked the fragrant rose from Anna's golden hair and brushed its delicate petals over her face and shoulders and breasts.

Brit scowled darkly and stuck the dried rose back between the book's pages as anger overcame sentimentality. He slammed the book closed and threw it forcefully across the room.

It hit the wall with a thud and fell to the plush carpet below.

At first he couldn't believe it.

He blinked, rubbed his eyes, looked again.

She was still there.

Brit anxiously sat up, thrusting a pillow behind his back, never taking his eyes off her.

His beautiful Anna had swept in through his open balcony doors and was floating gracefully toward him, as if she were walking on clouds. Her long golden hair was unbound, its shiny silkiness framing her exquisite face and flowing down her back. Her white nightgown with its long sleeves and high yoke covered her from throat to bare feet, but to his delight it was totally transparent.

His eyes wide, he could see her tall, slender body through the filmy fabric as if she were wearing nothing at all. Her full, creamy breasts were clearly visible, the pale pink nipples unthreateningly beautiful in their soft, sleepy state. Her delicate ribs were outlined beneath the flawless, pearlized skin, as were her flat belly and prominent hipbones.

Brit's mouth watered as he gazed at the tempting triangle of golden curls between her pale, perfect thighs. When he could bring himself to tear his eyes from those springy blond coils so effectively concealing and protecting her most feminine flesh, he noted that her knees were cutely dimpled, her ankles slender.

He was speechless as she drifted ever closer to his bed. When she stood directly beside it, she smiled at him and asked, "You won't send me away, will you? You did want me to come, didn't you, Brit?"

"God, yes," he managed to reply, his heart now thundering in his bare chest.

Anna reached down, cupped his dark jaw in her

hand, skimmed the pad of her thumb over his bottom lip and said, "Do you know why I'm here?"

"I hope I do," he said.

She smiled. "You made love to me once. Now I will make love to you."

He playfully bit her thumb and murmured, "Anything you want, baby, anything."

She slid her hand around the back of his neck, urged his head back, bent and kissed his lips. She thrust her tongue deeply into his mouth, and Brit sighed with pleasure and eagerly reached for her.

"No," she warned, abruptly tearing her lips from his and stepping back. "I told you, I am going to make love to you."

"I'm sorry."

She smiled at him again and said enigmatically, "Soon you won't be sorry, you'll be glad."

"May I get up and—"

"No. You're to stay where you are. I will join you."

Brit said foolishly, "Anna, I'm...naked."

"I would hope so," she said. "Let's see." And she reached for the covering sheet, pulled it free of him and the bed, and tossed it to the floor. "Yes, you are naked. Would you like me to be as naked as you?"

"Oh, yes, yes I would."

Brit almost lost his breath when Anna, standing directly before him, leisurely lifted the sheer nightgown up over her head and dropped it to the floor.

Gloriously naked, she sat down on the bed facing him. She placed her hands lightly on his shoulders.

"There is," she whispered throatily, "something I've wanted to do to you."

"There is?" Brit's hands tentatively lifted to clasp her narrow waist as he said, "Tell me, sweetheart."

"No," she said, "I will show you."

With that, she bent her head, flipping her long blond hair forward. For the next few, pleasurable minutes she expertly teased and tormented him with just her hair. Slowly, seductively, she moved down his body, her face never touching him, only her heavy hair pleasantly tickling him, arousing him.

Brit, overwhelmed, raised a hand, heard her warn, "No. Don't."

His heart raced in his chest and he felt as if he had never known such excitement. Her heavy hair was spilling over him, tantalizing him, the wispy ends tickling his belly and groin. And rising swiftly to thrust through those silky golden locks was his fully formed erection.

It was a sight to behold, one he would never forget—his own hard, heavy flesh piercing the covering blanket of shimmering blond hair. He was almost sorry when Anna abruptly lifted her head and looked into his eyes.

"Kiss me, Brit," she said.

"Baby," he murmured, and reached for her as she slid up to meet him.

His lips closed over hers in a fiery, penetrating **kiss that lasted** for several long seconds. When finally Anna tore her kiss-swollen lips from his, she said, "I know why you never came to me again after that night in the stables."

"No, you don't, I—"

"I didn't please you enough. I'll please you now. I'll make you happy."

Before Brit could reply, Anna wrapped her small, soft hands around his thrusting masculinity and gently stroked him.

"Oh, God, God, God," Brit breathed.

"Feel good?"

"You know it does."

Toying with him, Anna looked into his dark eyes and asked, "How much do you want me, Brit?"

"More than I could ever tell you," he said hoarsely, his hand lifting to gently cup a soft, pale breast. "More than I've ever wanted anything or anyone."

She brushed his hand away. She asked, "How can I believe you?"

"I'll make you believe me. I'll show you how much I want you."

She laughed softly. "No, I told you, you made love to me, now I will make love to you."

"I can think of nothing I'd like better."

Anna took her hand from him, put her arms around his neck and kissed him long and lovingly, licking at his lips, biting him playfully. Then she slipped out of his arms and rose from the bed. She put her hands on her hips.

"Lie down on your back," she commanded, and he obeyed.

Impatiently he waited as she danced provocatively around the bed, moving in and out of shadow, lifting her heavy hair atop her head, turning her back on him, then pivoting about.

By the time she climbed back onto the bed with him, Brit was so excited his breath was coming in loud gasps. She stretched out close beside him and pressed her soft, slender body to his.

"Baby, let me—" he began, but she stopped him.

"No. Not yet. Don't touch me just yet. Let me arouse you."

"God, I am aroused, can't you see that?"

"I can," she whispered. "But you must want me even more. And you will. You'll want me so much that you'll give up everything for me." She leaned over to kiss him, her hair cascading down around his face, enclosing him in a curtain of gold.

She kissed him passionately and pressed her soft curves against his hard body until he felt as if he couldn't wait one more second to make love to her.

But she made him wait.

And she didn't allow him to touch her. She scolded him each time he tried to caress her. She did all the touching, all the kissing, all the exciting.

It was exquisite agony for Brit. He lay there on his back in the hot darkness, more aroused than he'd ever been in his life. He wanted her so much he physically hurt. He had never known a woman more adept at titillation, more gifted at tantalizing him beyond endurance.

"Please," he begged huskily, "sweetheart, please."

When finally she agilely climbed astride him, Brit murmured his deep gratitude and relief.

Holding his breath, he watched, enraptured, as she rose up onto her knees and wrapped her hand around his throbbing erection. But just as she bent her knees and began lowering her spread thighs to impale herself upon him, she asked, "How much do you want me, Brit?"

"God, don't do this to me. I want you, I want you, what more can I say? How can I make you believe me?"

Anna lowered herself another couple of inches, and Brit's lean hips involuntarily surged upward, anticipating that much-longed-for meeting of hard flesh in soft flesh. She gave him just a taste. She skillfully placed the throbbing tip into her wet warmth, no more than an inch inside.

And then, to Brit's horror, her sensual smile became scarily evil and her eyes shone like shards of blue glass as she whispered, "You can't have it."

"Jesus," he rasped, grabbing her pale thighs and attempting to pull her down onto him.

But she was too quick.

Anna cast his hands away, shot to her feet, stepped over him and leaped down off the bed. "I must go."

"No!" Brit protested, beside himself with desire. "God, no, don't leave me like this. Have pity, baby."

She had no pity.

She laughed maniacally, and from behind her bare back she suddenly produced a legal-looking document. She waved it at him as she backed away and she said, "Know what this is? It's LaDextra's last will and testament." She laughed and added, "Guess what, Caruth? The Regent is now mine, not yours! You can't have it. And you can't have me."

"I don't care about The Regent, I just want you. Please, please…"

"Please, please!" Brit, muttering, bolted upright, waking abruptly from the dark, disturbing dream. Sweating profusely, a full-blown erection bobbing on his bare belly, he foolishly looked around, as if expecting the cruel blond beauty who had so exquisitely tortured him to be there in his room.

His breath labored, his heart hammering, he was greatly distressed by the erotic dream that had turned into a horrible nightmare. He trembled in the darkness.

"God, I *must* get her off The Regent," he said through clenched teeth, "whoever she is."

Twenty-Six

"Whoever she is," mused the tired, sunburned Pinkerton detective, Alex P. Hutchinson, to himself, "she's a clever little thing. She's managed to cover her tracks well."

Hutchinson, an eleven-year veteran of the famed Pinkerton Detective Agency, was a tall, rawboned man with thinning sandy hair, a ready smile and light gray eyes that were continually alert. No one was better at spotting the suspicious, ferreting out a helpful clue or knowing if a person being interrogated was lying. If Hutchinson was on a case, he was like a dog with a bone. He wouldn't rest until he had dug up the truth and solved the mystery.

Detective Hutchinson was proud of his reputation and frustrated that he had been unable to crack this present case to which he had been assigned. He had been sent down to the Arizona territory from the home office in Denver to investigate a woman who had shown up at the huge Regent ranch in far west Texas, claiming to be the long-lost heiress, Anna Regent Wright.

Detective Hutchinson had spent weeks on both sides of the border, questioning anyone and everyone who might know anything about the mysterious young woman. He had traveled countless miles in pursuit of the facts. Had tirelessly followed up on every lead, no matter how weak. Had interviewed dozens and dozens of people. Had interrogated whites, Mexicans and Indians alike.

And had hit a brick wall at every turn.

Now, as the Pinkerton detective approached the shimmering white adobe building housing the Border Convent at St. Peter's Mission, he felt a mild degree of optimism and hope. He had received only yesterday an urgent message from Sister Norma Kate, the convent's Mother Superior. He must come to see her at once. She had news concerning the case on which he was working. News that would be of great interest to him.

Detective Hutchinson had visited the peaceful convent two miles east of Nogales many times since his arrival in Arizona. He had spoken at length with the Mother Superior regarding the young woman who had spent five years at the mission before leaving for Texas less than five months ago.

But the nun had been of little help. She had known only that the woman had been taken as a child by the Indians and had lived with them until ranger captain John Russell had spotted her in an Apache stronghold south of the border. The ranger had ransomed her and brought her to the Arizona convent. The ranger had indicated that the Apache had not revealed to him who the girl was or how long she had been with them.

Now, as the Pinkerton detective dismounted in front of the vine-covered adobe mission, he hoped this wasn't another wild-goose chase. The home office had told him that their client, Brit Caruth, was growing increasingly impatient. This case needed to be solved pronto. Time was running out.

Detective Hutchinson smiled broadly as the tiny, white-garbed Mother Superior warmly greeted him. Her eyes as bright and alert as those of a young girl, she said, "Thank you for coming so quickly, Detective. There isn't a great deal of time, I'm afraid." Extremely curious, the tall detective said nothing, but followed the nun down the quiet corridor to her office.

Inside, he was promptly served strong black coffee by a young, unobtrusive sister. The Mother Superior, seating herself behind a desk that was bigger than her, leaned forward, clasped her hands together and said, "Finally, you are in luck, Detective. I know someone who may be able to tell you who the girl claiming to be Anna Regent Wright really is."

His pulse quickening, the detective set his coffee cup on the large desk with shaking hands. "Where is this person? When can I speak with him or her? Why haven't they come forward sooner? Why have—"

"Young man," the Mother Superior mildly scolded, "please be still and let me tell you what I know."

"Yes, of course. Forgive me."

"As I said, there isn't much time and I'll explain why. The person who may have the missing pieces of the puzzle is an ancient Apache warrior. The old Indian is very ill and has been brought to a relative's home in Nogales to die. It is said that his memory is as unclouded as that of a thirty-year-old, although he is nearing ninety. He is called Black Eagle, and he has lived since 1868 in the remote hideout in Mexico where Mary was found by the ranger. If anyone knows who she is and where she came from, Black Eagle is surely the one.''

Detective Hutchinson was already on his feet. ''Where is he? Where can I find this old Apache warrior? I'll go there at once, before it's too late. I must speak to Black Eagle.''

Brit's image kept intruding.

She had wrestled with herself, trying to forget him. Hoping that being far away from The Regent would obliterate the dark, handsome face that seemed to possess her every conscious moment. But it was her head talking to her heart, and her heart would not listen. She knew that she would never forget, would always remember. The memory of him making love to her would stay with her throughout her life.

Brit filled Anna's restless dreams at night, and while awake, she compared his distinctive countenance with every gentleman to whom she was introduced.

She had been in San Antonio for almost a week. Justin and Olivia were, as expected, excellent hosts. The minute she had stepped down from the train at the crowded depot, she had felt wanted and welcome and certain she was going to thoroughly enjoy herself.

If she had not enjoyed herself, it was through no fault of Justin's and Olivia's. They had done everything in their power to show her a grand time. On her very first evening in the city they had hosted a fabulous ball in her honor in the elaborate white-and-gold ballroom of their handsome, two-story riverfront mansion.

As predicted, there had been no shortage of eligible bachelors in attendance. Anna had danced and laughed with them all and, before the evening was over, she had promised a carriage ride in the country to the handsome blond real estate magnate, Franklin W. Cain. A night at the opera to the noted young attorney, Douglas Peterson. A dinner engagement to the wealthy young banker, Robert LaMar.

And she had accepted more invitations to parties than she could possibly hope to keep.

The days that followed had been an exhaustive whirl of shopping with Olivia for beautiful new ball gowns, sharing elegant luncheons, attending Thoroughbred horse races, taking walks along the river and meeting interesting people.

The nights had been a blur of fancy seven-course dinners and glittering galas and dances under the stars and hand-in-hand strolls in the moonlight with handsome, eager suitors. The never-an-idle-minute visit in this big, bustling city had been the kind of exciting adventure most young women could only dream of.

Now, at well past midnight, Anna undressed after yet another grand affair attended by the city's elite. She had been escorted to the splendid soiree by

Bradley Dexter, a fourth-generation San Antonian who was attractive, polished and attentive. It had been a gay, glamorous evening, yet she felt anything but exhilarated. The parties, the faces, the nights all ran together, and she found herself wishing that she could spend a nice quiet evening at home.

Not here.

Not here in this elegant San Antonio riverside mansion, where a steady stream of gay, witty people flooded in and out both day and night, but back home.

At The Regent.

She missed the nighttime silence, when all you could hear was the plaintive cry of whippoorwills or the distant yelp of a coyote or the mournful sigh of the hot desert wind. She missed the brilliance of the starry sky and the subtle scent of greasewood and the faint lowing of cattle from the pastures closest to the mansion. The pastoral existence at The Regent was soothing and peaceful, so unlike the hectic tempo of San Antonio.

Here in this teeming city the sidewalks were always filled with people, carriages jammed the streets and vendors hawked their wares. Loud music poured out of the many saloons and laborers shouted from down on the riverfront. There were constant crowds, constant activity, constant noise. Never, it seemed, never a time when it was calm and serene the way it was at home.

Anna smiled wistfully and sank down onto the bed, her fabulous new ball gown half-on, half-off. She realized with a welling of emotion that she had, in just a few short months, come to think of The Regent as home. *Her* home. And it was her home; she was convinced of it. She *was* Anna Regent Wright—she was sure of it, knew it in her heart.

And she wanted to go home, in spite of Brit. Or because of Brit. She wasn't sure which. But Brit or no Brit, she wanted to go home.

The next morning Anna wasted no time in telling her surprised hosts, as diplomatically as possible, that although she had had an absolutely wonderful time, she felt she should be going home.

Justin and Olivia looked at her, speechless. They looked at each other, then back at Anna.

Justin spoke first. "Why, child, you just got here. We're enjoying you so much and we had thought sure you would stay with us for a while."

"Justin's right," Olivia said softly. "We had anticipated having you here for two or three weeks. Won't you at least stay on through next week? The Hamiltons are having their annual costume party at the Menger Hotel a week from Saturday, and it's always such great fun. I'll help you find just the right costume and we'll—"

"No, I'm sorry," Anna gently interrupted. "I really feel that I should go home. It's LaDextra. She's been unusually tired and pale of late, and I'm worried about her. It was selfish of me to leave her."

Justin smiled at Anna. "And it's selfish of us to try and keep you here," he said graciously. "Shall I make the travel arrangements?"

"Would you please?" Anna replied.

He nodded. "Want to leave tomorrow morning?"

Anna needlessly cleared her throat. "Today, if possible."

Justin pushed back his chair. "I'll see what I can do, and then I'll wire the ranch that you will be coming—"

"No, don't bother," Anna interrupted. "I'll surprise them."

Twenty-Seven

If he had known she was coming home, Brit wouldn't have been out on the front gallery that blazing hot Sunday afternoon. He wouldn't have been anywhere near the house.

LaDextra had told him that Anna had gone to visit the Boxes in San Antonio, and that she would be gone for at least a couple of weeks. Only one week had passed since she'd left, so Brit felt comfortable in spending some time at home. He had, in fact, promised LaDextra that he would join her and Will Davis for dinner that evening.

Earlier in the afternoon Brit had ridden in from the Columbine division headquarters, where he'd spent the past three days. Now he planned to spend the night—perhaps two or three nights—at home. Sleep in his own bed for a welcome change.

He felt amazingly relaxed with Anna away and out of his sight. He realized with relief that once she was gone for good, he would be fine. Life at The Regent would return to normal, and in no time at all he would forget he'd ever met her. Held her. Kissed her. Made love to her.

At shortly after three o'clock, Brit finished his hated paperwork on the ranch's many complicated books, stood, stretched and decided he was sleepy. His bedroom, he knew, would be hot and stuffy. There might be a breeze out on the front gallery. It seemed like the perfect time for taking a nice little nap in the big canvas hammock that hung at the east end of the gallery. LaDextra was in her room resting. The servants were all taking their siestas. The house was as quiet as a church.

Brit exited his office, stepped out onto the wide, shaded veranda. He crossed to the front steps, raised a hand to shield his eyes and gazed uneasily out over the dying brown pastures stretching to the horizon. He walked down the steps and into the sun-splashed yard. He stared long and hard in every direction, anxiously searching for any sign of smoke rising to the cloudless sky.

Satisfied that, for the moment at least, there were no dangerous grass fires threatening The Regent, Brit yawned and returned to the gallery. He approached the inviting hammock, noting that it stirred not at all. There was not a hint of a breeze. Even here on the shaded gallery it was as hot as Hades.

Since no one was around, Brit flipped open the first two buttons of his chambray shirt, raised a hand behind his head and, in one fluid masculine movement, yanked the shirt up and off. He sat down on the edge of the hammock and removed his boots and socks. He yawned again, turned about and stretched out on his back.

He lifted his slim hips, unbuttoned the top buttons of his faded Levi's, exhaled heavily and scratched his bare abdomen. He crossed his ankles, wiggled his toes, draped a long arm over his chest and closed his eyes.

And fell instantly asleep.

The train bringing Anna home reached The Regent's private rail spur at three o'clock on that stifling Sunday afternoon. The uniformed conductor, placing her three matching valises on the wooden platform, looked around curiously and said, "Miss, are you expected? Is someone supposed to meet you?"

Anna smiled and lied. "Of course. My driver will be here any minute."

The conductor frowned. "I hate to leave you here alone in the middle of nowhere."

Anna laughed musically. "Ah, but it isn't the middle of nowhere. It's home. *My* home."

The conductor smiled, jumped back up onto the train as the wheels began to slowly turn. "Better put that bonnet on, miss," he called as the train began to pick up speed.

"I will."

Anna stood on the platform and waited until the locomotive, snaking slowly westward toward El Paso, became a small black ribbon moving in the heat-shimmering distance and she could no longer hear the clickity clack of the wheels turning on the tracks.

Blinking in the harsh Texas sunshine, Anna took the conductor's advice. She put on her big-brimmed straw hat and tied the blue taffeta streamers under her throat. She was unconcerned about her luggage.

A servant would be sent to fetch the heavy valises. So she lifted her long skirts, jumped down off the platform and set out for the ranch.

Soon Anna was thankful that she had chosen one of her coolest dresses, a pale blue organdy with short cap sleeves and a low, gathered bodice. It was, right now, the hottest part of the afternoon, and before she had walked a quarter of a mile, her face was shiny with perspiration and her petticoats were sticking to her legs.

Despite the discomfort, Anna was happy to be right where she was. She was glad to be home. She envisioned LaDextra's surprise when she showed up unexpectedly. There was no doubt in her mind that LaDextra would be genuinely delighted she had returned early. Anna gave a great yelp of joy. How incredibly wonderful it was to possess the sure knowledge that after all the lonely years, she finally belonged somewhere, was loved and wanted.

At least by LaDextra.

The same could not be said for Brit Caruth.

At the thought of Brit, Anna made a misstep, almost stumbled. She told herself she didn't care what he thought, that she hated the heartless Britton Caruth and would hate him with the last breath of her body.

But deep in her heart of hearts she knew that Brit was really the reason she had come back. To see him. To hear him. To be where he was. She was, she knew, a hopeless fool. She only hoped that he didn't know it, too.

Anna abruptly shook her bonneted head, determined to put Brit out of her thoughts. She looked around as she climbed the slowly ascending road and was horrified by what she saw. Here at the *Tierra Verde*, the vast fenced pasture on either side of the ranch road, nothing grew save a few scattered walking stick cholla, some prickly pears and brittle rabbit bush. The grass was burned brown by the continuing lack of rain and the relentless summer sun. No contented cattle grazed here anymore. The starving herds had long since been moved. The majority had been placed on the farthest eastern pastures, where traces of grass still dotted the burning land. Others—the best of the herds—had been taken to the lush green pastures of the mountain tract. Thousands more had been sold at a loss.

Anna frowned worriedly.

Everyone—including her—depended on Brit to guide them through this terrible drought, to make all the hard decisions, to take the necessary actions, to keep the big beleaguered ranch running. To prevent the loss of any or all of The Regent's empire. What, she wondered anxiously, would happen if Brit were not here and firmly in charge?

It was a sobering thought and with it came Anna's decision to immediately start learning all that she could about the day-to-day operations of the ranch. She couldn't count on Brit to be of any help, of course. But she could speak to LaDextra about enlisting one of the ranch's most trusted cowhands or vaqueros to educate her. And what the ranch hand couldn't tell or teach her, LaDextra surely could.

Anna's mind was made up. She had wasted

enough valuable time. She had to think about the future. A future in which she—not Brit—would be sole owner of The Regent. And therefore responsible for the ranch's operation.

When Anna had walked more than a mile, she was hot and thirsty. A sheen of perspiration covered her face, throat and slender arms. She could feel moisture beading behind her knees and between her breasts.

But when she had gone another quarter mile, she began to smile. There directly ahead, in the mammoth shadow of *El Capitán,* a huge eight-columned, antebellum mansion—so out of place in this hot, dry desert—rose starkly white in the blazing summer sun. An oasis in the savage Texas wilderness.

Anna felt a surge of fresh energy. She picked up her pace. She hurried eagerly toward the beckoning haven of home, happily anticipating a nice, cool bath, followed by a short rest on her big soft bed. At this time of the day everyone would be sleeping, so she would quietly let herself in and slip up the stairs.

Anna moved quickly up the pebbled drive and silently entered the iron gate. She hurried up the long front walk and sighed with relief when at last she ascended the steps onto the broad gallery. There in the welcome shade she paused, removed her straw bonnet and fanned herself. She hooked a finger in her dress's low bodice, pulled it out from her sticky skin and blew down inside, attempting to cool her heated, prickled flesh.

She stopped as the wispy hair at the nape of her neck rose suddenly.

A chill skipped up her spine despite the blazing heat of the afternoon. She had the eerie feeling that she was not alone. She looked down the west end of the long veranda and beyond. Nothing there. She turned her head and looked to the opposite end of the gallery.

And the straw hat dropped from her hands.

Brit lay sprawled in the hammock, sleeping soundly. He wore only a pair of faded Levi's, which were open down his brown belly. His muscular arms and broad bare torso glistened with sweat. His handsome face, in repose, was incredibly appealing. He looked like an innocent young boy, despite the high chiseled cheekbones and strong masculine jaw. With those dangerous lips slack in slumber and the dark penetrating eyes safely closed, he appeared far less threatening than usual.

Hardly realizing what she was doing, Anna tiptoed closer. She stopped a few feet from the hammock and stared at him, fascinated, enchanted. He looked so harmless and vulnerable, so like a guileless child. Seeing him this way, so defenseless and unguarded, it was easy to envision him as the sweet little boy left orphaned at age twelve.

As if he were that same sweet little boy now, Anna had an almost overwhelming urge to touch him. To reach down and push a wayward lock of blue-black hair back off his shiny forehead and then gently cup his lean cheek in her hand.

As she was gazing adoringly at the slumbering boy, the sleeping man awakened.

Anna winced as all traces of the innocent little boy disappeared, leaving only the cynical, intimidating man.

Their gazes locked. They stared at each other for a few breathless seconds, each swamped with his own impulsive, guilty yearnings.

For Brit the temptation to gather the beautiful blond temptress into his arms was almost more than he could resist. The blood beat in his temples, his body tensed with passionate longing and fierce desire rushed over him.

For Anna the urge to lie down and press herself against this handsome seducer's gleaming chest was almost more than she could stand. The pulse beat heavily in her throat, her body was taut with ardent yearning and primitive need washed over her.

Brit, recollecting his recent nightmare, recovered first.

"I wasn't expecting to find you here this afternoon," he drawled in a low, sleepy voice that sent a tingle of sensation through Anna.

"The same could be said for you," she replied, in a voice that sounded weak and strained even to herself. "I'm sorry if I disturbed your nap."

Brit's hooded eyes darkened and his lips tightened and curled in a hint of a sneer. "It's the darnedest thing," he said. "Anybody stands over me staring while I'm asleep, I wake up every time. You that way?"

"I said I was sorry," she replied.

Brit levered himself up into a sitting position, swung his long legs to the floor. Coming lithely to his feet, he looked her in the eye as he leisurely buttoned his Levi's, enjoying the flustered look on her flushed face.

Taking a step toward her, he charged, "It was my understanding that you were to be gone for at least two weeks. Was I misinformed?"

Instinctively backing away from him and all that lurking sexuality, Anna said, "No, you were not."

Brit lifted wide bronzed shoulders in a shrug. "Then what are you doing back?"

"I was homesick," she stated emphatically, knowing he'd be annoyed that she called The Regent home.

"Ah, I see. Well, I'm sure LaDextra would have me rush out and kill a fatted calf to welcome you *home*." He shook his dark head thoughtfully and added, "Only problem is, there are no fatted calves on The Regent this year. You see, we're having a little drought in west Texas this summer and—"

"I know that," she snapped. "I'm not stupid."

He advanced a step. She retreated a step.

"No, you're sure not stupid. In fact, I'd say you're a remarkably clever woman. One of the cleverest I've ever known."

Not quite sure how to take that, she said haltingly, "Well…thank you."

"Oh, don't thank me. Thank your momma and your daddy," he said, smiling cynically, "*whoever* they may be."

Immediately defensive, she lifted her chin defiantly and said, "You know very well who my mother and father are and I—"

"Do I?" Again he advanced on her. "Do you?"

"Yes. Yes I do. I *am* Anna Regent Wright and my—"

"I don't think so."

"I don't care."

"You will."

"Don't bet the ranch on it," she said, before she whirled about and stormed away.

He was trapped.

He had promised LaDextra his presence at dinner and he couldn't very well beg off just because Anna would be there, too. Damn her to hell.

Brit finished brushing his freshly shampooed hair, slipped into his navy linen suit jacket, shot his long arms out so that the cuffs of his white shirt showed exactly one inch beyond the jacket sleeves, and headed for the stairs.

His luck was running true to form today. Just as he exited his room, Anna stepped out into the corridor.

"We meet again," he quipped, wishing they hadn't, wishing she didn't look so fresh and lovely in an off-the-shoulder dress of pale yellow chiffon.

"What an unexpected pleasure," she said sarcastically, wondering why she had picked that minute to leave her room, wondering why he had to look so sinfully handsome in a dark navy linen suit and snowy white shirt.

"Shall we?" He offered his arm.

"Let's," she replied, wrapping a hand lightly around his biceps and feeling the muscles tighten at her touch.

Anna, so glad to be home that even Brit's indifference couldn't dampen her high spirits, was lively and charming at dinner. The seriously ill LaDextra, knowing that every fleeting moment counted, was thrilled that Anna had come back early. It gave the dying matriarch genuine pleasure to be able to look across the table at the two people she loved most in all the world.

How beautiful they were, her precious Anna and her cherished Brit. How young and healthy and vigorous. Their lives lay ahead of them, full of promise and challenge. Her weak heart fluttered in her chest. How could she possibly choose one over the other?

Dismissing her troublesome indecision, LaDextra said, "Anna, we want to hear everything about your trip, don't we, Will? Brit?"

Will, who made no bones about the fact that he thought Anna hung the moon, said enthusiastically, "We sure do, honey. Don't leave out anything now, you hear?"

No one noticed, except Anna, that Brit remained silent. She hazarded a glance at him. The frosty expression in his dark eyes assured her that he was not in the least bit interested in hearing of her escapades in the River City. Which promptly made her decide that she would indeed regale them all—including him—with her many adventures.

LaDextra and Will beamed and listened with interest as Anna spun tales of the glittering parties she had attended, one where she had even danced with the governor of Texas. Anna left nothing out.

She reeled off the names of the eligible bachelors who had been thrilled to escort her to the many social functions.

LaDextra asked pointedly, "And did any one of those handsome young men steal your heart?"

Anna smiled enigmatically. "Well...there was one who..." She let her words trail away and laughed girlishly.

LaDextra and Will laughed with her.

Brit did not.

His black eyes now stormy beneath heavily lashed lids, he drained his wineglass and refilled it. Anna continued to entertain and amuse her enraptured audience with vivid descriptions of the soirees she had attended. As she gaily went on and on about the dances and moonlight strolls and carriage rides, Brit found himself growing more and more irritated.

Never one to turn away from the truth, he faced the reason for his building annoyance. He was jealous. He didn't like the idea of her dancing with another man. Or holding hands. Or kissing. Or...or—

Abruptly Brit tossed his napkin on the table and pushed back his chair. Anna stopped speaking in midsentence. She, LaDextra and Will all turned to look at him questioningly.

Unsmiling, he rose to his feet and said, "Please excuse me, I have an engagement in town."

"Why, Brit, honey, you haven't had dessert,"

LaDextra said, frowning. "Maggie Mae baked a blackberry cobbler especially for you."

"Tell her to put a bowl of it aside for me," he said, and exited the dining room without another word.

LaDextra shook her white head. "I swear, I don't know what's gotten into Brit lately. I've never seen him turn down blackberry cobbler." She sighed and was silent for a moment. Then she brightened, turned back to Anna and said, "Now go on with the story. You were with…"

Nodding, Anna picked up where she had left off.

But continuing to talk about the parties, dances and flirtations was no longer enjoyable now that Brit was gone. She had, she realized with despair, desperately hoped to make him jealous with all her talk of eager beaux.

Obviously, it hadn't worked.

Twenty-Eight

The dog days of August dragged listlessly by as a smothering blanket of heat continued to cover the dry, parched land of southwest Texas.

The sleepy little town of Regentville was sleepier than usual. The wooden sidewalks and benches on the plaza were deserted most afternoons.

The heat was too much for Will Davis. He came to his downtown office each morning bright and early, but left at the noon hour, leaving a Closed sign hanging on the door. He would have departed for cooler climes if not for LaDextra. She hadn't much longer to live. He couldn't leave her.

It was so devilishly hot that Sally Horner no longer visited The Regent every day as she had at the beginning of the summer. She hadn't the energy to make the long ride. She missed seeing Anna, but needed to preserve what little energy she had for the long romantic evenings with her always vigorous beau, Buck Shanahan.

So Sally stayed pretty close to home, amusing herself as best she could by watching the comings and goings of her neighbors and townsfolk on the streets below her house. The three-story Horner mansion sat on a gentle rise of land just above Regentville. From her bedroom window, Sally had a bird's-eye view of all activity going on in town.

If and when there was any.

The uncomplaining Dr. McCelland, finding his sweltering square office almost unbearable in the broiling afternoon heat, was more than willing to make house calls. When a young messenger popped in to tell him that Mrs. Beverly Harris was in need of his immediate services, the physician eagerly grabbed his black bag.

Sally was at her bedroom window when the slender young doctor exited his office. Curious as to who might be sick, she watched with interest as Dr. McCelland rushed up the sidewalk heading north, left the plaza, went a block and turned onto Yucca Street.

Sally was still watching, wide-eyed, when, minutes later, Dr. McCellland stood on the porch of the pale yellow Victorian mansion where Beverly Harris lived. He raised his hand, but before he could knock, Beverly opened the door.

His first thought was that she didn't look sick. She looked completely healthy and absolutely beautiful. Her flaming hair was expertly coiffed atop her head, and her full lips were painted a bright scarlet. She wore a stylishly cut afternoon dress of crisp, sky blue piqué, the neckline of which dipped low enough to reveal a generous expanse of her pale, soft bosom. She smiled at him and her eyes were glittering.

The doctor stepped awkwardly inside, cleared his

throat needlessly and said, "I was told you are in need of my services, Mrs. Harris."

"Please, call me Beverly," she said, and immediately began leading him up the stairs.

"Uh...what seems to be the problem, Mrs.—Beverly?"

"It's my heart, Doctor. It's been about to speed right out of my chest all day and I'm so frightened."

His brows immediately knitted. "Sounds like it could be rather serious," he said, solicitously taking her arm in case she was weak and needed his support.

Inside her dim, cool bedroom, where all the heavy curtains were drawn against the blistering Texas sun, Beverly walked straight to the bed, turned about and sat down on its edge, folding her hands in her lap. She arched her back slightly and her breasts swelled against the low-cut blue bodice.

"I'm sure you'll want to listen to my heart," she said.

His skilled physician's hands suddenly gone clammy, Dr. McCelland said, "Yes, it will be necessary to...to..."

He swallowed hard, took the stethoscope from his black bag and, standing above her, cautiously slipped the listening end of the instrument down inside Beverly's dress and pressed it to her bosom.

"Hear anything, Doctor?" she asked, gazing up at him.

He shook his head to silence her, listened intently for several long seconds, moving the stethoscope farther down inside her dress to position it at the underside of her left breast, directly over her heart. Again he listened intently, trying very hard to ignore the soft, warm flesh pressing against his trembling hand.

At last he took the stethoscope away, hung it around his neck and told her in a soft, kind voice, "Perhaps this terrible heat has made you weak and caused you to feel as if your heart is racing." He smiled boyishly at her then and added, "Let me put your fears to rest, Mrs. Harris. There is nothing wrong with your heart."

Beverly wet her scarlet lips, reached up and took hold of both ends of the stethoscope dangling from around his neck. She slowly reeled his face down close to hers and said, "You're mistaken, Doctor. There's something very wrong with my heart."

"No...no, I—I assure you, your heart is just fine."

"No, it isn't. It is hollow, just like me." His eyes widened and he inhaled anxiously when she added, "Fix it for me, Doctor. Fill my empty heart...and me."

Shocked by such bold behavior, Dr. McCelland stammered, "I—I sincerely, ah, wish I could—that I could be of help, but I—"

"You can," she said, and pulled his face closer still, so close that only a couple of inches separated them.

"H-how?" he asked, perspiring nervously now.

"Doctor, do you find me attractive?"

"Well, yes, I...why certainly, you—you're extraordinarily beautiful."

Beverly smiled like the cat that got the cream. Her eyes focused on his mouth, she asked, "Do you ever get lonesome, Doctor?"

"Sometimes," he replied. "Usually I'm too busy to—"

"*I'm* lonely, Doctor." She lifted her eyes to meet his. "*So* lonely."

"I'm sorry, I had no idea that someone like you..." His words trailed away.

"You don't want me to suffer from severe loneliness, do you?"

"Of course not, but I—"

"Kiss me," she cooed. "Please. Kiss me."

Not waiting for him to comply, Beverly lifted her wet, red lips and kissed him soundly.

Then it was *his* heart that raced alarmingly. Knowing how she was affecting him, Beverly drew the stethoscope from around his neck. She put the earpieces into her ears, unbuttoned his shirt, slipped the stethoscope inside, placed it over his heart and listened.

"Oh, my," she said, removing the earpieces, "your heart is fairly thundering in your chest, Doctor. Better sit down here until you've calmed a bit."

Dr. McCelland said nothing, just sank down onto the bed beside Beverly and didn't protest when, again slipping her hand inside his half-open shirt, she spread her fingers on his naked chest and adroitly urged him down onto his back on her soft bed.

"There, isn't that better?" she whispered, and finished unbuttoning his shirt.

By the time Dr. McCelland, totally spent and
smiling foolishly, left Beverly's house, the biting
sting was gone from the heat because the searing
summer sun was sliding toward the western horizon.

Sally Horner, dressed and ready for the evening's
engagement with Buck, took one last glance out her
bedroom window before going downstairs. Her eyes
grew big as saucers.

Dr. McCelland was just now leaving Beverly's
house. He had been there all afternoon! Surely Beverly Harris wasn't *that* ill.

At The Regent, life had slowed just as it had in
town. Anna was so hot and miserable herself, she
naturally supposed that LaDextra's worsening lack
of energy was due to the sweltering summer
weather. LaDextra assured her such was the case.
Still, Anna insisted that the pale, weak LaDextra rest
all afternoon, and to make sure she did, Anna sat
with her. She read to her. She passed on any interesting gossip she could recall. She listened as
LaDextra reminisced about the days when she herself was young and had first come to Texas.

Anna kept the older woman company.

It was a satisfying time for them both. The tired,
aged LaDextra was the indulgent, loving, white-
haired grandmother Anna had never had. The young,
healthy Anna was the spirited, golden-haired granddaughter LaDextra had lost and finally found.

Anna had been back from San Antonio for only
a couple of days when she confided to LaDextra that

Complete Subtotal   16.98

Chilada Chix   8.99
Taco Sal Beef   7.99

Areai Grotto
Reprint #: 1
Guests: 2   30036
Table 281/1   3:49 PM
Server: JONATHAN   06/15/2000

she wanted to start learning—immediately—more about the day-to-day operations of The Regent. At her admission, LaDextra's pale eyes brightened and she quickly agreed that it would be a wise thing to do.

"I know just the man to teach you and—" LaDextra began.

"Not Brit," Anna anxiously interrupted.

"I wasn't going to suggest Brit," LaDextra said. "He's far too busy these days to bother with you."

"Yes, of course," Anna replied.

"No, I was thinking of Cheno Martinez. Cheno's one of the oldest vaqueros on the ranch, but he's still a vigorous man at age seventy-three, and he knows everything there is to know about the workings of the ranch."

Anna brightened. "Do you suppose he'd mind educating me a little?"

"Why, Lord knows, he'll be thrilled to death," LaDextra said with a smile. "Cheno's not only one of the most knowledgeable men on the ranch, he's the most patient, as well."

"Could Cheno start teaching me tomorrow?" Anna asked excitedly. "I could ride with him every morning, except, of course, those days when I'll be going with Dr. McCelland to visit the various division headquarters."

"My, my," said LaDextra, "you're going to be mighty busy, honey."

"Yes," said Anna, hoping she'd be so busy she wouldn't have time to think about Brit more than a thousand times a day.

* * *

At sunup the very next morning, a short, stocky, silver-haired vaquero stepped up to the back fence, smiling sunnily. He was leading a big roan gelding, along with Anna's gentle sorrel mare, Dancer.

When Anna came out of the house, Cheno swept the big straw sombrero from his head and bowed grandly.

She reached him and he greeted her warmly. "Señorita Anna, I am Cheno Martinez."

"So nice to meet you, Cheno," Anna said, extending her hand.

The vaquero took it in his own brown, work-roughened fingers and said, "*La Patrona* has told me you wish to learn more about The Regent."

"Yes, yes I do. I want you to teach me everything you know about this ranch and the way it runs."

"It will be my great pleasure," said Cheno, smiling widely.

Anna smiled back at the portly, sun-wrinkled vaquero and said, "I hope you'll still think it's a pleasure when I've driven you half-loco with my stupid questions."

Cheno threw back his head and laughed heartily, his dark eyes twinkling. "No, no, señorita, ask anything you wish and I will answer as best I can."

Anna nodded and said, "Cheno, you and I are going to be good friends, no?"

Pleased, the old vaquero beamed and replied, "Señorita Anna, we are going to be good friends, yes! Now, are you ready to take a little ride?"

"I can't wait," she replied.

The two rode together each morning thereafter, Cheno taking Anna out on far-reaching excursions of the big spread. As they rode farther and farther from the house, he was often amazed by her ability to correctly identify the various landmark mesas and washes and canyons that cut across the rugged ranchland.

She was, he had no doubt, a true Regent.

He gladly explained to her the need for the four divisions and the many separate pastures that made up The Regent. He was a well of information, and Anna felt she learned a lot from the old vaquero.

Cheno talked fondly of his life on The Regent, said he had been at the ranch for the past fifty-five years. He remembered well the day that the *patrón*, Robert Regent, had brought his bride home to Texas from Kentucky.

Anna loved to listen to the vaquero tell of those early days at the ranch. She encouraged him and he told of how, in the beginning, there had been only a handful of ranch hands, several hundred longhorns and a small two-room house in which the newlywed Regents had lived.

Then Robert Regent had slowly expanded— bought up land surrounding his spread, stocked it with cattle and hired more men—and built for *La Patrona* the big mansion he had promised her.

Cheno was telling about the first blooded cattle to arrive at the ranch when he stopped suddenly and asked, "Can you keep a secret, *señorita?*"

"Try me."

"I should not be disloyal to the good man who

brought me to The Regent, but the truth is the young *patrón,* Brit, is a much better rancher and business-man than Robert Regent ever was.''

At the mention of Brit's name, Anna stiffened. But the vaquero never noticed, and he began to speak affectionately about the capable man who he remembered as a sullen, suspicious twelve-year-old boy, and of all the trouble *La Patrona* had had with the orphaned, rebellious Brit.

"He wasn't really a bad boy, but he felt that he was in the way, that nobody wanted him and he didn't belong here.''

Anna said, "I know the feeling well.''

Cheno went on as if she hadn't spoken. "Finally *La Patrona* convinced Brit that she loved and wanted him, that The Regent was his home for as long he wanted to stay.''

"That was very kind of LaDextra," Anna coolly commented.

"It was, and Brit has repaid that kindness. As he matured, he became a very responsible, hardworking man. And so smart. *Muy inteligente.* So, four years ago *La Patrona* made him the general manager of the entire Regent, the boss over all bosses.'' Cheno shook his head as he added, "She loves Brit like a son.''

"Yes, I know.''

"Brit, he is a good boss. First thing he did when he took over was gather a few trusted advisors and draft a code of rules for the ranch. The first rule is that the abuse of horses, mules or cattle by a cow-hand will not be tolerated on The Regent. Brit made it clear that if any man strikes a horse or in any way abuses the creature while in his charge, the offender will be immediately dismissed."

"Has he ever actually dismissed anyone?"

Cheno shook his silver head and smiled. "Never had to. Brit possesses that—how you say—mysterious quality that makes people want to please him."

"Really?" Anna managed to ask, then gritted her teeth. Cheno spoke the truth. Everyone, it seemed, wanted to please Brit Caruth. The servants adored him, his men respected him, LaDextra loved him to death. Even Anna, knowing full well that he meant to have her exiled from The Regent, had wanted to please him so badly she had fallen right into his arms.

"...And to insure the suitable functioning of this vast enterprise," Cheno was saying, "Brit demands regular reports from his division foremen." The vaquero thought for a minute, then continued, "I tell you, *señorita*, the livestock affairs of this gigantic ranch are so, um, complex they demand Brit's constant care."

"I'm sure that's true. What are the biggest concerns?"

"Always there are the pressing problems of adequate pasturage, water, herd handling and control. And with this long terrible drought..." Cheno paused, drew a breath and said, "Brit has the weight of the world on his shoulders."

Eager to get off the subject of Brit, Anna said, "Tell me more about the roundups."

The somber vaquero brightened as he began to

talk about his favorite of all ranch tasks, the spring and fall roundups. He told her that the last roundup had been in April—right before she had come back home. He said that on roundups the cowhands each had twelve to fifteen horses—circle horses, cutting horses, roping horses and night horses. He talked for the next half hour about the hard work and satisfying rewards of a roundup, explaining exactly what happened from the time they began herding the cattle out of the many distant pastures until the day the beef were shipped to market.

When Cheno had imparted every detail he could think of, the two of them were far, far away from the house, out on the eastern boundaries of the ranch.

"*Señorita,* look there!" Cheno drew rein and pointed at a trio of riders in the near distance. "Is the *patrón.*"

Anna squinted. Sure enough, there was Brit astride his stallion, Captain, surrounded by a bawling herd of Hereford cattle.

Cheno said, "Ah, I know what they are doing now." He turned in the saddle and looked at Anna. "This is something to see, *señorita.* A bull has gotten in with the cattle. Brit and the others are going to cut it out of the herd and get it out of here. Is dangerous work. That's a mean Spanish bull and he can hurt a horse badly."

Anna nodded, then watched as Brit, controlling his mount with his knees, sailed a lasso up over his head, whirled it several times, then threw it. He didn't rope the bull. He roped a large thorny cactus, pulled it with the rope until it came out of the ground. He drew the cactus up, got hold of it by the roots and slung it at the bull's back. The prickly cactus hit its target squarely. The angered bull made a lane right through the herd of cattle, scattering them. A cowhand waited at the open pasture gate to shoo the snorting beast out.

Cheno laughed and applauded.

"Shh," Anna cautioned, not wanting Brit to know that she was here watching him. "Let's go, Cheno," she said, and turned her mare away.

The vaquero followed.

Knowing that she had been there all along, Brit finally turned tortured eyes in her direction and watched her ride away. She was bouncing slightly in the saddle, her small waist and flaring hips accentuated by her tight-fitting riding britches, her long golden hair spilling from under her hat.

Brit felt his chest tighten.

God, how he wanted her gone.

God, how he *wanted* her.

Twenty-Nine

The torpid, torrid month of August had finally taken its last dying gasp. The horrible heat, however, remained.

On Monday, the first day of September, Anna was to accompany Dr. McCelland out to the Texas Star, The Regent's western division headquarters. Located far out on the lowland deserts of the sprawling rangelands, the Texas Star was a good eight mile ride from the ranch's foothills mansion.

Since that was the case, it was an irritated Anna who paced back and forth on the front gallery, wondering what was keeping Dr. McCelland. She had been pacing off and on all morning. It was now nearing noon and she was pacing again. The doctor had promised he'd be here no later than 9:00 a.m. It wasn't like him to be late.

Finally Anna spotted a plume of dust on the southern horizon. She exhaled heavily and exclaimed aloud, "It's about time!"

In minutes Dr. McCelland, riding his black-and-white paint gelding, galloped into view. Hands on her trousered hips, Anna was waiting for him on the steps as he dismounted and hurried up the front walk.

"Thank heaven you're here at last," she called out. "I had about given up on you."

The physician reached the gallery steps. "I am sorry, Anna. I got, ah, tied up and I just couldn't break away."

Anna was immediately contrite. "Oh, then I'm the one who should apologize. Has someone in town fallen seriously ill and…?" Anna stopped speaking. She studied the doctor's face, which was rapidly turning red under her close scrutiny. Immediately she sensed that it wasn't a sick patient that had made him so late. Her intuition told her it was something much more exciting.

Anna tilted her head to one side, began to smile and said, "Tell me, Doctor, exactly what, or should I say who, held you up?"

Dr. McCelland's red face grew redder still. He didn't dare admit to the real reason for his tardiness. He couldn't tell Anna—or anyone—that he hadn't been delayed by a seriously ill patient, but by an incredibly healthy woman who had held him willing prisoner in her luxurious bedroom until she was finally sated and had fallen asleep.

The doctor said, "Anna, there's no time for explanations, we're way behind schedule."

"So I noticed," Anna teased, and followed him into the house.

She noticed something else, as well. Although the doctor looked haggard, as if he hadn't had enough sleep, he appeared to be strangely serene. Pleased with himself and his world. So content he couldn't hide it.

And when she followed him down the hall to LaDextra's sitting room, she detected a new spring to his step, a prouder set to his shoulders, a strong sense of command that hadn't been there before.

Anna puzzled over the startling change in this good friend who no longer seemed to be so shy, so boyish. There was about him the appearance and carriage of a totally confident man. What, she wondered, had brought about this amazing transformation? She could hardly wait to talk to Sally. If anyone knew what was going on, it would be Sally.

At LaDextra's door, Dr. McCelland stopped and said, "Wait for me here, Anna. I won't be long."

"I most certainly will not," she replied, shaking her head. "I'm going in with you and—"

"No," he stated decisively, "you are not."

Anna blinked in surprise. He had never spoken to her like that. He calmly continued, "LaDextra is my patient. Privacy between patient and physician is absolutely necessary."

Anna frowned, confused. "But you let me assist you with your patients when we're at one of the division headquarters."

"Yes, I do. But we are not at one of the division headquarters now," the doctor pointed out. "So let me repeat, you are to wait right here."

He gave her no chance to respond. He stepped inside LaDextra's sitting room and closed the door firmly behind him.

"How are you feeling this morning, LaDextra?" he asked in a soft, caring voice, crossing to the seated woman.

The white-haired Regent matriarch looked up at him with dull eyes and admitted, "Doctor, I'm not going to lie to you. I feel really awful. Not fit for nothing. Totally useless."

He was already getting his stethoscope out of his bag. "Are you having chest pains again?"

"No, those pills you gave me have helped control the pain. It's just that I am so tired and worthless all the time. I can hardly sit up in this chair."

He nodded, placed the stethoscope to her heart. For several long seconds Dr. McCelland listened to the aging heart that clearly would not—could not—beat much longer. When he withdrew the stethoscope, he patted LaDextra's age-spotted hand.

"Don't sugarcoat it for me, Doctor," she said, managing a faint smile. "Tell me the truth. I'm not going to last much longer at all, am I?"

"No, LaDextra, you're not," he said, his expression somber. "Time is rapidly running out, I'm afraid." He paused, cleared his throat and said, "Are you ready now to let Anna and Brit know that—"

"Not on your life!" LaDextra said with as much force as she could muster. "Surely I've got a couple of weeks left." She lifted white eyebrows questioningly. "Haven't I?"

"I hope so."

"Well, I need just a little more time to make up my mind about something." She didn't tell the physician that she was still struggling to reach a decision regarding the contents of her last will and testament.

"Don't wait too long," he advised. Then he murmured, "I could make an excuse to Anna, tell her I don't need her to go with me to the Texas Star. Leave her here to keep you company."

"Don't do that," said LaDextra. "She's been looking forward to going." The aged woman again smiled and added, "Besides, I don't plan on dying today."

Dr. McCelland smiled back at her. "It may be quite late when we get back this evening."

"That's fine," said LaDextra. "Don't worry about it. If it's too late when you finish up out there, just spend the night with the division boss and his wife."

The doctor picked up his black bag. "I hope an overnight won't be necessary, but I'm told that several children on the Texas Star have come down with chills and fever so..." He lifted his shoulders in a shrug.

"Do what you have to do, Doctor. If the two of you don't get back tonight, I'll know where you are."

"Very well," he said. "You get some rest."

"I will."

He hastily crossed the room, but LaDextra stopped him before he could open the door. "By the way, Doc..." she began, and he turned around. He saw that her dulled eyes were now twinkling mischievously. She pursed her lips, then said, "Who is she?"

"I beg your pardon?"

"Who's the lucky woman that kept you up all night?"

Dr. McCelland blushed, but didn't deny it. "How did you know?"

"Actually, I didn't," she said, eyes really flashing now. "You just told me."

"So I did," he said, and grinned. "I'm sorry it made me late and—"

"Don't be," she interrupted. "I've a feeling it was worth it."

"Yes," he confessed, "it certainly was."

"Good!"

"LaDextra Regent, you're a very kind lady," he said, grateful to her for being understanding.

"Not kind," she corrected, "but wise, perhaps. Wise enough to know that you better grab all the happiness you can get wherever and whenever you can." Her blue eyes clouded slightly then, and she added, "Because it all goes by—" she snapped her fingers "—just like that."

On the long, hot ride out to the Texas Star, Anna finally figured out what had caused such a change in Dr. McCelland. The two of them talked little as they galloped across the barren deserts under a high white sun, but each time Anna cast a quick glance at the doctor from under her lowered hat brim, she caught him sighing with seeming satisfaction. Or blushing at some vivid memory. Or simply grinning foolishly.

It took her a while to figure it out, then all at once it dawned on her.

Dr. McCelland was behaving exactly as she had behaved the morning after Brit had made love to her! How well she remembered awakening with a warm, wonderful feeling of incredible well-being. She had lingered in bed for a few precious moments of sweet contentment, sighing and smiling and stretching and blushing at the recollection of their wildly intimate lovemaking. How unbelievably happy she had been from the time she had opened her eyes until that horrible moment when she had stepped inside the dining room and had had her dreams—and her heart—so callously stepped on.

Anna glanced back at the doctor. He was grinning again, unable or unwilling to hide his sheer delight. Apparently he was more fortunate than she. His lover hadn't tired of him as soon as they had surrendered to desire. Anna was glad. Happy for him. And happy, as well, for the woman who had captured this kind man's heart.

The hot, perspiring pair reached the Texas Star shortly before one o'clock. There was no time to rest for a few minutes and cool off. At the salmon-hued adobe division headquarters, dozens of sick, feverish children awaited them, many crying, all needing immediate attention.

The pair worked tirelessly side by side throughout the long, scalding afternoon, caring for their patients and calming the worried mothers. Dr. McCelland diagnosed the illness as a mild strain of influenza that had spread quickly among the children.

Dispensing aspirin and instructing the mothers to

put their sick children to bed and give them plenty of fluids, the doctor was unruffled and tolerant. His calm demeanor and sympathetic manner worked like a soothing balm on both crying children and anxious parents.

When finally, late that afternoon, every single child had been seen, treated and sent home to bed, one young Mexican boy remained.

Anna and the doctor spotted the child at the same time. He stood against a wall, waiting patiently, his short arms crossed over his narrow chest. Doctor McCelland recognized twelve-year-old Miguel Hernandez. He crossed to the boy and placed gentle hands atop Miguel's slim shoulders.

"Miguel," the doctor said, "you were so quiet, we missed you. Are you sick, too?" He moved a hand up to the boy's smooth forehead, ruffling his dark hair.

"No, I am well," said Miguel, brushing the doctor's hand aside. "It is my brothers and sisters," he explained. "All have the coughing fever. Very sick. My *madre* says they are too sick to come here. She ask can you come to them?"

"Well, of course I can," said Dr. McCelland. "Right away."

"Gracias," Miguel said, bobbing his head as he started to turn away.

"Wait." The doctor caught his arm, drew him back. "Did you walk here?"

"Sí."

Dr. McCelland smiled, patted the child's head, turned to Anna and said, "His home is four miles from here.'' Then to Miguel, he added, ''You can ride with me.''

''*Gracias.*''

The sun was westering when Anna, Dr. Mc-Celland and Miguel reached the remote little house where the Hernandez family lived. The hot, trying day had left Anna extremely exhausted. Her back ached and her head throbbed from the punishing sun.

She glanced at her companion and was amazed to see that Dr. McCelland was still smiling to himself. Behind him, Miguel Hernandez dozed, his dark head resting on the doctor's back.

Thirty

Anna's fatigue lifted as soon as they entered the small, three-room home where a half-dozen children lay sick and miserable. Their distressed mother, a tiny, slender woman who had been anxiously tending her feverish brood, thanked them both for coming. Tears of relief filled her large, dark eyes and she immediately ushered them into a small, hot bedroom where three young girls lay shivering on a single bed.

To her son Miguel she said, "Where are your manners, Miguel? Go get some water for the doctor and the *señorita*." To them, she said, "You must be thirsty, no?"

Dr. McCelland examined the three sisters, then covered them up again, carefully tucking the thin blanket around their shoulders.

To their hovering mother, Consuela Hernandez, he said, "Your children have influenza, as do many of the children on the Texas Star. They will be fine, so stop worrying. I have given each girl an aspirin." He held up a half-full bottle of the white tablets and added, "I'll give the boys their aspirins and then I'll leave the bottle here. You are to give them all another aspirin in four hours, and every four hours thereafter. That should bring down their fever and give them some relief from the muscle aches.''

"Gracias, gracias," she said, nodding and following them out of the room.

In the only other bedroom, three sick boys lay on pallets. While the doctor examined them, Anna doled out the aspirin, kneeling beside each child, helping to lift his head so he could take a drink to make the pills go down. Her task finished, she turned away, handed Consuela the aspirin bottle. Clutching it to her breasts, the grateful mother left the room praising God and them in rapid Spanish.

After Consuela had gone, Anna heard someone singing nearby. It was a male voice, singing softly in Spanish. Curious, she moved across the room to a pair of windows that opened onto a small back porch. She pushed back the curtains and looked out.

And she began to smile. An old rocking chair, its back to her, sat at the far edge of the wooden porch. In the rocker a man with midnight hair was holding a tiny little boy in his arms, gently rocking the child, singing to him softly in Spanish.

Anna was deeply touched.

When the physician concluded his examinations, she whispered to him, ''Come look, Doctor.'' He crossed to her and glanced outside. ''Isn't that sweet?'' she said. ''A loving father rocking his sick son and singing to him.''

Dr. McCelland said matter-of-factly, ''The Hernandez children have no father, Anna.'' Her head snapped around and she stared up at him. He explained, ''Raul Hernandez was killed in a riding accident on an autumn roundup a few years ago. It was shortly after Arto—the four-year-old you see being rocked—was born."

"Then who is...?" She stopped speaking. Her breath grew short. Her pulse quickened.

The doctor smiled. "Go out and see."

Without another word, Anna exited the bedroom, crossed the spartan sitting room and stepped quietly out onto the back porch. She did not make her presence known. In silence she stood directly behind the man and boy in the slowly moving rocker. Watching. Listening.

Her heart began to pound. She trembled in the late afternoon heat. The low baritone voice, the noble head, the broad shoulders, all were disturbingly familiar.

Brit Caruth, with the tiny boy cradled in his muscular arms, sat rocking to and fro, singing to the child, comforting him, caring for him as if he were his own son.

Anna bit her lip. She was suddenly overcome with emotion. She had the strong desire to cry and she didn't know why. Tears stung her eyes and she blinked them back. But an aching tightness continued to squeeze her chest painfully.

There at that modest little house far out on the barren Texas Star, Anna saw a side to Brit Caruth that had never been in evidence before. He had a tender heart. He would make an excellent father. Her own heart hurt as she envisioned him holding his son.

Her son.

Their son.

Clamping her jaws tight and making her mouth hard in an attempt to conceal her feelings, Anna quietly turned away.

Back inside, Consuela Hernandez asked, "You saw the *patrón* rocking my baby?"

"Yes, yes I did."

Consuela smiled and exclaimed, "The *patrón*, he is nice man, good man. So kind to me and the children. He visits us, brings the children food and presents. When he heard they were sick, he came right away. Pronto." She looked past Anna, and her smile widened. "Ah, there he is now."

Brit walked inside, the tiny boy in his arms now sleeping peacefully. Nodding to Anna, he carefully handed the child to Consuela, who carried him into the bedroom.

For a long awkward moment Anna and Brit were silent. Then he said, "You look tired."

"A little," she admitted.

"It's getting late. Too late for you and Dr. McCelland to ride back tonight."

Anna was quick to protest. "No, not really. We can—"

"You heard me," said Brit. "You will spend the night at Jim and Tessie Martin's place. Jim's the Texas Star division boss. They have a big house with a lot of empty space. They'll be expecting you."

With that he stepped around her, bid a quick farewell to Consuela Hernandez and left.

* * *

Not a half hour later, as the burning sun completely disappeared behind the western mountain range, leaving only a bright orange glow in the September sky, Anna and Dr. McCelland rode up to the rambling ranch house where Jim and Tessie Martin lived.

Anna had barely dismounted before the front door flew open and a big, barrel-chested man with sandy hair and a wide, toothy smile, followed by a pleasant-looking dark-haired woman, stepped out onto the front patio.

The friendly Martins warmly greeted their arriving guests. Introductions were made and hands were firmly shaken.

"Now you two come on inside," said Tessie Martin. "I've got a big ole supper cooked for you. You hungry? You better be."

"Welcome to the Texas Star," boomed big Jim Martin, slapping Dr. McCelland on the back. "We're always glad to have company. Gets mighty lonesome around here since all our kids grew up and left."

Inside, Tessie Martin directed the pair to their respective guest rooms and said, "Now, y'all get washed up and come on into the dining room." She chuckled then, and added, "I don't know how much longer I can keep Brit out of the ham and potato salad."

"Brit's here?" Anna blurted out.

"Sitting at the table, hungry as a bear," said Tessie with a laugh.

Anna smiled weakly. "We'll be right there."

* * *

Anna attempted to keep her eyes off Brit during dinner. It wasn't easy. He sat directly across from her and it seemed that he had never been more ruggedly handsome, more genuinely charming. He was, if anything, more appealing than ever now that she'd seen him gently rocking little Arto Hernandez.

It was evident that both Martins were immensely fond of Brit and that their relationship was more that of good friends than of employer and employees.

Brit, Anna realized, never treated his division bosses or any of the cowboys and vaqueros as anything other than equals. Which was a definite talent and largely responsible for his running the big cattle empire so successfully.

Big Jim Martin poured another splash of madeira into Anna's stemmed wineglass and said, "Drink up, Anna. It'll make you sleep like a baby. Right, Tess?"

His wife made a face, as if disgusted with him. But she was smiling when she said, "If that were the case, you'd never stay awake past nine."

The meal progressed pleasantly enough, and afterward Anna helped Tessie with the dishes. When the final dish had been dried and put away, Anna said to the small woman, "Think I'll step outside for a minute. You don't mind, do you?"

"Go on. It's so peaceful and pretty out here in the evening," said Tessie, "and there's a full moon tonight."

Anna went out onto the Martin's back porch, descended the steps and walked out to the very back edge of the big yard. A full white moon was already beginning to rise from behind the towering Guadalupe Mountains.

Enchanted, Anna stood there in the fading twilight with her arms folded over her chest, enjoying the quiet, majestic beauty surrounding her.

When Brit walked out into the yard and came to stand beside her, it seemed somehow completely natural. There was no need to turn and acknowledge him. She knew that he knew she was vitally aware of his presence. Neither spoke. In companionable silence the two of them stood side by side and watched the huge harvest moon slowly rise above the soaring mountain range.

Before them, floating across the empty, darkening sky, a golden eagle leisurely winged its way toward its mountain nest. Red-tailed hawks rode the mountain thermals below *El Capitán* Peak. And, silhouetted against the evening sky, an imperial mountain lion took a regal stance on a lofty peak. It seemed that nature itself wished to please the pair.

They were pleased, and neither wanted the interlude to end. Both felt somehow that if they didn't speak, didn't say a word, that the other wouldn't turn away and leave. Would stay to share the magic of the night, the beauty of the savage land.

Not daring even to let himself so much as look at her, Brit wondered what Anna would say if he admitted that he had followed her outside because he was helpless to do otherwise.

Her eyes fastened on the rising moon, Anna wondered what Brit would he think if he knew that she was fighting hard to resist the strong urge to touch him.

While they stood there watching the spectacular moonrise, Anna was struck with the sad realization that her time with Brit was short—that this time next year, or perhaps even this time next month, he wouldn't be here.

Or she wouldn't.

For Brit the strain suddenly seemed to become unbearable. He had to speak to her, to have her acknowledge that he was here and that it was okay with her.

He said softly, in a low, drawling voice, "The full moon striking the top of *El Capitán* Peak is really something to see, isn't it?"

"It is," Anna replied, nodding. Then she stunned Brit by adding, "Now in just a minute…one more minute…it's almost there…yes…yes, there it is! The moon's starting to touch the top of Washboard Peak."

Brit turned and looked at her hard. Anna felt his eyes on her and stiffened, wondering what she had done wrong.

Uneasy, she said, "Good night, Brit," turned and hurried away.

Brit swallowed hard.

Washboard Peak. That's what she'd said. That's what she had called the jutting rise of rock just below and a little west of *El Capitán*. LaDextra had told him, many times, that when Anna was just six years old she had looked up at the strangely configured spire of rock with deep ledges cut across its face and declared it looked just like a giant washboard.

Nobody else called it Washboard Peak. To everyone but Anna it was known as Cathedral Peak.

Brit felt a shudder ripple through his tall frame. Could it be that she really was Anna?

Thirty-One

"No!"

"Yes!"

"Dr. McCelland and Beverly Harris?" Anna said, incredulous. "I can't believe it!"

"Well, believe it," said Sally Horner, "because it's the gospel truth."

The two friends were out in the shaded grape arbor on a blistering Saturday morning. Sally had come to spend the day at The Regent for the first time in weeks. She had just arrived and was full of gossip to share with Anna. The best—and most shocking—being the news that the good doctor and the red-haired widow were the talk of the town.

"But they are so…mismatched," Anna said, unable to envision the two of them together.

"Apparently they aren't," said Sally with a meaningful look. "I know for a fact that every free minute the doctor has is spent at Beverly's house."

"Really?" Curious, Anna asked, "Do you suppose they…that is…do you think that the two of them are…?"

"Intimate? That the word you're looking for? You bet your boots they are," Sally stated emphatically. "I've seen the doctor leaving her place in the wee small hours of the morning. Besides, haven't you noticed how different he is?''

"Yes," Anna admitted. "I have. I noticed it this past Monday when I went with him out to the Texas Star. He couldn't quit smiling and I knew then that something was up." She sighed, shook her head worriedly. "But Beverly Harris? Poor Dr. McCelland." Her delicate jaw tightened and she added, "She seduced him, I know she did."

"So what?" said the practical-minded Sally. "She did him a big favor, if you ask me."

"You don't mean that," Anna said.

"Oh, yes I do," Sally replied. "I like Dr. McCelland. But he's always been painfully shy and therefore needs an aggressive woman. If Beverly Harris has made him a happier man, then I'm all for it."

"I know, Sally, but think how miserable he'll be when she tires of him."

"Looks like that isn't going to happen," said Sally slyly.

"What do you mean?"

"Word has it that the two of them are unofficially engaged."

Anna's lips fell open. "They are going to get married?"

"Yes, indeed."

Anna felt a quick rush of excitement at the news. But she tried to sound nonchalant when she said, "But I thought Beverly was—was..." She stopped talking, shrugged slender shoulders.

"Brit's woman?" Sally finished for her. "Nope. Not since the Fourth of July."

Anna's heart kicked against her ribs. "What do you mean?"

"Exactly what I said. Buck told me that Brit lost interest in Beverly sometime back in June, and that as far as he knows Brit hasn't been with her—or anyone else—since July 4." Sally then tilted her head, peered thoughtfully at Anna. "Know anything about that?"

"No," Anna said, but she was secretly overjoyed to hear that Brit had not been with another woman since he had made love to her.

"I don't believe you," Sally said.

"What?" Anna said, distracted, her thoughts on Brit.

"I said I don't believe you. I think something happened between you and Brit that Fourth of July night when you both disappeared for hours." Sally paused, waiting for Anna to say something. When she didn't, Sally added, "I think you are madly in love with Brit Caruth and just won't admit it."

Anna was silent for a long moment, then mused aloud, "Any woman would be a fool to love Brit."

"Not if she's the right woman," Sally said, pushing a wayward lock of red hair out of her eyes. A hot wind had blown up from out of the west, rustling the vines covering the grape arbor and irritating Sally. "Dang these west Texas winds," she complained. "Guess it's going to blow all day like it did yesterday."

"I wouldn't doubt it," Anna agreed. "Come on, let's go inside."

The pair headed to the house as the winds grew stronger, catching their full skirts and blowing them out like bells around them. They squealed as they made a mad dash across the dying lawn, past the wishing well and up onto the back gallery. Inside, they rubbed their watering eyes and smoothed their wind-tossed hair.

Except for a half hour at noon when they joined LaDextra for lunch in the dining room, the two friends spent the day upstairs in Anna's room, gossiping, listening to music and cursing the rising winds that sighed and moaned and rattled the windowpanes.

At midafternoon, Sally glanced at the clock on the mantel, made a face, quickly levered herself up off the bed and said, "Good Lord, it's past four o'clock. I have to go. Buck's coming for dinner tonight."

Rising, Anna said, "It's really getting serious between you two, isn't it?"

"Grave," Sally quipped, deadpan. Then she laughed heartily and said, "Buck doesn't know it yet, but he's going to marry me."

It finally happened.

The telegram that Brit had been anxiously looking forward to receiving arrived later that same windy September afternoon.

Brit had just ridden in from three days down on the border at the *Agua Fría* division headquarters.

Still dirty with trail dust and sweat, he had stopped by his office to check the mail.

He was seated behind his desk when the Western Union messenger arrived. Brit heard the hoofbeats, glanced out the French doors and saw a rider galloping up the long drive. He watched as the rider reached the front gate and he recognized cotton-haired Corky Stewart, a youth that Dub at the Western Union office frequently used to deliver telegrams.

Brit felt his heart slam against his ribs. He licked his dry lips and swallowed with difficulty. His first inclination was to jump up out of his chair and go rushing out to meet Corky. He made himself stay where he was. Nervously he waited as Corky dismounted, came jogging up the front walk and knocked on the door.

Brit heard Connie, LaDextra's personal maid, say to one of the other servants, "That's okay. I'll get it."

Seconds later Connie knocked on his office door, then entered bearing a small silver tray. She crossed to him and held out the tray. On it lay the telltale yellow envelope. Brit picked it up. Connie continued to stand there looking at him and at the telegram.

"Thank you, Connie," Brit said, dismissing her. "That will be all." Clearly curious, she reluctantly turned away. "Please close the door behind you," he requested, and heard her sniff indignantly.

Alone again, he withdrew a silver letter opener from its holder and neatly sliced the top flap of the envelope. He replaced the opener and took out the

folded message. He laid the envelope aside and unfolded the yellow telegram.

He drew a quick, shallow breath and began to
read:

Saturday, September 6, 1890

Mr. Brit Caruth,
Your suspicions have been confirmed. The
young woman claiming to be Anna Regent
Wright is in fact an Arizona woman named
Margaret Sue Howard. Miss Howard was cap-
tured...

Brit read the entire message from the Pinkerton
Detective Agency. Then he read it again. He carefully refolded the telegram. He put it inside the
breast pocket of his soiled blue chambray shirt. Then
he folded his hands atop his desk and stared off into
space.

Here, at last, was the proof he'd been waiting for.
He'd been right all along. This beautiful woman
claiming to be Anna was indeed an imposter. Time
for celebrating. Or it should have been.

But, oddly, he felt no satisfaction.

Brit exhaled heavily and closed his eyes.

His eyes quickly opened and he looked up when
Buck Shanahan abruptly burst into the office, saying
excitedly, "It's happened, Brit. Fire on the *Tierra
Verde!*"

The telegram resting against his heart instantly
forgotten, Brit shot to his feet.

"Oh, Jesus," he swore as he strapped on his gun

belt and took a sharp-bladed hunting knife from the bottom desk drawer. His mind was racing. The only water left on the ranch was Manzanita Springs and the springs were surrounded by solid rock. The water couldn't be channeled down to the fire and it was too far away for a bucket brigade. Brit rushed out of the house with Buck close on his heels. Cowhands, interrupting their free Saturday afternoon, were already gathering at the stables, saddling their mounts.

Brit shouted instructions. "Slim, take a dozen men, ride up to the mountain tract. Round up twenty or thirty head and bring them on down."

"On my way, Brit," said Slim.

Brit turned his attention to the old silver-haired vaquero, Cheno. "Cheno, you'll drive the hack with a barrel of water. And load it down with feed sacks, brooms and saddle blankets. Get three or four men to help you. See to it that every feed sack and blanket on the place is wetted down and ready for the firefighters!"

"*Sí, Patrón,*" said Cheno, already turning away to do Brit's bidding.

Brit quickly pivoted, addressed a tall, bowlegged cowboy with a cigarette dangling from his lips, one of the best horsemen in the desert southwest. "Jake, I'm depending on you to corral the remuda once we've reached the fire. Keep the horses out of harm's way and have fresh mounts ready when we need them."

"Count on it, Boss."

"Jaurez," Brit shouted, "you and your brother,

Juan, take some of the boys and get a back fire going to protect the house."

"*Sí, Patrón.*"

Already climbing into the saddle, Brit shouted, "The rest of you men, mount up and follow me."

Anna and LaDextra had heard the commotion and had come out onto the front gallery. They saw the thick black smoke far to the south and bright orange flames shooting skyward.

"Dear Lord in heaven," exclaimed a horrified LaDextra, "it's heading this way. If they can't put the fire out, the house will go up."

Anna squeezed the older woman's hand reassuringly. "Surely they'll be able to put it out quickly."

LaDextra said, "You're forgetting, child, they have no water. How can you fight that kind of blaze without water?"

Anna had no answer.

The two women watched as Brit and the men galloped away, heading directly toward the growing inferno. LaDextra wondered what had happened. Had a careless cowhand flicked a cigarette away despite all Brit's warnings? No, none of the men were that foolish. Most likely a bolt of heat lightning had struck the *Tierra Verde* pasture. The dead, dry grass had quickly caught and the flames, pushed by the dry, hot wind from out of the west, were now rapidly roaring northward.

Straight toward the house.

Thirty-Two

In minutes Brit and his men reached the roaring fire, dismounted and began to fight the blaze. But they had little ammunition to use against the rapidly spreading inferno. All the water tanks on and surrounding the *Tierra Verde* were nearly dry, most without an ounce of water.

Side by side, Brit and Buck beat at the raging flames with dampened saddle blankets, but knew they were making little or no progress. Fueled by the strawlike dead grass and whipped by the strong west winds, the fire was already becoming a fearsome, encompassing monster.

The wind was so high the blaze had jumped the fireguards as if they were not there. There was nothing to break the sweep of the roaring, raging flames. The awesome fire was quickly exploding into a holocaust that could burn thousands of acres, as well as any man, animal or structure that stood in its way.

With heat scorching their faces and thick clouds of smoke choking them, the cowhands beat at the flames with sacks, saddle blankets, brooms and chaps. It was simply an exercise in futility as they waited for the horses and cattle to be brought down.

Jake and his wranglers soon arrived with thirty or

forty nervous, snorting saddle horses. Minutes later Slim showed up, herding thirty head of prime cattle and a couple of big Spanish bulls.

Brit looked around.

He now had enough men, horses and cattle.

He threw down his blanket and drew his pistol. He was glad that Slim had thought to bring a couple of bulls. They were much bigger than the cattle, and the heavier the carcass, the better the job.

Brit took aim and fired.

The first shot rang out above the roaring den and one of the huge Spanish bulls sagged to its knees, dead. Brit fired a second shot. The other bull keeled over.

Brit holstered his still-smoking revolver, hurried to the first fallen bull, even as Buck went to the other. Knives drawn, they swiftly split the dead bulls open down the middle so there'd be plenty of fresh blood, then turned them flesh side down. Both men swiftly mounted dancing saddle ponies that Jake had brought forward. Then they waited impatiently in the saddle as the men tied the dead bulls together side by side in order to cover a wider space.

With one rope tied to Brit's saddle horn, another to Buck's, the pair dug their heels in the horses' bellies and dragged the bulls down the fire line. Behind them shots rang out as the rest of the cattle were being slaughtered. Other mounted cowboys dragging bleeding carcasses would follow Brit and Buck on the line.

Dragging the heavy cattle was harder work for the horses than for the men. Because of the rapid speed of the fire, the horses had to lope while they dragged their heavy cargo. The thick smoke exhausted them quickly, so the cowhands had to change horses every half mile or so.

All the men knew that if they rode a horse too long over the burning grass, its hooves would be ruined. A horse with burned hooves took a year to heal. So Jake kept fresh horses saddled and ready to put into the line.

Working together like a well-oiled machine, the cowboys and vaqueros spaced themselves out to fight the little tongues of flame still ablaze after a drag had gone by. They had to run to keep up, so a new man was dropped every hundred yards for just that purpose.

He'd leave his horse where he started for the man fighting the fire to pick up and bring back to the main fire, there to drop out again when his turn came.

With amazing precision, the well-trained Regent cowboys soon had the drag line running smoothly. Every man was riding a horse and taking time about, dragging the cows, dropping out again to fight the remaining spots of fire when his time came.

While Brit and his bunch fought the lead fire, Juarez and Juan Valdez were busy setting back fires at the northern edge of the pasture in a valiant attempt to protect the mansion.

Up at the house, Anna heard the gunshots, jumped and turned questioning eyes on LaDextra.

"Brit's doing what has to be done, Anna." And the Regent matriarch explained the necessity of slaughtering the cattle.

The two women watched in growing horror as the inferno continued to blaze despite the unflagging efforts of the cowboys on the drag line. Wind driven, the flames were moving ever closer to the house.

"Oh, Robert, Robert!" LaDextra addressed her long-dead husband, wringing her hands. "Looks like the fire's going to get this beautiful home you built for me."

"That's not going to happen," Anna soothed, but she, too, was afraid the spreading fire would engulf the stately mansion. She had to keep her wits about her in case they needed to flee quickly.

Down at the lead fire, Brit felt a growing sense of frustration and despair. Night had fallen, but the wind continued to blow. His eyes watering, throat raw, he watched helplessly as the strong west wind whipped around and checked its speed, almost stopping at times, like a whirlwind, only to blaze up again, higher and hotter.

Brit's main concern was for the house. He knew how much that big old white mansion meant to LaDextra. They had to save it for her.

By ten o'clock that night the firefighters were out of cattle carcasses and out of fresh horses. Exhausted, hot and thirsty, the men again took up their dampened feed sacks and saddle blankets. Beating wildly at the flames, Brit and Buck advanced aggressively forward, followed by a half-dozen cowboys.

It was Brit who first realized that they had maneuvered themselves into a dangerous position. Behind them the blaze had caught again. And spread.

Ahead there was a wide wall of flames, shooting a hundred feet into the night sky. In every direction was fire. Hot, breath-stealing fire. Racing, deadly fire.

"God almighty," said Jake, back at the north edge of the fire with his tired remuda, "Brit and his boys are cut off."

"Looks that way," said Slim, shaking his head.

"Madre de Dios," murmured old Cheno, and crossed himself.

"Look, LaDextra." Anna pointed to the line of fire, which had not moved northward in the past half hour. "The back blaze the men set has stopped the forward march of the main fire. I'm sure the house is safe. You're not going to lose your beloved mansion."

"Oh, thank God," said LaDextra, sagging down onto a chair.

But she was up again in a minute when a young horseman, galloping at full speed in the darkness, approached the house. Out of breath, shaking with excitement and emotion, he hurried toward the gallery and the two worried women waiting there.

"Patrona, señorita," he said, "it's—it's…"

"What? What is it, Ricardo? Calm down and tell us," ordered LaDextra.

"Is the *patrón,*" said the young, frightened vaquero. "He and Buck Shanahan and a half-dozen men…*Dios*…they have been cut off. They're surrounded by fire!"

Anna automatically took a couple of steps forward, before she caught herself. Her heart pounding fiercely, she had the overwhelming desire to hurry down the steps and rush out to the fire. To Brit. To her darling Brit. To run headlong through the smoke and flames until she found him and knew he was safe.

She checked herself, knew that she had to stay right where she was and watch after LaDextra.

Brit felt the intense heat on his face as the shooting flames raced steadily closer. Anxiously he looked around. He saw no way out. They were trapped. There was nothing to stop the blaze. They were going to perish.

He remembered the telegram in his shirt pocket. If he died in the fire, the telegram might survive. He couldn't let that happen. If he was gone there was no reason to break LaDextra's heart. She believed that she had found her long-lost granddaughter. He would let her go on believing it.

Brit stopped beating at the flames long enough to reach inside his shirt pocket. He took out the yellow telegram, tossed it into the flames and watched it quickly catch and burn.

And the fire steadily advanced.

Midnight.

Word came that the fire had finally been brought under control. The house was no longer in any danger. There was no word as to the fate of the men.

LaDextra refused to go to bed until there was news of Brit, Buck and the others. Anna understood and stayed up with her, anxiously looking southward, waiting, hoping, praying.

Anna remained totally mute while LaDextra went on and on about how she couldn't bear it if anything happened to her boy, to her precious Brit. She talked nonstop about him, laughing about things he had done as a child, bragging about things he had done as a man.

When finally she paused for breath, she looked up and studied Anna's pale, drawn face. She had never seen such naked misery in a pair of eyes. How foolish, how selfish she had been not to see, not to know.

LaDextra reached for Anna's hand and said softly, "Oh, Anna, forgive me, I didn't realize. You love him, too, don't you? You're in love with Brit."

Anna bowed her head, but did not deny it. She squeezed the older woman's hand and fought back the tears that were threatening to fall.

The women stayed there on the shadowy gallery as another long, nerve-racking hour dragged slowly by.

The clock inside the mansion was striking one o'clock when, at long last, Brit appeared. Dirty. Sweaty. Exhausted. His face was blackened and scorched by the flames.

But he was unhurt.

To both women, he had never looked better.

"Brit, Brit," cried LaDextra as he came up the front walk, "you made it, you escaped! Thank God. Thank God!"

"We all made it," Brit called out. "There was a brief lull in the wind and the boys were able to beat out a narrow corridor through the flames and pull us to safety."

When he came up onto the gallery, LaDextra

threw her brittle arms around his neck and began to cry happy tears of relief.

Over her head Brit glanced at Anna. He could see the sweetness of her lips as they turned up into a smile and the way her expressive eyes clung adoringly to him. And he knew, all over again, that what he had been trying hard to deny within himself could never be denied.

Brit smiled warmly at Anna, reached for her hand and held it firmly in his own. He gazed at her with a look in his eyes that he knew mirrored the telling expression in hers. No words were needed. The message that passed between them was unmistakable.

Brit gave Anna's soft hand one last squeeze and released it.

"Now, now, darlin'." Brit turned his full attention to the weeping LaDextra, soothing her. He lifted her up in his powerful arms and carried her inside. Anna followed, but stopped in the entryway, turned and went into the lamplit parlor.

To wait.

Brit carried LaDextra straight down the hall to her room, all the while assuring her, in a low, gentle voice, that he was fine and so were the rest of the boys. At her door, he stepped inside and nodded to her waiting maid, Connie. Brit gently laid the tired woman on her bed and turned her over to Connie.

"Rest easy, dear," he said to LaDextra. "Everything's fine. Just fine."

Thirty-Three

In the parlor, Anna waited nervously.

At first she sat down on one of the plush velvet sofas and very carefully arranged the skirts of her blue summer dress. She wanted to look just right when Brit came in.

In seconds she was up pacing, her heart beating erratically. She crossed anxiously to the white marble fireplace to peer into the gold-framed mirror that hung above. She pinched her cheeks and bit her lips. She smoothed her hair, arranging the golden locks to fall appealingly on her shoulders, taking care, as she did so, to make sure a shiny curl concealed the ugly black tattoo below her right ear.

She turned away from the mirror.

She glanced at the clock and shook her head. What was keeping him? Why hadn't he come?

Brit quietly closed LaDextra's door, but he didn't go straight to the parlor. He turned and rushed down the dim corridor to the back stairs. He anxiously climbed the steps, taking them two at a time. When he reached the second floor and the door to his room, he'd already removed his badly scorched shirt.

Inside, he wasted no time in stripping down to the skin, leaving his soiled, smoke-blackened clothes where he dropped them. Naked, he made a beeline for the bath. Nervous as a schoolboy, Brit rushed to bathe, wash his hair and get his clothes changed so he could hurry down to the waiting Anna.

In the big marble tub, he washed away the soot and sweat and grime from his lean body. He soaped his hair and scrubbed his scalp with nimble fingers.

Out of the bath, toweling himself dry, he studied his face in the mirror and frowned. He needed a shave, but there was no time. It would take too long. She might not wait.

Brit tossed the towel aside, stepped into clean underwear and reached for a freshly laundered shirt. Not bothering to button it, he drew on a pair of black, neatly pressed trousers, hastily buttoned them, then hopped on one foot, then the other as he put on his shoes and socks.

With the minutes ticking away, Anna kept glancing at the clock, so tense she felt she was going to jump out of her skin. She couldn't sit still. She paced restlessly before the cold marble fireplace, wondering what was keeping him.

When twenty long minutes had passed, Anna stopped pacing, shook her head sadly and told herself she was once again behaving like a fool.

Brit was not coming to the parlor.

He was not coming to her. She had imagined everything. She had let herself read a meaning into his look on the gallery that was never really there. The way he had gazed at her, the way he held her hand so tightly in his, had meant nothing.

Nothing at all.

How could she have believed that, just because he had smiled at her and squeezed her hand, he'd meant her to know that he would come to her? He wasn't about to. Now or ever.

Her face immediately grew hot with embarrassment and shame. Dear Lord, what if he learned that she was waiting here for him like a lovestruck girl? What if he casually wandered into the parlor and found her here? How could she ever explain?

Eager to get away before he could catch her, Anna quickly crossed the spacious room, stepped out into the foyer and hurried to the front door. She slipped quietly outside, crossed the broad gallery and went down the front steps.

Raking his hands through his still-damp hair and buttoning his shirt as he came, Brit skipped down the back stairs and rushed toward the parlor. His heartbeat quickening, he stepped, smiling, into the arched doorway of the lamplit parlor and looked eagerly around.

The room was empty.

Brit's smile instantly fled. Confused, disappointed, he frowned and shook his head. His wide shoulders slumped wearily.

She wasn't here. She wasn't waiting. Had he really expected her to be here waiting for him? Just because she had smiled so sweetly at him and gripped his hand as if she would never let it go?

That was no reason to suppose she'd be here where he'd left her, eagerly anticipating his return.

All at once exhaustion settled over him, consumed him. The long, hard day of fighting the raging blaze had left him with absolutely no energy. He was tired to the bone. The thing to do was to go right back upstairs and go to bed.

But Brit wasn't sleepy, despite his weariness.

He was restless. Disillusioned. Edgy.

He exhaled heavily and headed for the front door, feeling as he had felt while fighting the fire, as if he were suffocating. Like he couldn't get a breath. Outside on the front gallery, he glanced at the hammock, considered stretching out in it.

It was no use. He couldn't lie still. He lit a cigar. The late-rising moon was up fully now, brightly illuminating the sprawling grounds and the vast valley below the house. And revealing the hundreds of blackened, still smoking acres of land that had burned in the fire.

Cigar in his mouth, Brit went down the front steps and out onto the manicured lawn. With no particular destination in mind, he circled the big house, choosing—he didn't know why—the east side. He unhurriedly rounded the eastern corner of the mansion and stopped dead in his tracks.

His lethargy instantly departed.

Anna stood at the old wishing well, her long golden hair gleaming silver in the moonlight, the skirts of her blue summer dress lifting in the night breezes.

For a long moment Brit stood there unmoving,

staring, awed, wondering if he could trust his eyes. Was she actually there or was she only an illusion brought forth by his yearning heart?

Anna moved slightly.

She *was* real.

She was there.

Brit dropped his cigar, crushed it out under his heel and started toward her.

Anna sensed his presence, turned and watched him approach, her pulse quickening at the sight of him so tall, so dark, so devastatingly handsome, coming toward her in the bright moonlight.

Brit reached Anna, smiled down at her and asked softly, "Were you making a wish?"

"Yes," she said truthfully, gazing up at him, "and I got my wish. You have come to me." She took a half step closer and asked, "Haven't you?"

"Yes," he said, his voice a warm caress, "I have. I have come to you, Anna."

"Brit!" She murmured his name on a sigh.

"Sweetheart," he responded huskily.

Then, slowly lifting a hand to brush back a wind-blown lock of golden hair from her ivory cheek, he said, letting her know his intent in case he might still be misreading her, "I am going to kiss you."

She smiled a dazzling smile and replied, "And I am going to let you."

Brit quickly closed the gap between them and took Anna in his arms. He looked into her eyes for several seconds, a muscle dancing in his lean jaw, then lowered his head and kissed her. It was the sweetest, most tender of kisses. His warm, smooth lips settled on hers in a soft caress so caring, so unthreatening, she melted with bliss.

When the brief buss ended, Brit lifted his head and drew Anna closer against his tall, lean frame. Anna sighed with happiness and laid her forehead against Brit's chest. They stood like that for several peaceful moments, their arms around each other, their hearts beating together, their bodies taut with longing.

Holding her, wanting her, Brit cautioned himself to let her set the pace. He was not going to rush her. He was, if need be, willing to take all night to win and woo her completely. She meant too much to him. More, much more than any woman ever had.

At last Anna raised her head, tipped it back and looked up at Brit. She said, "Kiss me again?"

"Ah, baby," he murmured, and kissed her.

This time what began as that same kind of sweet, gentle brushing of lips swiftly escalated into a fiery kiss of budding passion. Both were breathless when the long, penetrating kiss ended, but they hastily changed positions and kissed again.

For the next half hour the two of them stood there in the brilliant September moonlight at the wishing well, kissing, touching, straining against each other, pressing their sensitized bodies together through the increasingly vexing barrier of their clothes.

Brit stood with his back braced against the wishing well, his feet apart. His hands at Anna's small waist, he held her close against him, his knees on either side of her legs. Their lips combined in probing, prolonged kisses, and Brit could feel her passion-hardened nipples rubbing against his chest, her pelvis pressing temptingly against his own.

He wondered if she knew what she was doing to him. Already she had him so aroused he wished that he didn't have to wait, wished that he could just take her right now, right here where they stood. He had to fight the strong temptation to swiftly turn her about, press her up against the well, rip away her underwear, open his trousers and quickly bury himself inside her.

He didn't do it.

He was not going to behave like an animal this night. He loved this woman, no matter who she was or was not, and he meant to give her so much patient pleasure she would never want to be in any arms but his.

Brit kept kissing Anna, and kissing her, until she was sighing and clinging to him in unquestioned surrender. Wordlessly he swept her up into his arms and carried her back inside the big, silent house.

He climbed the shadowy stairs and took her directly to the privacy of his room.

Thirty-Four

Once inside the spacious, masculine room, where a lone lamp burned beside the bed, Brit pressed Anna up against the closed door and began kissing her once more. Again and again they kissed, and soon they were so weak and excited they sagged to their knees on the carpet, continuing to kiss anxiously, as if they could never get enough of each other.

And as they kissed, Brit began to undress Anna. Lost in him, loving the feel of his fiery mouth searing her lips, his warm hands on her tingling flesh, Anna made no move to stop him when he dexterously opened her dress down the back.

She helpfully lifted her shoulders when he began to ease the short puffy sleeves down her arms, the bodice past her breasts. When the dress was lowered and lay bunched around her hips, Brit took his lips from hers, looked into her eyes and relieved her of her lace-trimmed camisole, peeling it up her ribs and over her head.

Naked to the waist now, Anna shivered when Brit cupped her left breast in his hand and, rubbing his thumb back and forth over the nipple, said, "God, you are so beautiful, so incredibly perfect. I could look at you forever.''

Her hands clutching his hard biceps, she said, ''I'm not perfect, Brit.'' And she tried to turn her head away when he pushed her heavy golden hair back from her face on the right side. ''No,'' she said, ''don't.''

''Sweetheart, you don't have to hide anything from me,'' he told her. He leaned down and placed a kiss on the disfiguring black tattoo that was her only flaw. Leaving his lips there, he said, ''You're as beautiful here as anywhere. This may become my favorite place to kiss.''

Relieved, she said, ''You don't mean that.''

He raised his head, smiled and said, ''I'm not sure. I haven't kissed every other place yet, have I?''

''N-no,'' she managed to reply.

''But I will,'' he promised, ''If you'll let me.''

Then his lips were back on hers, coaxing, persuasive, arousing. During one long, heated kiss Anna felt herself being slowly lifted up off her knees. She tore her lips from Brit's and gave him a questioning look.

His hands at her waist, he effortlessly raised her to her feet, while he remained kneeling before her.

''What are you doing?'' she asked, placing her hands atop his broad shoulders.

''I can't finish undressing you while you're kneeling,'' he explained. He then tugged her blue dress down over her hips and let it fall to the floor. At only a look from him, Anna stepped out of the dress and he swept it aside. Her petticoats came next. Then her slippers and silk stockings.

She shivered with giddy delight when, after peeling the last stocking off, he raised her foot and kissed the instep, then her toes, one at a time, before lowering her bare foot to the floor.

Now that she wore only her lace-trimmed underpants, Anna experienced a quick flash of embarrassment. She was almost naked, while he was still fully dressed. She didn't understand why. And she didn't understand why they didn't get into his big comfortable bed, which had been turned down for the night.

"Brit—" she began.

"I want," he hoarsely interrupted, brushing heated kisses on her delicate ribs, "to smell and touch and taste every precious inch of you, baby."

She flushed hotly at the brash statement, and her breath grew short. She was sure he didn't mean it, and if he did mean it she wouldn't let him, of course, but it was thrilling to hear him say it. She felt her underwear sliding down her belly, and her breath came out in a loud rush. His lean, dark hands gently, but surely eased the last remaining garment from her now trembling body.

Feeling suddenly too exposed, too vulnerable, Anna grabbed futilely for the underwear. But he withheld it, tossed it out of her reach. Her heart now pounding, she stood there totally naked before him, both excited and frightened by the passionate look in his midnight eyes.

She shuddered when he cupped her hips in his

dark hands and laid his hot, handsome face against her bare belly. His silky black hair brushed against her sensitive skin and his warm cheek, in need of a shave, was mildly abrasive, tickling her. Exciting her.

His breath was furnace hot, and when he began to kiss her stomach, her hips, her thighs, her knees, his mouth felt like a flame against her skin. She couldn't stand still. She squirmed and stirred and murmured his name and wondered when—and where—he would stop kissing her.

His tongue made a teasing swirl around the small indentation of her navel, and he said in an enticing tone that sent the blood scalding her veins, "I want to love you in every possible way a man can love a woman. But remember this, sweetheart, I'll never do anything you don't want me to do."

He put out the tip of his tongue and slowly licked the fine line of pale baby hair going down her belly to the thick triangle of curls between her thighs. He added, nuzzling his nose in the springy coils, "But I'll do anything you want me to do for as long as you want me to do it."

"I…Brit, let's go to bed now and…"

"We'll go to bed," he promised. "In just a minute."

"Well, at least take off your clothes," she urged, not wanting to be the only one naked.

"In just a minute," he repeated.

His hands slipped down to wrap around the backs of her knees, and he tipped his head, gazed up at her and said, "Look into my eyes, sweetheart. Tell me what you see there."

Anna looked into his flashing obsidian eyes and trembled. "Hunger," she stated. "Passion. Desire. Lust."

"All of those," he readily agreed. "But you left out one thing."

"I did?"

Brit nodded and said, "Love."

"Love?" She couldn't believe what she was hearing.

"Love. I love you as I've never loved anyone else. I love you, baby, and I'm sorry that I—"

"Oh, Brit, I love you, too," she eagerly interrupted. "I love you, I do, I do. I love you more than life itself."

"If you love me," he whispered, his hands tightening on her legs, "you also trust me. Don't you?"

"I trust you completely."

"Then let me show you all the sweetness of love," he said, and released her legs. He brought a hand up and spread his long, tapered fingers on her quivering stomach. Touching her lightly with just his fingertips, he said, "Will you do something for me, sweetheart?"

"Of course, my darling. Anything. Everything."

"Move your legs apart just a little."

"But, Brit, I—"

"For me, baby. Do it for me."

Anna took a shallow breath, pressed her shoulders back against the solid, heavy door, and moved her bare, slender legs slightly apart.

"All I want is to make you feel good," he whispered, and letting his hand slip down her bare belly, he swept apart the thick golden curls. She gasped when, with only the tip of his middle finger, he tenderly touched that most feminine spot of all. Gently caressing her, he asked, "Feel good, sweetheart?"

She couldn't lie. It felt good. Marvelous. Enjoyable beyond belief. "Yes, yes it does."

But then she winced in shock when Brit bent his dark head and put his lips where his finger had been. With his lips completely closed, he kissed her there, just as if he were kissing her mouth. The soft butterfly touch of his warm lips on her tingling flesh instantly brought on an involuntary throbbing of that ultrasensitive flesh.

Brit took his lips from her, raised his head and asked, "Doesn't that feel even better?"

She didn't answer. She couldn't. She couldn't breathe, much less speak. She couldn't believe that he had actually kissed her there and that it had felt so scarily wonderful. The kiss had caused a strong pulsating sensation that now surged throughout her entire groin. She was stunned to realize that she wanted to have his lips back on her, wanted him to kiss her there again. She didn't dare ask him to do it, but she hoped that he would.

She felt as if she needed it badly. Had to have it.

Her face aflame with the shame of her forbidden desire, Anna pressed her flattened hands against the door when Brit—as if he were reading her guilty thoughts—cupped the twin cheeks of her bottom and slowly bent back to her.

Anna gasped with delight when she felt his beard-stubbled face pressing between her legs before his hot, smooth lips settled on her again. She shuddered violently when he opened his mouth and warmly enclosed that highly responsive nubbin of flesh that was throbbing between her parted legs.

Sure that the tingling ecstasy she was feeling could rise no higher, could get no better, Anna soon changed her mind. With the first masterful stroke of Brit's tongue on her swollen flesh, her joy increased. It felt so good. *Too* good.

"Oh, God, no," she begged, wanting him to stop, or thinking she did. "Please, Brit, I can't stand it."

Brit's reply was several long, loving licks that made her moan and squirm against him as she tried to free herself from his teasing, tormenting tongue. Her nervous hands went into his thick raven locks and she anxiously drew his head up. Obeying her wishes, Brit pulled back and looked up at her, his lips gleaming with the wetness flowing from her.

"If you want me to stop," he said softly, "I will. But if you'll let me love you this way for just a few more minutes, I promise you'll experience a wonderful kind of wild ecstasy that you have never imagined." His dark eyes flashing with desire, he blew his hot breath on her as he waited for her decision. He watched the golden curls dance before his face and caught a fleeting glimpse of the slick wet flesh he had kissed.

"You...you'll stop if I really want you to stop?" she asked, trembling, undecided, torn.

"I will, sweetheart," he vowed, leaning close,

brushing kisses to her trembling belly, her prominent hipbones, her luminous thighs. "Whenever you say the word."

And he waited no longer. His face was back between her legs, his mouth and tongue upon her, giving her immediate joy. Moaning with surprise and with pleasure, Anna no longer fought the building, blinding passion, but gave in to it, offering herself completely to him. Brit sensed her total yielding and began to give her what she wanted, what she needed.

He licked her lovingly, slowly, very gently. He languidly circled that pulsating button of flesh that was the source of all her sexual pleasure. Unhurriedly, he made bold, burning love to her with his mouth.

Sighing and swallowing anxiously, Anna looked down upon the handsome, dark-haired lover stroking her so expertly with his talented tongue, and her growing desire blazed out of control.

What a powerfully erotic vision it was: her standing above Brit, totally naked, her legs parted to him; him fully clothed, kneeling between her legs, feasting on her as if she were a delicious banquet of which he couldn't get his fill.

The sight of them together this way was so incredibly arousing, Anna wanted to stay right where she was forever, gloriously naked and shamelessly open to her lover. She wanted to keep Brit's dark, whiskered face buried in her for all eternity. She longed to stand here in the shadowy darkness of his room and gaze down upon her one and only love as he so exquisitely pleasured her.

But the vision was too erotic, the heat of his slightly abrasive face and the masterful touch of his tongue too thrilling. The sight, the feel caused her to ignite with a raging, all-consuming heat. His tongue and lips were fanning the flames, spreading the blaze, setting her body on fire.

Where she'd once been afraid he wouldn't stop, she was now just as worried that he would. She grabbed him by his temples and pressed him closer even as she bent her knees slightly and thrust her pelvis forward.

"Don't stop, don't stop," she begged, near to tears of erotic hysteria. "Please, Brit, don't. Don't leave me, don't stop!"

He didn't.

His mouth opened wider. His tongue stroked faster. His whiskered jaws flexed against her tightly gripping thighs. He licked and lashed and loved her until she was calling his name in a frenzy, frightened by the intensity of the waves of carnal pleasure buffeting her, shocked beyond belief at the height of the euphoria he was bringing her to. So potent was her pleasure it bordered on pain. She moaned and tossed her head and flung her hand over her mouth to quiet herself.

But she couldn't be quiet, couldn't be still. His flickering tongue was magical. It whirled around and around her tiny bud of pure sensation until she quivered with jolts of stunning joy over which she had no control. She felt herself erupting helplessly in a volcanic response, coming again and again.

Her hands gripping his head, she frantically

pressed Brit to her, terrified he would take his marvelous mouth from her before her stunning, startling climaxes had fully ended. It was he who had made her burn this hotly, and only he could put out the blaze.

Sensing her anxiety, Brit buried his face more deeply in her and carefully guided her all the way to the top until she was bucking and quivering and crying out in absolute orgasmic ecstasy. Making certain she wouldn't hurt, even for a second, he lingered until all the little aftershocks had washed over her and she finally slumped against him, her weak knees folding beneath her.

Only then did he raise his head. He caught her before she could fall, swung her up into his arms and rose to his feet. She trembled in his arms, crying with happiness. She looked at him through tear-filled eyes and saw that he was pleased with himself. He had every right to be. She was certainly pleased with him.

Brit brushed a kiss to her damp forehead and said, "If you didn't like that, I'll never do it again."

She sighed and said, "I can't lie to you, Brit. I did like it, but it was so thrilling, so intense, it frightened me. I was afraid that…that…"

"You never have to be afraid with me, sweetheart," he told her as he crossed the room and gently laid her in the very middle of his bed. "I'll always take good care of you."

She sighed, flung her weak arms up over her head and stretched against the silky white sheets like a

contented feline. "In that case, will you please do
that to me again sometime?"

Brit smiled and began undressing. "As often as
you wish, my love."

Thirty-Five

And so began a long night of loving that neither Brit nor Anna would ever forget.

Content, so well satisfied she was sure she couldn't be aroused again anytime soon, Anna lay on the bed, sublimely lazy. She placidly watched Brit undress and was struck anew by the magnificence of his lean male body.

Her gaze slowly traveled down his broad chest to his flat belly, and she flinched inwardly. He was fully aroused, while she was totally sated. The prospect of having that rock-hard flesh thrust into her right now was not pleasant. It would surely hurt, because she was no longer excited.

He had seen to that.

Still a novice at lovemaking, Anna wondered what she could do to give him the same kind of unequaled joy he had given her—without having him inside her. The answer came to her as Brit put a knee on the mattress and started to climb into bed.

"Wait, darling," she said, and rolled up into a sitting position.

"What is it, love?"

She smiled at him, came up into a kneeling position and moved across the bed to him. She put her arms around his neck and said softly, "You trust me, don't you, Brit?"

"With my heart," he said.

"And with your body as well?"

"Certainly."

She pressed a quick kiss to his lips and said, "Then do me a favor."

"Name it."

She released him, scooted around and jumped off the bed. He turned about to face her, giving her a questioning look. She said, "Sit down on the edge of the bed, please."

Brit shrugged his bare shoulders and sat down. Anna stepped between his spread knees, laid her hands atop his shoulders and began kissing him. She cupped his face in her hands and kissed his temples, his cheeks, his mouth, his chin.

His breath short, his hands eagerly caressing her bare bottom, Brit said, "Baby, let's get in the bed."

"In just a minute," she said, and continued to kiss him.

Her lips slid down over his firm chin to his throat. She placed several plucking, sucking kisses there before moving on down his chest. As she kissed and teased him, Anna slowly began sinking to her knees.

"Oh, God, baby," Brit rasped, as her warm face nuzzled in the thick black hair covering his chest and she put out the tip of her tongue and licked his right nipple.

He held his breath as her golden head continued to move lower and lower down his tense, bare body. Just as he had done with her, she swirled her tongue around his navel, carefully nudging aside his throbbing tumescence. But her soft cheek was against it and her silky hair was tickling it.

Abruptly she lifted her head, then bent and kissed his right knee. Slowly, tormentingly, she kissed her way up his hair-dusted thigh to the warm inside. She stopped an inch short of where the thick, raven-black hair swirled around his pulsing erection.

She repeated the erotic exercise, kissing and licking her way up the inside of his left thigh. She nuzzled her nose and mouth in the dense black curls of his groin, and Brit felt as if his heart was going to explode. She put out the tip of her tongue and dabbed at the crisp springy coils. She blew her warm breath up and down the hard, jerking length of him.

Brit was now at the stage where he'd had her earlier. If she didn't kiss it, if she didn't take him in her mouth for just a moment, he wouldn't be able to bear it.

As if she had read his thoughts, Anna raised her head, swept back her long hair and, boldly wrapping her hand around him, asked, "Doesn't that feel good?"

"God, yes," he managed to answer.

She smiled at him, took her hand away, bent and kissed the throbbing tip, opening her mouth slightly to touch him with her tongue. Again she raised her head and, looking like the cat that got the cream, asked, "Doesn't that feel even better?"

Brit shook his head, unable to speak. He was momentarily terrified. His heart hammering, his blood pulsing, he felt that he would surely die if he couldn't feel her warm, wet mouth on him for just a moment. At the same time he was worried that he would immediately explode if she kissed him again.

Anna didn't wait for his permission. Led by instinct, she held him with one hand and slipped her open lips down over him. She heard him groan, but knew it was with pleasure, not pain. Very, very gently she sucked on him and heard him groan even louder. Wanting to excite him as much as he had excited her, Anna took a lesson from Brit. She raised her mouth from him momentarily, then put out her tongue and licked him lovingly, starting at the very base and sweeping all the way up to the jerking tip.

On fire, so aroused he was beside himself, Brit allowed himself the incredible pleasure for only a few short minutes. He looked down on the golden head bent to him and almost climaxed. What an erotic sight the two of them made. He, Adam naked, sitting on the edge of the bed with his knees spread. She, as naked as he, kneeling between his legs, her head down, her lips on him, her golden hair spilling over them both.

How incredibly thrilling to watch her love him like this even as he felt her soft, sweet lips tugging at him, her sleek tongue spreading liquid fire. He wished the two of them could stay like this forever. He wanted to keep her just as she was, naked and kneeling between his legs, for all eternity.

But as he fantasized, the vision became too electrifying. He felt himself slipping dangerously close to an erupting orgasm.

Brit put his hands in Anna's hair and gently raised

her face from him. He bent and kissed her and said into her mouth, "Let's get in bed."

To her surprise, Anna found that she was aroused again. Pleasuring him had had a similar effect on her. Her skin felt feverish. Her nipples ached. And a gentle throbbing had begun between her legs.

When Brit stretched out beside her on the bed, she happily lifted her face for his hot, probing kiss. By the time the kiss ended, Brit had moved between her legs. His weight supported on a stiffened arm, he put his hand between her legs, touched her gently and found her hot and wet and ready.

He glanced at her face and she blushed. "I'm a shameless wench, aren't I?"

Brit slid the smooth tip of his erection into place and slowly thrust until he was fully inside her. "Yes," he said. "Thank heaven you're my shameless wench."

Grateful that he didn't have to spend long moments arousing her, Brit began to pump forcefully into her. He had held himself in check for as long as he possibly could. Her body was too hot, too tight, too sweet. He couldn't hold back any longer.

"Love me, baby. Take me, take it all," he implored as he drove into her, the lean cheeks of his brown bottom flexing, his pelvis slamming into hers, his hard, seeking flesh plumbing the very depths of her hot, yielding softness.

His climax soon began and it was potent, powerful. Anna could feel him growing to an unbelievable size inside her and then felt the hot liquid gushing until it overflowed. She watched, entranced, as his eyes helplessly closed and his dark handsome face contorted in ecstasy. Thick veins stood out on his neck and the sleek muscles of his upper arms bulged and knotted.

When at last he groaned out his final release and collapsed tiredly atop her, Anna held him and hugged him closely. She supposed that when his breath returned to normal, he would move off her and stretch out beside her.

When he shifted slightly, she started to pull away, but he stopped her.

"No, don't move," he said. "I'm going to stay right here where I am, inside you, until you make me hard and hot again. Then I'll love you properly."

His flaccid flesh remaining inside her, Brit lay between Anna's slender legs and began to excite her all over again. He kissed her lips. He fondled her breasts. He sucked her nipples. He spoke in a low, sexy voice of all the things he wanted to do to her, with her. Of all the ways he wanted to make love to her.

Responding, Anna kissed him back. She playfully bit his sleek shoulders. She ran her nails down his deeply clefted back. She drew her right leg up and wrapped it around his hips. And she agreed, in a soft, sensual voice, that she wanted him to show her everything there was to know about lovemaking.

In minutes they were both aroused.

Anna could feel Brit swelling inside her as the blood rushed to that most male part of him. It was, she thought happily, a wonderful experience to feel her lover's flesh changing from soft and harmless to rigid and powerful while inside her.

"I'm ready to make love to you," Brit murmured.

"I know," she said, "I can feel it."

This time Brit took it nice and easy, and it was heaven for them both. They lay in the mellow lamplight and made slow, sweet love. Brit no longer had to coach Anna to look at him; she gazed steadily into his eyes as he filled and stretched and moved within her.

Through the cooling September night, Brit patiently taught Anna all he knew about lovemaking. He showed her the incredible pleasure that could be had when a man and a woman made sweet, hot, unhurried, uninhibited love.

If Brit was the patient teacher, Anna was the eager student. No matter how astonishing his request, she didn't hesitate to comply. When he left the bed, sat down in an armless rocking chair, spread his knees wide and invited her to climb astride his lap, she accepted. And found that making love while rocking rhythmically back and forth was very pleasant indeed.

More shocking, but every bit as enjoyable, perhaps more so, was when Brit turned her about on the bed so that she was facing the same direction as he. His arm around her, his hand caressing her breasts, her stomach and that burning place between her legs, he entered her from behind, and it was wonderful.

And so it went.

Anna lay trustingly in Brit's arms as they made

love, her body and soul open to him, her heart his to keep or break. When finally the exhausted Brit fell asleep, Anna continued to lie there in the lamplight, wide awake, gazing at his beautiful brown body, wishing once again that everything could stay just as it was at this moment. That she could stay here forever in this bed with this man whom she loved so completely.

That, of course, was impossible.

Her blood beginning to cool, her doubts surfacing, Anna rose from the bed. She dressed in the shadows, blew out the bedside lamp, slipped out into the silent hallway and went to her room.

But she couldn't sleep.

She lay there in the silvery moonlight reliving every touch, every word, every moment of ecstasy they had shared.

Still wide awake with the dawn, Anna rose, put on her riding clothes, slipped out of the still-sleeping house and went down to the stables.

Tiptoeing past a dozing young groom, she hurriedly saddled Dancer and led the gentle mare outside. She climbed into the saddle and rode away as the first pink tinges of light streaked the eastern horizon.

Thirty-Six

Anna headed for the cool uplands of the mountain tract as the summer sun began to strike *El Capitán's* soaring peak. Soon leaving the pastures below, she urged the mare onto the path that would take her past Manzanita Springs.

At the springs, she dismounted, patted the gentle mare and tethered her to a nearby tree. Dancer neighed loudly, bent her head and began contentedly cropping at the patchy grass. Anna laughed and walked away.

She approached the hidden springs, batting aside willow limbs until she stepped out into the clearing. She smiled with delight. Despite the lingering drought, the springs still splashed and bubbled with cool, clear water.

Anna didn't waste a minute considering it.

She stripped off all her clothes and jumped in. She shivered as the chilly waters closed over her bare shoulders, but she wasn't cold for long. She swam the width of the springs and back again. She turned onto her back, pushed away from the rocky bank with her feet and floated on the surface, blinking as the sun began to fully illuminate the mountains.

When she pulled herself up onto the bank, the rapidly rising sun felt good on her wet, chilled skin. With both hands she swept back her saturated hair, wound it into a thick rope and squeezed the excess moisture from it. She then sighed and stretched out on her back to let the sun completely dry her.

She realized, as she squirmed around to make herself comfortable, that she had chosen the very spot where she'd come upon Brit that afternoon in May. He had been lying right here where she was, and he'd been stark naked, save for the Stetson covering his groin. She had been shocked and outraged, while he had laughed and teased her.

Anna smiled now, thinking that a person would have to get up pretty early to best Brit Caruth. He was a man who knew what he wanted and how to get it. He was, no question about it, good at everything he did.

LaDextra had told her that Brit was a self-made man who, from the time he was a boy, had been dependent upon his own ingenuity for survival and success. She said Brit was the epitome of the tough Texas rancher. He could ride like a Comanche, rope like a Mexican and shoot like a Texas Ranger.

Anna felt herself flush.

There was something else at which he was quite good. He was a tireless master of passion who could make exquisite love for hours. She shivered as she recalled last night's incredible loving. His body, she had learned, was not only extraordinarily beautiful, it was a well-honed instrument over which he had amazing control.

He had, it seemed, that same control over *her* body. He knew just when and where to touch her to set her on fire. Just what to do to get her so excited she gladly shed all inhibitions. Just how to turn up the heat until he knew she was ready for him to bring her to those earth-shattering climaxes that lasted and lasted.

Shivering with the recollection of all the things they had done during the long romantic night, Anna rolled up into a sitting position. He was a magnificent lover, but did he love her? He'd said he loved her, but that was in the heat of passion. Had he really meant it?

Only time would tell.

Anna rose to her feet. Her tall slender body was now perfectly dry, although her thick, long hair was still damp. She hurriedly dressed, wove her way back out through the maze of willows and mounted the patiently waiting Dancer.

She neck-reined the mare higher up the mountain slope, planning to ride all the way up to the mountain tract and perhaps even through McKittrick Canyon. Relaxed in the saddle, reins loose in her hand, Anna studied the awesome scenery. She turned and looked back over her shoulder at the parched lowlands, saw the blackened acres of *Tierra Verde*. Her gaze swept over the craggy brush country spreading to the west and she realized that she had truly come to love this big, rugged land, just as she had come to love the big, rugged man who ruled over it.

Anna slowly turned back around in the saddle and

gazed up at the stark, rocky beauty above her, unaware of the danger directly below her horse's hooves.

A huge diamondback rattlesnake, disturbed by the horse and rider, slithered out of its rock-concealed nest. With its gleaming silver body bowed in an S-curve, its deadly fangs dripping venom, it prepared to strike the horse.

When Dancer heard the rattler's deadly warning, the frightened creature whinnied and reared in terror, avoiding the diamondback's deadly strike. But Anna, caught totally off guard, was unseated. She was thrown to the ground and her head struck a boulder. All went black.

Anna lay there unconscious as the September sun climbed high in the cloudless sky.

Dr. McCelland was the first one to reach The Regent.

Will Davis was a close second.

Other carriages began pulling up before the eight-columned mansion as the word quickly spread.

When the physician and the attorney arrived, Brit was at LaDextra's bedside, consoling her, promising he would have Anna found and brought straight to her.

"Don't you worry, darlin'," he said, patting LaDextra's age-spotted hand, "she's probably gone for a little ride and will be home any minute."

Tears in her pale eyes, LaDextra said, "I wanted to see her one last time before…"

"You'll see her lots of times, LaDextra," Brit calmly replied, not really believing it.

"If you'll excuse us..." said Dr. McCelland as he hurried into LaDextra's room.

"Certainly, Doctor." Brit rose to leave. "I'll be right outside," he promised LaDextra.

While Will Davis stood silently across the hall from LaDextra's door, Brit paced back and forth, up and down the wide corridor, wondering where Anna was and hoping she got back before...before...

Brit stopped pacing and turned to the attorney and close family friend. "Will, did you know about this? Did you know that LaDextra was so ill that she..."

"I did," Will admitted. "I knew."

"Why didn't you tell me? Did you tell anyone? Did you tell Anna?"

Will shook his head. "No. LaDextra asked me not to say anything to either of you."

"Why, for God sakes?"

Will wearily shrugged. "You know LaDextra. She wanted—"

He was interrupted when the doctor stepped out into the corridor. Both Brit and Will turned anxiously to him.

"How is she?" Brit asked. "Is she—"

"LaDextra has suffered a major heart attack. I've been expecting it." McCelland looked from one man to the other. "She won't live out the day. I'm very sorry."

"Oh, God," Brit said, and started for LaDextra's door.

But the doctor put a hand on his arm to stop him.

"Wait, Brit, LaDextra has asked to speak with Will alone."

Brit nodded and began his pacing once more.

Will Davis drew a deep breath and went inside. Connie, LaDextra's maid, was there by the bed, crying quietly.

Near death, LaDextra Regent was still formidable. "Connie, will you stop that infernal bawling and give me a minute with Will!"

Dissolving into loud sobs, Connie exited the room.

"Not doing so good today, dear?" Will asked as he reached the bed and squeezed LaDextra's thin shoulder.

"Will, listen to me, I am dying and I know it."

Will looked at her with deep affection and did not correct her. Tears filled his eyes and his voice broke when he said, "Oh, God, LaDextra, how will we ever get along without you? How will I?"

She said softly, "Dearest Will, you'll be fine. So will the others. And as for me, I don't mind so much, really I don't. I've been mighty tired and useless this summer. Besides, I got what I wanted. My beautiful granddaughter is back home where she belongs."

"Yes," Will said, nodding, tears spilling down his cheeks. "And I—"

"Did you know that Anna's in love with Brit?" LaDextra interrupted.

"I didn't," Will admitted, "but I'm not all that surprised. Most women are."

She managed a weak smile. "That's true. But I'm

gambling that he loves her, too,'' LaDextra mused, adding, ''I know Brit so well. I've finally got it all figured out. If I leave The Regent to Anna, Brit will never admit that he loves her. He'll go away. He'll leave this land he loves so much.''

Will nodded. ''I wouldn't doubt it. He's a proud man.''

''But if I leave everything to Brit...'' She smiled and her words trailed away.

''So there is to be no change in your last will and testament?''

''None. It all goes to Brit.'' She sighed as if a load had been lifted off her shoulders, and said, ''Now send Brit back in here. I want to look at his face one last time. And find Anna! I want to see my granddaughter!''

Anna moaned as she began to come around. Her eyes opened, then immediately closed against the harsh midday sunlight. For a time she lay there with her hand shading her eyes, wondering how badly she was hurt. Dizzy, suffering from a pounding headache and feeling half-nauseated, she struggled to sit up.

Finally she managed it. She cautiously felt her arms and legs. She was pretty sure no bones were broken, and for that she was grateful. *Better not try to move around too soon,* she told herself.

She sat there resting, holding her aching head in her hands, waiting for the terrible dizziness to pass before she tried to walk. Unconnected thoughts began drifting through her mind. Things she hadn't thought of in years.

All at once Anna's lips fell open and her blue eyes widened.

Dear God, the blow to her head had made her remember things she had long since forgotten. Her heart racing, Anna sat there on the ground in stunned disbelief as her memory miraculously returned. She now remembered everything. Everything!

She was *not* The Regent heiress. She was Margaret Sue Howard and she had been taken by the Apache from her southern Arizona home. Chill bumps popped out on her flesh as she recalled, with horror, that hot summer day when a band of hostile Apache had ridden onto their property and killed her father, mother and brothers.

A choking lump rose in her throat as she remembered seeing her family brutally butchered before her very eyes. She remembered screaming and crying and being the only one left alive and praying that they would kill her quickly as she waited in fear for her turn to be murdered.

But they hadn't killed her.

The savages had taken her with them when they left. With her home engulfed in flames behind her and her dead family left where they had fallen, she had been carried down into Mexico.

It was there, in the Apache mountain stronghold, that she had met another white girl who was about her same age. She, too, had been taken from her home and spirited down to Mexico. The blue-eyed

girl whose hair was gold like her own was Anna
Regent Wright.

The two of them had quickly become friends.
Both frightened and lost, they had turned to each
other for comfort. Day after day they had worked
side by side, their bare feet bloody, their fingers raw,
their backs breaking. And as they toiled they had
talked about their homes and happier times.

It was the real Anna who had told her so much
about The Regent and her family. That's why she
had known things that even Father Fitzgerald had
not known. The real Anna had told her.

Tears sprang to Margaret's eyes. Her poor friend!
She had died of starvation in the winter of '77. Until
now she hadn't remembered. She hadn't remembered knowing her or that she had died. She hadn't
remembered anything after the cruel blow to her
head.

She reached up and touched the fading scar on
her right temple. She gritted her teeth as she recalled, with vivid clarity, the excruciating pain that
followed the forceful blow to her head all those
years ago from a sadistic brave's tomahawk. She
could remember all the other evil, laughing faces of
her tormenters before she had mercifully passed out.

Shaking her aching head to clear it, Margaret now
knew—for certain—that she was not the long-lost
Texas heiress. She was immediately overcome with
guilt. She couldn't continue the charade. Before, she
had told herself there was a chance that she actually
was Anna Regent Wright. Now she knew better.
And she knew what she had to do.

She could not, in good conscience, lay claim to The Regent when she knew without doubt that it didn't belong to her. The vast desert-and-mountain ranching empire rightfully belonged to Brit and he should have it. She wanted him to have it.

Margaret Sue Howard rose unsteadily to her feet. She looked around for Dancer, saw the mare a few yards down the mountain, calmly swatting insects with her tail. She would ride straight back to the ranch. She would go to LaDextra and confess the truth.

It was the only decent thing to do.

Before she reached the house, Margaret saw the many carriages parked in the front drive and immediately grew alarmed. Something awful had happened. She felt it. She knew it.

At the stables she swung down out of the saddle and ran anxiously toward the house. Will Davis met her at the back door.

"Thank God, you've come home," he said, then put a fatherly arm around her slender shoulders. "It's LaDextra, Anna. She's had a massive heart attack."

"Oh, no! Is she…"

"She's still alive, but barely," Will told her. "Dr. McCelland says she won't last the day."

"Dear God," murmured Margaret, and she began to tremble with emotion. Tears sprang to her eyes.

"Now you must calm yourself, Anna, for La-Dextra's sake," Will instructed. "She's asking for you. You're to go right in."

Nodding, blinking back her tears, Margaret composed herself and hurried on ahead to LaDextra's room. There, just outside the door, she took a spine-stiffening breath and knocked.

Brit opened it. "Why, here she is now," he said over his shoulder to LaDextra.

"Anna?" LaDextra's weak voice came from across the room, and Margaret, exchanging worried glances with Brit, went directly to her.

"I'm here, LaDextra," she said, stepping up close to the bed, smiling down at the pale, white-haired woman. "I'm right here." She took LaDextra's hand in both of hers.

"Thank God," LaDextra murmured, gazing up at her. "I did so want to see my precious granddaughter one last time this side of heaven."

Margaret swallowed hard. She said, "LaDextra, there's something I must tell you."

LaDextra smiled at her. "What is it, child? You can tell me anything, you know that." And her pale, sick eyes shone with deep affection.

Margaret battled with herself for only a second. She couldn't do it. She couldn't tell this dying woman that she was *not* her long-lost granddaughter. It was too late for honesty. She couldn't unburden herself now. LaDextra Regent was dying. She should be allowed to die in peace.

Margaret leaned over and laid her cheek against LaDextra's sunken cheek. She said softly, "I just wanted you to know how much I love you, Grandmother, and to tell you that this past summer here at The Regent has been the happiest time of my life."

LaDextra said, "Oh, child, how I've longed to hear you call me Grandmother. And now you have. Bless your heart."

"Can I get you anything? Do anything for you, Grandmother?"

She made no reply.

Margaret anxiously lifted her head, looked down at LaDextra. Her breathing had changed. She struggled for air. Margaret shouted for Dr. McCelland. The doctor rushed in, with Brit right behind him.

But it was too late.

LaDextra Regent had peacefully passed away.

Thirty-Seven

Twenty-four hours after her death, LaDextra Regent was buried beside her husband in the family plot high up the sloping valley behind the house, in the shadow of *El Capitán* peak. Her final resting place was high above the parched desert floor, in the cool shade of an elm tree.

After the brief morning services, the mansion was filled with mourners, as it had been since the moment of LaDextra's death. While old friends talked and visited, Will Davis quietly called Brit into the study.

Producing a packet of papers from the inside pocket of his dark suit jacket, Will said, "LaDextra's last will and testament." Brit felt his knees go weak, his throat go dry. He said nothing, just looked at the attorney, who told him, "Brit, she never changed the will. You are the sole heir. Everything goes to you."

Stunned, Brit said, "What about Anna?"

"She left nothing to Anna." He handed the document to Brit and asked, "Shall I tell her?"

"No, don't," Brit said. "I'll tell her."

Will nodded, recalling what LaDextra had said shortly before she died: "If I leave The Regent to

Anna, Brit will never admit he loves her. But if I leave everything to him…''

The two men exited the study. Brit immediately began looking for Anna. He'd had no chance to speak with her alone since they'd made love. There was so much he had to say to her. He spotted her across the crowded room.

''Excuse me, Will,'' he said, and started toward her.

But he never made it.

An out-of-breath ranch hand arrived and intercepted him.

''Sorry to bother you at a time like this, Brit,'' said the cowboy, ''but I figured you'd want to know. There's a large portion of fence down on the mountain tract. Lots of cattle getting out.''

''Be right there,'' Brit said.

Ever the concerned ranch manager, Brit quickly made apologies to the guests and left without saying anything to Anna. That would have to wait. He'd talk to her as soon as he got back. She would understand.

The crowd of friends and relatives began to thin out by late afternoon, and Margaret was relieved. She had acted as hostess since the moment LaDextra had died, organizing the help, greeting callers and making sure everyone had something to eat and drink.

She hadn't minded being busy, but she had minded the fact that there had been no opportunity to talk to Brit, to see him alone. Overnight guests had quickly filled the house. There hadn't been a single minute when the big mansion wasn't full of people.

By sunset the great house was quiet again. Nearly everyone had gone. At bedtime only the closest of friends remained.

In her room Margaret waited anxiously for Brit. Surely he would come to her tonight. She bathed in a tub full of bubbles and brushed her long hair a hundred strokes. She slipped into a shimmering white satin nightgown that clung to her body. She dabbed her most expensive French perfume between her breasts and behind her knees.

But the sleepless hours of night went by and Brit did not come. Doubts torturing her, Margaret worriedly walked the floor, wondering if he even meant to come to her. Was she once again being foolish to suppose that he would? She needed reassurance. She needed to have his arms around her, to hear him say he loved her.

Those troubled hours between darkness and dawn gave Margaret far too much time to think, far too much time to worry and wonder. With uncertainty plaguing her, guilt nagging, she told herself that there was only one thing to do.

Before the dawn broke she had decided that she would—that she had to—leave The Regent. She knew the truth now. She wasn't Anna and she had no right to be there. The Regent was not hers and never would be. It belonged to Brit. It belonged to the man she loved.

The man who did not love her.

Sure, Brit had repeatedly murmured "I love you" as they had made love, but she had no reason to believe that he had meant it. He had, she felt sure, told dozens of women that he loved them. He hadn't meant it when he'd said it to them and he hadn't with her, either. She was nothing more to him than all the others.

LaDextra had told her that Brit Caruth had been loved by many women, but that he had never loved a one of them.

Dark, ominous clouds filled the sky the next morning. It looked like The Regent was finally going to get some much needed rain. The blazing heat of summer had cooled and there was a slight nip in the heavy air.

Brit, Margaret learned from a servant, was still away from headquarters.

It didn't matter. She had made up her mind. She would leave today. Now, while Brit was away.

Margaret packed a few of her dresses and shoes. She was about to close the valise when she remembered something. She stopped, turned and hurried to the bureau. She pulled out the top drawer, reached underneath some lacy underthings and withdrew the little tied bundle she had brought with her to The Regent.

She returned to the bed and spilled the contents out onto the beige counterpane. The turquoise-handled knife. The bits and pieces of cloth. The baby teeth. The gold locket.

And the gleaming silver concho she had twisted

from Brit's *charro* trousers. She had added the concho to her valuables. She bit the inside of her cheek, lifted the silver circular disk and pressed her lips to it. It was all she had of Brit.

All she'd ever have.

Margaret slipped the concho down inside the bodice of her dress, allowing it to come to rest directly over her aching heart.

She then lifted the gold locket with the initials M.S.H. She could now wear the locket. She would wear it. She was Margaret Sue Howard and she would tell the world that's who she was.

She lifted it, draped the delicate chain around her neck and smiled when she realized that it was too small. It was a child's necklace and she was a woman. She wrapped it twice around her wrist and closed the clasp. The locket dangled on her hand.

She gathered up the few remaining keepsakes, put them back into the bundle and tossed it into the open valise. She left the room without turning back for one last look.

She slipped down the stairs and, seeing that the coast was clear, let herself out the front door before anyone knew she was gone.

Margaret rushed down to the carriage house and ordered one of the old Regent drivers to take her to the rail spur to meet the eastbound morning train.

When she alighted from the carriage at the platform, she pointed a finger in the old man's face and said, "Now, Roberto, promise me you will not tell anyone that I have gone. You understand me? You know nothing. You didn't know I was gone. You don't know where I went, *comprende?*"

The puzzled Mexican driver frowned worriedly. "Where are you going, Señorita Anna?"

"Away," she told him. "Far, far away. Tell them that, if you must tell them anything. Tell them that I have gone away and I won't cause any more trouble."

She heard the train whistle. "Here it comes. Goodbye, Roberto," she said, then turned and hurried up onto the wooden platform.

A few sprinkles of rain struck her face as she waited for the train to reach her. She lifted her eyes heavenward. The clouds had darkened. Off to the west a bolt of lightning streaked down out of the sky, followed by a low rumble of thunder.

The rain began in earnest as she stepped onto the train. Her valise in her hand, she moved down the aisle and took a seat beside the window. She looked out and saw that old Roberto was still sitting there in the carriage, letting the rain fall on him. She waved him away, but he didn't budge.

The train began to move and Margaret felt her heart lurch along with its jerky movement. The locomotive slowly began to pick up speed. Margaret looked out the rain-splattered windows, thinking that at long last the dry, dead pastures were going to get a good soaking.

She smiled wistfully and gazed out on The Regent rangelands, stretching as far as the eye could see in every direction.

The rain was coming down in thick blinding

sheets now, pounding against the train's steel roof, drenching the dry soil and starting to fill the long-empty water holes. Lightning streaked brightly across the night-black sky and thunder boomed across the plain.

Fighting back the tears that were stinging her eyes, Margaret sighed wearily, leaned back in the seat and wondered if she would ever forget the summer she'd spent at The Regent. She knew that she wouldn't. She had told the dying LaDextra that it had been the happiest time of her entire life, and it had.

No matter how it had ended.

Daydreaming, reminiscing, Margaret was jolted from her musings when the fast-moving train abruptly began slowing.

Puzzled, curious, she leaned over, tried to look out the window. She could see nothing through the rain-spattered glass. Annoyed, wanting to know why they were stopping, Margaret impulsively raised the window, stuck her head out and looked up the tracks.

Nothing.

No reason at all for the train to be stopping.

She turned her head, looked back down the tracks and felt her heart race out of control.

A hard-riding cowboy astride a big iron-gray stallion was thundering after the train in the pouring rain.

"Brit," she murmured. "Brit," she said more loudly as the fleet-footed stallion, galloping at full stride, easily overtook the locomotive.

Unable to move, unable to think clearly, she stayed in her seat as the train rumbled to a complete stop. Tense seconds ticked away and then the handsome, hatless Brit Caruth stepped into the car. He stood unmoving for a minute, booted feet apart, flashing eyes fixed on her.

Then, while passengers stared and mumbled, he stalked up the aisle, decisively plucked Margaret out of her seat, swung her up into his arms and hauled her right off the train.

With the rain peppering their faces and saturating their clothes, Brit lifted Margaret up across Captain's saddle, swung up behind her, reined the gray stallion about and turned toward home.

Soaked to the skin, laughing and crying at once, Margaret shouted above the tempest, "Brit, you don't understand. I'm not Anna. You were right about me all along. I'm an imposter. I don't belong here on The Regent."

His strong arms protectively enclosing her, his handsome face wet with rain, he laughed and said, "Of course you belong here on The Regent. Where else would my wife, the mother of my children, belong?"

Her heart swelling with so much happiness she could feel the silver concho pressing against her left breast, she said, "You mean it, Brit? You...you love me?"

"Yes, I love you, sweetheart," he said, and in his dark eyes was the testimony of that love. "You're the only woman I have ever loved, will ever love."

"Brit, oh Brit," she sobbed, her tears mixing with

the rain on her flushed cheeks. "You're not angry with me for—"

Interrupting, he said, "I wanted you the minute I saw you and I've loved you from the first time I held you. I don't care who you were before, only who you are now. And now you're mine. My one and only love. The woman I want to spend the rest of my life with. Marry me, sweetheart. Marry me and let's share this vast, wild land called The Regent."

SHE WOULD GIVE HIM EVERYTHING...BUT THE TRUTH.

MARY LYNN BAXTER

ONE SUMMER EVENING

One summer evening, Cassie Wortham's life changed forever.
Now she's returned to Louisiana: to her childhood home, to
her parents...and to Austin McGuire.

Nine years later, Cassie must face the man she brazenly
seduced. The man who fathered the son he doesn't know
exists. He's still as desirable and disturbing as ever...and still
as forbidden.

When danger follows her home, Cassie must risk everything to
protect her son by turning to the only man who can save them.
She came to Louisiana seeking safety and peace. Instead, she
found the man who first gave her love.

MIRA

On sale mid-July 1999 wherever paperbacks are sold!

Look us up on-line at: http://www.mirabooks.com   MMLB523

New York Times **bestselling author**

JAYNE ANN KRENTZ

Having a baby was supposed to be the greatest event in her life, but for Pru Kenyon, it was bittersweet. Her relationship with her baby's father was exciting and satisfying...but Case McCord refused to commit.

She knew she could have this baby on her own and love her child enough for two. But Pru hadn't bargained on what Case would do for love.

THE FAMILY WAY

MIRA

If you enjoyed what you just read,
then we've got an offer you can't resist!

Take 2 bestselling love stories FREE!

Plus get a FREE surprise gift!

Clip this page and mail it to The Best of the Best™

IN U.S.A.	**IN CANADA**
3010 Walden Ave.	P.O. Box 609
P.O. Box 1867	Fort Erie, Ontario
Buffalo, N.Y. 14240-1867	L2A 5X3

YES! Please send me 2 free Best of the Best™ novels and my free surprise gift. Then send me 3 brand-new novels every month, which I will receive months before they're available in stores. In the U.S.A., bill me at the bargain price of $4.24 plus 25¢ delivery per book and applicable sales tax, if any*. In Canada, bill me at the bargain price of $4.74 plus 25¢ delivery per book and applicable taxes**. That's the complete price and a savings of over 10% off the cover prices—what a great deal! I understand that accepting the 2 free books and gift places me under no obligation ever to buy any books. I can always return a shipment and cancel at any time. Even if I never buy another book from The Best of the Best™, the 2 free books and gift are mine to keep forever. So why not take us up on our invitation. You'll be glad you did!

183 MEN CNFK
383 MEN CNFL

Name	(PLEASE PRINT)	
Address	Apt.#	
City	State/Prov.	Zip/Postal Code

* Terms and prices subject to change without notice. Sales tax applicable in N.Y.
** Canadian residents will be charged applicable provincial taxes and GST.
   All orders subject to approval. Offer limited to one per household.
   ® are registered trademarks of Harlequin Enterprises Limited.

BOB99   ©1998 Harlequin Enterprises Limited

From the middle of nowhere—
to a place of new beginnings

CURTISS ANN MATLOCK

LOST HIGHWAYS

Meet Rainey Valentine: thirty-five, twice divorced, a woman with broken dreams but irrepressible hope. After her mother's death, Rainey packs up her inheritance—a horse trailer, an old barrel-racing mare and a lifetime's supply of Mary Kay cosmetics—and heads off, leaving Valentine, Oklahoma, in her rearview mirror.

Somewhere outside Abilene she finds him. Dazed and wandering after a car accident, Harry Furneaux is a man as lost as she is. With nowhere else to go, he joins Rainey's travels. And when their journey leads them back to Valentine, Harry and Rainey find an unexpected new direction....

On sale mid-August 1999 wherever paperbacks are sold!

This fall,
HARLEQUIN HISTORICALS

is proud to introduce four very
different Western men who will
change the way you look at romance....

In August 1999, look for
THE MIDWIFE #475
by Carolyn Davidson
and
THE SURROGATE WIFE #478
by Barbara Leigh

In September 1999, look for
THE DOCTOR'S WIFE #481
by Cheryl St.John
and
BRANDED HEARTS #482
by Diana Hall

Available at your favorite retail outlet.

From *New York Times* bestselling author

Barbara Delinsky

Jenna McCue needs a favor—a very big favor—and Spencer Smith is her only hope. She's counting on his sense of adventure to give her something she wants more than anything: a baby.

But Spencer has a plan of his own. He just might give her that baby, but it will be the old-fashioned way! Since what Jenna doesn't realize is that he isn't willing to be *just*...

"One of this generation's most gifted writers of contemporary women's fiction."
—*Affaire de Coeur*

MIRA

On sale mid-June wherever paperbacks are sold!

New York Times Bestselling Author

DIANA PALMER

Maggie Turner returned to her Texas hometown with her daughter, seeking comfort and safety. Instead she found sexy, dangerous Gabe Coleman. *Ten years* Maggie had been gone, and Gabe was still cold and distant…still irresistible. Maggie thought marriage had cured her of desire. Then the raging passion of a Texas cowboy taught her about love.

RAGE OF
Passion

"Nobody tops Diana Palmer."—Jayne Ann Krentz

On sale mid-August 1999 wherever paperbacks are sold!